Readers love
How to Be a Normal
by TJ Klune

"Fans of TJ Klune will not be disappointed…. The well paced and well developed story hits all the emotional highs and lows that all I can say is I recommend this to everyone who loves MM romance!"
—MM Good Book Reviews

"It's a feel good, be good kind of book. It's a book that says, be who you are, love who you are, and find people who are searching for the same thing. Well done!"
—Diverse Reader

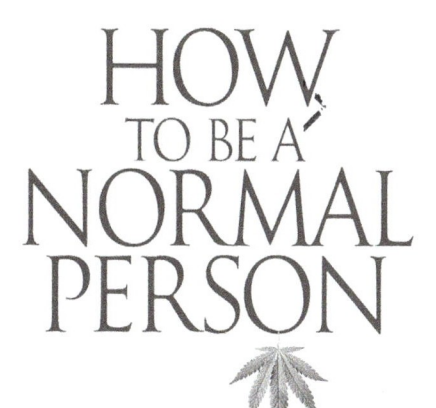

"I've got a lot of love for this book and for the author. He constantly surprises me, amazes me, gives me Wookie cry face, and makes me snort water out of my nose. Mostly though, he makes me feel…."
—Rainbow Book Reviews

HOW TO BE A NORMAL PERSON

TJ Klune

By TJ Klune

Into This River I Drown
John & Jackie
Murmuration
Olive Juice

AT FIRST SIGHT
Tell Me It's Real
The Queen & the Homo Jock King
Until You

BEAR, OTTER, AND THE KID CHRONICLES
Bear, Otter, and the Kid
Who We Are
The Art of Breathing
The Long and Winding Road

ELEMENTALLY EVOLVED
Burn

GREEN CREEK
Wolfsong
Ravensong

HOW TO BE
How to Be a Normal Person
How to Be a Movie Star

TALES FROM VERANIA
The Lightning-Struck Heart
A Destiny of Dragons
The Consumption of Magic
A Wish Upon the Stars

Published by DREAMSPINNER PRESS
www.dreamspinnerpress.com

HOW TO BE A MOVIE STAR

TJ Klune

DREAMSPINNER PRESS

Published by
DREAMSPINNER PRESS

5032 Capital Circle SW, Suite 2, PMB# 279, Tallahassee, FL 32305-7886 USA
www.dreamspinnerpress.com

This is a work of fiction. Names, characters, places, and incidents either are the product of author imagination or are used fictitiously, and any resemblance to actual persons, living or dead, business establishments, events, or locales is entirely coincidental.

How to Be a Movie Star
© 2019 TJ Klune.

Cover Art
© 2019 Reese Dante.
http://www.reesedante.com
Cover content is for illustrative purposes only and any person depicted on the cover is a model.

All rights reserved. This book is licensed to the original purchaser only. Duplication or distribution via any means is illegal and a violation of international copyright law, subject to criminal prosecution and upon conviction, fines, and/or imprisonment. Any eBook format cannot be legally loaned or given to others. No part of this book may be reproduced or transmitted in any form or by any means, electronic or mechanical, including photocopying, recording, or by any information storage and retrieval system, without the written permission of the Publisher, except where permitted by law. To request permission and all other inquiries, contact Dreamspinner Press, 5032 Capital Circle SW, Suite 2, PMB# 279, Tallahassee, FL 32305-7886, USA, or www.dreamspinnerpress.com.

Trade Paperback ISBN: 978-1-64080-783-9
Digital ISBN: 978-1-64080-782-2
Library of Congress Control Number: 2018941443
Trade Paperback published February 2019
v. 1.0

Printed in the United States of America
∞
This paper meets the requirements of
ANSI/NISO Z39.48-1992 (Permanence of Paper).

This book is dedicated to all my queer readers.
You deserve every happiness.
Never stop fighting for what you believe in.
And also to Chuck Tingle. Thanks for all you do.

Chapter 1

Now, it could be said that Josiah Erickson was an actor of the highest caliber. Granted, there were only two people who'd said this in his lifetime, but he believed them completely. They had no reason to lie.

First, his fourth-grade music teacher, the incomparable Mr. Stefan Alabaster IV, who, on the first day of auditions at Cornerbrooke Elementary School in Wooster, Ohio, told his breathless students that he had come from Akron to mold them into the Next Big Thing. He was going to be ruthless, he said, and his critique would be sharp. "There is no time for tears in theater," he said, straightening his ascot. "Unless, of course, the script calls for it. In that case, there is *always* time for tears."

Josiah was enthralled.

And when he won the coveted role as a block of American cheese in a production on the importance of the four food groups, he couldn't have been more excited. "You must *be* the cheese," Mr. Stefan Alabaster IV told him. "There can never be anyone more cheese than you in this entire world. Do you understand me?"

Josiah did. He'd never understood anything more.

His costume had been a particularly violent orange, one that would have been offensive had it been seen outside of a fourth-grade production of health food in a small Ohio town. It was made of Styrofoam and smelled of paint and glue. The fumes made Josiah dizzy, and he usually spent the rest of his day after rehearsal with a headache. It was near impossible to move in, and he ended up falling more than he stood. Mr. Stefan Alabaster IV, as any good theater director should, solved this dilemma by shoving a broom up the back of the costume and telling Josiah he was absolutely not to move. "Sometimes," his director said, "we must suffer for our craft."

In his acting debut, Josiah Erickson had one line and delivered it with the grace of a wheel of gorgonzola: "It's not cheesy to want to be healthy."

At least seven people in the audience of dozens chuckled.

It was a monumental moment for young Josiah. He understood, then, his destiny.

He would be a movie star.

After he booked his first commercial in La La Land in 2011 (a one-day local production where Josiah told the undoubtedly rapturous viewers who were awake at two in the morning that *no* one sold mattresses like the Mattress Dictator: "Because he will take all your decisions away so that you have no choice but to do what he says and get a good night's rest!"), Josiah returned to Cornerbrooke Elementary with a copy on a VHS tape, sure that Mr. Stefan Alabaster IV would want to see what his mentee had achieved in such a short amount of time.

The *problem* was that Mr. Stefan Alabaster IV was no longer the music teacher/theater director at Cornerbrooke Elementary. He had found himself starring in what was perhaps his greatest role, that of a resident of the Federal Correctional Institution in Elkton after embezzling almost fifty thousand dollars from the Wooster City School District. If he were lucky, he would get time off for good behavior and be released in eight years to supervised probation.

But Josiah thought Mr. Stefan Alabaster IV could take comfort from the fact that he was listed under the Notable People section on Wooster's Wikipedia page, regardless of his crimes. Josiah himself had been on it for sixteen hours before someone had gone in and taken his entry off.

It might have been the greatest sixteen hours of his life up until that point.

THE SECOND person who told Josiah that he was an actor of the highest caliber was his agent, the indomitable Starla Worthington. It had been rather like fate, their meeting, as if the stars had aligned in the heavens above because they *knew* Josiah was fated to become something more.

It occurred in the La Brea Coin-Op Laundry.

He stood in his underwear and a white undershirt, trying to figure out why the washing machine kept rejecting his quarters (he would find later he was trying to use pesos), when a rather colorful curse came from the line of machines opposite him. He looked up in time to see a small black woman with a lit cigarette clenched between her teeth pull out a healthy selection of undergarments, all of which had been turned pink.

"What the bitch is this?" the woman growled.

"That's the pink machine," Josiah told her. "It always turns everything pink."

She looked over her shoulder, eyes narrowing. "Don't try it, you fuck."

And because Josiah was a fan of the classics, he *knew* what the next line was. He was pleased to meet another cinephile. He squared his shoulders and twisted his lips in a snarl. His flip-flops slid a little on the dirty floor. "You talkin' to me? You talkin' to me? You talkin' to me? Then who the hell else are you talking—" He glanced back over his shoulder before looking back at the woman. "He… you talking to me?" He pointed at himself. "Well, I'm the only one here. Who the *fuck* do you think you're talking to? Oh yeah? Okay."

The woman stared at him.

Josiah broke character and grinned at her.

"One moment," the woman said, and she turned toward an oversize purse sitting in a laundry basket.

Josiah waited.

To say he was surprised when he received a face full of Mace a moment later would be an understatement. He was not proud of the way he screamed as he ran out of the La Brea Coin-Op Laundry.

Later, after LA's finest had come and gone and the world was slightly less blurry, the woman said, "Travis Bickle. You were doing the scene from *Taxi Driver*."

Josiah sighed. "You shouldn't say lines from movies unless you're planning on acting out the entire scene. It's the law. Okay, it's not *actually* the law, but it should be."

"You an actor?"

Josiah puffed out his chest. Yes, his eyes were leaking and his skin was swollen and red, and he was pretty sure there were snot bubbles hanging from his mustache, but dammit, he *was* an actor. "Absolutely. You ever hear of the Mattress Dictator?"

The woman coughed out a puff of blue smoke. "Kiddo, everyone's heard of the Mattress Dictator."

"Well, *I* was in one of his commercials. The Dictator himself cast me after seeing me working at the car wash. Said that I had a certain appeal that would be sure to get people onto mattresses." Josiah frowned. "I don't know why I had to take off my pants for the audition at his house and jump on a trampoline in a Speedo while he smoked a cigar, but it all worked out in the end. It was my big break. Well, sort of. It's the *start* of my big break. I'm still waiting for it to actually break. It's more cracked right now."

"A trampoline in a Speedo," the woman repeated. "And you don't know why he asked you to do that."

Josiah shrugged. "I expect it was because he wanted to test my endurance. It's not the weirdest thing I've had to do for an audition. This one time, I had to pretend to eat a parrot while wearing a skirt. I think it was for almond milk or Toyota or something."

The woman looked toward the sky. She took a deep breath. "Oh my sweet, sweet summer child."

"I was born in January," Josiah told her, because even though she had maced him for his Robert De Niro impression, he didn't want her to think he was something he wasn't.

She stuck out her hand. "Starla Worthington. Agent."

It took him a second to find her hand because everything was still blurry. "Josiah Erickson. Actor. Waiter. Car washer. Dog walker. Sometimes. I don't do well with picking up poop. I always gag and—" He paused. He frowned. And then his eyes widened, which was not the best move given that he was still in quite a bit of pain. "Ow. Did you say you were—motherfucking *ow*. It burns! Holy god, it *burns*." He sneezed. It felt wet. He wiped his nose with his arm. "Did you say what I think you said? You're an *agent*?"

"That's what I said, kid."

"This is—oh my god, I need to—hold on. Don't move. Stay *right* here."

He spun on his heels to head back inside. He misjudged the distance to the door and walked into it. The glass rattled. "This is the best day ever," he breathed, even though there was a good chance his nose was bleeding. He managed to get inside the coin-op without further injury and grabbed his backpack. It hadn't been stolen, which was lucky. He shouldn't have left it in here, but he hadn't had much choice when he'd run screaming after getting maced. He went back outside, heart beating rapidly in his chest.

Starla hadn't moved. He opened his backpack and pulled out the portfolio that had cost him three months of his food budget, but it'd been worth it. *Yes*, it could be said that surviving on crackers and hot dogs and sneaking bites off near-finished plates at the restaurant was unbecoming of an actor who had once been a block of American cheese in Ohio, but he was one of *thousands* who had big dreams and a small amount of cash. You couldn't walk very far in Los Angeles without tripping over someone who had a script that just *needed* to be produced or had stood in line for seven hours for an audition that was cast before they'd made it in front of the firing squad.

But here he was, in his underwear and flip-flops, face on fire and most likely bleeding, and he had managed to stumble upon an agent. He would be foolish to let this moment pass him by.

And besides. She had actually *helped* him by causing him great amounts of pain. He wasn't hungry at all now. In fact, he felt slightly nauseous. He wouldn't need to eat tonight, no sir!

It was finally happening. It was all finally happening.

"My portfolio," he said, thrusting the folder at her. "As you'll soon see, I have a wide range. I can be happy." He grinned. It hurt. He wondered if his nose was broken. "I can cry on cue! But... you can't tell that right now because I'm already sort of crying because I was temporarily blinded and might have fractured my nose. I can be *menacing*." He growled at her. "I can play a teenager. 'Like, totes mcgoats!' I could be a scientist." He brought his hand to his beard and rubbed it scientifically. It was coated with snot and blood. "'The earth will be destroyed by a meteor unless we avert this crisis by changing the polarity of the axis and using the ozone to cause a gravitational reaction that will expel the meteor back into space where it belongs.' I can be a *villain*." He twirled the ends of his mustache. There was definitely snot and blood. "You'll never get to the girl in time, Agent Magnum von Saviorface. She's trapped on top of the volcano laser, which will certainly mean her *doom*." He cackled maniacally.

"Wow," Starla said, obviously impressed by his range. "That's... something."

He nodded furiously. "And if you'll just...." He helped her open the portfolio. "Okay, so this is from the series I call *The Many Faces of Josiah Erickson*. Here is me being pensive in black and white. Here is me being pensive in color." He flipped the page. "Oooh, and this one is me pretending I'm getting chased by a killer with a large knife who just murdered all of my friends using a combination of drills, hammers, and a table saw. And *this* one is me at the beach letting the water cascade down my chest and stomach. And *yes*, I do have ab muscles, thank you for noticing. The only reason I do is a combination of not enough money for food and a gym membership I won in radio trivia for knowing the answer to the question of, on average, adults do this about seventy times per day. The answer was *complain*. I'm really good at radio trivia. Now, as you can see, I have hair on my chest and stomach, but I have *no* problem in getting that waxed should the situation call for it. And *this* one is me with the face I would make if I were in a period piece and the love of my life just suffered a horrible death from the plague. Obviously, it's a mixture of anguish, horror, and disgust because the love of my life is most likely leaking pus out his and/or her eyes and mouth. And *this* one is me—"

Starla snapped the portfolio closed. "You fuck around?"

Josiah blinked. "Like, a love scene? Because I have no problem with nudity if that's what you're asking. Every morning I practice flexing my butt muscles in the mirror in case I have to—"

"You ever screw someone for a job?"

Josiah was aghast. "Never! That's—that's *terrible*. Why would you—"

"So if a big-name director came to you and said you can have this role that will most likely open big doors for you, but you have to fuck these three studio execs, what do you say?"

"Um. No?"

She snorted. "Really."

"Well, I mean, I don't—I wouldn't *enjoy* it. I'm not—I'm demisexual."

She stared at him.

"It means that I don't experience sexual attraction until I—"

"I know what that means. I have a Tumblr account. And it was a trick question. If a big-name director came to you and said you can have this role but you need to screw studio execs, you tell him to fuck off because the patriarchy is *bullshit* and you don't have time for that crap. Take it from me. Men can be disgusting, but men in power? Ain't nobody got time for that."

"Ha!" Josiah said. "References. I got that one. I saw it on… and now you're glaring at me."

"Do you have any tattoos?"

"No? I mean, almost everyone I know does, but needles scare me, so I don't have any. I mean, why would you want to sit in a chair and get repeatedly stabbed—"

"You do drugs?"

"No? Wait. I smoke weed, but—"

"Kid, everybody smokes weed. *I* smoke weed. It's for my arthritis that I will probably get at some point when I'm older. You shove shit up your nose?"

Josiah frowned. "A marble once. But I was fifteen, and it was a dare. It got stuck until I sneezed so hard it shot out and cracked a window."

"Jesus," she muttered. Then, "Your beard. And that mustache."

"What about them?"

"Why do they exist?"

"Oh. Well, I mean, I suppose I can get rid of them if I need to—"

"Don't. Keep them. It makes you look like you'd spend seven hundred dollars on a framed Washington State license plate from the seventies."

"Wow," Josiah said. "They sell those? That would look so awesome next to my—"

"The haircut."

He frowned. "What's wrong with it?" It was long on the top and shaved on the sides. He'd done it himself. He thought it looked pretty good, especially since he only had one mirror.

"You look like every white guy on the Internet ever."

"Oh. Thank you?"

"Is that your natural color?"

"Um. Yes? It's brown, so. Does it not... look natural?"

She ignored him. "Are you wearing contacts, or is that your natural eye color? I can't tell, given how swollen your face is."

"Natural. They're blue like ice, or so this random stranger told me at a bar once. He was really drunk and trying to put his mouth on me—"

She reached into her purse and pulled out a case. Inside was a card she shoved into his hand. He squinted down at it, trying to make out the wording.

Above an address and a phone number, it said:

Worthington Talent Agency
We see what you're Worth!
Starla Worthington

"Once your face clears up, you call me," she said. "I'll have you come in, sign your life over to me, and we'll see what we see."

This was it.

This was going to change everything.

This was the moment he'd look back on when he stood in a tuxedo on a stage and spouted the bullshit that first and foremost, he wanted to thank god, because with him all things are possible and—

"Are you *crying*?" Starla demanded.

"No," Josiah said in a choked voice. "It's just the Mace."

"You're an actor of the highest caliber," Starla told him a few months later. He sat in her smoky office, the ancient ceiling fan creaking overhead. "I got you an audition for a commercial."

Josiah fist-pumped.

"Don't ever do that again."

He put his fist down. "What's it for?"

"Does it matter? It's an *audition*. I called in a couple of favors. The director is the son of an old friend of mine."

"Wow," Josiah said, suitably impressed. "Connections."

Starla waved at him dismissively. "My friend is a scumbag who probably should have been arrested years ago. I've got the photographs to prove it. Which means you've got an audition."

Josiah nodded. "What's my motivation? My character arc? Do I have a backstory?"

She handed over a sheet of paper. "Congrats, kid. You've got genital herpes. Sell it."

AND THAT was how Josiah Erickson earned his first nationally televised role, that of Basketball Guy in a commercial about medication for a sexually transmitted disease. It played in over forty different markets *during the day*, often sandwiched between babies crawling in diapers and a random celebrity looking pensive and broody in a luxury car.

In it he wore tiny shorts that clung to the muscles in his thighs, and a tank top. The director—a greasy-looking man named Dan who told him they were going to bring the *sex* back to sexually transmitted diseases—all but demanded it. It took thirty-seven takes, mostly because Josiah needed to be reminded that there was no ad-libbing. It didn't help that Josiah had already given Basketball Guy a backstory in which he'd gotten his STD from a sex worker he'd fallen in love with named Salient Sal, a high-priced escort in the City of Angels. Their love was doomed, given that Salient Sal's pimp had an iron grasp around him, and the only thing that Basketball Guy had gotten to prove their love was real was sores on his junk.

Dan didn't want to hear about any of that, so Josiah made the decision to focus on the script.

There were shots of him dribbling a basketball with a group of guys, wide smiles on their faces because life was *good*. He'd take a couple of shots, and they'd high-five each other, all while Josiah was thinking about Salient Sal and how he needed to forget about him. So while the others were just boys being boys, Josiah's joie de vivre was tinged with the sadness of a love lost to the ravages of the sexual desires of men with money. Josiah's new teammates faded to the background as he turned to face the camera. And as he opened his mouth to speak *only* the lines that had been written for him, he made sure he remembered kissing Salient Sal at night in the rain under a streetlamp.

"I don't let a flare-up of genital herpes affect my game," he said, holding the basketball under his arm. "With Herpetrex, I can get back to doing what I love most. Genital herpes?" He shook his head. "Not today. They're gone in a *swish*."

He turned and shot the ball toward the basket.

The first time, he whiffed it and the ball hit one of the extras in the back of the head.

It took another sixteen takes, but the ball eventually went where it was supposed to go.

Sports were dumb.

THE COMMERCIAL was released.

It was *huge*.

He gained thirty-two Instagram followers because of it. The world was his oyster.

He became extraordinarily successful and went on to become the world's biggest movie star. He also found love in the arms of an Armenian businessman and started a charity that built shelters for homeless dogs, who were given all the squeaky balls and rawhide bones they could ever want.

And it all happened because of genital herpes, which was the point of this story all along.

Therefore, this is the end.

JUST KIDDING.

That's not what happened at all.

HERE WAS Josiah Erickson now, three years after having met Starla Worthington while wearing nothing but his underwear and flip-flops, in what could be his greatest role.

The target was sitting at the table in the crowded restaurant. Sweat trickled down the back of his neck. He only had one chance to make this right. The president was dead. The vice president had been kidnapped. No one was running the government, and the world was descending into chaos. He was undercover, having been thrust into this role after inadvertently witnessing the assassination of the leader of the free world. The girl he loved was in danger (she had been the president's secretary), and he was going to do what he had to in order to save the day.

Which meant serving the food to the mark.

The mark who could lead him to the shadow organization that had taken everything.

The tray was ready.

He straightened his apron and brushed back his hair.

The presentation was immaculate. *He* was immaculate. He lifted the tray and plastered a smile on his face.

"Action," he whispered.

"*Cut*," an annoyed voice called.

The lights went up. An alarm blared.

Josiah blinked. "What? What happened? What's going on?"

A man standing near a row of windows scowled at him. "You said action. *Again*. For the *fourth time*. You're not supposed to say action. *I'm* supposed to say action. *I'm* the director."

"Right," Josiah said hastily. "My bad. I'm just really excited about working with you. I've seen everything you've ever done."

"I've directed four commercials," the man said. "And a music video for a punk band called Writhing Death Maggots of Festering Doom who sang songs about shooting up heroin and having their hearts broken."

Josiah had no idea who the Writhing Death Maggots of Festering Doom were, nor did he know this director before meeting him literally two hours ago. "Exactly. All that… heroin. They're so authentic."

The man (Dave? Keith? Esteban?) snorted. "They're four white rich kids from Brentwood. I worked for one of their fathers at the time and was forced to do it."

"I, too, suffer for my art," Josiah said seriously. "Also, I've been thinking about my role. So since the president was assassinated and I'm delivering this blooming onion to the mark who—"

Dave/Keith/Esteban threw up his hands. "This is a *commercial*. For *Applebee's*. The only reason we hired you was because you're hot and have experience. And also, it was cheaper because this is where you actually work."

"Thank you," Josiah said, because he was humble.

"Can you do this?"

He could. "Yes."

"*Without* saying action?"

He could. "Yes."

"Okay. Get back to your mark. We're going to go again. Places, everyone."

The director's minions scurried around him. One came to Josiah and took the tray from him. Another dragged him back to stand on a small piece of blue tape on the carpet.

"How's my makeup?" Josiah asked her.

She rolled her eyes. "Fine. Seriously. Don't piss this guy off any more. He will ruin you for Applebee's commercials forever. And then where will you be?"

"Working at Applebee's."

"Yeah. Exactly."

And since Josiah was nothing but a consummate professional, he stood where he was supposed to and waited for the gaffer to fix the lighting. He told himself to forget the backstory, forget Katrina, the woman he loved who was being held prisoner, forget the *goddamn vice president*, because he had a *job* to do. A job that was paying scale, which was barely more than the tips he made but would still allow him to survive in this cutthroat world.

He could *do* this.

"Annnnd... *action*."

He smiled.

He lifted the tray.

He carried it to a smiling interracial lesbian couple with their adopted Russian children (backstory) and said, "Gosh, I hope y'all are ready for a treat. I've got your bloomin' onion right here and ready—"

"*Cut*."

The adopted Russian children glared up at him.

"Y'all," Dave/Keith/Esteban said. "*Y'all*. Why. Why would you do that?"

"I can do accents," Josiah said, handing the tray back to the harried assistant. "I am very versatile."

"This asshole," one of the adopted Russian children said, sounding very much like she was from the Valley. "Would someone get my agent on the phone? I don't have *time* for this. Do any of you know who I am? I was on the *Disney* Channel. And where the hell is my mother? I swear to god, if she's not here with my grande quad nonfat one pump no-whip mocha in the next four minutes, the ride home is going to be a *nightmare* for her." She pushed her way up from the table and shoved Josiah as she stalked away.

"That amount of coffee is bad for your tiny body!" Josiah called after her.

She flipped him off without looking back at him. It was rather intimidating coming from an eight-year-old.

"One more take," Dave/Keith/Esteban warned. "I will give you *one more take*. If you don't do it like you're supposed to, you're fired, and I will make sure you *never* work in this town again. In commercials. For Applebee's. Do you understand me?"

Loud and clear.

An hour later he had delivered what he thought would go down in history as the most riveting performance of an Applebee's waiter bringing a meal to an interracial lesbian couple and their adopted Russian children.

When they'd finished, he thought about asking if there was going to be a wrap party, but it wouldn't have mattered. He still had a ten-hour shift ahead of him.

So the bright lights and the cameras were all gone, leaving behind only Josiah Erickson, standing in his brightly colored uniform, his apron adorned with pins with cheerful legends such as *HAPPY HOUR 2-4-1 M-F!* and *ASK ME ABOUT THE APPETIZERS!*

He was very blessed.

(Mostly. His feet hurt. As did his back. And after his shift, he had to go twirl a sign on a street corner while wearing a crown and cape, trying to get people to pull over into the check-cashing place behind him. But still. Blessed.)

Chapter 2

"How'd it go yesterday?" Serge asked as Josiah slumped into his usual chair for Tuesday brunch. Even though it was mid-September, they still lived in Los Angeles, which meant it was hot as balls. He was already sweating through his tank top. The air-conditioning in his car had gone out six months ago, and he hadn't had the funds to get it fixed. There were more important things than air-conditioning. Like headshots. And facials to keep his pores clear.

"Good," Josiah said, because he was eternally optimistic. "I didn't get fired, and they only had to yell at me six or seven times."

"You're holding yourself stiffly. Have you not been centering your chakras as I've shown you?"

Josiah didn't... well. He didn't quite *understand* the concept of chakras. Oh sure, he knew they were inside him, and if he was thinking of the right place, they were somewhere near his pancreas (whatever *that* was), but they were important to Serge, so he tried his best to feign as much interest as possible. "Every morning," he said. "I do the chants and everything."

Serge frowned as he reached up to rub his designer stubble. His massive eyebrows did a complicated dance as his eyes narrowed, and Josiah wondered if Serge was seeing his chakras *right now* and would find out he wasn't doing his morning chants as often as he should. The eight months Serge had spent in India had changed him (as had the three weeks in the hospital where most of his insides had tried to leave to his outsides), and Josiah was convinced that Serge had some sort of mystical powers now. Serge, for his part, never denied it.

"Maybe you should come down to my studio. I have learned a new pose I believe you must try. It is the kala bhairavasana. The Destroyer of the Universe."

"That sounds...." Terrible. It sounded terrible. "Amazing. And complicated. And potentially life-threatening. I doubt I'd be able to do it, so it's probably best that we don't try. Remember what happened the last time you tried to bend me? I accidentally kicked that woman in the face."

Serge shrugged. "Mrs. Wellington didn't mind."

"I gave her a black eye!"

"She's developed her prana. Pain is but an illusion of the mind. I also gave her three free classes, so she promised not to sue you."

"Which is awesome, because if she'd taken the twenty-six dollars I have, it would make me sad. I worked hard for it."

"I can give you a loan if—"

Josiah shook his head. "I don't want your money. I told Xander the same thing. And Casey, especially when he offered to let me use his house here, even though it's in the middle of bumfuck nowhere."

Serge sighed and, for a moment, dropped the Yogi act. "Josy, you know you can—"

"I know. But I don't *want* to. It's not bad. At least not yet. I'm not late on the rent or anything. And I still have my phone, so I can update my followers on every single thing I do. Speaking of which." He pulled out his phone, grabbed Serge by the back of the neck, and squished their faces together. They smiled perfectly as he snapped the picture. "What filter should I use? I'm thinking something black and white. It'll show I'm artistic and think deep thoughts about the welfare of the ocean or the lives of sheep farmers in Middle America."

Serge rolled his eyes. "Instagram is so twelve seconds ago. It's all about Moi Mir now. It's Russian, and anyone who is *anyone* is using it."

"What? But I don't speak Russian!"

Serge waved him away. "No one does. It's, like, a made-up language. Just download the app and try to create an account. It took me seven hours to figure it out, but I already have sixteen thousand followers. They like it when I pose in my yoga pants with my legs over my head."

"Dammit," Josiah muttered. "Just when I think I know what I'm doing, the Russians come in and change everything. The world is unnecessarily complicated. I guess I'll just post this on Instagram for now. Do we still use hashtags, or is that not a thing we do anymore either?"

"If you must. It's so… retro."

Right. Retro. "But that will make it cool again. Like when we wore snap bracelets ironically for three days last summer."

"We are front and center of the cultural revolution," Serge agreed.

It was hard being so influential all the time. "Hashtag Josy's modern life. Hashtag Tuesday brunch is the best brunch. Hashtag bearded queers. Hashtag I love Serge. Hashtag Instagays. Annnnd… posted. Now where is Xander, and why don't I have a mimosa in my hand? I have been sitting here for almost four minutes."

"There's a line at the bar," Serge said. "We may have to relocate again before the masses descend even more. It's why a large group of people is known as a No Thank You."

Josy hoped it wouldn't be *too* far. They'd already switched their Tuesday brunch places three times in seven months, and each time, it got farther from his apartment. Gas was expensive, and he hated taking the bus. "Maybe we should just stick it out for as long as we can."

Serge looked horrified. "We're *hipsters*. We're fickle creatures. Nothing we do is supposed to be predictable. Or make sense. It's our job to keep everyone guessing."

"Yeah, yeah," Josy mumbled, sinking lower in his seat. He slid his mirror shades off the top of his head down to his eyes. He sighed in relief as he stretched his legs. It felt good to be off his feet for once.

Xander appeared a few minutes later, carrying three champagne glasses. He looked like he'd gained at least three pounds of muscle since Josy had seen him on Saturday. The colorful tattoos up and down his arms were bright in the sunlight. "Saw your selfie on Instagram. About time you got here. And no one posts on Instagram anymore. It's all about—"

"Russia," Josy muttered. "I know. Serge told me. I don't know why you guys couldn't send a Snap to let me know. I probably look ridiculous now."

"You're wearing socks with pumpkins on them. In public."

Josy didn't know what *that* had to do with anything. "I love them."

"Don't stifle his creativity," Serge said. "You know he likes to express himself through socks."

"It's for Halloween," Josy said, turning his head as Xander bent down and kissed him on the cheek.

"It's September," Xander reminded him as he sat down in the empty chair.

"Close enough. Also, I won tickets on the radio on my way over. Whose turn is it to go with me?"

"*Again?*" Xander asked, sounding aghast. "How the hell do you do that?"

Josy shrugged. "I dunno, man. Just something I'm good at, I guess. You know how I get when I smoke a bowl. Like, philosophical and shit."

"That's not—" Xander sighed. "What was the question?"

"Thirty percent of adults have this stolen from them at work."

"Tape," Serge said.

"Nope."

"Yogurt," Xander said.

"Nope. God, you guys suck at this. The answer is *ideas*. Thirty percent of adults have their *ideas* stolen at work."

Xander and Serge stared at him.

Josy shrugged. "I've never had that happen to me. Most times whenever I have ideas, I'm told to stop it and stick to the script." He cocked his head. "They tell me that at Applebee's too. I don't know why."

"How… sad." Xander took a drink of his mimosa. "What are the tickets for?"

This wasn't going to go over well. But if Josy could stand on the sidewalk and twirl a sign to convince people to cash their checks and possibly take out a loan while they were at it, he could do anything. "A poetry slam."

"Oh no," Serge said. "Of all the luck. I already have plans."

"I didn't even tell you when it is yet!"

"I know. But I guarantee I'm already going to have plans."

He looked at Xander.

"No."

"Oh, come on! You know I have to go!"

"You don't."

"I *do*. If I don't, then my luck will run out and I won't win anything ever again! Everyone knows when you win a prize on the radio, you have to go to whatever it is that you've won, even if you'd rather scratch your eyes out instead. It's the law of averages."

"That's not what any of that means," Xander told him.

"Regardless, I have to go. What if I don't, and then the next time, it's not radio trivia but a movie role that will allow me to pose on a movie poster with a big gun while something explodes behind me? *Josiah Erickson is… Johnny Destruction*. You know it's my dream to be photoshopped onto a movie poster with an explosion behind me. Why would you want to take that away from me?"

Serge and Xander exchanged a look before Serge said, "That's… Josy, that's not how things work. At all."

Josy scowled at them. "You don't know that! Serge, did I try and crap all over your dream when you decided you wanted to open a yoga studio after you randomly went to India?"

"No," Serge said slowly. "But you initially thought yoga was a type of Chinese food."

"And when I found out it wasn't?"

Serge sighed. "You did the splits and asked if that was yoga. And then screamed that you'd broken your balls."

"Exactly. And Xander, when you wanted to open your tattoo parlor, did I tell you it was a bad idea?"

Xander sat back in his chair, crossing his arms. "You said that if it was my dream to give sorority girls tramp stamps, then you would support me. But that's not what I—"

"Damn right," Josy crowed. "So *yes*. Whatever you guys do, I'm there for you. And now all I'm asking for is for one of you to go to a poetry slam with me so I don't lose my streak of good luck that will one day land me a pilot on the CW where I will play a sixteen-year-old, even though I'll be, like, thirty."

Xander looked at Serge. "I went with him to the monster truck rally when he won tickets. That should count for at least six times."

"You also ended up fucking the man who drove the monster truck that looked like a llama," Serge reminded him. "I had to go to the wrestling match where the drunk guy sitting next to us told me he wasn't into that *queer shit*, but that my mouth was wide and to meet him in the bathroom."

Xander sniffed. "It's not my fault you didn't go."

"He was there with his wife and fifteen children! He had a Confederate flag on his shirt! And who the hell hits on someone by telling them they have a wide mouth?"

"You would think for as little you get laid, you wouldn't be fighting opportunities to—"

"That's disgusting!"

"It was a joke. I don't have to—who are you calling?"

Josy glared at both of them as he held the phone up to his ear. "My best friend, seeing as how my *other* best friends are being stupid and I don't want to talk to them right now."

Xander groaned. "Jesus. I can't believe you think he's your best friend. He's fucking weird."

"Don't be mean," Serge chided him. "Josy is allowed to—"

"Thank you for calling Pastor Tommy's Video Rental Emporium, where we offer recommendations based on your every need. This is Casey. How can I help you?"

"Casey," Josy moaned into the phone. "I need him."

"Oh man," Casey said. "I was wondering what took so long. You've been at brunch for fifteen minutes already. You normally call before then. Gus was getting worried. Hold on."

"You've done it now," Serge muttered.

"It's not my fault Josy has this dumb thing with—"

Josy ignored them, instead focusing on what sounded like a scuffle coming on the other end of the phone. He heard Casey say, "Just take it. You know you want to," and a grumpy voice replied, "You have to know how that sounds. You're doing this against my will, and that's *illegal*."

Josy already felt better.

There was an aggrieved sigh, and the grumpy voice spoke into the phone. "Gustavo Tiberius speaking."

"Gustavo!" Josy cried. "I need you."

"No," Gustavo said. "No, no, no. Casey said it was a customer with a question. My trust has been betrayed. Do you have any idea what day it is?"

"Tuesday," Josy said. "The same day I always call you."

"It's ninety-nine cent rental day. I'm busy."

"But I need your advice. You know that you're the only person in the world who I trust to give me advice. It's why you're my best friend."

"I am no such thing! I barely even know you!"

"Don't lie, man. We talk every Tuesday, and you always pretend that you don't like it. Casey told me you were worried."

"I wasn't worried. I merely wondered why you hadn't bothered me yet. For all you know, I have a line of customers out the door and don't have time for your inane prattling."

"Do you have a line of customers out the door?"

Silence. Then, "No."

"Good," Josy said, relieved. "Because this is important."

Gustavo made a strangled noise. "Fine. But make it quick. The We Three Queens will be here shortly, and I'll need to reshelve the movie they return before they select the next one. I need to focus."

"What are they up to now?"

"A German film called *Mein Bruder, Der Vampir*, or literally translated, *My Brother, the Vampire*, even though for some reason, it was released in the United States under the title *Getting My Brother Laid*. Apparently Americans won't go see an obscure foreign film about a mentally disabled man falling in love with his brother's girlfriend unless there is the promise of sex. I don't understand people."

"Right? That's exactly my problem!"

"Your problem is *Mein Bruder, Der Vampir*?"

"No," Josy said. "My problem is that Xander and Serge won't tell me which one of them will go with me to the poetry slam I won tickets for by getting the right answer on the radio."

"What."

"You don't understand German vampires have sex, and I don't get why people won't go with me to a poetry slam."

"I don't like you."

"Yes, you do. Casey said—"

"Casey is stoned right now. Anything he says can't be trusted."

"Huh. I'm also stoned, though it was shitty ragweed—"

"You're so—ugh. Fine. If I tell you what to do, do you promise never to call me again?"

"You know I can't do that, Gustavo. You're one of my best friends. What would I do without you?"

"Fall into a river of lava and die?" Gustavo asked hopefully.

"Probably, which is why I need you."

Gustavo groaned. "Fine. Xander has to go with you because of how he ditched you at the monster truck rally to go have sex with the llama monster truck driver, and if you *ever* make me repeat a sentence like that again, I will cancel your video membership to the Emporium that you made me give you under duress, and you will never be allowed to rent a movie from my store again. Do you understand me?"

"Oh no," Josy said. "Wherever else would I go to watch movies? If only there was some newfangled technology where I could download anything I wanted online."

"The Internet is a *fad* that is full of Tumbling and children who write explicit fan fiction pornography based upon my boyfriend's books. They should be outside playing with pinecones or hula hoops or whatever it is children do these days, *not* talking about a fictional threesome that will never happen."

"Did you read the one I emailed Casey where Desmondo and Martindale had tentacles for hands and stuck them up Catarina's—"

"Never call here again!"

The phone beeped in his ear as Gustavo disconnected the call.

Josy immediately felt better. Gustavo did that for him. Ever since he'd run his lines for his audition for Campbell's Chunky Classic Chicken Noodle Soup with Gustavo that had somehow turned into a harrowing tale of familial strife and patricide, they had had a close bond. Granted,

Gustavo hadn't seen it that way for a very long time, but Gustavo was a whale and Josy was his barnacle. It was just meant to be.

"Gustavo said Xander has to go with me because of the llama monster truck guy," Josy announced, setting his phone down on the table.

"And why, exactly, do I need to do anything he says?" Xander asked.

"Because you ditched me," Josy said slowly, "to screw a guy who drove a monster truck shaped like a llama."

Xander blinked. "That's—okay. I've got nothing to say to that. I'll go to your poetry slam thing."

"Good. Now that that's settled, someone better bring me some eggs and hash browns. Is this brunch or is it communist China? Also, what's communism?"

LATER, AS he smoked another bowl while getting ready for work, he sent a quick text.

Xander sez he goin. Thks.

He got a response less than a minute later. *I don't know what any of that says. Use full words like a normal person. You have somewhat of a grasp of the English language. Use it.*

It was followed by a second text.

You're welcome.

"I CAN'T believe this is how I'm spending my Friday night," Xander muttered as they walked toward the building lit up in front of them. "I at least thought this was going to be at a coffee shop. You didn't say anything about a library. Who the hell goes to a library?"

"Librarians," Josy said. He straightened his suspenders over the gnarly Hypercolor shirt Serge had given him as a birthday present. Serge had found it on eBay, and though it didn't change colors anymore, just the fact that he had one was enough for Josy. Well, mostly. Yes, he had spent a good hour and a half blowing on it to see if it would work, even going as far as to consider shoving it in the microwave, but he didn't know if the Hypercolor technology would start a fire, so he just accepted it for what it was: a piece of history that he could wear whenever he wanted. "People who like books. Older men who can't look up porn online at home."

"I'm so mad at you right now."

"That indica tablet kicking in yet?"

Xander rolled his eyes. "Mellow, right?"

"Supposed to be."

"Yeah. It's working. I like it."

"Casey sent it to me. And this topical lotion infused with THC. I rub it on my feet."

"I didn't need to know that."

"My feet feel good."

"Don't talk about your feet."

"My socks have cows on them. I don't know where I got them."

Xander sighed. "I bought them for you."

"Oh. Right. Sorry, man. I'm like, *really* mellow right now."

"Jesus fucking Christ," Xander muttered. Then, "Why are there so many people here?"

And there were a lot more than Josy expected. Granted, he wasn't an expert when it came to library-based poetry slams, but even he was surprised how many people were already lining up outside. And none of them were wearing berets, which he thought was practically a requirement. He was thankful he'd decided to leave his own beret at home. It hadn't matched his outfit.

"People must really like poetry," Josy said as they reached the end of the line, others already starting to gather behind them. "Culture or whatever."

"We could be having culture in a bar right now."

"Yeah, but this is free. And maybe for once, I don't have to sit next to you as your wingman while you and Serge try to find your next conquest."

That wiped the scowl from Xander's face. He almost looked uncharacteristically concerned. It was probably just the tablet, but still. "You don't like going out with us?"

Josy shrugged and looked away. He hadn't meant to bring this up. "I mean... I don't know. I love you guys, but it gets kind of old after a little while. I don't like the same things you guys do. It was better when Casey was here. You know, Aces Unite! Or whatever. But now that he's in Oregon with Gustavo, it's just... different."

"I didn't even think about that," Xander admitted, and Josy felt a little bad. "I'm not trying to make you feel left out. And I know Serge isn't either."

Josy didn't want to talk about this right now. His tablet was kicking in pretty good, and he didn't like feeling down when he was stoned. It made things worse. "I know you don't. Let's just—"

"You want like… a boyfriend? Or something?"

Well, yes. Of course he did. Didn't everyone? Someone who could laugh with him and go to poetry slams without being guilted into it by a video store owner in Oregon. Someone who wasn't necessarily preoccupied with getting laid all the time. It wasn't that Josy didn't like sex. It just took him a long time to ever get to the point where he thought sex was something he wanted with a person. And usually the guy was long gone by then. Josy had learned rather quickly that people didn't put time into things without a payoff. And it sucked, because he couldn't ever guarantee there'd *be* one. It wasn't how he was wired.

But a boyfriend who liked to get stoned and maybe lay on top of each other on a couch while they called in to radio stations to win tickets for things? Josy could be okay with that.

He shrugged. "I dunno, man. I mean, it's like—okay. You and Serge like sticking your dicks in things, right?"

The woman in front of them turned slowly to stare at them.

"He means people," Xander said quickly. "Not things. I like sticking my dick in *people*."

"Well, you'd be in the right place," she said before turning back around, whatever *that* meant.

Xander punched Josy on the arm. "Maybe think before you speak?"

Josy shrugged. "I'm stoned, man. You know how I get when I'm stoned. Like, words. All the words."

"You really miss Casey, huh?"

"Yeah. I mean, of course I do. I know he's all small-town hipster lumberjack now. And he's happy, which is awesome. He gets to write his books, he gets to be around Gustavo all the time—"

"Oh, because that's such a great thing," Xander muttered.

Josy ignored him. "And he even got to open his 420-friendly bed-and-breakfast in Abby. That's living the life, man. Go for the strawberry festivals, stay for the edibles at Baked-Inn & Eggs."

Xander stared at him strangely. "Is that what you want?"

"To run a bed-and-breakfast called Baked-Inn & Eggs? Nah. I mean, I wouldn't say no. Did you see the new updated menu? He made pot peanut butter! The chunky kind. You can put it on toast and everything." He frowned. "Now I'm hungry. Did you bring snacks?"

"No, I didn't bring—I'm not talking about the bed-and-breakfast. I'm talking about the whole… life that's he's living. If you could even call it that."

Josy squinted at him. "That's not nice. I don't get why you can't be happy for him. I know you don't like Gustavo for reasons that make absolutely no sense, but they're good for each other. Casey is happier than he's ever been. And Gustavo even smiles once a week now by himself."

"I'm not talking about Gus," Xander said as he rolled his eyes. "I'm talking about you."

The line slowly began to move forward. "Oh. What was the question again? I'm pretty high right now and I totally forgot what we're talking about. Did you say you brought snacks?"

Xander rubbed a hand over his face. "Do you want a boyfriend?"

"Oh yeah! I mean, sure. I wouldn't say no to a boyfriend. But you know how people get when I tell them I'm demi. I had one guy say it wasn't a thing because there's a lot of people who don't want to have sex until there's a more meaningful connection. I mean, *yeah*, but it's not the same thing."

Xander scowled. "People like him aren't worth your time. Why didn't you say anything?"

"Because then you'd get that pissed-off look you have on your face right now when you're trying to figure out how to murder someone and get away with it."

"I don't like it when people make you feel like shit. It's not fair."

Josy linked his arm through Xander's and tugged him close. "I know. It's why I love you."

"You get so sappy when you're stoned."

"You like it."

"No one will ever believe you."

They reached the stairs and slowly began to climb them. "It'd be easier if I could love you like that. Or Serge."

Xander choked. "Oh dear god."

"Hey! We'd be good together!"

"Josy, don't take this the wrong way, but I would never, ever want to have sex with you."

"Oh no," Josy breathed. "I'm taking it the wrong way. I don't like being high and sad."

"I told you not to," Xander said. "You're like my very annoying little brother. Sure, I thought you were hot when we first met—"

"Was that when I was dancing and you stuck your hands down the back of my pants?"

"—but then you started talking and talking and *talking*, and I realized I liked you too much to throw it all away for a quick fuck."

Josy was absurdly touched. "I wouldn't have had sex with you anyway."

Xander sighed. "I know, Josy. I know. But the fact remains I would rather have what we have now than anything else. You know that, right?"

Josy did. Xander was a dick and had a reputation as a muscle ice queen, but if he loved you, it was for life. There weren't many people in the world Xander felt that way about, and Josy considered himself one of the lucky few. "I know. I just get…. I dunno, man. It gets a little lonely, sometimes."

Xander kissed the side of his head. "You'll find someone. I promise. And they'll like you for you. The demi thing, the sock thing, the fact that you like radio trivia and make us go to poetry slams in libraries even though we could be literally anywhere else in the world. What about that ace dating app I made you download? What was it called?"

"Nuzzlr."

"Yeah, that. Anything come from that?"

"Definitely. Some guy wanted to tie me to my bed and tickle me."

"Yikes."

"Yeah, I think the app still has a few kinks it needs to work out." He laughed. "Literally. Get it? Kinks to work out? Because the guy wanted to tickle me—"

"I get it, Josy."

They were nearly at the top of the stairs. "There wasn't a lot of people on it, even for LA. And it just feels weird, you know? I'm not made for that kind of thing. I need to be friends with someone first."

"We'll figure it out," Xander told him, squeezing his arm. "And I promise not to ditch you all the time, okay?"

"Nah. It's just the indica talking, man. I don't know if you know this, but I kind of get sappy when I'm stoned."

Xander snorted. "I know, Josy."

"And besides, we'll—"

"Got your tickets? I need to scan—Xander?"

They looked toward the large dyke standing near the door. Her head was shaved, and she had beautiful tattoos along her neck and the sides of her skull. It looked like a burst of wildflowers was blooming on her skin.

"Dee," Xander said, sounding surprised. He let go of Josy and took a step toward her. They did a randomly complicated handshake that Josy could barely follow. "What are you doing here?"

"I'm the event coordinator for Q-Bert."

Josy squinted at her. "The video game character from the eighties?"

"Sorry," Xander said quickly. "This is my friend Josy. Josy, this is Dee. I do her ink."

"I like the sides of your head," Josy told her seriously.

"Thanks." She sounded amused. "I like your mustache."

He grinned at her. "We should be friends. Let me give you my phone number—"

"He's a little stoned right now." Xander sounded apologetic. "Tries to give his phone number to everyone when he's high. We have to keep an eye on him so he doesn't get kidnapped and held in a basement."

"Probably a good idea," Dee said. "Q-Bert is who you're here to see. Tickets?"

"That's a weird name for a poet," Josy muttered, pulling the tickets out of the back pocket of his skinny jeans.

Dee snorted as she took the tickets and scanned them. "Poet. That's funny."

"What's funny about it?" Xander asked.

She looked back up at them. "I don't think the Q-Man has ever been called a poet before."

Josy was confused. "Is that like an artistic thing? I don't know the rules of a poetry slam. I've never won tickets to something like this before. Last time I won, I got a week's worth of free tacos from Umberto's. They told me not to come back after the second day because of how many tacos I'd ordered. Did you know that Umberto's doesn't appreciate someone pulling up in the drive-thru and ordering one hundred tacos? *I* didn't know that."

"No," Dee said. "That's not something I would have known."

"Right? I mean, what's the difference between ten people in a row ordering ten tacos and me just doing it all at once? I had to go back in line over and over, and by the time I was done, the tacos I got at the beginning were cold!" Josy frowned. "Now I'm hungry. Xander, you wanna go get some tacos? I think we should go get tacos." He looked up at the bright lights of the library. "What were we doing here again?"

Xander sighed. "Poetry slam."

Dee blinked. "Poetry slam? Do you... do you not know who Q-Bert is?"

"Uh, no," Xander said slowly.

She smiled at them. Josy had never seen a dyke smile evilly before, but he figured there was a first time for everything. It was actually pretty great. She looked like a movie villain, Tattoo Head, and she'd probably try and take over the world's supply of honey. It would be up to Johnny Destruction to stop her. "Oh, my sweet, sweet baby queers," she said, and Josy wished she had a mustache like his so she could twirl it. "This isn't a poetry slam, and Q-Bert is most definitely not a poet." She pointed to a sign on a stand near the door.

Josy was very stoned, so it took him a moment to read it.

> Q-BERT EVENTS PRESENTS
> A Q-BERT PRODUCTION
> A READING BY THE ONE AND ONLY Q-BERT
> "GETTING POETRY SLAMMED IN MY BUTTHOLE BY SASQUATCH"
> A LOVE STORY

"The fuck," Xander said faintly.

"The Q-Man doesn't write poetry," Dee said gleefully. "He writes monster porn. And he's doing a live reading. Better get to your seats, boys. You're in for a wild ride."

Chapter 3

"What the hell is this?" Xander hissed as he dragged Josy inside.

Josy couldn't be sure he was sober enough to answer that question with any certainty. "I have no idea! I thought it was going to be poems and snapping and berets!" He paused, considering. "Though it makes sense why the guys on the radio were laughing at me when I told them I liked poems that rhymed because it made me happy all the time. I thought they just liked my poem."

"Jesus Christ," Xander groaned. "I can't believe I agreed to this. Maybe we should go—"

"We *can't*. I already told you that I have to go to every single event I win tickets to. For luck! Don't you want me to be Johnny Destruction with explosions who stops lesbians from stealing all the honey?"

Xander's face was in his hands. Behind him, an ethnically aware poster showed a group of multicultural children jumping on a trampoline while holding books. Josy didn't understand how they could read while jumping. He could barely read while sitting. "I don't know what any of that means," Xander said, though it was muffled.

Josy didn't either. "Why don't we just see how it goes?" He tilted his head. "Also, what's monster porn? I mean, I get what monsters are. And what porn is. But monster porn? Is that like the tentacles that Desmondo and Martindale shoved into Catarina—"

Xander dropped his hands. "You really had no idea?"

"Nope. You know how I get when I'm high. Apparently I hear monster porn and it somehow turns into a poetry slam. I don't know."

"You were high when you called the radio station."

"Man, I'm pretty much high a lot of the time."

"And we really have to stay?"

"Yes," Josy said. He didn't think he'd ever been more serious about anything in his life. "If we break the chain now, for all I know, I'll wake up tomorrow with no eyebrows and—okay, really. You can't *read* and jump on a trampoline at the same time, you ethnic rainbows of joy!"

"Would you stop yelling at the poster?" Xander growled at him. "I'm trying to find out how you've managed to survive this long."

"A combination of timing, luck, good beard oil, and that mustache comb you got for me two Christmases ago."

Xander looked toward the ceiling. "I love you."

"Thanks, man," Josy said happily. "I love you too."

"But I don't like you very much right now."

"Oh. That's a bummer to hear so soon after the whole love thing."

Xander shook his head. "This is important to you?"

Josy shrugged. "I mean, yeah. Right? Totally."

Xander took a deep breath. "Okay. We'll stay. But I swear to god, if this gets weird, we're leaving—"

"Wow," Josy said, pointing toward the crowd gathering in the library. "That guy is dressed like a unicorn. Do you think his tail is a butt plug? I want to go ask him if his tail is a butt plug."

"We're leaving," Xander snapped, trying to pull Josy toward the door.

"What? Why?"

"It got weird!"

"Oh, please," Josy said, jerking his arm out of Xander's hand. "We saw weirder things when we went to the Folsom Street Fair. Remember that guy sitting on the exercise bike outside of the Korean restaurant?"

"He was working out!"

"The seat was a dildo, and he was wearing nipple clamps attached to a car battery!"

"Dammit," Xander muttered. "I hate it when you remember things that negate any point I could make."

"Awesome," Josy said. "And notice how I'm not pointing out the lady that appears to be a mermaid. Or maybe she's some kind of salmon trying to swim upstream. I'm not sure."

Xander was getting twitchy again, so Josy pulled him farther into the library.

A small stage had been set up on one side of the room with rows of chairs in front of it, each with a number on the back. Josy looked at the tickets and saw they were damn near the front, which made him giddy. He couldn't exactly be sure what was happening (and he was *really* jonesing for some tater tots), but he led Xander to their seats.

He took the chair on the end of the row, and Xander sat next to him. On the other side of Xander was an older woman whose face was painted like a tiger.

Xander looked particularly aggrieved when she bared her teeth at him and growled, but he didn't say anything, for which Josy was eternally grateful.

"Hi," he said. "I'm Josiah. This is my friend Xander."

She stopped growling, her face splitting into a smile. "It's nice to meet you. I'm Tigress. I don't know the Josiah and Xander characters. Which Q-Bert book are they from?"

"Those are our real names," Xander muttered.

The woman looked surprised. "Oh. Well, I like your costumes."

"This is what we normally wear," Josy said.

"Oh," Tigress said. "Wow. You guys sure are… unique."

Since this was coming from a woman who was wearing tiger face paint, Josy took that as a great compliment. "Thank you. I think so too. I like your face."

"Oh my," Tigress said. "Aren't you just a sweetheart. What's your favorite Q-Bert book? Mine is *Blasted in the Behind by the Failed Patriarchy Who Learned Feminism Was a Good Thing.*"

Xander choked.

"Whoa," Josy said in awe. "I didn't know there were books like that. We'd never heard of Q-Bert until I won the tickets and the nice villain dyke outside told us who he was."

"You're *virgins*?" Tigress squealed. "Oh my god, we have to tell them when they ask!"

Xander's eyes narrowed. "Tell them what, exactly?"

"Oh, you'll see," Tigress said, clapping and sitting back in the chair. "Virgins are beloved here."

"But I've had sex," Josy said, confused. "It was all right, but it means more when—"

"Not that kind of virgin," Xander said.

"Oh."

"I'm never forgiving you for this."

"Nah," Josy said easily. "You will. You tell me that all the time, and yet here we are."

Before Xander could respond, the crowd started to roar as the lights began to flicker. Tigress jumped to her feet, tilting her head back and howling, which was something Josy didn't think tigers could actually do. He would need to watch more NatGeo documentaries to make sure.

He turned toward the front in time to see Dee take the stage. She stood at the podium, adjusting the microphone a bit. "We all know why you're here. You're here, in this place of literature and knowledge, to bear witness to the man. The myth. The *legend*. He who writes stories that fuel the imagination. He who spins tales of your darkest fantasies. He who has a finger on the diseased pulse of Americana. Ladies and gentle-Qs, I give you the one, the only... *Q-Bert*."

"Yay!" Josy said loudly...

...which was apparently the wrong thing to do because everyone else was silent.

"Ah," Dee said, smiling evilly once again. "At least we know where the virgins are."

"Oh my god," Xander moaned.

"I think I did it wrong," Josy whispered loudly to him. "Do you think I did that wrong?"

"Oh my god," Xander said again.

The people around them begin drumming their hands on their knees and stomping their feet as Dee left the stage. No one spoke. No one cheered. Josy wondered if this was what being in a cult was like. He reminded himself not to drink the Kool-Aid if there was any, but then he started to think about Kool-Aid, and he *really* wanted some, which led to thoughts of tater tots again, the kind covered in cheese and chili and maybe some cake and—

A man walked onto the stage, and all thoughts of the best foods to eat while stoned left his mind.

Now, it must be said that Josiah didn't necessarily experience attraction right away. Oh sure, he could appreciate when someone looked interesting, but he didn't feel that pull of *want* and *lust* that many others did. He never really had.

And that, of course, didn't change when he saw Q-Bert for the first time. Why would it? There was nothing wrong with him, and definitely not anything that needed to be fixed.

But there was *something*, wasn't there? Because Q-Bert was not at all what Josy was expecting.

He was... different. He looked around Josy's age and was skinny, with short, messy blond hair that stuck out in all directions like he'd been running his fingers through it. He wore thick blue glasses and a black tie over a plaid shirt. He looked nervous, his mouth twitching slightly upward. His eyes crinkled at the corners into these little lines that Josy was fascinated by. He started to smile, and his teeth were a little crooked, and Josy found them *endearing* for reasons he couldn't quite explain. Q-Bert waved, his hand jerking awkwardly side to side as the people in front of him continued to pound their feet. His fingers were thin and long, and Josy had to stop himself from waving back frantically.

He decided right then and there that he needed to be friends with Q-Bert, no matter what it took. Anyone who wrote monster porn and was the leader of a cult where people dressed as salmon and tigers and unicorns definitely could make Josy's life more interesting.

The *problem* with that was Josy didn't have many friends, and he wasn't necessarily sure how to make them. Oh, he had Xander and Serge and Gustavo and Casey. And, to a certain extent, he had Lottie—Casey's aunt—and the We Three Queens. When Josy found someone he wanted to know, it tended to be forever.

He didn't really even know how he'd made friends with Casey and Serge and Xander to begin with. Xander had wanted to bone him, hence the whole hands-down-the-back-of-Josy's-pants thing, but that had stopped almost immediately when Josy told him he wasn't into sex like that. Normally, someone he rejected would leave right away, but Xander had stayed. And then came Serge and Casey, and Josy decided he wanted to keep them all.

So he did.

It certainly didn't hurt that Casey had taken a sabbatical to Oregon where he met Gustavo Tiberius, a man that Josy was convinced could quite possibly be the greatest human who ever existed. He had a ferret named Harry S. Truman, and when Josy and Gustavo had met, they'd managed to turn soup into murder. Even though Josy hadn't gotten the part in the commercial, he'd gotten Gustavo, which was ultimately more important.

(Though it should be said that the people from Campbell's Soups did *not* appreciate his audition, where he somehow forgot that what he and Gustavo had rehearsed wasn't what the actual commercial was going to be about. They'd cut him off when he started to ask his little bro about being locked in the closet and said that they needed to use quicklime to keep the smell of a decomposing body from getting too bad, something he'd learned in his brief stint as a corpse on *Criminal Bad Guys: Topeka*,

Kansas. Since he was a professional, he thanked them for their time before leaving and asked they keep him in mind for any future projects. They still hadn't called Starla back.)

So yes, his friend group was small, but he liked it that way. And besides, it'd recently doubled because of a guy who owned a video store, a trio of women who wore pink jackets and drove Vespas, and the proprietor of Lottie's Lattes, who liked him a lottie.

Maybe Josy didn't know how to make friends, but he seemed to be good at it. Maybe he could be good at it with Q-Bert too.

"Hello," Q-Bert said into the microphone, and his voice was softer than Josy expected. It sounded like how he thought clouds felt.

"I'm so mellow," he whispered to Xander.

"I will have my revenge," Xander whispered back.

"Thank you for coming to my reading," Q-Bert said. He was fidgeting worse now. Josy wanted to tell him everything was all right and maybe bring him some hot chocolate. Hot chocolate always made Josy feel better. "I know that I said I'd try to do these more, but things have been a little difficult for me lately."

"We love you, Q-Man!" someone in the audience shouted.

And Q-Bert *blushed*. Josy wanted to give him all the hot chocolate in the world. Even the kind with the little marshmallows in it that always got stuck in his mustache. "Thank you," Q-Bert squeaked. He coughed, clearing his throat. "Thank you. I'm trying, and to see all of you here makes it all worth it." The microphone screeched, and Q-Bert looked a little stricken as Dee came up to help him.

"He's so brave," Tigress breathed.

"What's wrong with him?" Josy asked her. "Is he sick?" The thought worried him greatly.

She narrowed her eyes. "*Nothing* is wrong with him. Just because he has social anxiety disorder doesn't mean he's broken. He's very up-front about what he goes through, and being here in front of all these people is scary for him. But he's always honest, and it helps the rest of us going through the same thing. It took a lot for me to come here by myself, but here I am."

"And as a *tigress*," Josy said, almost reverently. "That's so cool of you. You're doing a great job."

Her face softened. "You really have no idea who he is, do you?"

Josy shook his head. "Nope. But I want to."

"I like you," Tigress told him.

He grinned at her. "I like you too."

Dee was whispering something into Q-Bert's ear. He nodded slowly and took a deep breath. He gripped the sides of the podium and closed his eyes. Josy knew that positive reinforcement was always something he liked, so he said quite loudly, "I think you're doing amazing and that you're a good person!"

Q-Bert's eyes snapped open and looked directly at Josy.

Josy waved at him.

Q-Bert almost smiled. Dee whispered something else to him as she winked at Josy.

"What are you doing?" Xander asked.

"Making sure he knows that it's okay to be nervous."

"It sounds like you're flirting with him."

Josy's eyes widened. "What? That's not—I'm not trying to do that!"

"Uh-huh."

"Being nice isn't always flirting, Xander. Maybe if you stopped trying to bone everyone, you could see that."

"Wow," Xander said. "That almost hurt. I'm impressed."

Josy bumped his shoulder. "Dick."

"Asshole."

"Sorry about that," Q-Bert said as Dee left the stage, though she didn't go far. "Technical difficulties with the mic and my brain. You know how it is. I—I appreciate you all being here. Like I said, I'm trying to get better at these things. I know I canceled the last two events, but I made myself a promise for tonight. I told myself that I could do this, that I could get up in front of all of you, because I owe it to you. But more than that, I owe it to myself. Some days are harder than others, but today is a good day." He glanced at Josy before looking back out to the rest of the crowd. "And I've been reminded that I'm a good person, so let's do this."

The crowd roared. Tigress howled. Josy clapped a little maniacally. Xander crossed his arms.

Q-Bert looked taken aback, but he continued as the crowd quieted. "I guess we should start as these things do. With the virgins."

The crowd laughed, and a few people stood up from their chairs as their friends jostled around them.

"That's you," Tigress whispered excitedly. "You're so lucky. I remember when Q-Bert took my virginity. It was amazing."

Josy was a little alarmed. "Um, okay? I like you, and I'm glad you decided to paint your face, but I don't know if I want to get naked in front of all these people. I mean, I could do that if it was an audition. I've had to do it before." He frowned. "Though I still don't know what that had to do with Japanese energy drinks. But at least they let me hug the body pillow with the naked anime girl on it. *Konnichiwa*!"

"You don't have to get naked," Tigress told him. "It's not about sex. It's about cupcakes."

"Dude," Josy breathed. "I was just thinking about food, like, five minutes ago! Granted, I always think about food when I'm stoned, but still! It's like you're reading my mind."

"It's destiny," Tigress said. "You have to stand up."

Josy stood up immediately.

"Sit down," Xander hissed.

He looked down. "I can't. I'm a virgin. And there's cupcakes."

"Oh. Well, then. Cupcakes sound pretty good right now."

"I know, right? Stand up before they think you're not a virgin!"

Xander rolled his eyes. "No one in their right mind would think I'm a virgin." But he stood up anyway.

Josy adored him.

There weren't as many virgins as Josy expected. He started counting, got to seven, but then got distracted by the poster of the ethnic children jumping on the trampoline while reading and began to think about the last time he was on a trampoline, which for some reason led to thoughts of horseback riding, and how was it that he was twenty-five years old and had never ridden a horse? He couldn't even be sure he'd ever *seen* a horse up close. He then wondered if miniature ponies were the result of genetic experimentation and if there were any videos on the Internet of cats riding dogs wearing saddles. He needed to look that up when he got home.

He was snapped out of his daydream of a cat wearing a sheriff's uniform riding its horse in a dusty western town ("You think you can come and rob my bank? You've got to be kitten me!") when the standing virgins began to form a line in front of the stage.

He pulled Xander to the back of the line.

"You owe so much for this," Xander told him.

"I got you high and brought you to a library. I think we're even."

"What? That doesn't even make sense."

"I know. Isn't it great?"

Q-Bert moved to the front of the stage and sat at the edge, his feet hanging off the side. He was wearing green Chucks and pink socks under his jeans. Josy wondered if he was colorblind, but since he had a Hypercolor T-shirt on under his suspenders, he didn't know if he had room to discuss the fashion choices of others.

Dee came to stand next to him, carrying a white bakery box. Josy wanted a cupcake so bad he could almost taste it. He wondered if they also brought milk, which would make this the best night of his entire life. He didn't see any milk, so it was only equal to the last best night of his life, which involved a bong named Vlad the Inhaler, a stack of black-and-white monster movies on DVD, and a pizza bigger than his head. That had been the best night.

This was close, though.

The line moved quickly.

Josy was very excited.

He barely noticed the people walking past him back to their seats.

Xander did and was mumbling under his breath, but Josy ignored him.

And then it was his turn.

Q-Bert sat at the edge of the stage, the tips of his toes scraping against the floor. He was shorter than Josy had thought when he'd first walked out on the stage. The top of his head probably barely came to Josy's chin if they were standing side by side. Since it wasn't polite to ask someone if he could keep them in his pocket, he didn't.

It was close.

"Hi," Josy said. "I'm a virgin. But not in real life. Just a virgin in the library."

Q-Bert blushed and his eyebrows twitched. "I can see that. I like your shirt."

"Thank you," Josy told him seriously. "I like your socks. I have a thing for a good pair of socks."

"Cool."

"Yeah, cool."

"Cool, cool, cool."

Xander groaned from behind him.

"This is Xander's friend," Dee told him, that evil smile back on her face. "Xander's the guy who does my ink. And this is Josy."

"It's short for Josiah," Josy told him helpfully.

"That's… nice," Q-Bert said, sounding slightly strangled. He reached into the box for a cupcake. It had red frosting. Josy was so on board with all of this. He was going to eat the shit out of that cupcake. "Hold out your hand."

Josy did.

Q-Bert placed a Wet-Nap on his palm. And then he said, "Sorry about this. I'll try to not get any on your shirt."

"What? Why would you—"

And then Q-Bert shoved the cupcake onto Josy's forehead.

It took a moment for Josy to figure out what was happening. One moment he was just standing there, waiting for this… this *guy* to give him food he hadn't expected to get, and the next his forehead had cake and frosting on it.

All in all, Josiah Erickson was very confused.

Dee snorted. Josy decided she *was* evil.

"You've been devirginized," Q-Bert said quietly, pulling his hand back. "Thank you for coming."

Josy was speechless. And he couldn't help but smile. Because *what*.

Q-Bert dropped the smashed cupcake into the box.

It was about this time Josy wondered what would happen to all the smashed cupcakes and if he was stoned enough to forgive himself for asking if he could eat them.

In the end, he decided against it.

He stepped out of the way. Xander took his place, and even though he was scowling, he didn't try to fight getting a cupcake to the face. Dee laughed at him.

He followed Xander back to their seats.

"I feel like I've been betrayed," he told Tigress. "By you. By Q-Bert. By god."

Tigress nodded solemnly. "And yet you've been anointed by Q-Bert. You are no longer a virgin."

"But… but all those *cupcakes*. What'll happen to them? They'll be all alone and scared with no one to eat them."

"It's in my hair," Xander muttered. "You owe me so bad for this."

"You took it to the face like a champ," Josy told him, patting his hand. "But then, you're used to it, so I wouldn't expect any less."

"I don't know why I forget how much of a dick you are when stoned. A sappy, sappy dick."

"I regret nothing."

Xander sighed as he wiped a glob of frosting off his cheek. "That's fine. I regret enough for the both of us. Why haven't you wiped your face yet?"

"I forgot. Oh! Before I do—" He pulled out his phone and demanded Xander and Tigress smoosh in close for a selfie. Tigress came willingly. Xander came too, though he didn't look happy about it. Josy took the picture, and though he looked ridiculous, he knew his followers would appreciate seeing that even though he was an actor, he still knew how to have a good time with frosting on his face, a scowling best friend on one shoulder, and a woman with tiger face paint on the other. Hashtags were involved, of course. He'd tried using the new Russian thing Serge had told him about, but it'd been confusing, and he figured when Instagram became cool again, he would be at the forefront of that retro wave. By the time he put his phone away, he already had eleven likes and three comments. Granted, one of the comments asked if Clifford the Big Red Dog had jacked off on him, but still. It was the thought that counted.

Once the virgins were finished, Dee closed the lid to the box. Josy stared at it mournfully as she took it away. Since he was above eating face cupcakes (barely), he decided to let them go. It was one of the hardest decisions of his life.

By the time Q-Bert stood again at the podium, Josy had managed to get all the frosting off his face. He handed his Wet-Nap to Xander, who demanded to know what *exactly* he was supposed to do with it. Josy told him that his pants were vintage, and he didn't want to get frosting on them.

Q-Bert cleared his throat. "Thank you to those who offered their virginities to me. I will never forget your sacrifice. I shall now read to you from one of the good books." He held up a thin tome. "*Getting Poetry Slammed in My Butthole by Sasquatch.* Chapter 1."

The audience cheered.

Josy could barely stand the anticipation.

Xander looked as if he were dying on the inside. And also the outside.

Q-Bert began to read.

Daxton Shepherd awoke one morning, unaware that his life was about to change. He was tall and fit, with heavy muscles in this arms and legs and chest, a testament to his twice-daily workouts. His body was a temple, and he resided in said temple as its king.

"Wow," Josy whispered. "He gives Casey a run for his money in terms of prose."

"When you tell Casey that, please let me be there," Xander whispered back. "I'll record it and everything."

He raised his arms above his head and yawned as he stretched, working out the kinks in his back and shoulders. His body felt pleasantly sore. He struggled to remember what had happened the night before. He remembered going to the poetry slam at the local haberdashery, where he'd gone to get fitted for a new top hat. He'd needed the hat to attend an upcoming business meeting where he would conduct his business. He hadn't expected there to be a poetry slam at the haberdashery, but since life was unpredictable and wonderful, he just went with it, as one should.

"So many hidden meanings," Tigress whispered reverently.

Josy didn't know what a haberdashery was, but he nodded in agreement.

He was about to get out of bed when he realized he was....

Q-Bert coughed, looking almost embarrassed.

When he realized he was nude.

"Oooh," the audience said.

"Oooh," Josy said, trying to get in on that action. He appreciated a good audience *oooh*.

Now this was strange, because Daxton didn't like sleeping in the nude. He always preferred wearing tight boxer briefs that showed off his considerable package. His girlfriends always appreciated them, and he knew that men at the gym eyed him on the regular too. He wasn't gay, but he still liked to be looked at.

He wiped the sleep from his eyes, and it was only then that he realized he wasn't in his own bed at all, or even in his own bedroom. He was in a bed. But it was in... a cave.

Josy didn't know how to handle any of this. He'd never been so transported by a piece of fiction. It was like he too was in the cave. He could hear the water dripping off stalactites, could smell the moss growing on the walls. Q-Bert was obviously a master of his craft, and it had absolutely nothing to do with the fact that Josy was stoned.

Well. Mostly nothing.

Daxton looked around, sure that he'd been kidnapped. He pressed his hands back against the bed, only to feel what seemed to be a warm piece of shag carpeting underneath his fingers.

"I don't think that's carpet in the bed," Josy whispered to Xander.

"I never understood when people said they couldn't even," Xander whispered back. "Until this very moment. I can't even."

Daxton turned his head slowly to look back on the other side of the bed. And there, eyes closed and lips flapping from heavy snoring, was a large, hairy ape creature.

"What in the ever-loving F," Daxton managed to say.

"My thoughts exactly," Xander muttered.

The large, hairy ape creature looked to be at least eight feet tall and was heavily muscled under all the hair. Daxton couldn't help but let his gaze trace along the muscles of his chest and stomach to where the sheet pooled around his hips. There was an enormous bulge under the sheets where his crotch was, and even though Daxton had never even considered looking at a male before (human or otherwise), he found himself getting aroused. He thought that probably made him bisexual, since being gay for one person (or an ape creature) was preposterous and didn't actually occur in the real world. He understood that erasing the bisexual label was problematic and that people should be accepted for who they are.

"Q-Bert is very woke," Tigress said to Josy.

When Daxton brought his gaze back up that long, hairy, muscled body, he found the ape creature's eyes were open and watching him. The ape creature smiled, his large lips pulling back over gigantic square teeth.

"Hello," Daxton said. "I'm sorry. I'm having a hard time remembering coming back here. I hope I wasn't too much of a problem. I think I might have drank too much last night."

And then the hairy ape spoke in a deep, erotic voice. "That's all right. We had a good night. You shouldn't feel mortification after our bout of perceived fornication."

"What," Xander said flatly.

Josy slowly turned to look at him. "Sasquatch *rhymes*." He was pretty sure this had now surpassed any night with Vlad the Inhaler. "You thought there would be no poetry. You were wrong. *All* of this is poetry."

"Yes, well," Daxton said. "I still feel terrible. I don't remember much of what happened. I know I went to the haberdashery and found a poetry slam, but not much after that. I didn't mean to drink all that wine."

The hairy creature propped himself up on one of his elbows. "You did come to the haberdashery, and then you decided to stay, which flattered me. There was something about the way you looked. I thought I could read you just like a book. You watched me like you'd never heard a poem before, and I knew I just had to have you, either here in my bed or on the cave floor."

Tigress sighed dreamily. "I love romance."

"That's unexpected," Daxton admitted. "I go in to get a hat sized and instead find someone like you. Life is strange. I never thought I would be into someone like you, but even now, I find myself craving your touch."

The hairy ape creature arched an enormous eyebrow. "Someone like me? What does that mean? What do you see?"

Daxton once again let his gaze trail down the long, muscled body of his bedmate. "A beast who looks like he is capable of ravaging me. I never knew I wanted that until this very moment."

"Oh," the hairy ape creature said. "You realized that last night, much to my ever-loving delight. Once you heard my poetic rhymes, I knew you would be mine for all of time."

This time when Tigress sighed dreamily, Josy joined her.

"All of time?" Daxton asked, confused. "But I can't even remember your name. How could you want someone like me, whose body is the only thing that can recall our first time together?"

"We haven't had our first time yet," the hairy ape creature said. "I respected your autonomy, even at the beginning of our tête-à-tête."

"Then why am I so sore?" Daxton asked, looking away. "You know. Down there."

The hairy ape creature reached up a hairy monkey hand and cupped the side of Daxton's face. "Because you fell down a set of stairs. I tried to save you but was caught unawares. I am afraid 'twas the price of drink. But fear not, after I picked you up, I made sure our arms were linked."

"So we haven't experienced our first time yet?" Daxton asked, heart racing in his chest.

The hairy ape creature growled. "No, we have not. Though I want to have you with all I've got."

"I am really uncomfortable right now," Xander mumbled.

Q-Bert looked as if he could agree. He hesitated, blushing harder before continuing.

Daxton felt himself... harden. A spike of arousal flooded through him. He was barely holding himself back from launching across the bed at the hairy ape creature. "Please," he begged. "Tell me your name."

"Sasquatch is what they call a-me. But to you, I am Sassy, and that's all I want to be."

Daxton could hold himself back no longer.

From there, Josiah Erickson heard things he never thought he would. Descriptions of carnal acts that would make even the most amorous of hairy ape creatures flush. The fact that it was described by Q-Bert's soft voice only made the strange dissonance of what he was reading that much sharper. Josiah wasn't experiencing a full-body high—the tablets weren't strong enough for that—but by god, it *felt* like it. He wasn't aroused by what he was hearing (and he hoped no one else was either, but to each their own), but he was entranced by it. He listened to Sassy poetry slam Daxton in the butthole, where such excruciatingly wonderful dialogue was uttered like "With my member I shall split you in half, since it's almost as long as the neck of a giraffe," and "Take it, take it, take it from me, and next time we'll see what happens with you over my knee."

In his short, eventful life, Josiah Erickson had been transported to the place Serge had described as Nirvana perhaps only four times.

First, it was the time he wore a bright, blocky orange costume and spoke a line that caused people in the audience to laugh. The sound of them reacting to something *he'd* said had caused his body to be flooded with a joy like he'd never experienced.

The second time was when he'd inhaled for the first time, thick smoke going down his throat, causing it to burn and his eyes to water. He'd coughed almost instantly, a waste of his turn in puff, puff, pass, but he'd been allowed to try again, and he was sure nothing was happening, sure that he wasn't feeling it, until all of a sudden, *everything* felt good.

The third was when he realized he wasn't alone. It'd been before Casey had gone to Oregon on his sabbatical. They'd been at Tuesday brunch, and it'd hit Josy out of nowhere, the realization that he'd built a family on his own. He would do anything for them, knowing they would do the same in return. He hadn't had that before. The audience had *laughed* when he'd been the cheese, but no one there had been related to him. His parents just... they hadn't understood him, even back then. It'd only gotten worse as he grew older. He had dreams. To them, they were flights of fancy that weren't ever going to be real. They thought he was *special*, that word so coded to mean all sorts of things. He didn't start speaking until long after he should have; he didn't get the best grades, couldn't necessarily understand complexities that others could. Words were thrown around him, things that sounded like *Asperger's* or *high-functioning autism*, but it hadn't amounted to anything. He wasn't *slow*, though his father had used that word quite a lot when talking about him.

And maybe he *was* something. Maybe he was disordered. Maybe he had something wrong with his brain. Or maybe, just *maybe*, he was exactly the way he was supposed to be. And it wasn't until Casey and Serge and Xander that he realized it didn't matter. He was the way he was, and he was always going to be that way. They were happy when he was happy, and when he wasn't, they would do everything they could to fix it, knowing he would do the same for them. It wasn't that he didn't know *how* to be any other way than how he was, but that he didn't want to be. He had found people who didn't talk shit about the whole demi thing, didn't give a fuck if he wasn't the smartest guy in the room. They loved him stoned, they loved him sober. They loved him for all the things he was and not all the things he wasn't. They supported him in his acting career and let him bitch and moan when he didn't get a part. Sure, Xander could be a dick sometimes, and Serge tended to pose more often than he didn't, and Casey decided it was a good idea to move to another state entirely, but they were his and he was theirs, and nothing was going to change that.

The fourth time he'd achieved Nirvana (though Serge had decided Nirvana wasn't quite what was going on) was when he'd met Gustavo Tiberius. Even if Gustavo would deny it, Josy knew they were kindred spirits, though Casey said Gustavo was a beautiful rain cloud and Josy was a ray of sunshine. While Casey and Gustavo were meant to be in love forever and do cute couple stuff like hold hands and shotgun into each other's mouths, Gustavo and *Josy* were destined to be brothers for the rest of their lives.

Gustavo didn't understand that yet, but it was okay. Josy had time.

And here, now, was the fifth time Josy had achieved Nirvana, hearing a man named Q-Bert reading about a rhyming Sasquatch plowing his newly bisexual bed partner into the mattress in his cave.

(Either that or the tablets were a hell of a lot stronger than Casey said they were.)

He knew he was staring, mouth gaping, but there was nothing he could do to stop it.

And when Q-Bert finished chapter one of *Getting Poetry Slammed in My Butthole by Sasquatch*, Josy was the first to stand, clapping furiously, sure he was feeling the same way scientists felt when they saw the light from newborn stars.

Which, of course, meant he had to go and screw it all up.

Chapter 4

"I just—I can't *believe* this," Josy exclaimed to Xander.

"Odd," Xander said. "I was thinking the exact same thing."

"I know, right? Why have we never heard of Q-Bert before? He's the greatest author in the history of the entire world!"

"Josy, you don't read books. You told me once your favorite book was a magazine."

Josy blinked. "I did? Was I stoned?"

Xander sighed. "Probably."

"Oh. Well, that explains a lot. And so what if I don't read much? That doesn't mean I'm not allowed to have an opinion. I've read Casey's books, and I think *those* are good."

"They're young adult postapocalyptic vampire/werewolf books."

"Yeah, and I still don't really know what that means. Like, the world ended, right? But then there are werewolves and vampires? And one of each just happens to fall in love with a human girl? That's dumb. No offense, Casey."

"He's not here."

"Oh. Right. Oregon with Gustavo." He grinned. "I'm so happy for him."

"Focus."

Josy tried. "What were we talking about again?"

Xander leaned against the wall near the entrance to the library. The poster with the multicultural trampoline children was behind him. Josy was getting used to it by now. He wondered what else a library could normalize for him. "The travesty we just bore witness to."

"Oh yeah! Did you know about him? About any of this literary wonderment?"

"No, Josy. If I had, I would have also needed to fuck the guy who was in the monster truck that looked like a sombrero in order for this to make us even."

"Monster trucks are weird."

"I feel like that sentence aptly sums up the type of life you live."

"*We* live," Josy reminded him. "Because you're part of my life, and I will never let you leave me. I have too much blackmail shit on you."

Xander looked like he was struggling not to smile. Josy knew his aloofness was a facade, but Xander had spent years cultivating it, so he didn't call him out on it. "Lucky me," Xander said, maybe not scowling as much as he had been.

"My life is forever altered," Josy announced grandly. "Because of a rhyming filthy Sasquatch read by a man named Q-Bert."

Xander eyed him strangely. "If I didn't know any better, I would think you have a crush."

"Huh," Josy said, cocking his head. "That's weird. I don't know if I've ever had a crush on someone I didn't know before. How do I know if it's a crush?"

"Do you want to talk to him?"

Josy thought hard. "Yes."

"Do you want to make him smile?"

That sounded nice. "Yes."

"Do you want to hear him laugh?"

That sounded *really* nice. "Oh yeah."

"Do you want to stick your dick in his asshole?"

Josy grimaced. "No. Definitely not. I don't even know him. Why would you even ask me that?"

Xander shrugged. "That's how things usually work."

"Not for me." Josy's smile faded a bit. "And there's nothing wrong with that."

Xander squeezed his shoulder. "I know, Josy. You're good exactly the way you are. You just… go about things differently."

"Man, don't I know it. Not everything needs to be about sex, you know? I mean, sure, it can be nice, but why worry about it right off the bat? It's like sex in movies."

"I… don't follow."

"This critic I read once. He said sex scenes in movies are pointless. What's a sex scene supposed to add that imagery and dialogue can't show you much better? Intimacy doesn't need to be about fucking."

"Most people like fucking," Xander pointed out.

"And that's fine. But I don't want to sit next to dudes in a theater getting boners because the woman's boobs are bouncing on screen." He paused, considering. "I think I forgot what we're talking about again."

"Honestly, I have no idea."

"Pretty good tablets, huh?"

"Casey doesn't disappoint," Xander agreed. "Something having to do with your crush on monster-porn guy."

"Right," Josy said. "Except we don't know if it's a crush because I don't know what that feels like."

"You've had boyfriends before."

This was true. Three in fact. The first was when he was seventeen. Jason had been a year older, and they'd gotten stoned in a church parking lot on six different occasions. They'd given each other hand jobs three of those times, though Jason seemed to enjoy it a lot more than Josy had. It hadn't been… bad, not really, but Josy would've liked if they'd just passed the spliff back and forth and maybe kissed a little.

The second was when he'd been twenty. Armando had been older, in his late forties. He'd been sweet and kind and most of all patient, though he didn't quite understand Josy's views on sex. He hadn't pushed, exactly, but in the end, the sex thing had led to frustration on both their parts. Josy tried to give more than he was ready for, and Armando had put a stop to it. They still talked every few weeks or so, and Josy had been one of the groomsmen in his wedding last year to a dog walker named Scott. He'd cried because it'd been such a happy event.

The third hadn't gone so well. Nothing bad had happened, per se, but Elliot hadn't gotten Josy's… entire existence. Those had been his exact words, at the end. They'd worked together at Applebee's, and Josy was feeling a bit sorry for himself since Casey had moved to Oregon to be with the best dude in the entire world, and Xander was casually seeing three or six guys, and even *Serge* had a sort-of boyfriend who liked to touch his chakras, whatever that meant. Maybe Josy had been feeling a little lonely and down on himself, so when Elliot had asked him out for the seventh time, he'd said sure, yeah, why not.

It'd been okay for a while, Elliot respecting his boundaries on being touched or taking things further. It wasn't that Josy didn't like him, just that he didn't *know* him, not really. It'd been friendly at first, and maybe Elliot didn't like that Josy got stoned, but whatever. Josy didn't like the way Elliot wouldn't help him practice his lines for whatever audition he had coming up. You didn't have to like everything about someone to actually have feelings for them.

Elliot stopped his supposed understanding of Josy's boundaries and began to push. Josy told him he wasn't ready, and he'd get attitude in return. Elliot would scoff or roll his eyes or ask if Josy just wasn't attracted to him, all the while making it sound like the very idea was ludicrous. In someone Josy knew well, like Xander, that kind of ego wouldn't have bothered him, given he knew that wasn't all Xander was.

But on Elliot?

It rankled him, though Josy wasn't quite sure how to put it in words. And who gave a fuck that Josy liked weed? He rarely drank, never did hard drugs, and still showed up on time for work and was ready for every single audition Starla got for him. What did it matter that Josy liked to smoke out of a bong named Vlad the Inhaler? It was better than popping pills that were supposed to calm his head but instead made him not give a shit about anything. He didn't like not feeling in control.

It had taken longer than it should have for Josy to realize he wasn't happy with Elliot. Sure, he had a wicked sense of humor and he let Josy ramble at him sometimes, but he was also a fucking dick.

So Josy had broken things off. Elliot had been angry, but Josy no longer had time for petty bullshit or for people who didn't accept him for who he was, smoking habit and sexual identity be damned. Life was too fucking short to be involved with stupid people named Elliot.

Xander and Serge had been awesome about it, bringing him fat buds and the collector's edition of *The Wolf Man*. Gustavo and Casey had been on Skype watching it in Oregon at the same time, Gustavo allowing Josy to quiz him on Academy Awards trivia for damn near twenty minutes. They'd all gotten stoned and talked about how dumb Elliot was, and by the time Josy nodded off, his head in Xander's lap, Serge rubbing his feet, and Gustavo on the screen talking to Casey about something to do with a monkey on an island, he felt better about most everything.

Yes, he'd had boyfriends before. And some of them had even been pretty good.

(Except Elliot. Fuck that guy.)

But he'd never had a *crush* before.

"I think I just want to be his friend," Josy said now, doing his best to articulate the weird little flutter in his stomach. "Do you think he'd be my friend if I asked?"

Xander's expression softened. "I don't know, Josy. But if he doesn't, he's a dick who doesn't deserve you." He pulled out his phone and began to type on the screen. "I just need to let Serge know you have a crush on someone who writes dirty bestiality porn."

"I do not," Josy growled at him.

Xander glanced up at him, a cocky smirk on his face. "Why are you blushing?"

"It's moderately temperate standing near the door, and my skin is heated. Also, I'm high, and you know my skin turns red when I'm high."

"Uh-huh." He pointed his phone at Josy, snapped a picture, and grinned down at it.

"You better not post that to the Russians!"

"Too late. You ready to go, or...."

"I'm thinking."

"Oh boy."

Josy gnawed on his bottom lip. "Dee said he's doing a meet and greet right now."

"So I heard," Xander said, sounding amused.

"And maybe we should go to it. You know. To get the full experience."

"That right."

Josy nodded furiously. "Also, there are cookies, and I swear to god, if I don't get food in my mouth in the next six minutes, I'm probably going to die."

Xander's eyes were a little glassy. "I could go for a cookie or seven."

"Maybe there's even some punch."

"Like, fruit punch?"

"Oh yeah."

"You know what'd be awesome right now? Capri Sun. You remember those?"

Josy did. Vividly. "I was one of the cool kids who turned it upside down and poked the straw through the bottom. I didn't have time for rules. Don't like it? Die mad about it."

"Badass," Xander said fondly. "I suppose we should go if there's going to be cookies. And maybe you can talk to Q-Bert for a minute too."

Josy shrugged as he rubbed the back of his neck. "It would be rude not to, right? He was pretty good. Tigress said he's got anxiety, so it must have been hard for him to do that. He needs to hear that he did a great job. Positive feedback always makes me feel better when I'm nervous."

"Right. Positive feedback."

Josy glared at him. "I'm being serious!"

Xander reached out and patted his cheek. "I know. And it's adorable. Let's go make you a friend." He pushed himself off the wall and started walking into the library.

Josy was slightly panicked. "What do you mean, *make a friend*? Xander? Xander!"

THE LINE was long.

That was good.

And also bad.

Good, because it gave Josy time to plan out what he was going to say.

Bad, because it gave Josy time to overthink what he was going to say.

And for one of the first times in his life, he wished he wasn't as stoned as he was. Yeah, he was feeling fine, but he was also *not feeling fine*, and he kept getting distracted by the damn cookies that they'd forgotten to get before they joined the line. Xander tried to leave him to go to the cookies, but Josy demanded he stay right by his side. He took Xander's hand in his for support, and also to keep him in place. Either they would go for the cookies together or they wouldn't go at all. And since Josy couldn't take the chance of losing his place in line, the cookies would have to wait.

Besides, Josy liked holding hands.

Also, Xander couldn't be trusted.

"Okay," Josy said as the line slowly moved forward. "How's this? 'Hi, my name is Josiah. I like ferrets named after presidents, and sometimes I turn on music really loud in my apartment and dance in my underwear.'"

"That… might not be the best thing to open with."

"What? Why?" Josy thought it perfectly summed up his life.

"Because ferrets are creepy, and half the time, you forget to put on underwear."

"You do *not* get to talk about Harry S. Truman that way! And it's my apartment! I can wear whatever I want. Including not wearing anything."

Xander rolled his eyes. "Just tell him that you liked his book and let the conversation flow from there."

That sounded reasonable. "But what if he asks me questions I don't know the answer to? How tall is Mount Everest?"

"I have no idea."

"Dammit. If only there was a place we could go to that had such knowledge."

"Like a library?"

Josy rolled his eyes. "No one goes to libraries anymore."

"I don't even know what to say to that."

"We should probably just go," Josy decided. "We can grab a pocketful of cookies and then get an Uber and eat the cookies on the way home."

"How many cookies is a pocketful?"

Josy thought hard. "I guess it depends on the size of the pocket. Sometimes three. Sometimes thirty. I guess we'll have to—oh my god, you're distracting me! Villain!"

Xander snorted. "Darn. And I would have gotten away with it too, had it not been for you—"

Josy felt the blood drain from his face. "We're only six… seven… nine, ten people away from the front of the line!"

Xander squeezed his hand. "Just be yourself. Or something like it."

"How do I do that?"

"For better or worse, you're doing a pretty good job of it right now."

Josy groaned. "Being an adult and making adult friends is the worst thing in the entire world."

"Weed is only legal for recreational use in a handful of states."

"Okay, *that's* the worst thing in the entire world. If it was legal everywhere, making friends would be so much easier." Then a terrible thought struck him. "Oh my god, I'm stoned."

"Wow," Xander said. "We really need to work on your self-awareness."

"What if he doesn't like stoners?" Josy demanded. "What if he thinks marijuana is evil and tries to give me pamphlets about drinking the blood of Jesus and eating his little body crackers?"

"I don't know how those things are related."

"Of course you don't! You're not the one trying to make a new friend! I don't want to drink Jesus—oh look, it's Tigress. Tigress. Tigress!"

She looked startled as she was walking by, a book with the impossible title of *I Almost Got Fisted by a T-Rex but Its Arms Couldn't Reach* clutched to her chest. On the cover, a half-naked man stood in front of a tyrannosaurus that was nuzzling his neck. Josy wasn't sure how that made him feel.

"Hi," Tigress said happily. "You guys in line to meet Q-Bert? He's so wonderful."

"I knew it," Josy groaned. "I knew he'd be wonderful. And I can't figure out what to say to him to make him be my friend."

Her face scrunched up. Josy had never seen a confused tiger before. It was enlightening. "Why not just ask him?"

Josy gaped at her.

She cocked her head. "What? What did I say?"

"Something very easy," Xander reassured her. "He's just processing. It takes him a moment."

"Oooh," Tigress said. "Well, he's very nice. He'll probably be just as nervous as you are. I know you said you don't know him, but he has a blog where he writes a lot about his struggles with social anxiety and depression. He makes a lot of us feel better because he helps remind us that we're not alone with our mental health issues. He's built a great community where we can all talk about what it's like for us."

"Did you hear that?" Josy asked Xander with wide eyes. "He's *perfect*."

Xander squeezed his hand. "I don't think that's quite what she meant."

Tigress smiled. "Sort of. It's just… it's hard for him to be out there. In front of a crowd and then meeting people face-to-face. But he also knows how hard it is for someone like me to step out of my comfort zone and come to a library with my face painted like my favorite Q-Bert character. It's weird, but he says that it's okay to be weird. And that makes me feel better. I don't have to justify myself to anyone here. For a little while, I feel like I can breathe."

"Can I hug you?" Josy asked seriously. "It's okay to say no."

"Thank you for asking," Tigress said. "And thank you for understanding that I'm going to decline. I don't… I don't like being touched like that."

Josy grinned at her. "I totally understand. You do you, boo-boo."

"You're a nice person," she told him "That's all you need to be. Don't worry too much about all the rest."

"Easier said than done."

"Maybe. But if you worry too much about all the things you could be, you'll miss out on all the things you actually are." She shuffled her feet and glanced toward the door. "Now if you don't mind, I think I'd like to go back into my shell for a little while at home. Maybe I'll see you again at the next reading?"

Josy nodded. "I look forward to it."

She backed away slowly. "I'll hold you to that. Bye." She whirled around and hurried toward the door.

Xander squeezed his hand. "Feel better?"

Josy turned slowly toward him. "Absolutely not. Just be myself? Do you know how hard that is? Oh my god, what if he—"

"Next!"

Josy jerked his head to see how much farther away the front of the line was.

And to his horror, saw that *they* were the front of the line.

Dee was waving her hand at them, beckoning them toward a large table where Q-Bert sat, nervously fiddling with his glasses, books stacked around him. Josy had only known of Q-Bert's existence for a little more than an hour, but even he could see that Q-Bert was always moving, leg bouncing, foot tapping. He was twitchy. Josy wanted to hold his hand to make him feel better.

"Oh no," Josy whispered. "I'm doomed."

"Gross," Xander muttered. "How did your palm get so sweaty so fast? It's like you just dunked it in water."

Josy ignored him. His mouth was dry, and he tried to chalk that up to the indica tablet and not his nerves. Then he realized he didn't like to lie to himself and thought it was most likely a combination of both.

Dee arched an eyebrow at him. "Feel free to step forward any time now. It's not like there's a gigantic line behind you and we only have so long before we have to clear out."

Sarcastic lesbians were Josy's jam. He could dig it. Granted, he wished she hadn't chosen *this exact moment* for sarcasm, but still. He would have to ask Xander later if Dee ever hung out with stoner hipsters, because that would be epic.

He tried to take a step forward. Funnily enough, his feet weren't working, and he stayed where he was.

Xander sighed. "Come on." He pulled Josy forward.

Q-Bert swallowed thickly as they approached the front of the table. Stacks of books were piled on either side of him. Josy glanced at some of the titles (*Locked in a Loch with the Loch Ness Monster: Sea of Love* and *Probed in the Anus by a Neoconservative Alien Who Realized Its Politics Are Terrible* and *A Triceratops Got Me Pregnant and Now I've Given Up My NRA Membership*) and was struck by the idea that he was in the presence of a literary genius. What were the chances that he would know two of them in his lifetime? He needed to make this work so Q-Bert would be his friend, and then would meet Casey and become *his* friend. After a six-month period of getting to know each other, they would decide to co-author a book and eventually go on to win the Man Booker Prize.

He had no idea what the Man Booker Prize was.

He had no idea how he'd even heard of it.

He was so stoned.

He stood in front of the table staring down at Q-Bert.

Q-Bert stared up at him, fingers tapping on the table.

Josy opened his mouth to say something to make Q-Bert his friend, but no sound came out.

He hadn't expected that.

He closed his mouth.

Dee looked back and forth between them. "Huh."

Xander apparently decided to use his powers for evil, because he said, "Josy, isn't there something you wanted to say?"

Josy wasn't feeling very fond of Xander at the moment. "Um."

"Hi," Q-Bert said.

"Hi," Josy breathed.

"Huh," Dee said again.

"Jesus Christ," Xander muttered.

Josy ignored them. "Hi," he said again. Then, "I already said that. Sorry."

Q-Bert smiled. "That's okay." He looked down at the table, then back up at Josy. "Do you—"

"You shoved a cupcake in my face," Josy blurted.

Q-Bert winced. "Yeah, sorry about that. It's this whole… thing."

Josy nodded furiously. "Oh, it's okay. I just thought we should get it out there. I mean, cupcakes. On my face. I wasn't expecting that. I mean, I wasn't expecting a rhyming erotic Sasquatch having sex with a newly minted bisexual frat boy either."

"You… weren't?"

"No."

Q-Bert pushed his glasses back up on his nose. He looked nervous. "What did you think was going to happen?"

"A poetry slam."

Dee coughed roughly. Josy hoped she wasn't choking.

"A poetry slam," Q-Bert repeated slowly.

"Yeah," Josy said. "You know, with people snapping and berets and long cigarettes and flapper girls and saxophones and…." He frowned.

"Wait. That doesn't sound right. Poetry slams aren't 1920s jazz clubs." He glanced at Xander. "Right?"

Xander sighed again.

"Did your boyfriend not tell you what this was?"

And *that* got Josy's attention. He looked back at Q-Bert. "My boyfriend? I don't have a boyfriend."

Q-Bert flushed. "Oh. You're… holding his hand, and I thought—"

"Not his boyfriend," Xander said dryly. "Josy just likes holding hands. And trust me when I say this wasn't my idea. At all. This is all on Josy."

Josy pulled his hand out of Xander's. "We aren't *dating*." He didn't know why he sounded so scandalized.

"Sorry," Q-Bert said again. "I didn't mean to—"

Dee leaned down and whispered something in his ear, squeezing his shoulder gently. Q-Bert closed his eyes and nodded as he listened. Dee kissed his cheek before stepping back again.

Q-Bert shook his head as he opened his eyes. "I apologize a lot." He sounded chagrined. "Dee likes to remind me that I don't have to."

"She's right," Josy said seriously. "You didn't do anything wrong. Xander does the same for me. So does Serge. And Casey. And Gustavo. And—"

"I think he gets the point," Xander said.

"Right," Josy said quickly, trying to find his way back to Friendship Station, where he and Q-Bert could board the train and be friends and hope the train didn't get derailed by a penny on the tracks and kill dozens and cause an ecological disaster when chemicals leaked into a nearby river. "You get it. The point I was making. About everything."

Q-Bert looked like he didn't get it at all but was too polite to say otherwise. Josy liked those kinds of people. "I do."

And since Josy knew that friendships were built upon honesty and trust, he said, "And it's probably my bad about the whole poetry slam thing. I wasn't really paying attention to what the prize was when I called in to the radio station to answer the trivia question. But to be fair, the prize doesn't matter because it's not about what you get when you win as much as it's about winning in the first place."

"Radio… trivia?"

"I'm very good at it. No one knows why."

"It's one of his quirks," Xander added helpfully. He was a good friendship wingman.

"So you really had no idea what this was going to be about when you got here?" Dee asked, sounding rather gleeful for a person in a library this late on a Friday night.

"None," Josy said.

"Oh my god," Q-Bert moaned, flushing brightly. "I'm so sorry—"

Dee cleared her throat.

"I mean, I know it probably wasn't what you were expecting, and it can be a lot to take in if you've never heard of me before, but I swear that—"

"I liked it," Josy said quickly because Q-Bert looked like he was about to get up from the table and run. "Like, so much, man."

Q-Bert's eyes widened. "You did?"

"Xander, tell him."

"He liked it."

"See?" Josy said. "Xander always tells the truth, even when you don't want him to. Like that time I used beard wax to curl the ends of my mustache and he said I looked like I was going to tie a woman to train tracks while wearing a black cape." A terrible thought struck Josy. "Which I would never do, of course! I don't remember the last time I actually saw a train."

"We took the train to get here," Xander reminded him.

"That's the Metro. Everyone knows when you tie someone to train tracks, it has to be for one of those steam-powered trains." He looked back at Q-Bert. "But I would never do that, regardless of what kind of train it is. So, in summation, I liked your monster porn."

"Thank you," Q-Bert said, voice cracking slightly. "That's very nice of you."

Josy was feeling very good about this. Maybe this would work out after all. He knew the key to any artist's heart was gushing praise. "I especially liked the part where Sasquatch really seemed to care about whether Daxton Shepherd was in pain after they had to use the slime from the cave wall as a lubricant. It showed that even though he was a monster on the outside, he was considerate on the inside, which is not something I expected from a large, intelligent primate."

"That's... thank you. I know it's not—"

"Come on, man!" someone said loudly from behind them. "We're all waiting here!"

Q-Bert blanched.

Josy felt awful. "Oh crap. I didn't mean to take up so much of your time. I just—you seem really cool, and I like talking to you."

"It's okay," Dee said, glaring at the crowd behind Xander and Josy. "Some people don't know when to *keep their mouths shut*." She looked down at Q-Bert. "But we might need to wrap this up. We only have the library for another half hour."

"Do you want me to sign something?" Q-Bert asked Josy. "I can sign whatever you want."

"I didn't bring anything for you to sign," Josy said morosely. "I didn't even know you existed until I got here. I feel bad." And even though the sign on the table said the books were only ten bucks, Josy couldn't afford that. Ten bucks could buy a shit ton of Cup of Noodles when things got rough.

"Which one do you want?" Xander whispered because he probably knew what was going through Josy's head. He was scary like that.

"Oh, hey, no, you don't have to do—"

"Just pick one, okay? It's my way of saying thank you."

"For?"

"Being alive."

"Oh. Wow. Well, when you put it that way." He looked down at the table. "I'm going to buy one of your books. Well, Xander's going to buy it, but it's going to be mine."

"That's not going to work," Dee said gravely.

Josy squinted at her. "It's not? Do you… oh. Is ten dollars code for something else? Like, some secret monster-porn thing? Are you going to shove more food on my face? Because I'm okay with that, but could you maybe aim for my mouth this time? I'm starving."

"Oh, he'll aim for your mouth all right," Dee muttered.

"Dee!" Q-Bert growled. His hands twitched on the table.

"What I *mean* is that since you're a newbie and more precious than even the ring of power, Q-Bert here is going to gift you one of his books. Aren't you, Q-Bert?"

"You don't have to do that," Josy said. "We can pay for it. It's—"

"It's okay," Q-Bert said hastily. "I want you." His eyes bulged. "I mean, I want to. Give you one, that is. For free. As a gift. From me. To you." He pulled at the collar of his shirt. "Is it really warm in here? It feels really warm."

"My hands are sweating," Josy told him. "So probably."

"What book do you want?" Xander asked.

Oh god. He had no idea. He pointed at one. "I guess I'm curious how the triceratops convinced the guy to give up his NRA membership, and also managed to get him pregnant."

Q-Bert reached for the book and proceeded to knock a couple of copies to the floor in front of Xander and Josy. He sputtered another apology, but Josy told him it was fine. He bent down to pick up the books, Xander crouching down and helping him.

"I think it's going really well," Josy whispered.

Xander snorted. "If you say so."

"When do I ask him if he wants to be friends?"

"Just… play it cool. You'll know when the time is right."

They stood up, putting the books on the table.

"Thanks," Q-Bert said, gnawing on his bottom lip. "Who do I make this out to?"

"Me," Josy said promptly.

"Uh. Yeah, great. Cool. I just need to know your name."

"Oh crap. I never told you my name."

Q-Bert waited.

Josy panicked, wondering if it was too late to start this whole thing over.

Xander groaned. "His name is Josiah."

Xander for the save! "Josiah Edward Erickson," Josy said. "It's nice to meet you." He held out his hand, because he would salvage this. He *would*.

Q-Bert stared at it for a moment.

Maybe he didn't like to be touched? And here Josy was, practically *forcing his hand on him*—

Q-Bert reached up and gripped his hand. His fingers were long and slender. His skin was warm and dry. They didn't quite shake hands, as much as they just *held* hands. Maybe now was the perfect time to ask Q-Bert if he wanted to hang out sometime. Josy started making plans. They could go to a farmers' market and look at tomatoes. Or they could hike to the Hollywood Sign and breathe in that hot, dank Los Angeles air. Or they could go to a park and swing on the swings and then get frozen yogurt, even though frozen yogurt was literally pointless. It didn't taste bad, it didn't taste good, it just *was*.

"Huh," Dee said again.

Q-Bert pulled his hand away as if scalded. He opened the book as he picked up his pen. He stared down at the page for a moment before he muttered something under his breath and started writing. It took him only a few moments before he finished with a flourish. He closed the book and handed it to Josy.

Josy, who was running out of time.

Now, it should be said that Josiah Erickson was not a coward. It takes a certain amount of gumption to be able to repeatedly stand in front of a line of producers and casting directors and overworked PAs and be scrutinized down to the tiniest little detail, only to find out that he's not right for the role, with little to no feedback given. Most of the time, it's just *no*. In fact, he'd heard that word more than any other in his lifetime.

But he still got up every morning, telling himself that today was going to be the day he got his big break, even when he didn't have any auditions scheduled. For all he knew, he'd be on shift at Applebee's and a producer would see him and say that his face was *exactly* what he was looking for in his latest movie involving gigantic robots fighting each other and destroying cities with little regard to human life and/or property damage. He would most likely have to run in front of a green screen in slow motion while holding the hand of a beautiful woman who was inappropriately dressed for a robot apocalypse, but he could do it. As long as it wasn't directed by Michael Bay, he could *do* it. And if Mr. Bay *was* involved, he would have to politely decline this random man in the booth at Applebee's who had ordered artichoke dip, because there was a dude in Oregon who Josy cared for very much who believed Mr. Bay was a soulless husk of a human being and potentially a mass murderer.

But if Mr. Bay wasn't involved in any capacity, Josy could run with it. He practiced in the mirror what he referred to as his *gritty face*, the expression he would wear when he was barking orders at the soldiers around him as they took their last stand against Mega Death Annihilator, who had machine guns for fingers and could shoot laser beams from its elbows. He would get the girl in the end, and he would get revenge against the robots who had murdered his father, the king of the northern hemisphere.

So no. Josiah Erickson wasn't a coward. He knew rejection. One could not be an actor of his caliber and *not*.

But funnily enough, when faced with a blushing author in glasses handing him a book where it appeared a triceratops would get a gun-toting man pregnant even though it defied human anatomy, Josy couldn't find the words to say just how much this moment meant to him.

So he said, "Um. Thank you. I can't wait to read this, even though I don't read a lot."

And Q-Bert said, "Wow, that's great, I hope you enjoy it."

And then Josy said, "Sure. Nice. Neat. Great. Wonderful."

And that was it.

They stared at each other for another moment, and then the woman who was either a mermaid or a salmon pushed by them to talk to Q-Bert.

For a brief moment, he thought about telling her to swim back upstream and *wait her goddamn turn*, but Josy wasn't mean.

Xander, on the other hand, *could* be mean and looked as if he was going to try to wrestle the shiny woman. Since Josy figured that wasn't allowed in a library, he took Xander by the hand and dragged him toward the exit.

"That was it?" Xander demanded. "I thought you were going to be his friend!"

"I tried," Josy snapped as he reached the doors. The children on the trampoline looked as if they were laughing at him. God, how he hated their joy of reading and jumping. "I couldn't make the words come out. Being an adult in a library and trying to make friends should not be this hard."

"That's… an uncomfortable sentence."

"How do you think *I* feel?"

"Why are we leaving? What have I told you? Don't ever let someone in a costume try and push you around, especially when they are supposed to be some kind of sea animal."

"I know," Josy muttered. "And it's so oddly specific I never thought it'd come true. But here we are."

"A drag queen dressed as Ursula tried to get me to go home with her," Xander said. "She was really rude about it, and so that's why the rule exists."

"Uh, you *did* go home with her."

Xander shrugged as they pushed their way through the doors. "I have oddly hypocritical tastes."

The air outside was warm as they started down the steps. The end of the line was just inside the doors, but people gathered in front of the library, talking and laughing. Josy was still high, though it seemed to be the least of his problems. He remembered the young, naïve person he'd been, standing on these steps only an hour before, not knowing how his life was going to change. He envied that man.

They hadn't even gotten any cookies.

This was pretty much the worst night ever.

And also pretty great, because they'd had fun. Tigress had been really cool, and he'd learned that Sasquatch could be erotic.

It was quite the conundrum.

"We could just wait here until he leaves," Xander told him.

"That's kind of creepy."

Xander rolled his eyes. "What if you had just gotten done with an event and people were waiting to talk to you?"

"I would be touched and give myself to my adoring fans."

"Then why can't you do the same thing now for Q-Bert?"

"Because I don't want to be an adoring fan. I want to be his *friend*. There's a difference. With the fans, you smile and nod and take selfies and then hope they don't follow you back to your house and murder you by shoving their underwear down your throat. With friends, you go get McFlurries and go to the park and eat them on the swings."

Xander stared at him. Then, "Do you want to get McFlurries and then go to a park and eat them on the swings?"

"It's dark. The only people who go the park in LA this late are the people cruising public bathrooms or the ones that want to get murdered after accidentally stumbling upon a drug deal."

"That's very seventies. I like it."

Josy shrugged. "Retro, right? Can we just go to your house? I want to smoke a bowl and lie down and talk about my feelings. I'm staying the night, by the way. I don't have to work until two tomorrow, and I am feeling pretty down. I might need you to make me popcorn."

Xander wrapped an arm around his shoulders. "With M&M's in it?"

"It's the only way to eat popcorn."

"I think I can manage that. Let's get an Uber and we can—"

"Josiah!"

They turned in time to see Q-Bert rushing down the steps. He had a strange look on his face, and his hands were balled into fists. Josy wondered if he was about to get punched. He hoped not. He couldn't go to auditions when he had a black eye.

But Q-Bert, in fact, did not punch him. If anything, he looked like he was about to throw up as he stopped in front of them. He glanced at Xander, then back at Josy. "Hi. I want to ask you something."

"Oh boy," Xander said, taking a step back. He didn't go too far, which Josy was thankful for. He couldn't be sure what was happening, but he didn't want Xander to leave in case it was bad. The other people outside the library were staring at them, some of them taking pictures with their phones. Josy wondered if they were fans of his or Q-Bert's. Probably Q-Bert's. He didn't often run into people who were fans of his commercials.

"Okay," Josy said slowly. "You can ask me something. But if it's how tall Mount Everest is, I have absolutely no idea."

"What? No, that's not what I want—I thought you were good at trivia?"

"I am. But that's not trivia. That's mountains."

"Oh my god," Q-Bert mumbled. "You're so… you."

Josy shrugged. "I do okay."

"Dee said she'd murder me if I didn't come after you."

Josy didn't know what to do with that. Well, he believed it, but beyond that, he had nothing. "Oh. She's… scary. I mean, lesbians are awesome, and lesbians with neck tattoos are even better, but I would never want to make her mad."

Q-Bert looked frustrated. "She's not… she wouldn't get mad. Not unless I asked her to."

"Please don't ask her to."

"I won't," Q-Bert promised, and Josy believed him.

But it also raised questions. He leaned forward and lowered his voice. "Have you ever asked her to?" He liked Q-Bert's eyes. They were brown like the chocolate chips in the cookies he would never get to eat. Unless Q-Bert had brought him some, but that didn't seem to be the case.

"Once."

Josy felt a chill run down his spine. "She murdered someone for you? That's awesome."

"What? No! She didn't—it wasn't *murder*. Some guy was getting a little too close and wouldn't take no for an answer, and she grabbed him by the back of the neck and threw him into a wall."

"Dude," Josy breathed.

"Right? It was—okay, that's not why I'm out here."

Maybe there *would* be cookies. "What's up, man?"

"I don't—I don't do this often." He cleared his throat. "Scratch that. I don't do this ever."

"Do what? Chase after people in front of a library? I mean, that's cool if that's your thing. I can respect that. I have a pair of socks with Ewoks on them, so no judgment here."

"No," Q-Bert said forcefully. "That's not—this shouldn't be so hard." His face screwed up as he looked down at his feet.

Josy wanted to hug him, but his shoulders were tense, and he didn't think it'd be appreciated. "It doesn't have to be."

Q-Bert nodded, head jerking up and down. "Right. Like, okay. Just. I think... I think you're weird."

"Thank you," Josy said promptly.

"And I like weird."

"Well, that's good for me, I guess. This is going well."

"And I like your shirt."

"My friend got it on eBay. You can blow me, but it doesn't change colors."

He heard Xander groan behind him as Q-Bert appeared to choke on his tongue.

"Holy crap, that's not what I meant," he said quickly, doing his best to keep the train out of Friendship Station from falling into a canyon that was filled with lava. "You don't need to blow me. Or even *on* me. I didn't mean it like that. I'm stoned, and when I get stoned, I say stupid things. Well. I say stupid things when I'm *not* stoned, but it's worse when I'm high."

"Right," Q-Bert squeaked. "Of course. No blowing. That's—wait. High?" He took a step back. "Are you on heroin?"

Josy blinked. "What? No. Of course not."

Q-Bert took another step back. "Bath salts? Are you going to turn into a zombie and eat my face?"

"I'm not going to eat your face," Josy promised. "I mean, even if I was on bath salts, I wouldn't do that. I think. I'm not really sure how that works. I mean, is it... soap? Are people eating soap and turning into zombies?"

Q-Bert looked as if he was about to run.

Josy needed to salvage this situation. "It's just pot."

Q-Bert's shoulders slumped. "Oh. That actually makes a lot of sense."

"It does?"

He waved at hand in Josy's direction. "Just... all of this."

Josy looked down at himself. He didn't see anything different than what he'd seen in the mirror back at his apartment. "Sure?"

"It's not bad," Q-Bert said quickly. "In fact, I like it. I don't even know you, but I like a lot of things about you."

"Wow," Josy said, awed. "That was a nice thing to say. Thank you."

Q-Bert looked as if he were steeling himself for something. He squared his shoulders and clenched his jaw. "Would you want to go on a date with me? Maybe? Possibly?"

And that's when Josy did the absolute worst thing in the world.

In fact, the absolute worst *two* things in the world.

He was surprised into laughter.

And he said, "No."

He didn't mean for it to sound like it did. In fact, anyone who knew him well enough would say it was almost impossible for Josy to be mean about anything. It'd led to him getting walked over every now and then, and he'd had to learn to take a firmer stance, but Josiah Erickson didn't know *how* to be an asshole. Serge said once that he was literal sunshine and that whatever made human beings act like dicks was missing from Josy. They agreed it must have all been given to Xander, who scowled at the both of them.

He laughed, yes, but only because he wasn't expecting Q-Bert to say what he said.

And he said no because he didn't want to go on a date. Dates usually meant expectations. And expectations led to situations that Josy wasn't comfortable with. It was easier to just avoid it entirely.

But the blood was draining from Q-Bert's face like he'd just been shot down and, worse, *laughed* at in the process.

Which is exactly what had happened.

Josy never wanted to see that look on his face again, especially when he was the one who put it there. "No," he said, reaching for Q-Bert, who took another step back. "That's not—that's not what I meant. I swear. I wasn't expecting it, and it caught me off guard. You're awesome, man. Like, you have no idea. Your entire existence is gnarly. I just don't date." He smiled because he wanted Q-Bert to see how great things could be if they were friends. "It's not something I like to do, especially with someone like you who I think could be—"

Well, that certainly didn't come out right, if the expression on Q-Bert's face was any indication.

Q-Bert's eyes were wide, and he was gnawing on his bottom lip again. "Sorry. I didn't—that's not—I shouldn't have—" He looked around, and Josy realized they had an audience and people were staring at them. "I should probably go. I couldn't—" He made a strangled noise before spinning on his heels and rushing back up the steps into the library.

"What the hell just happened?" Josy demanded of no one in particular.

"Shit," Xander muttered, coming up to stand beside Josy. "You okay?"

"What did I do wrong?"

Xander sighed. "Nothing, man. It just... escalated. I think. Quicker than even I could follow. You were saying one thing, and he was thinking another. It was just a miscommunication."

"Miscommunications are so pointless. Should I go talk to him? I think I should go back and try and talk to him. I didn't mean to laugh. Honest. I was just trying to be his friend!"

"I know you were. But the guy dressed like a unicorn is glaring at us, and I think we should just cut our losses and get out of here before it turns into a mob and I die at the hands of someone with sparkly eye shadow and a horn tied to their head."

"But—"

"We know who he is now," Xander said quietly. "If anything, we can stalk him online and find out where he's going to be next." His phone beeped. He pulled it from his pocket and looked down at the screen. "Uh, scratch that. We should probably forget he exists. I just got a text from Dee, who said she's going to kick your ass."

"Oh my god," Josy whispered. "Angry lesbian. We have to run."

And so they did.

They made it four blocks before they remembered they needed an Uber.

Ten minutes later they were in the back seat of a minivan belonging to Milton, who talked about himself in the third person. Normally such a dude would pique Josy's interest immensely, but since he decided to feel sorry for himself, he stared out the window instead, brow furrowed as he watched streetlights flash by.

It wasn't until they were almost back to Xander's apartment that he remembered the book in his hand.

He looked down at the picture of a half-naked man with a rifle slung over his shoulder, his belly distended from the dinosaur baby that grew inside him. A triceratops nuzzled his horn against the man's stomach. Josy wondered if he'd ever find a dinosaur or a person to love him that much.

He opened the book to see black ink in shaky scrawl across the title page.

It read:

> *Josiah—*
> *Thank you for being a bright light in all the darkness.*
> *Q*

Chapter 5

Josiah Erickson had a problem.

Well, that went without saying.

But this was a *big* problem.

He had taken Xander's suggestion to heart.

He was being creepy.

It wasn't until he was fifty-six weeks into Q-Bert's Instagram that he realized just *how* creepy he was actually being. He most certainly didn't intend to let it get that far, of course. He'd told himself in the days that followed his piss-poor attempt at making friends he would just put the entire thing behind him and move on with his life. He'd made a mistake, but the chances of him actually running into Q-Bert again without actively looking for him were minimal. Los Angeles was a big place filled with millions of people. He would probably never see Q-Bert again.

Unless he decided to stalk him.

Which he did.

And was.

In the bathroom at Applebee's while on his lunch break.

He wasn't trying to be malicious. Having never stalked anyone before, Josy wasn't quite sure how to go about it. But it was twenty minutes into his thirty-minute break, and he was sitting on the toilet, scrolling through Q-Bert's Instagram, and he was a failure at being a real person.

"I should stop," he'd muttered to himself when he first started.

"I should really stop," he muttered to himself twenty minutes later.

Which is where he was now, fifty-six—no, fifty-*eight* weeks into Q-Bert's Instagram, and even though he knew he should put his phone away and attempt to poop before he had to go back into the dining room, he was now on week *fifty-nine*, and it was just freaking endearing.

Oh sure, Q-Bert was terrible at Instagram. For one, he apparently didn't see the need to use filters. All his photographs were… normal. They weren't stylized. And don't even get Josy started on the lack of hashtags. How was someone supposed to know what Q-Bert was thinking about each photo without hashtags? Yes, maybe Josiah was a little annoyed that Q-Bert had approximately seventy thousand more followers than he did, and that there was the tiny little blue check mark next to his name that showed he was pretty much better than anyone who didn't have it, but Josy was not a vindictive person. He didn't know how to be.

What he *was* on this Monday afternoon in the bathroom at Applebee's was utterly charmed. Q-Bert apparently didn't understand the art of the selfie, so he was barely in any of the posts. But what he did post were pictures of dogs he saw while out for a walk, close-ups of lolling tongues and pointy ears and captions that said things like *This is a good boy* and *Made a new friend, his name is Baxter and his owner says he likes broccoli*. There were pictures of flowers growing from cracks in the sidewalk, women in professional attire doing double Dutch with a long jump rope, coffee art shaped like a leaf, a burrito bigger than Josiah had ever seen, leaves changing colors, the temperature on the dashboard of a car with a caption lamenting on how it could be April and almost a hundred degrees.

There was one photograph that captured Josy's attention more than the others, from just over a year back. Q-Bert was standing in front of a full-length mirror. There were bookshelves in the reflection behind him, stuffed full of books and what looked like sleeves for hundreds of records and a plant that looked like it had died at least a month prior.

Q-Bert was wearing loose pajama pants and a thin tank top, and he looked *exhausted*. His skin was sallow, and there were dark circles under his eyes. His fingernails were bitten to the quick on the hand that held the phone toward the mirror. His hair was disheveled and greasy, as if it hadn't been washed in days.

It wasn't flattering by any stretch of the imagination.

But Josy thought it might be the realest thing he'd ever seen.

The caption read: *I've talked a lot about mental health, and how important it is to take care of yourself. You need to get out of bed, even if the very idea hurts. You need to take a shower. You need to eat. You need to get dressed. You need to go outside and get sun on your skin. But no matter all the platitudes I spout, sometimes I forget my own words. For the last few days, I've forgotten how to practice self-care. It can come without warning. I don't know why it happens, but it does. Three days ago, I woke up and I was drowning for no reason at all. Instead of pushing myself to get up, I pulled the blanket over my head and stayed there. I only moved to use the bathroom. I haven't eaten. I haven't showered. I was tired and sad for reasons I can't quite explain. But this morning, I opened my eyes and realized I couldn't let this be who I was. I wouldn't let this thing beat me. So I pushed myself up. Here is what I look like now. It's not great, but I'm going to be okay. I have an appointment with my therapist. I'm going to take my SSRIs. I am going to go outside and breathe that sweet, sweet smoggy air. Because I'm worth it. And so are you.*

It was the only photograph like it. The photos that followed were brighter. Happier.

And even though Josy knew that Q-Bert was better now—he'd just seen him, after all—he couldn't help but breathe a sigh of relief.

It was when he was *sixty-three weeks* in that he made a mistake.

It was on a mundane post, a photo of water sluicing down a window with the caption *I love rainy Sundays*. It was nice, and while it didn't speak to him like some of the others, it still fit in with Q-Bert's aesthetic.

The *problem* was that the bathroom door opened, and an awful voice said, "Josy, are you still in here? I swear to god, if you're getting high again, I'm going to get your ass so fired," causing Josy's thumb to slip and skitter along the screen.

A little heart blossomed over the rainy picture.

Josiah Erickson had just liked a year-old photograph on the Instagram account of the writer he was stalking.

He stared down at his phone in horror.

There were only three people in the entire world that Josy despised.

The first was Filipino president Rodrigo Duterte, who was responsible for numerous human rights violations.

The second person was Mason Grazer, a fellow actor who had beaten Josy out for some roles in commercials but still managed to find the time to aggressively flirt with Josy, telling him it was only a matter of time before Josy said yes. He had also sent Josy an unsolicited dick pic via direct messenger. Josy had replied that Mason should really get those varicose veins on the underside of his penis checked out before blocking him.

The third and final person that Josy despised was Frank, a dictator—er, *manager* at Applebee's. He was a lifer, or so he liked to claim, having been employed with "the Apple" (as he called it, much to Josy's dismay) for almost ten years. There was absolutely nothing wrong with gainful employment and being proud of where you worked, but Frank was everything wrong with humanity wrapped into one five-foot-six package whose sole purpose on this earth was to make the lives of the people under him a living hell.

And yes, maybe Josy sometimes partook in a little herb before his shift (and maybe during, too, if he was being honest), but who the hell hadn't? It wasn't like it affected his job performance. He absolutely was still able to serve sliders and chicken tenders while stoned. And *yes*, there was that one time that, while high, Josy had *accidentally* eaten some french fries from a plate that was about to go out, *but who the hell hadn't?*

Frank hadn't, apparently.

Frank, who had decided to make it his mission to follow Josy's every move.

Frank, who had stood behind Dave/Keith/Esteban while Josy was filming the commercial, a scowl on his face, interrupting every now and then to tell Dave/Keith/Esteban that *he* could take over if there was a need to fire Josy.

Frank, who had just caused Josy to accidentally double-tap a photo of a rainy Sunday that had been posted *over a year ago*.

"Oh my god," Josy mumbled. "No. No, no, no. Take it back. Take it back!"

For the first time in his life, Instagram was failing Josiah Erickson. Because there was no way *to* take it back. No matter how many times he tapped the photograph, that little heart beneath it remained bright red and mocking, whispering to him that his life was over, that Q-Bert was going to see that *TheRealJosiahErickson* had been scrolling through his profile like a *stalker*.

And he couldn't fix it.

A fist pounded on the stall door. "Josy!"

"I'm taking a shit!" he snapped. "For Christ's sake, let me do my business in peace."

"Are you on the reefer?" Frank demanded. "I can smell the reefer!"

No, Josy wasn't "on the reefer." He wasn't stupid enough to light up a joint in the bathroom at Applebee's. Well, sure, he'd gone through a wake-and-bake this morning, but that was normal. It was how he functioned. But Frank was a liar when he said he could smell anything aside from bleach and hints of hamburger meat wafting in from the kitchen.

"I'm not smoking," Josy growled. "If you don't stop harassing me while I'm in the bathroom, I am going to call the anonymous corporate line and leave a strongly worded voice mail that you won't leave your employees alone while their pants are down. Where will you be then, Frank? *Where will you be then.*"

Frank sputtered. "That's—you wouldn't dare!"

"Oh, wouldn't I?"

"Ugh. Fine. But if you're not out in the dining room in three minutes, I am going to write you up and put it in your permanent file."

"Oh no. Not my permanent file. Please, anything but that."

"Jessica just sat a group in your section. Get your ass—oh, hello, sir. Welcome to Applebee's. I hope your visit is enjoyable."

"Uh, thank you?" a man said before the stall door next to Josy opened and closed.

"Josy," Frank hissed. "Get out there. *Now*. The Apple waits for no man!"

"I will. Can you take their drink orders?"

"Yes, fine. No more reefer!"

There was nothing about how to make it look like you weren't stalking someone's Instagram page in the FAQ section. Josy couldn't even find a phone number to call to see about getting the *like* removed. He gave very real consideration to just deleting his Instagram entirely, but then thought that his seven thousand, six hundred and thirty-seven followers would be bereft at losing insight into the life of an actor on the rise.

Besides. Each of Q-Bert's photographs had thousands of likes. He probably wouldn't even notice.

HE NOTICED.

Josy was opening the front door to his apartment when his phone vibrated in his pocket. He fumbled with the keys as he pulled the phone out.

In the top left corner was an Instagram notification.

He slid his thumb down the screen.

He read four words that caused his heart to stutter.

Q-Bert started following you.

"What, pray tell, the fuck," Josy whispered.

What, pray tell, the fuck indeed.

"—AND NOW I don't know what to do. Do I follow him back? Do I ignore it and pretend it never happened? Do I pretend that I'm a *different*

Josiah Erickson even though we look exactly the same? There is no protocol for this. Believe me, I've looked, man. Do you want to know how bad this is? I got through this morning on air to answer trivia. It said almost one-third of Americans are embarrassed by this. You know what I said? Their nose hairs. Their *nose hairs*."

Xander and Serge stared at him blankly from over glasses of mimosas.

"It's not their nose hairs!" Josy bellowed. "It's the cleanliness of their cars! Why the hell would I say nose hairs unless I was so distracted by the fact he follows me on Instagram!"

Okay, so maybe Josiah had been ranting for the past ten minutes, having begun as soon as he arrived without even saying *hi*, but this was an emergency. He was allowed to freak out.

His phone vibrated on the table.

"And *that*," he said. "That keeps happening. Q-Bert only followed thirty-seven people before, and I'm the thirty-eighth. So now all *his* followers are starting to become *my* followers. I've gotten sixty new people on my Instagram account since last night. The last time I got so many new followers was after I played basketball in those tiny shorts with genital herpes!"

"He's kidding," Xander said quickly to all the people who had turned to stare. "He's an actor. It was acting. He doesn't have genital herpes. *I* don't have genital herpes."

"Isn't it a good thing that he followed you?" Serge asked, his mirror shades reflecting Josy's rather unattractive irate face back at him. "Won't it mean he has no hard feelings when you basically shot him down in front of all his fans on accident? He's obviously looked inside himself and centered his chakras, expelling all the negative energy, replacing it with light."

"But what if he looks at my page and thinks I'm just one of those Instagays who only posts flattering pictures of themselves?"

Xander and Serge exchanged a look. "You *are* one of those Instagays who only posts flattering pictures of yourself," Xander said. "We all are. I actually used hashtag Instagay this morning before coming to brunch because the veins on my biceps were really noticeable after my workout. I already have my half-naked accidentally-trapped-in-Christmas-lights photo planned for December."

"And it's not like you put unflattering pictures of yourself online," Serge pointed out. "No one does that."

"He does," Josy moaned. "Because he's a good person that cares about other people. And I have no idea how to even begin to handle that. It's like he's Jesus and Ryan Gosling all wrapped in one."

Serge squinted at Josy. "This is going to sound sort of weird, so I apologize in advance. But do you… do you have a crush on this dude?"

Xander rolled his eyes. "That's what I said. You should have seen him at the reading. It was surreal. It was like he'd been taken over by some weird Bizarro Josy."

"I have a *friend*-crush," Josy retorted.

"Is that a thing?" Serge asked. He frowned. "I don't think that's a thing."

"It is. It's something that I've decided is real, because it's the only thing that makes sense for why I'm freaking out as much as I am. And it's really not doing me any favors that you aren't giving me the advice I want to hear. I need to speak to the expert."

Xander groaned. "I swear to god, you have all week to talk to him, and yet every Tuesday brunch, it's the same damn thing."

"Well, maybe if you told me how to fix every problem in my life, I wouldn't need to!"

"You don't have problems," Serge said sagely. "Only obstacles waiting to be overcome."

"That's what problems are," Xander said slowly.

"Exactly," Serge said with a serene smile.

"I don't understand your mysticism," Josy told him, phone already ringing in his ear. "And I don't think you do either."

"Thank you for calling Pastor Tommy's—"

"I need him!"

"Josy?"

"Hi, Casey."

"How's it going, man?"

Josy sighed. "My life is in shambles and I've got a friend-crush on a guy who writes Sasquatch porn who I laughed at when he asked me out on a date. And then I accidentally stalked his Instagram and Frank made me like a photo in the bathroom, and now he's following me and I don't know what to do!"

Silence.

Then, "Jesus, I am way too stoned for this. Hold on, man. I'll get him."

"Thank you. Wait! Wait. Before you go."

"What?"

"How are you?"

Casey laughed. "I'm all right. It's been a good morning so far. The ferret with merit woke me up by chewing on my hair, so I can't complain."

"Harry S. Truman is pretty rad."

"Oh, totally. I've almost got him trained to play dead when I shoot him with finger guns. Gus says it's a pointless waste of time, but he has no idea how cool it's going to be."

"Gustavo thinks a lot of things are a pointless waste of time."

"Yeah," Casey said fondly. "He's the best."

Josy slumped farther down into his chair. "Okay, now that we've got that out of the way, I need to talk to him to have him tell me how to fix all of this."

"Ten-four, good buddy. Hold on."

"Wait! One more thing."

"What?"

"I have a confession to make."

"Uh-oh. I'm listening."

"This person. This *guy*."

"What about him?"

"He's…." Could Josy do this? Could he really tell Casey this?

He had to. He owed it to his friend. Aces Unite.

"He's also an author. But I want you to remember that you were always my first author friend, and nothing can take that away from us. Even if I end up liking what he writes more than your young adult postapocalyptic vampire/werewolf books, you will always be special to me."

"Whoa, really? Dude, rock on. That's righteous. Do I know him?"

Josy frowned. "Do all authors know each other?"

"Sometimes."

"Oh. Q-Bert. He writes monster porn."

"Monster porn."

"Yeah. Like full-on Sasquatch having sex with newly woke bisexual frat boys. And sometimes there are dinosaurs."

"Huh. Respect. No idea who that is. I'll have to look him up."

"It spoke to my soul when I heard him read it," Josy said seriously. "Like, you have no idea."

"I can only imagine. No worries, my dude. I got you. Bros forever."

"Bros forever," Josy agreed. "I'm done with you now."

Casey laughed again. "Later days. Good luck with your friend-crush."

The phone was muffled. Josy could almost picture it in his mind. They would be standing inside the video store, a line of customers out the door. Gustavo would be working hard, but as soon as he heard it was Josy on the phone, he'd tell all of his customers that he had to take a very important call and they'd have to come back later.

Gustavo really was the best.

"What do you want now?" Gustavo asked gruffly.

"Everything is terrible and I made it worse," Josy moaned into the phone.

Silence. Then, "And you thought you'd call me about it for reasons I don't care to understand."

"It's Tuesday. I always call you on Tuesdays."

"Yes. But *why*."

"I can't afford a therapist."

"I'm *not*—that's—oh my god. Casey said you had a problem with your Instabook."

"I can't believe you're a real person."

"What's that supposed to mean?"

"Nothing. Yes. I'm having a problem with my Instabook. I met someone who I wanted to be friends with, but then I messed it up and I don't know how to fix it."

"And you're asking me… what."

"How to fix it!"

Gustavo sighed. "How did you mess it up?"

"He asked me out on a date, but I don't like him like that. I mean, maybe one day I could, but why can't we just be friends first? I laughed at him, though, when he asked. I didn't mean to. And then I stalked him on his Instabook, and now he started following me."

"Wait. What? He's following you? Like right this second? That's something you need to involve the police over. You're kind of famous to insomniacs who watch infomercials at two in the morning. He might try and murder you and wear your face like a mask."

Josiah couldn't even with Gustavo. "Not literally. He's following me online."

"Oh. Is he a scammer, then? Casey made me get an email address, and I got a message from a Nigerian prince that said I had forty million dollars waiting for me. I thought it was too good to be true, and guess what?"

"What?"

"It *was*," Gustavo said savagely. "It was a *lie*. Did you know that people can lie on the Internet about anything they want to? Who does that?"

"Apparently Nigerian princes," Josy said. "What the hell."

"Right? This is why I don't Instabook or FaceSnap or whatever. And the only people who send me emails are the We Three Queens. Bertha forwards me dog videos. I hate them, oh my god."

"Ooh, did you see the one where the husky howls at his owner when he doesn't want to leave the park?"

"No. That sounds terrible." Then, "Send it to me later."

"Will do. Now fix my problem."

"You're asking me how to talk to other people."

"Yes," Josy said. "Exactly."

"I don't know *how* to talk to other people."

"You're doing okay right now."

"Dammit. Okay. Fine. He asked you out. You laughed at him and said no. Now he's following you on Instabook. Is that right?"

"Yes. You're very good at keeping up, unlike other people I know." He glared at Xander and Serge. Xander flipped him off. Serge was taking a selfie. He looked good. His teeth were very white.

"Okay," Gustavo said slowly. "Why not just apologize?"

That was baffling. "What? Just… say sorry?"

"Yes. Tell him you're sorry, that you didn't mean it the way it sounded, and then ask him to go do whatever it is kind-of-famous people do. Bowling or whatever. I don't know. I'm not famous."

"You're famous to me."

"That doesn't make sense at all," Gustavo said. "Oh my god. You should be ashamed of yourself. Are we done now?"

"Yes. No! How do I talk to him and make him be my friend?"

"I have no idea. I have friends only because none of you will leave me alone. Whatever you do, though, don't look it up on the Internet. You'll see things you'll never be able to unsee before you get terrible advice from websites that should be illegal. I have to go. Someone just came into the store and asked Casey if we have a copy of *Transformers*. I need to ban them for life for asking such a ridiculous question. Sir? Excuse me, sir? You stay *right* there, and I'll deal with you. Don't you even think of running out that door. I work out, and my stamina is really high. Josy, I am hanging up now."

"But you haven't told me how to fix this!"

"You resemble something close to an adult. Figure it out. And don't call me about this again. Until next Tuesday. And send me the dog video."

The phone beeped in Josy's ear.

Josy put his head on the table. "I'm so screwed."

"There, there," Serge said, patting the back of his head. "You'll figure it out. A yogi gave me some advice when I was in India that I think fits this situation aptly. He said, 'Do or do not. There is no try.'"

"That wasn't a yogi in India," Xander said. "That was Yoda in Star Wars."

"Oh," Serge said. "That… changes nothing. It's still sound advice. The Jedi aren't that different than those of us who are enlightened."

Worst. Brunch. Ever.

Now, it should be said that Josiah Erickson wasn't usually in the market to follow advice that came from a tiny green puppet that had a human arm shoved up its backside. It wasn't that he necessarily thought there was anything wrong with that, it just wasn't for him.

But the more he thought about it, the more it made sense.

"Do or do not," he muttered, staring up at the popcorn ceiling of his apartment. Thick bluish smoke swirled around him. "There is no try."

"Do or do not," he whispered, clapping along while his coworkers sang happy birthday to a screaming six-year-old who was throwing silverware across the restaurant. "There is no try."

"Do or do not," he mumbled as he scrolled through Q-Bert's blog at three in the morning while sitting on his futon in his underwear. "There is no try." He ate another Chicken in a Bisket cracker because it reminded him of Thanksgiving and he was blazed out of his mind.

"Do or do not," he said. "There is no—"

"Kiddo, what in the actual fuck are you talking about?"

He blinked, startled out of his reverie. Starla sat across from him, a cigarette dangling from her lips. They were in her cluttered office. When he'd arrived, she'd asked him if he wanted a cup of coffee. He'd politely declined, but she'd barked for one anyway. A harried-looking intern had rushed in and set the mugs on the desk on top of papers that were apparently important, if the way she'd yelled at him was any indication. The intern had apologized before running out of the office and closing the door behind him.

"He's my nephew," she'd told Josy. "Useless, but I apparently owed my sister a favor. I'm seeing how long it takes before he cries. He started yesterday. I give him two more hours until he breaks."

"You're very scary," Josy said.

She grinned. It was deliciously evil.

Except now he hadn't realized he'd been talking to himself again. *Do or do not. There is no try.* It'd become a mantra that he hadn't known he'd needed in his life.

The *problem* with having it as a mantra was that Josy had done absolutely nothing about anything. Here he was, a week out from the disaster that had been his first meeting with Q-Bert, and he was no closer to finding an answer to his problems. He'd almost convinced himself to follow Q-Bert back on Instagram but couldn't bring himself to do it, unsure if it would be seen as an invitation of sorts. He'd posted a few more pictures over the past couple of days, but Q-Bert hadn't liked any of them.

Josy was terribly vexed over the entire situation.

There was a contact email on Q-Bert's website. Josy had almost used it to send Q-Bert a message, but he wasn't sure what to say to convey the depths of his friend-crush while also apologizing for laughing in the face of someone who had anxiety and depression. He quickly learned while reading through Q-Bert's blog that he didn't *suffer* from anxiety and depression, he just *had* it. He'd written that he didn't like the word *suffering* because it implied losing, and he was far from losing. He was fighting. He was locked in battle. Suffering meant weakness, and sure, some days brought setbacks, but he'd pick himself up, sword in hand, and get ready to go again to slay the beast.

Josy was impressed. Because of Q-Bert's strength, but also with the idea of him having a sword and killing shit.

Which, of course, made things worse. Because Q-Bert had this… he had this whole life. He was so put together, even when he seemed to be falling apart. He used his social media pages not to flaunt himself but to show the world through a different set of eyes. He answered questions from his followers who needed his help with their own mental health. He said he wasn't an expert by any stretch of the imagination and always pointed people to those who were. And it was all so very overwhelming, because what did Josy have to offer in return? He lived paycheck to paycheck, and his most expensive possessions were his three-foot bong and his flat-screen TV that he bought so he could watch his black-and-white horror movies. He'd had to eat nothing but off-brand dollar store Hamburger Helper called Burger Assistant! for weeks after that, but it'd been worth it to see the creature from the black lagoon rising out of the water on fifty-five inches.

But those were just *things*. Things that, in the great and grand scheme of things, didn't matter in the slightest. What mark was he leaving on the world? Was he ever going to be in the *Oh My God That One Person from That Thing Died* montage at the Oscars?

So instead of figuring out what to do about Q-Bert, he only succeeded in making things worse. He didn't even know how. One moment he was nervous about emailing Q-Bert, and the next, Josy had convinced himself he was the most narcissistic person who had ever lived.

Do or do not. There is no try.

Do not is exactly what he was apparently doing.

And it was awful.

Which is why when Starla had summoned him to her office, he'd jumped at the chance. Maybe this was the opportunity he was waiting for. Maybe he would get to audition for something amazing that would also change the world. He would get the part and suddenly become the face of saving apes or stopping fracking, whatever that was. The only fracking he knew was from *Battlestar Galactica*, but he didn't think that was what the news kept talking about. But if it was, then at least he would know how to defeat those damn Cylons.

But this could be it. His big break. Starla wouldn't tell him what it was about, no matter how much he begged. He'd even arrived two hours early to her office, and she'd made him wait because apparently appointment times were set for a reason. There were two people waiting ahead of him, one guy Josy recognized from such roles as Guy in Bar #4 in the moderately successful TV show *I Got Your Mother Pregnant* and Priest in Street #77 in the ill-conceived rom-com called *Mansplain*, which turned out to be horribly misogynistic and ruined the careers of at least four people. The other person was a woman who was apparently double-jointed and even offered to show Josy. He politely declined and was grateful when Starla called her in before she wrapped her knees around her own neck. Granted, she'd left crying for reasons Josy wasn't privy to, and he wondered if he was about to be let go.

Do or do not. There is no try.

So when Starla asked him what the fuck he was talking about, he couldn't be quite sure. There'd been no wake-and-bake this morning since he was a professional. One would think it would help to clear his mind, but that didn't seem to be the case. Professionalism was hard.

So he gave her his best smile and said, "It's nice to see you today."

She stared at him.

He smiled a little wider.

She sucked on her cancer stick before blowing smoke out above his head. He'd tried to get her to quit last year, but she'd told him that if he ever tried to take her Virginia Slim 120s away from her again, he would have to go through life explaining to any potential future partner that he only had one testicle due to a woman who was barely above five feet and weighed a buck ten only after a big meal.

He believed her. And not just because he was a pacifist, but also because Starla was terrifying.

But the severe expression on her face softened slightly, as it sometimes did around him. "How you been?"

He shrugged. "Complicated."

She snorted. "That right."

"I've had a very strange week. It's this whole… thing. Learned some stuff about myself."

"Like what?"

"I don't know how to talk to people I don't know. And also, I'm materialistic."

"I've seen your apartment, kiddo. I don't think you have enough materials to be called materialistic."

"Right? That's what *I* thought, but then I was watching my gigantic TV that I almost got punched for when I bought it on Black Friday, and I realized that I wasn't doing things like battling depression or fracking, and I don't know. It just hit me."

She ashed the cigarette into a 7-Eleven Big Gulp. "Depression? Kid, you are literally the happiest person I know. It's honestly disgusting. What's this about depression?"

"Oh, it's not me. It's someone else who I tried to be friends with. But then I messed up, and now I'm stalking him even though I don't mean to."

The gaudy ring on her finger flashed in the light overhead as she pointed at him. "You get a restraining order against you, I'm going to kick your ass."

"Not *actually* stalking," he said quickly. "Just… his Instagram. And his blog. And his Tumblr. And Twitter. And Facebook, though he's not sixty years old and posting photos of his grandchildren or shouting with memes about people taking his guns, so I don't know why he's on that one. It's not even ironic yet."

"Sounds like a mess."

"Got any advice?" he asked hopefully.

"Oh sure. Got the best advice. Gonna lay it on you. You ready?"

He was so excited. "Yeah!"

"You gonna listen to me?"

Damn right he was! "*Yeah!*"

"Okay. Here it is."

He leaned forward.

She said, "Shut up. I don't care about any of this."

He blinked. "That's… not helpful."

She reached across the desk and patted the back of his hand. "You're wonderful. Stop wasting my time. I called you in here for a reason. Do you know who Roger Fuller is?"

"No. Should I?" He frowned. "Wait. Hold up. Roger Fuller. The producer? The guy who made all those terrible horror movies in the seventies and eighties where men tried to fight gigantic radioactive frogs or gigantic radioactive ants or gigantic radioactive aardvarks and somehow always ended up mostly naked?"

"He did like his gigantic radioactive monsters," Starla agreed. "And cock. The one and the same. *Attack of the Frogs* and *The Ants Are Eating Our Picnic and Our Faces* and *Aardvark Terror on the Titanic*. Shit films with shit budgets that tried to be allegorical takes on the Cold War but instead turned out to be an excuse to have his beefcake du jour pose nude on camera as they snarled at terrible special effects."

"The aardvark one was actually pretty cool," Josy said thoughtfully. "I mean, James Cameron probably wouldn't have gotten to make his version of *Titanic* without it."

"Keep telling yourself that, kiddo. Roger Fuller has apparently decided to embrace this weird and stupid world we live in, and crowdfunded his next film." She started to flip through the many papers on her desk. "Can't get the funding from a studio or production company? Have the masses pay for it instead while offering producer credits that'll get them a pointless IMDb page and nothing else." She paused her search and looked up at him. "You keeping your IMDb page updated?"

"Yes, ma'am. Uploaded another headshot two days ago."

She resumed flipping through the papers. "Good. It's important you do that." She grunted as she found a thin stacked set of pages and set it in front of her. She dropped her cigarette into the Big Gulp, where it hissed in what was most likely three-day-old Dr Pepper filled with other butts. "He was able to raise the budget he needed for his next film. Calls it a *prestige picture*, though I doubt he barely has a passing acquaintance with the concept. He apparently had some goodwill left, as the project was fully funded in less than a week. Either that or people are idiots and hardwired to choke on nostalgia for movies they barely remember. It's even worse when it comes to gay men. All that disposable income."

Josy knew nothing about disposable income. "What does that have to do with me?"

She leaned forward on her desk, folding her hands in front of her. "You don't know Roger Fuller?"

"Personally? No."

"You didn't go to one of his pool parties slash orgies that are supposed to be secret but everyone knows about? Maybe stick your ass in the air and your face in pile of coke?"

"Wow," Josy breathed. "Is that what people do to get famous? Because if so, I think I've been going about this whole thing wrong. I mean, not that I would actually do that, but still. It would have been nice to at least get an invite that I could have politely declined and then regretted not going to."

"You're serious."

"That I wouldn't go to an orgy and do cocaine? Yeah, man. I don't like that kind of thing."

"No, Josy. Not the cocaine orgy. You've seriously never met him?"

He thought hard before shaking his head. "Why?"

She tapped her fingers on the stack of papers before she slid it across the desk. "Because he's asked for you by name to come and audition for a part in the film."

"*What?*" he asked, staring down at what appeared to be a script. There were only thirteen words on the top page in bold black ink.

The Stories of My Father
A Roger Fuller Production
Screenplay by
Quincy Moore

"I don't know what to tell you, kiddo." Starla lit another cigarette. "This was delivered by courier yesterday. I had to sign a nondisclosure agreement before I could even put my hands on it. And it's only a few pages, a specific scene. Apparently the entire script is being kept under wraps. And there was a note on the top requesting you specifically audition next week."

This was it.

This was going to be his moment.

He could barely breathe.

"Do I have to put my ass in the air and/or do cocaine?" he whispered reverently.

"You better not. I will pin you down with my heel in your throat and shave off that ridiculous beard if you do."

He reached up and traced a finger along the top page. Starla was right; it couldn't have been the entire script, as it only seemed to be a handful of pages. But still. It was real. And he had been asked for by *name*.

He'd often thought about what this moment would be like. Late at night, when he couldn't sleep, he'd stare at the ceiling and think about his phone ringing. He'd pick it up and the voice on the other end would say, "Josiah Erickson, this is Steven Spielberg, and I want you to be in my upcoming war movie," or "Josiah Erickson, this is Chris Nolan, and I want you to be in my next sixteen-hour masturbatory fantasy with an ending that frustrates the hell out of everyone," or "Josiah Erickson, Tarantino here. I want to put you in a suit so you can say *fuck* a lot and shoot people in the face."

(There were days too, pre-Gustavo Tiberius, when these fantasies also involved "Josiah Erickson, this is Michael Bay, and I want you to star in my next movie, where you run in slow motion as a monster robot alien thing destroys Washington, DC, behind you on a green screen." Post-Gustavo Tiberius, that one was put on hold.)

They were the daydreams of someone who wanted something bigger. Something more. And he'd put in his time, sure. STDs and Applebee's and infomercials and dead guys on *Criminal Bad Guys: Topeka, Kansas*.

Of course he dreamed. He had to. Ever since he was that block of cheese in Wooster, Ohio, he'd dreamed of nothing else. He'd barely graduated high school. He hadn't gone to college, much to the disappointment of his parents. He'd scrimped and saved every single penny he could, packed up his meager belongings into his shitty car, and headed west with only a dream.

And it was finally paying off.

Here. Now. In this moment.

"Are you *crying*?" Starla demanded.

"No," he said as he wiped his eyes and sniffled. "It's just the cigarette smoke." He looked up at her. He trusted her more than almost anyone else in the world. "You think I should do this, right?"

Starla sighed as she sat back in her leather chair. "Yeah, kiddo. I guess I do." Her eyes narrowed. "Though if Roger Fuller tries anything on you, you tell me. I won't have any of my clients being put into a position where they're made to do something they don't want to. I believe in you, Josy. You piss me off, and I swear the more you smoke, the dumber you get, but I know you're going to do big things. I wouldn't have taken you on if I didn't think so. Out of everyone I represent, I think you've got the best shot here." She blew out another stream of smoke. "Though if you tell anyone else I said that, I'll rip out your tongue and shove it down your throat. Are we clear?"

"Yes, ma'am."

"Good. Now, I've read through the audition scene. It's absolutely ridiculous and gave me heartburn. Here's how I think you need to play it."

Chapter 6

If Josiah Erickson's life were a musical, the moment he exited the office of his agent, the sun would be shining and he would burst into song about how his whole life had been building to this moment and he was going to make it after all. Men in suits and women in pretty summer dresses would begin to dance around him, and he would belt his heart out, building toward a rousing climax where a chorus would sing behind him, fireworks exploding overhead.

A few things stopped that from happening.

First, Josiah Erickson's life was absolutely *not* a musical.

He couldn't sing.

It was cloudy.

There was only a homeless man pushing a shopping cart down the sidewalk.

And California was in the middle of a severe drought, so fireworks were illegal.

But still.

"I have an audition for a movie!" he exclaimed to the homeless man.

"That's great!" the homeless man replied. "I was abducted by aliens when I was twenty-six, and they implanted a device in my head that makes me see ghosts!"

"Whoa," Josy said. "You win. I don't have any cash, but I have this coupon for McDonald's that I can't use since I'm going to be in a movie and have to watch my diet. You can have it."

The man took the coupon and smiled at him. He was missing a tooth, and Josy thought it gave him character. "Thanks! There's a man standing next to you who says he was murdered in this exact spot fifty-seven years ago by a falling piano dropped by his business partner who was having an affair with his wife. Have a great day!" He whistled as he pushed the shopping cart away.

Josy looked over his shoulder.

There was nothing there.

But that was okay.

Because he was going to *nail* this audition.

"Jesus *Christ*," Xander moaned the next night. "Why in the hell are we watching this? It's Saturday and none of us are working. Why aren't we going out?"

Josy scowled as he paused the movie playing on the television in Xander's house. On the screen, a man attempted to look terrified while wearing nothing but a loincloth and running away from a gigantic radioactive Claymation aardvark on the deck of the *Titanic*. Granted, the aardvark looked fake as fuck and the *Titanic* was obviously a large tugboat in a parking lot getting sprayed with a couple of hoses. And *yes*, okay, maybe the guy's hair was feathered, and the costumes weren't exactly appropriate for the time period, but still. "This is research," Josy insisted, annoyed he'd had to stop the film for what had to be the seven hundredth time. He was sitting on an ottoman right in front of the TV, trying to soak in the atmosphere. "I need to know what I could expect before the audition on Tuesday. It's important, Xander."

"Dude's hot," Serge said, squinting at the screen from his spot next to Xander on the couch. His eyes were bloodshot. He'd been smoking since early afternoon. He'd offered his pipe to Josy when he arrived, but Josy had refused. He needed all his faculties while he prepared for what was probably going to be the biggest moment of his life. "I like his bangs." He paused, considering. Then he giggled in that way he only did when he was really high. "I'd like him to bang *me*. Get it? Because of the bangs. Yeah. You get it. I want pizza rolls." He pushed himself up from the couch and wandered toward the kitchen.

"Important," Xander repeated. "You think this is important. A revisionist take on the sinking of the *Titanic* that involves aardvarks the size of buildings. *This* is important."

"Yes," Josy said promptly.

Xander sighed as he looked toward the ceiling. "Okay, Josy."

A crash came from the kitchen. Silence. Then, "My bad! Apparently the drawers come out and fall on the ground when you pull them really hard. I don't know why I'm even looking in the drawer. That's not where pizza rolls are supposed to be."

Xander rolled his eyes as he turned his head back to Josy. "I don't even have pizza rolls."

"You gonna tell him?"

Xander shrugged. "Nah. He'll get distracted by something else in a minute and will forget all about them. You know how he gets when smokes."

"Lucky," Josy muttered. He looked at the cached pipe longingly where it lay on the coffee table before he shook his head. No. He needed to focus. "I want to—"

His phone beeped. He swiped the screen and pulled up the text thread. The new message said, *Gussy's yelling at aardvarks on TV. Sez its not historically accurate. No aardvarks on titanic?*

Mybe n cargo bay? Josy wrote back.

Oh, Casey replied. *Makes sense. Gus sez movie is dumb, but I kno he likes it. He's excited 4 u. I am 2.*

Josy grinned. *Thnks.*

Other messages waited for him under a different thread called W3Q.

B1: *Oh dear, why do his clothes always fall off?*

B2: *I am going to burn our television. I hope you're happy.*

B3: *This is positively delightful. I hope you get to run naked on a boat.*

Hopefully! he wrote in response.

"What are you smiling about?" Xander asked suspiciously.

"Our people are pretty awesome," he said, setting his phone back down.

"I can't believe Gus had two copies of this movie at his store," Xander muttered. "Or that they agreed to watch it at the same time."

"It's *research*," Josy said again. "The more I know about the type of movies Roger Fuller makes, the better position I'll be in."

"He's only the producer," Xander said, picking up the partial script from next to Serge's pipe. "What about this guy? Quincy Moore. Any idea who he is?"

"Nope. I googled him, but all I got was the Kickstarter page. The only thing it said about him was that he was young and that it was his first script. I couldn't find anything else about him."

"Could be a pseudonym," Xander said, leafing through the script.

"For someone famous," Josy whispered to himself.

"What was that?"

"Uh. Nothing. It doesn't matter. They asked for me, Xander. Do you know how crazy that is?"

Xander sighed as he dropped the script back on the table. "I know. I just… I don't want anything to happen to you. You know? You're…."

"I'm what?"

Xander rubbed the back of his neck. "You're… naïve. Sometimes. And that's okay!" he added quickly as Josy started to frown. "You're just—you don't see things like other people do. And normally that's pretty rad, but I don't want to see you get hurt. I know you think this is your big break or whatever—"

"I don't think it. I *know* it."

"That's good," Xander said, not unkindly. "And I hope you're right. I need you to be careful, though, okay? Starla said this Roger guy is a tool."

"I can take care of myself."

"I know you can. That doesn't mean I'm still not going to worry. I don't want you to get taken advantage of with something you really want dangling over your head. You're good, Josy. Really good. I always knew you'd make it someday. I just hope it's for the right reasons." He looked away. "All of us do. It's why Casey and Gus and the We Three Queens are watching the movie too."

Xander was all hard lines and scowls. He was a dick. He could be coarse and blunt to the point of being mean. But sometimes he could be awesome, so much so that Josy couldn't help but hug him.

Like right now.

Xander gave a cursory protest as Josy tackled him on the couch, but he didn't really mean it. He wrapped his arms around Josy's back, holding him in place. Josy tucked his head under Xander's chin and breathed in happily. They didn't do this often—not like he and Casey used to do before he moved to Oregon—but when it happened, it was good. It was really good.

"Oh man, I am so going to get in on that," Serge said from the entryway to the kitchen. He was munching on baby carrots. "We need to combine our energies, you know? Get our auras in sync. You better make room for me. I swear to god I am going to cuddle the shit out of both of you for at least the next hour before I fall asleep."

And you know what?

They did exactly that.

(It wasn't until much, much later that he realized he hadn't thought of Q-Bert at all that day. Which, of course, promptly made Josy think about Q-Bert for the rest of the night. His brain was so weird.)

JOSIAH ERICKSON was ready.

He was going to nail this audition.

He was going to get the role.

He was going to become famous.

He was going to get *rich*.

And then he was going to start a charity to help homeless children feed starving whales or whatever.

"You have arrived at your destination," Waze announced on his phone. "Boodely-boop."

Josiah gulped as he looked ahead.

Maybe he was completely out of his depth.

Yes, he'd had an idea of what he was in for when he'd seen the address was located in Hollywood Hills. While not completely ritzy, it was still far above his tax bracket (though if he thought about it, he wasn't quite sure what his tax bracket was). The homes were older and often gated. And the farther into the neighborhood he went, the bigger they got.

Waze just happened to announce he had arrived in front of the biggest one yet.

It sat far back off the road down a long driveway lined with thick bushes. The house itself looked like it had turrets, and Josy wondered if this was where the orgy/cocaine parties occurred. He looked down at himself, hoping he wasn't underdressed. Or possibly overdressed, if what Starla had told him about Roger Fuller was true. He'd spent the night before freaking out on the phone to Gustavo, who made Casey look up what to wear to an audition that could be a big break. For some reason, Gustavo gave explicit instructions for Casey to avoid a Wiki something-something, but Josy had no idea what he was talking about.

Gustavo had put him on speaker, and they both listened to Casey as he read off from an undoubtedly reputable source that Josy should dress for the part, if possible. The *problem* with that was Josy wasn't quite sure what the part *was*. The script he was given said he was trying out for a character named Liam, who was listed in a brief description as an *everyman from anywhere facing life-changing events*.

Josy had asked if that meant a cowboy hat, and immediately began to panic because he didn't have a cowboy hat, and it was already almost *midnight on a Monday*, and where the hell was he going to find a cowboy hat this late?

Fortunately Gustavo and Casey vetoed the cowboy hat.

So here he was, sitting in his shitty car outside a black gate that was probably made of ground diamonds, and he was wearing maroon skinny jeans, boots, and a gray sweater over an untucked dress shirt.

It was ninety degrees outside at ten in the morning, but Casey had said he looked cute, and Gustavo had said they were hanging up now because he had a business to run, and that business was *not* offering style advice over Facetagram or PictureSnap or whatever the heck app it was that Casey made him download that added absolutely nothing to his life.

Also, the air-conditioning in Josy's car was broken.

He was sweating.

It probably wasn't a good look.

Unless the role was like any of the other Roger Fuller movies and he would have to be running away from monsters a lot. If that were the case, then he would be sweating a lot. Which meant he looked perfect for the role.

It was quite the conundrum.

He reached up and pulled down the sun visor, checking to make sure his mustache and beard were still as perfect as they'd been that morning. Maybe his mustache was a little wilted, but he still looked good. He had this.

He *had this*.

He pulled up next to a black box in front of the gate. There was an intercom above a button. And naturally, as one does, he miscalculated how close he needed to be to reach it. He groaned as he put his car in Park and leaned out the window, grunting as he barely hit the button with the tip of his finger.

A buzzer sounded.

Silence.

More silence.

Then a static-filled voice said, "Yes?"

"Uh," Josy said, unsure if he needed to put his mouth right on the box. Since that didn't seem sanitary, he decided against it and hoped for the best. "I'm here for an audition? My name is—"

"Pull in and park by all the others."

The box buzzed again, and the gate swung open as Josy mouthed *all the others* to himself.

He hadn't been so naïve as to think that he would be the only one auditioning, even if they had asked for him by name. He figured there'd be others up for the same part. But *all the others* didn't do much to settle his nerves as he drove down the driveway, gravel crunching underneath the tires.

He was relieved to see only about a dozen vehicles parked to the right of the house in a paved lot. Most of them were nicer than his. Gustavo had tried to tell him that there were forums for cars like theirs online, but he hadn't had time to look any of them up. He wasn't sure what people who drove decades-old Toyotas would have to talk about, aside from how sad they were. He could already do that with his friends.

He parked and got out of the car. He blinked up at the house in front of him in the harsh sunlight.

Those were definitely turrets.

He was a little out of his depth, both financially *and* spiritually.

"You can do this," he whispered to himself as he straightened the tail of his shirt. "Do or do not. There is no try."

He squared his shoulders.

He stuck out his chin.

He was calm.

He was cool.

He was *confident*.

He walked into the car door he'd forgotten to shut.

"What the *frig*, man," he growled, rubbing his knee. "So not cool, dude. Come on!"

He shut the door.

Now he was ready, even if it felt like his knee was most likely broken and he was going to lose his leg.

He expected the doorbell chime to be epic. He was not disappointed.

But before he could marvel on the chimes that rang inside the house, the door opened and there, with a smile on her face, stood—

"Dee?" Josy asked, surprised. "Are you real?"

Dee rolled her eyes. "Yes, Josiah. I'm real."

"Oh. Because, like. You're here. And so am I. And that's... weird."

"You're wearing a sweater in September in Southern California. I don't know if you're the best judge of weird."

Josy looked down. "Is it too much? Gustavo and Casey said I needed to dress for the part, but since I have no idea what the part is, I just dressed like a fancier version of myself."

She grabbed him by the arm and pulled him inside, shutting the door behind them. "It's fine. You look fine. If I was into stoner hipsters with penises, I would probably consider trying to get all up on that."

"Oh. That's... swell. Thank you. I think. I just want to be friends, though. I mean, no offense. You seem nice."

"I'm not hitting on you."

"That's good," he said, relieved. "I'm not very good at figuring out when people are doing that."

"That's an understatement," she muttered, tugging him down a long hallway.

He barely had time to take in his surroundings, gauche though they were. Everything seemed to be made of *crystal* and *feathers* and large black-and-white nude prints of men in various poses that looked mostly painful. The walls and floors were dark wood, and Josy only caught glimpses through open doorways of offices and entertainment rooms and what looked to be a room filled with nothing but beanbags, something Josy desperately wanted to go into.

"What are you doing here?" Josy asked Dee as she pulled him around a corner. "Is this your house? Did I go to the wrong place? My bad. I do that sometimes."

She glanced back at him, a strange glint in her eyes. "You didn't go to the wrong place. I don't live here. This is part of my job."

"It is? What is it you—" A thunderous thought struck him. "Oh my god, *hey*. Dude. Look. I need to talk to you! I stalked Q-Bert online because I felt bad about the whole—"

"Being an asshole and laughing in his face thing when he tried to ask you out even though he was scared out of his mind and you probably set him back a good three years?"

Josy blanched. "Uh. Yeah. That. Has anyone ever told you that you're really good at making people feel worse about themselves? Because you are, in case you didn't know. I can be a reference if you ever put that on your résumé."

She laughed. "Good to know I can depend on you. Josiah, are you a bastard?"

"Uh, no? I mean, my mother and father are still married, if that's what you're asking. Is this for the movie—"

"Hoo boy," she muttered. Then, "Are you a dick?"

"I don't think so. Being stoned usually makes me want to be nice to everyone." He felt the blood drain from his face. "Not that I'm stoned right now. Or ever. Okay, that was a lie. The second part, not the first. I swear I'm not stoned. But if I have to take a drug test, I absolutely will not pass. Did you know that if you're bald, they take your pubic hair instead? I can't imagine someone trying to pluck out my pubes to see if I'm stoned. Like, dude. I'll just tell you I am." He coughed. "Though not right now. Because this is an audition and that would be bad."

"Christ. This is really how you are, isn't it? It wasn't an act at the library."

He shrugged. "I don't know how to be anyone else but me. Except when I'm acting, and then I can be anyone else."

She stopped and stared. "How have you survived in this town for so long?"

He grinned. "Do or do not. There is no try."

She gaped.

He grinned less.

"Here's how this is going to go," she said after she'd recovered. "Quincy doesn't know you're here. This was all my doing, with the assist from Roger. But if Quincy gets upset, this is your fault."

"I can dig that. I have no idea what you're talking about, but count me in. Also, who's Quincy?"

"Who's Quincy," she repeated slowly.

A light bulb went on in the attic of Josy's mind. It was mostly covered in cobwebs and wasn't very energy efficient, but it still worked. "Oh! The screenwriter. Right. Why doesn't he know I'm here? Also, can we still talk about Q-Bert? I really think I need to explain myself better. You need to tell him the next time you see him that I'm really nice and that I didn't mean to like that photo on his Insta from last year. My thumb slipped because Frank's a dick and wouldn't leave me alone."

Her eyes narrowed. "Who's Frank? Is he your boyfriend?"

Josy gagged. "Oh god no. Frank's the Rodrigo Duterte of Applebee's who wouldn't let me sit in the bathroom stall in peace and made me like Q-Bert's rain photo."

"I... don't know what to do with any of that."

"Right?" Josy exclaimed. "He's so annoying."

"You can tell Q-Bert yourself," Dee said. "He's here."

"Whoa," Josy breathed. "Unexpected. I'm sorry I'm so sweaty all of a sudden. Does he know Quincy? Are they friends? Do you think he can put a good word in for me?" Josy frowned. "Well, maybe not ask him that, seeing as how the last time I tried to talk to him, he ran away."

Dee looked toward the ceiling. "Oh my god."

Josy looked toward the ceiling too. There was some very nice crown molding. "Oh my god," he agreed. "Is that original to the house, you think?"

Instead of answering, she continued to pull him down the hall. "Did you prepare for your audition?"

"Did I prepare," he scoffed. "Of course I did. It's going to be amazing, though I have no idea what the audition is for. I looked up the Kickstarter, but it was really vague. And all the rewards involved promises of nudity, which seems like prostitution." He sighed. "Shit, I shouldn't have said prostitution. I should have said *sex work*. The word *prostitute* has a negative connotation, especially against women."

Dee coughed roughly. "Where did you learn that?"

"My weed dealer is a feminist. She teaches me a lot of things. Did you know that women only make seventy-eight cents for every dollar a man makes? And that's only about white women. It's even worse for women of color. That's just wrong."

"I know we don't know each other very well," Dee said, "but you need to know I love you."

"Aw, thanks. Ditto, dude."

"The Kickstarter was ambiguous for a reason. Quincy gets... nervous about these things. Roger decided it would be best to just keep his own name on it instead and only use Quincy as a last resort. He's protective of Quincy. Luckily it wasn't needed, though when everyone finds out, they're going to flip."

"That was a lot of information to take in. I have so many questions. Why are people going to flip, and what exactly are they going to flip about?"

She stopped in front of a large mahogany door. She turned and eyed him up and down. He wasn't sure what was going on, so he stood there awkwardly.

She reached out and straightened the collar of his shirt. "I got you in. Roger was fully on board, but the rest is going to be up to you. Don't blow this. You get this one chance."

"I have no idea what you're talking about," Josy told her seriously. "But I'm going to do the best I can."

She smiled. "I know you will. I watched your commercials on YouTube. You looked really cute in those tiny shorts, even though you were supposed to have genital herpes."

"Thanks! I was really proud of that spot."

She pushed open the door and motioned for him to walk through. "Take a seat with the others, and we'll call you in when it's your turn."

He took a deep breath, steeled himself, and stepped forward to face his destiny. Or rather, to wait to face his destiny, which was almost the same thing.

And that's when Dee said, "One more thing. You should know that Q-Bert's real name is Quincy Moore. He's the screenwriter, first-time director, and Roger Fuller is producing. He's also Quincy's grandfather, who loves his grandson more than life itself. And Quincy doesn't know you're here. So! Don't mess this up."

She shoved him the rest of the way through the door and slammed it behind her.

NOW, IT should be said that Josiah Erickson didn't do well with surprises. For his sixth birthday, his parents threw him a party. The *problem* with that was they didn't tell him about the party, and when people jumped out and yelled *surprise*, Josy screamed for a long time, to the point that the partygoers would later compliment him on his lung capacity and his ability to not pass out even when his face turned blue.

Everyone learned that day to avoid surprising Josiah Erickson if at all possible.

But since life is chock-full of surprises, Josy had to learn to roll with the punches. His friends knew in no uncertain terms to avoid surprising him with anything, lest he go into a tailspin that typically could only be resolved by Vlad the Inhaler, a copy of *The Bride of Frankenstein*, and kettle corn.

Dee loved him. She had just said as much. But she didn't know him. If she had, she probably wouldn't have dropped such a large bomb in his lap.

To say that he was befuddled would be an understatement. In fact, he was *beyond* befuddled. The idea that Q-Bert and Quincy were one and the same had never crossed his mind. He hadn't actually thought Q-Bert's real name was Q-Bert; that was ridiculous. It was just a stage name, a nom de plume, like Casey's C.S. Richards or the Rock. Josiah had considered adopting a different name for his acting career, but Starla had told him that Josiah Erickson fit his whole aesthetic, whatever that meant.

So there he stood in a mansion in Hollywood Hills, wearing a sweater in September, sweating profusely, with the knowledge that the man he'd tried to be friends with and then accidentally stalked was the same man who would now determine the fate of his movie career.

All in all, Josy was having a very strange day.

And it certainly didn't help that at least ten people were in the same room with him, staring while his brain went on the fritz.

Most sat in folding chairs against the walls. They were all men roughly his age, but he didn't recognize any of them. Oh, he knew they were most likely his competition, but that typically didn't bother him. As with any audition, the only thing he could do was give it his all and hope for the best. He'd been rejected more than not, and if he wasn't right for the part, there was nothing he could do about it. Do or do not. There is no try.

But this felt different.

Not only was this a part in a movie produced by the man who had once made a film where a seventy-foot-tall woman had destroyed the male-dominated United States government by picking up the White House and throwing it into space, he was also Q-Bert's—*Quincy's*—grandpa, and probably knew all about how Josy had laughed in his grandson's face, even if he hadn't meant to.

Josy stood against the door, waiting for the browser in his brain to install the new information and reboot.

It took a lot longer than it should have. The software didn't seem to be compatible with the hardware.

Finally he was able to move, though he wasn't quite able to bend his knees as one should. He managed to lurch to an open chair next to a man with devastating eyes and a jawline that looked as if it could cut through concrete.

"Are you okay?" the man asked him warily as Josy collapsed on the chair.

"No," Josy said honestly. "Have you ever been shoved into a room by a lesbian after she altered your entire world?"

"No."

"Oh. I have."

"Okay?"

"I don't recommend it."

Josy couldn't even find it in himself to be offended when the man scooted his chair away a little bit.

He sat back in his own chair, trying to remember the calming techniques Serge had taught him. Josy didn't understand what chakras were, but he figured now was as good a time as any to try to center them. He breathed in through his nose and out through his mouth. He wished he had a joint. That would be rad right now.

Another door opened on the opposite wall, and a harried woman stepped in, a clipboard in her hand. "I need Morgan Ecchols."

A man a few chairs down stood up. He had to be at least six four and looked as if he were an underwear model who liked to stand near the large windows in his loft and brood as he stared down at the city below, a cup of coffee in one hand, the other pressed against the glass.

He carried a ream of papers and followed the woman through the door. It closed behind them.

It looked as if everyone in the room had papers in their hands.

Everyone, that is, except for Josy.

He tried not to panic.

He leaned over to Jaw Guy. "Were we supposed to bring something with us?" he whispered. "My agent emailed my portfolio like instructed, but I didn't bring anything else."

Jaw Guy smirked. It didn't seem very nice. "Uh, *yeah*. The script? With the scene? You do know you're at an audition, right?"

Josy blinked. "Sure. But I memorized mine. Didn't everyone else?"

Jaw Guy laughed. "What are you talking about? Who the hell memorizes their auditions?"

"Actors," Josy said, confused. "Wait. Did *you* not know you were going to an audition?"

Jaw Guy scowled at him. "No one memorizes their entire auditions."

"Oh. I do."

"What are you, some kind of method actor?"

"I don't know," Josy said. "I guess I've never thought about it. Method actors are supposed to be in character all the time, right? I guess I could be. Wait. Hold on. Let me get in character."

He wiggled in his seat, shaking the tension from his shoulders. He took another breath and let it out slowly. And then suddenly he was Liam, a young man in his midtwenties who, according to the partial script he'd gotten, was weary and carried the weight of the world on his back.

"There," Liam said. "My life is difficult, and sometimes I remember just how bleak these dark days can be."

"Some of us take this seriously," Jaw Guy snapped at him.

"I do," Liam said morosely. "I take everything seriously." He looked away, staring into the distance, contemplating the cruel reality that he'd found himself in. "So seriously."

"Jesus Christ," Jaw Guy muttered. "Don't talk to me, you weirdo."

The door opened again, and the same woman reappeared. The underwear model wasn't with her. Liam/Josy wondered if he'd been so good in his audition that she was here to tell the rest of them they could go home. But when she said, "I need Alexander Gibraltar," Jaw Guy stood, and Josy figured underwear model probably had been shown out. Either that, or this whole thing was the front for a weird sex cult and he had already been sacrificed to multiple orgasms.

Josy really hoped that wasn't the case. Orgasms were nice, but getting stoned and cuddling with legs tangled together was even better.

"Good luck," Josy said, but since he was method, Liam added, "not that I care, because I'm weary."

Alexander Gibraltar (which *had* to be a fake name) glared at him as he followed the woman through the door.

Method was hard. Liam was angsty, and Josy by default was not. Josy decided that it was probably just better to let it go until it was time for his audition.

Besides, he was more nervous about the whole Q-Bert/Quincy thing. Auditions for life-changing movie roles were nothing in the face of getting a second chance at a first impression. Should he greet Quincy like they'd never met? Should he apologize up front? He still wasn't quite sure how to make friends, especially when said friend was potentially his future boss.

Unfortunately for Josy, he still hadn't figured it out when he heard his name called. He looked up and blinked when he saw he was the only one left in the room aside from the woman standing in the doorway. He hadn't even seen them leaving.

"Oh crap," he said.

"You coming?" the woman asked.

"Oh crap," he said again as he stood. Fortunately his knees had figured out how to bend properly, so when he walked toward her, it was mostly normal. Sure, his armpits and palms felt as if he'd just gone for a swim, and he was pretty sure the skin under his left eye was twitching, but still. His knees could bend. That was good.

He could do this.

He could *do* this.

"You look like you're about to run in the opposite direction," the woman told him. "Please don't do that. I don't want to have to chase you."

"I'm method," he told her. He immediately felt bad because he was lying, but he didn't know what else to do. "This is acting. I'm an actor."

"I don't get paid enough for this," she muttered. Then, "Come on. They're waiting for you."

Chapter 7

He didn't have time to learn her name or forge a connection with her before she abandoned him in front of another door down the hall. "Go in," she said over her shoulder. "I'll be here when you're done to take you out."

"Bye," Josy called after her. "Thank you for showing me the way!"

She ignored him. Josy hoped she would have a better day after this.

"You can do this," he muttered to himself. "You can do this. This is going to be it. Five years down the road, they're going to read your name off for the Best Supporting Actor Oscar, and you are going to thank god and Jesus and Starla, and then you're going to talk about standing in front of this door. And you are going to sniffle but not quite cry, because you have strength. You can do this. Do or do not. There is no try."

He raised his hand.

He knocked on the door three times.

"Come in!" a voice called.

He opened the door.

It wasn't what he expected. Granted, he didn't know exactly *what* he was expecting, but this wasn't it.

It was a large sunroom, the walls and ceiling made of glass and black metal. Two ceiling fans spun lazily above him, and an ornate rug lay beneath his feet over hardwood floors. There was a white sofa and what Josy called a fainting couch, something he'd always wanted to own but had no room for. Or money for.

A table had been set up at the opposite end of the room. On it lay a couple of iPads and an open laptop. Dee stood next to the table, that same evil smile that made Josy uneasy on her face.

Next to her was an older man in an electronic wheelchair that looked impractically futuristic, like something Professor Xavier from the X-Men comics would be in. On one of the armrests was a brightly lit control panel that had more buttons than a TV remote. The man himself was eyeing Josy with interest, his dark eyebrows looking as if they'd been painted on, and very recently. In fact, he looked as if he was wearing quite a bit of makeup, and Josy was instantly enthralled by him, almost forgetting that he was about to throw up. The man's lipstick had been expertly applied, his cheeks rosy. His hair was mostly gone, but what was left was white and curled artfully around his ears. He wore red velvet suit, the lapels black, with a white collared shirt underneath, open at the throat. Josy wished he owned such a suit. It looked dashing.

"Well, well, well," the man purred. "Who is this stunning creature I see before me?" His voice was wispy and effeminate, the words so airy they sounded like they would float away at the slightest of breezes.

Dee rolled her eyes. "You know who this is, Roger."

"Yes," he said, eyes glinting. "But I would like to hear it from him." The man held out his hand, fingers shaking slightly.

Josiah so had this. "Josiah Erickson." He walked forward until he reached the table. He took Roger's hand in his own, unsure if this was supposed to be a handshake. He made a split decision. He brought Roger's hand to his lips and kissed the cool skin. "At your service."

Roger squealed. "Oh my goodness. You are *darling*. Dee, you didn't tell me he was so... *this*."

"That's because I know how you get," Dee said dryly.

"Pishposh," Roger said, never taking his gaze off Josy. "I have no idea of what you speak. Ignore her, dear boy. She's confused." He pulled his hand away. "I am Roger Fuller, queen of the B movies, not to be confused with the Queen B, which is apparently Beyoncé. Lovely woman. I've never met her, but I assume she is. I must say, your portfolio doesn't do you justice. You are simply stunning."

"Thank you," Josy said, unsure if he just got compared to Beyoncé. "I like everything about you."

Roger gasped, a hand going to his throat. "Flattery will get you everywhere with me. Please, tell me more. And be quick about it. I fear that we only have moments left before our love affair is doomed. My grandson will return and you'll forget about little old me."

"I don't know that anyone could forget about you," Josy said. "Have you seen you?"

"Oh, the absolute *heartbreaker* you must be," Roger said. "But you have no idea, do you?"

Josy was confused. "Um, no? I try not to break any hearts. That's not nice, though I believe honesty is important."

"Is that right? Tell me, then, something. Honestly. The first thing that comes to your head."

"How do you have a grandson when you're so…." Josy blanched. "Uh—I mean, that's not what I meant to ask. I'm sorry. That was rude. I didn't mean to say—"

"Yes, you did," Roger said, sounding amused. "That's exactly what you wanted to know. How do I have a grandson when I'm so camp, people pitch their tents around me." He waggled his eyebrows at Josy. "I am staggeringly bisexual, if you must know. Josy's grandmother, may she rest in peace, was a lovely woman. And she knew how to wield a whip like you wouldn't believe."

Josy didn't know quite what to do with that. "How grand."

"Indeed. Now, when Dee told me about you, I knew we just *had* to have you audition for our little picture here. I do hope you're as good as you look. I would hate to be disappointed like I've been all day with these little shits that come in here and think they're doing *me* a favor. Do you want to disappoint me?"

"No, sir."

"Good." His expression softened. "And while I may play a part, just know that you're safe here. I would never make you do anything you're uncomfortable with. I may skirt the line, but I will never cross it. I've seen and heard too much of the so-called casting couch. Men and women should never feel uncomfortable or harassed. And I expect the same for the people I employ. I know there are… rumors of the sordid variety that float around about me, but most of it is hogwash. I treat you with respect, and I ask you do the same for me. Are we clear?"

Josy was relieved. "Yes, sir. Thank you for saying so."

"And if something comes up, you'll tell me, yes?"

"Absolutely."

"Good. Now, if we can just—"

The door behind him opened.

Josy turned to the sound of voices.

Q-Bert.

Quincy.

He spoke to someone over his shoulder. "And I know we haven't found the right person, but I'm hopeful. Chemistry is important for—"

He stopped when he saw Josy.

He blinked.

He blinked again.

And then he *squeaked*.

"Hi," Josy said, sounding rather breathless.

"Um," Quincy said. "Hi? And also, what?"

"Oh my," Roger said. "There it is. Dee, you absolute *minx*. How I treasure you."

Quincy continued to stare at Josy, who fidgeted. He wasn't sure what was cool here, if he should shake his hand or, hopefully, go in for an apology hug. He did neither and instead said, "I'm here to audition for the part in your movie. Congrats on that, by the way. I didn't know you were an author *and* a screenwriter." He paused, considering. "And a director. That's, like, so rad. Good job." Now or never. "Also, I wanted to apolo—"

And that's when he saw the person behind Quincy.

His blood boiled. Fiery rage consumed him.

But since he was good at what he did, he said, "Hello, Mason. It's nice to see you again. I didn't expect you to be here."

Mason Grazer stood behind Quincy, a blank expression on his handsome face. Mason Grazer, one of the three people Josy hated. He was blandly handsome in a way that suggested he'd been xeroxed from someone unique and had ended up slightly faded. He looked like any one of the interchangeable models on an Abercrombie & Fitch bag. Short sandy-blond hair with bright green eyes and muscles that seemed ridiculously fake. When he smiled, people swooned. Josy was not one of those people.

Add in the fact that he was standing so close to Quincy it made Josy's stomach twist in ways he didn't understand. Josy knew violence was wrong and should be avoided at all costs, but if an eagle swooped in through a window and sank its talons into Mason's face, Josy would feel absurdly patriotic and do very little to help.

"Josiah," Mason said, and for whatever reason, he'd decided today he wanted to sound British, even though he was from Seattle. "How delightful. How positively *droll*."

"You two know each other?" Quincy asked, sounding flustered.

"Hollywood is such a small town," Mason said, patting Quincy on the shoulder. "Of course we do. Josiah and I have auditioned for the same roles before." He smiled sympathetically at Josy. "He always tries his best. It certainly is a… quality he has. Tell me, Josiah, how are the residuals for genital herpes? Good, I hope."

"I don't have herpes," Josy said, just to be clear. "It was a commercial I did."

"He was really very good in it," Roger said. "I certainly believed that the herpes didn't get in the way of his game."

Josy looked back at Roger. "You know my work?"

Roger winked at him. "I googled you. You played a very good corpse on that television show. Maybe even the best I've ever seen."

"Thank you," Josy said. "I worked really hard on that."

"You're here to audition for my movie," Quincy said faintly.

Josy turned back to him, suddenly worried. "I hope that's okay. I just—I thought you knew I was going to be here. I don't mean to make you uncomfortable."

Quincy stared at him for a moment longer before shaking his head. "No. It's—it's fine." His smile looked forced. "I'm sure Grandad and Dee will explain it all to me later."

"We look forward to it," Roger said. "Isn't that right, Dee?"

"Sure," Dee said easily.

"Now, if you don't mind," Roger said, "I'd like to see what Josy can do. Shall we proceed?"

Showtime.

JOSY STOOD in the center of the room. Mason, as it turned out, had already been cast in the movie and would be his scene partner. Dee had a camera set up on a tripod, pointed at both of them. Before they could begin, Roger had Josy sign a nondisclosure agreement, telling him that the plot details for the movie were being kept under wraps and anything he heard in the room today must be kept secret. "If you blab, I'll sue you," Roger said cheerfully. "Please don't make me do that. My attorney would chew you up and spit you out."

Since Josy didn't want that to happen, he agreed.

Once he *did* sign, he was sure he'd get to hear more about the project itself, but apparently Roger had other ideas. He leaned forward from his wheelchair, resting his chin on his hands as he watched them avidly. Quincy sat beside him, staring down at the laptop. Dee fiddled with the camera before she gave them a thumbs-up.

Mason had taken a copy of the script from a bag near the table. Josy closed his eyes for a moment and reminded himself that he was capable, he was likable, and dammit, he could do this.

"Forgot your script?" Mason asked. "Figures. I suppose we'll have to get you a copy—"

"I'm ready," Josy snapped.

When he opened his eyes again, Josiah Erickson was gone. All that remained was Liam.

He was so method that if he were a superhero, people would call him Method Man.

Wait. No. That wasn't right. That was a rapper.

"You may begin any time," Roger said.

Mason rolled his eyes, looking down at the script. He scanned the page for a few seconds before looking back up at Josy. For everything that Josy disliked about him, Mason was certainly adequate. He'd beaten Josy out for more roles than not, so he had to have *something* that Josy just couldn't see as well as others.

He nodded at Josy.

At *Liam*.

Liam's gaze slid unfocused as his shoulders slumped. "Dante," he said, putting the weight of all the wrongs in the world in his voice. "What are you doing here?"

"I had to see you," Dante said softly.

"I told you I wasn't ready."

Dante looked frustrated. Damn him for pulling it off. "I know, but it's—you can't keep going on like this, Liam. You're going to kill yourself."

Liam scoffed. "You don't know what you're talking about. You have no idea what—"

"I *do*," Dante growled. "I know you try and keep all this shit from me, but I *do*. You forget. I know you. Maybe better than anyone else." He shook his head. "Or at least I did. I know your father is sick, Liam. And I know how much you love him. But what he's asking you to do… it's madness. You have to know that. He's lost his mind."

"You don't get to speak about him that way!" Liam shouted. "He's—oh god, he's *dying*. I'm going to give him whatever he wants while I still can. I haven't been the best son. I know that. So I need to do what I can while I still can." He looked away. A perfect tear slid down his cheek. His voice cracked when he said, "I need to do this." Granted, he didn't know *what* he was supposed to be doing, but that didn't matter. He was *nailing* this. He heard Roger sniffle, and he almost broke character to dance, but somehow he kept it together. He was supposed to be sad, goddammit.

"I'm not trying to…." Dante sighed. "They're just stories. That's all."

"Maybe," Liam said. "But my father believes them. And that's all that matters. I love you, Dante, but I have to do this."

Dante smiled sadly at him. "I know you do."

Now to go for broke. He stepped toward Dante and reached up to touch the side of his face. Dante looked surprised but covered it up well. "I'll come back." He leaned forward and kissed Dante's cheek. "I won't ask you to wait for me, but—"

Dante captured Liam's hand in his, turning his head to kiss his palm. "I know. Just… be safe."

And scene.

Liam fled deep within Josy as he took a step back. He reached up and wiped his face.

He turned to look at the others.

Dee gave him a thumbs-up, a big grin on her face.

Roger blew his nose into an embroidered kerchief.

Quincy was typing furiously on his laptop.

"Bravo!" Roger cried, dropping the kerchief on the table and clapping his gnarled hands. "Oh! That was wonderful. Dear boy, you are *marvelous*."

Dee coughed.

Roger rolled his eyes. "I mean, thank you for that. We appreciate your time today. We'll let you know. Please don't get your expectations up." He leaned forward and whispered, "Get them *way* up."

"That bit at the end," Quincy said, looking up from his laptop. "What was that?"

"Exactly," Mason said, glaring at Josy. "That wasn't in the script."

"I know," Josy said nervously. "But I thought… I mean, they have this history, right? The way the scene ended didn't… I didn't *feel* it. There needed to be more of a connection. I'm sorry. I didn't mean to go off script. Okay, that was a lie. I kind of did mean it."

Quincy shook his head. "No, it was fine. It was actually better." He continued typing on the laptop before he sighed and closed it. "I'll… look.

I'm...." He rubbed the back of his neck. "I'm trying to make something different here, okay? And honestly, I have no idea what I'm doing."

"He doesn't," Roger agreed. "But I have faith in him. Also, I happen to have people at my beck and call who *do* know what they're doing."

Quincy smiled at his grandfather before looking back at Josy. "When you think of queer films, what do you think of?"

"Cheap-looking," Josy answered honestly. "Especially if the queer characters are front and center. It's not fair, but the budget just isn't usually there. Or if it is, we're in the background. Or the sassy sidekick. And if we *are* the main characters and there's a good budget, it's because the queer character is going to get sick. Or die. Or end up alone. We're stereotyped or tragic or sometimes both."

"*Exactly*," Quincy said, his hands in fists on the table. He looked fired up. Josy liked it. "And I hate that. Why can't we be happy just like everyone else? Why do the Oscar-bait movies with queer people always end up as tragedies? I'm sick and tired of not having happy endings for us, and I want it to change. But since no one else is doing it, I figured I would try." He blanched. "Not that I think I'm making a better movie than anyone else. That's not what I mean. I wouldn't presume—"

"Wow," Josy said in awe. "That's so amazing. You're so cool. Like, maybe even the coolest."

Quincy flushed. "That's not—I'm not—" He groaned and covered his face. "You don't have to say that. But thank you."

"You're welcome," Josy said. "Thank you for letting me audition. Even if I don't get the part, I hope you get to make your happy gay movie."

"It's a fantasy," Quincy blurted as he dropped his hands.

"But even fantasies can become realities if you believe in them hard enough," Josy said sagely.

"What? No. The movie itself. It's a fantasy. Sort of. I wrote it because I wanted to see queer characters go on journeys that didn't end in death or putting their own wants or needs in the background. So there's this guy, okay? Liam. His dad is sick. He's going to die. But he has stories he wants to tell his son. About his youth. About this land he used to go to, this weird, fantastical land."

"It's like Narnia," Roger said gleefully. "Except instead of going in the closet to find it, he's bursting out of one."

Quincy rolled his eyes. "His dad is… not a nice person. At least he didn't used to be, but he's facing the end, and he's summoned his son for the last time. Liam thinks he wants to listen, but there's a lot of bad history there. And it's caused a lot of friction between him and Dante, his ex-boyfriend."

"Which is me," Mason said. "Because I've already been cast."

"Congratulations," Josy said, because even though Mason was a jerk, he still was in a movie that Josy was not.

Yet.

"And I'll be honest," Quincy said, "Dante is the showier role. Even though Liam is the lead, Mason is going to play a bunch of different characters that Liam comes across when he actually goes to his father's fantasyland. Creatures that only exist in his father's mind, though the line will blur so the audience starts to believe it's real." Quincy tapped his fingers on the table. He always seemed to be moving. "Because they do have this great love, and Dante will become part of the fantasy that Liam follows in his father's stories."

"Whoever gets cast as Liam will have to make out with Mason a lot," Roger said. "Especially when he's in creature makeup."

"Monster porn," Josy breathed. "You're making *monster* porn."

Quincy groaned. "It's not… it's not porn. I mean, sure, yeah, I write it as Q-Bert, but this—this isn't that, though it is an extension of it. This is *serious*. It's supposed to be mystical. It's supposed to be pure."

Roger scoffed. "Please. Like it's going to stay that way once the Tumblr people get their hands on it. I guarantee that whatever is pure and innocent in the world, someone has drawn graphic porn of it and posted it online. You of all people should know this. I've seen some of the fan art."

"Grandad!"

"What? You know it's true. Dee, tell him!"

"It's true," Dee said, fiddling with her camera.

"Whatever," Quincy muttered. Then, "Liam goes on this journey which brings him closer to his father and reminds him of what he left behind. Yes, his father passes, but not before you see the love they have for each other. And Liam gets his happy ending with Dante. It starts off angsty, but it turns into a celebration of life."

"Wow," Josy said, suitably impressed. "So, you essentially want to make gay *Big Fish*."

Quincy squinted at him. "What?"

"The Tim Burton movie? With Ewan McGregor? Sick, estranged dad tells him stories about his travels in a fantastical world and sees odd things. Son learns to love himself and his father. It's based on a book."

"No," Quincy said. "Not gay *Big Fish*. This is… different."

"Sure," Josy said easily. "Because of the monster porn. I get it. It sounds deep. Like, feelings and stuff."

Quincy made a strangled noise. "It's—it's nothing like *Big Fish*! Because the big twist in the film is that all of these monsters he finds are actually Liam's imaginary friends he had when he was younger! And they turn out to be *real*."

"They do?" Roger asked, squinting at his grandson. "I don't remember that part."

"Well, you wouldn't. Because I'm going to *add* that part."

"Ah," Roger said. "Rewrites. Got it."

"It's not gay *Big Fish*!"

"I believe you," Josy said. "It's going to be amazing. You wrote it, after all."

"Aw," Roger said. "That was sweet."

Quincy looked flustered. He was staring down at his twitching fingers. "I just want there to be happy gays. I'm tired of feeling like we exist only to prop up other people or to end in heartbreak."

Josy understood this. He really did. Maybe not completely, but he had a firm grasp on it. He knew the world that existed outside of Los Angeles. He'd lived in it once. He was queer. He had queer friends. They didn't get shit for it where they lived. Sure, maybe sometimes they got side-eyed every now and then when he held Xander's or Serge's hand, but it was rare.

But that wasn't how the world always worked outside of his little bubble. And to make it worse, it didn't necessarily exist in Hollywood. He was told early on that in order to be taken seriously, he needed to keep his sexuality on the down low. "You won't get the roles you want if they find out you're a homo," an oily producer had told him once. "Especially if you audition for a straight character. What's the point of having a queer play straight when it's just as easy to go hetero?" Of course, the producer had then propositioned Josy in the next booze-soaked breath. Josy had politely refused. He'd been a cater waiter at a party, his ass slapped at least once for every circle he made around the room, tray in hand piled high with hors d'oeuvres. He'd briefly thought about arguing that if it was so important for straights to play straights, then why did so many straight actors get to play queer or trans characters when there were already people who *lived* that life better suited for the part?

He hadn't, of course. He'd learned rather quickly that no one cared about the opinions of a cater waiter trying to catch his big break. He was one of thousands in the same position.

Besides. He'd never hidden who he was once he'd figured it out. He wasn't about to start now. Not for anyone. So if that meant he got passed over for a role after a producer had scoped out his Instagram or asked if he'd ever sucked cock?

So be it.

He understood what Quincy was saying.

And he really hoped he could be part of it.

"I think it'll be good," Josy said honestly. "I mean, I had imaginary friends when I was a kid."

"Me too," Quincy whispered as he looked away.

"I hope this turns out to be everything you want."

"Thank you."

"Well, Josiah," Roger said, clapping his hands. "It has been a delight. We'll be in touch. And by that, I mean if you would step outside so we can talk about you without you listening in."

"Um. Okay? Like, outside the house, or…."

"Outside the room would be just fine. Don't make me chase after you. You'd be surprised how fast this chair can go." He pulled out what looked to be a small walkie-talkie. It beeped as he pressed the button on the side. "Miranda? If you don't mind, please keep Josiah company for a moment."

The walkie-talkie screeched. "On it, boss."

The door immediately opened behind them, and the woman from before jerked her head at Josy. He glanced back at Quincy, who had slumped in his chair, eyes closed. He hoped he'd have a moment to talk to him before he had to leave. He wanted to apologize for the laughing and the stalking.

Miranda closed the door behind them and stood in front of it, clipboard clasped against her chest.

Josy smiled at her.

She didn't smile back.

Josy smiled less.

"None of the others were told to stay," she said.

"O… kay?"

"Except for you."

"Is that good?"

She shrugged. "Your facial hair is problematic."

He frowned. "For the movie? I mean, I suppose if I get the part, I can shave it—"

"For real life."

"Oh. I'm… sorry?"

Miranda huffed. "Have you ever bought a repurposed table that was once part of a fishing boat?"

"Whoa," Josy said. "Those things exist? That sounds awesome."

"Yeah, I figured as much. I don't like you."

Josy blinked. "Huh. That's new. Most people like me. Maybe you just don't know me?"

"I know your type."

Josy looked down at himself. He appeared as he always did. Maybe…. "A man?" he asked.

"A hipster."

Josy was relieved. "Oh. Yeah, no, I get it. It's not for everyone."

"You can take your gentrification and shove it up your ass."

"I don't know what that means," Josy said. "Do you mind if I take a selfie for my followers? This house is insane."

"I absolutely do not care."

"Thanks!" He pulled out his phone and opened the front-facing camera. His mustache *was* curled at the ends, but he thought he looked okay. Maybe Miranda was just having a bad day. He didn't know what life would be like if it wasn't socially acceptable to have a mustache. He hoped that women would one day feel comfortable to do what they liked with their own facial hair. Xander had once introduced him to a cool chick who had dyed her armpit hair bright blue. Josy had liked her immediately.

He held out his phone, grinned at the camera, and snapped the photo. It turned out pretty good for the first try. Sometimes he had to take nine or sixteen before he got the right one. Since he didn't know how long he'd have to wait, he figured it was good enough. He didn't spend long on his filter choice, deciding to go black and white because it gave him depth.

Audition day! he wrote. *I think it went well. Wish me luck! #actorlife #instagay #beardboy #mansionsarecool #iamhungry*

"Annnnd posted," he said. He put his phone away and looked back at Miranda. "My followers like it when they see what I'm up to."

"Wow, how interesting," Miranda said flatly. "I'm not one of them."

"Sure," Josy said. He hesitated. Then, "So, you think I have a chance to get the part? I mean, that would be so cool—"

"I'm Mr. Fuller's assistant. I do what he asks me to. If you'll recall, he didn't ask me to assuage your ego."

"Right, right. It's just—"

"Stop talking."

"But—"

"Hush."

Josy hushed.

They stood awkwardly for another five minutes. Josy thought he was going to go insane. He wanted to call Gustavo or Casey or Xander or Serge, but he didn't think Miranda would like that. He thought of suggesting that she smoke out to relax, but since she was glaring at him, he kept that to himself.

Fortunately the walkie-talkie attached to a clip on her belt burst to life. "Miranda?" Roger said. "Please escort Mr. Erickson back in."

She pulled it off the clip. "On it," she said. She stepped away from the door and jerked her head toward it. "Go in. And don't even *think* about trying to flirt with Mr. Fuller to get special favors. I see the way you walk. It's not going to work."

Great. Now he felt self-conscious. He didn't know there was something wrong with the way he walked. "Of course," he said. "I will try and work on that."

She scowled at him as she opened the door.

Mason stood next to Quincy, bulky arms crossed in front of him. Quincy was typing on his laptop again, muttering to himself. Dee was putting her camera away in a large bag on the table. Roger sat back in his wheelchair, fingers steepled under his chin.

Miranda slammed the door shut behind him.

"Hi," Josy said. "I just wanted to say thank you for—"

"Do you have a problem with nudity?" Roger asked.

"Like, in general?"

"For a part."

Josy was slightly alarmed. "Like... to get the part? Because I don't think that's very fair—"

"*In* a part," Roger said.

"Oh! No. I mean, I already had to once for a Japanese energy drink."

They stared at him.

He smiled his most charming smile.

Quincy coughed roughly.

Josy hoped he was okay. He knew the Heimlich maneuver if it was needed. He'd done a safety video two years ago where he played a scientist or a doctor or something.

"Right," Roger said slowly. "The script calls for a nude scene. Your bum would be shown. We will, of course, make you as comfortable as possible. A modesty pouch will be provided for your genitals."

"A cock sock," Josy said. "I know what those are. My friend Casey gave me one for Christmas last year. His boyfriend said it was traumatic to think about, but Gustavo thinks most things are traumatic—wait." His heart stumbled all over itself. "What do you mean *my* bum? *My* genitals?" There was a sharp stinging in his eyes. "Are you… am I getting the part?"

"Let's not get ahead of ourselves. First things first. Is there anything we need to know about from your past that could bite us in the ass down the road? I've perused your social media, and while there is an inordinate number of pictures of yourself, it seems relatively harmless." He frowned. "Aside from the numerous commenters who desire to see you naked and apparently consider themselves masters of the erotic with how many of them want to fellate you."

Josy's heart was pounding. "I have a very loyal following."

"Quite. Have you ever been arrested?"

"No."

"Ever been so strung out that you injected white lightning between your toes?"

"No. At least I don't think so? I don't know what half of those words meant. I mean, I smoke weed, but—"

"Everyone does. My doctor. My grocer. My priest, though I don't actually have a priest. If I did, I assume he would. Have you ever taken naked pictures of yourself in various states of arousal and sent them to a vindictive ex-lover who you spurned and will unleash them upon the world at the slightest hint of your success?"

"Um. No? I promised myself the only time I would ever put my junk on film was if I was in a Merchant Ivory production where I played a lord who lived in the British countryside and lay in the grass while my horse grazed nearby. I even have an accent ready and everything. 'Lost me knickers, I did, and I'm positively chuffed as pudding, wot, wot—'"

"There are contracts to be worked out," Roger said. "You're going to be paid, but it's not going to be much. This is a crowdfunded indie film, after all. The shoot will last six weeks, so any other employment will need to be put on hold, though we might have a problem with the shooting location, seeing as how we have none currently. We'll figure it out. I have… favors that I can cash in. But yes, Josiah. We would like to offer you the part of Liam Eagleton in the film *The Stories of My Father*." He frowned. "That's a working title, one I'm not fond of. It lacks a certain oomph. But no matter. You have a presence about you, one that I haven't seen since Joseph Zeiber auditioned for my film *Attack of the Killer Mongeese from Madagascar*. And, as you probably know, he went on to win a Daytime Emmy Award or some such thing before he died a horrible death involving an anvil and rampant alcoholism. Yes, I've got a good feeling about you. I think you could be something grand. An actor of the highest caliber."

And since Josiah Erickson had been dreaming of this exact moment for as long as he could remember, he did the only thing he could.

He promptly burst into tears.

"Oh dear god," Mason muttered.

"Are you all right?" Dee asked, sounding alarmed.

"Yes," Josy sobbed. "I'm perfectly fine. I promise. I'm just so happy."

"Miranda!" Roger barked into his walkie-talkie. "Can we bring Mr. Erickson some tissue? In addition, I would like cranberry juice. And god help you if it's anything but room temperature!"

FORTUNATELY NO one seemed to mind much that Josy needed a little time to compose himself. Except for Mason, that is, who rolled his eyes at Josy before leaving in a huff. Josy was okay with that. After all, it wasn't every day that he was cast in his first feature film, and he wasn't going to let someone like Mason Grazer ruin that for him.

He couldn't even find it in himself to be embarrassed. Maybe later it would hit that he'd cried in front of Quincy, but now he was just happy.

And crying.

But whatever.

They left him in the room with a wad of Kleenex Miranda had shoved at him. Roger told him he would fax all the paperwork over to Starla and they would talk soon. He said something about an announcement needing to be made, but they could work out the details later. Dee patted him on the shoulder, telling him that when he located his missing balls, find her and she would walk him out.

Quincy looked like he was going to say something, but instead swallowed it down and hurried from the room, laptop clutched to his chest.

Josy felt a pang at that, but since he had snot dripping from his nose, he thought it was for the best.

He eventually got himself under control, the sweet ache in his chest reduced to a warmth spreading through him.

He had done it.

Through all the crap slung his way, he'd told himself that if it was meant to be, it'd happen.

And here it was. This moment.

Validation.

He wished his former teacher, Mr. Stefan Alabaster IV, wasn't in prison. He would call him and thank him for casting him as a block of American cheese. Maybe he could send him a letter later, and a recipe for toilet wine if he could find one. It was the least he could do.

He wiped his eyes again, sure he'd gotten his emotions under control. He was tired, but it was a *good* tired, the one he always felt after having an exciting day. He needed to call his friends and tell them the good news, but that could wait until he left. He needed to find Dee. Maybe even see if Quincy had a moment.

He wasn't expecting to find Quincy on the other side of the door, hand raised like he was about to knock.

Quincy's eyes widened as he took a step back. "I… I was just…."

"Is this real?" Josy asked him. "Did that really just happen? I'm going to be in a movie?"

Quincy nodded slowly. "I guess so."

"I really need to hug something. Is it okay if I hug you? You can tell me no if you don't want to. Maybe Dee will—"

"No," Quincy said quickly. "I mean *yes*. I mean—" He coughed. "You… you can hug me. That's—that's okay. Just… not too hard."

Josy was more than okay with that.

In the history of hugs, it certainly wasn't the best. Not even close. Josy wrapped his arms around Quincy's back, hands clasped loosely. Quincy was stiff, and for a moment he didn't respond. Josy hooked his chin over Quincy's shoulder and held on gently. He was about to let go when Quincy reached up and carefully put his hands on Josy's back, patting once, twice, three times.

It wasn't the best.

But it was good.

Josy pulled away.

Quincy blushed, taking a step back, looking down at his shoes.

"Thank you," Josy said. "That was very nice of you. And I promise I am going to do everything I can to make this the best movie ever made."

Quincy cleared his throat. "It's not *that* good."

"Maybe. But we'll act like it is."

"Thanks, Josy."

"And I need you to know I'm sorry."

Quincy looked up, alarmed. "Oh, hey, no, you don't have to—"

"I do," Josy said firmly. "It's important. I didn't mean to laugh at you at the library. You surprised me. That's all it was. It had nothing to do with you. I was flattered. I *am* flattered."

"But you don't date."

Josy hated the look on Quincy's face. "It's not you. It's me. Wait. That sounded bad. But it really *is* me. I swear. I don't—I don't do attraction like that." He'd never had a problem saying it out loud before, but now that he was here in front of Quincy, it sounded stupid, and he didn't know why.

Quincy cocked his head. "What? What do you mean you don't— *oh*. Oh geez. Are you asexual? Or aromantic? Is that the right term? I always get them confused. That's okay! If you—"

"I'm demisexual. I mean, I thought I was gray-ace for a long time, but demi fits me better."

"I don't know what that means," Quincy admitted.

"It means that I have to get to know someone really well before I even think about wanting to do… anything with them." He frowned. "I've tried to force it in the past. I thought there was something wrong with me, that I wasn't normal. But it only made things worse. Just because I like the idea of something doesn't mean I can make myself want it. So it wasn't you. It was me. I promise."

"You don't have to apologize for being who you are."

"I know. It's just—" He groaned. "I wanted to be your friend really bad. And I made a mess of things. I… stalked you? But not physically! Like, online and stuff. And it wasn't really *stalking*. I just read about you and stuff. And looked at your pictures. And went through every entry on your blog."

"Wow," Quincy said.

Josy winced. "Yeah, it was probably getting a little out of control at the end. But I read about the things you've gone through, and I know how hard it must have been to ask me what you did. I should have had a better reaction. That's why I'm apologizing. You were being brave, and I wish I'd seen that."

"You didn't know anything about me," Quincy mumbled. "You couldn't have known."

"Maybe. But good people deserve to be treated with respect because everyone goes through things we don't know about."

Quincy shuffled his feet.

Josy wanted to hug him again but kept that to himself. Quincy had put some distance between them, and it was probably for the best.

"Maybe we could start over," Quincy said finally. "Because I'd really like to be your friend."

"Really? Oh man, that's so cool. Like, you have no idea how cool that is. This is the best day of my entire life. Holy crap." He stuck out his hand. "I'm Josiah Erickson."

Quincy stared at his hand for a moment before shaking his head. He reached out and took Josy's hand in his. "Quincy Moore. Also known as Q-Bert."

"It's nice to meet you," Josy said, squeezing his hand before letting it go. "I am going to be in your movie."

Quincy laughed. It was a lovely sound. Josy vowed to hear it as often as possible. "Yeah, I guess you are. There's still a lot of work ahead, but… we're getting there. We've got you and Mason. And since Grandad is going to play the role of Liam's father—"

"Shut up," Josy exclaimed. "Seriously? He's literally one of the most perfect human beings to have ever existed. I wish I could pull off lipstick like that."

Quincy snorted. "Don't let him hear you say that or he's going to give you every tip you never wanted." He frowned. "Seriously. Don't let him hear you say that."

"Uh, okay?"

"Good. There's a bunch of smaller roles to fill, but we'll get there. The only other issue is location. We don't have the budget for big sets, and I was hoping to film in Angeles National Forest, but we're having a hard time with the permits and finding the perfect small town where the first part of the story takes place. It would have been easier because we could have just traveled to the shooting locations each day."

"You need to film in a forest?"

Quincy shrugged. "Yeah, I mean, it's a big part of the movie. It's where Liam ends up through his father's stories and has all his adventures. You'll see what I mean when you get the full script after I make some changes to it."

Josy wished he could help. If only he knew of a small town in the middle of a forest where they could make this movie. If only he knew someone with connections in a small town in the middle of a forest where they could make this movie. But unfortunately, life wasn't that simple. It didn't just drop everything you needed into your lap like it was kismet, or whatever it was that Serge talked about.

"That sucks," Josy said. "Well, I'm sure you'll figure it ouuuohhhh my *god*."

"What?" Quincy asked, looking worried.

"What what? Oh, sorry. I just remembered that today was Tuesday brunch and I forgot to call one of my best friends. He's probably really worried about me. His name is Gustavo, and he lives with his boyfriend, who is one of my *other* best friends, in a small town in the mountains in Oregon." His brow furrowed. "Hold on. Wait a minute. That's… huh. I think I'm beginning to have the start of what might be an idea."

"What're you—"

"Shhh," he said. "I'm thinking."

And he *was*. In fact, Josiah Erickson was thinking as hard as he ever had in his life. He was thinking so hard that he was actually starting to get a headache.

Casey went to Oregon.

Casey met Gustavo.

Gustavo lived in Oregon.

Gustavo owned many buildings in Oregon.

Josiah had *been* to Oregon.

Oregon had trees. In fact, Oregon had a *lot* of trees. In fact, Oregon might have the most trees of anywhere ever, per Josy's approximation. Granted, he wasn't a tree expert, but he did have eyes and knew trees when he saw them.

Abby, Oregon, the quintessential small town in the middle of a forest.

With *trees*.

"Holy crap," Josy breathed. "I think I've just found a way to save our movie."

Quincy squinted at him. "I'm not sure it needs to be *saved*—"

But Josiah barely heard him. He was already pulling out his phone. He highlighted a name on the screen and pressed it against his ear. The person on the other end barely had time to speak before he exclaimed, "I have the best news you'll ever hear! We're coming to Oregon to make a movie about… okay, I don't really quite understand what it's about, but it's going to be amazing and rad and I need you to—sorry? Uh, this is Josy. Josiah Erickson? Isn't this Casey? I'm trying to reach Gustavo in… oh. Oh crap. Sorry. My bad. I didn't mean to yell in your ear. I must have called the wrong—who is this? Why do I have your number in my phone? Greg? I don't know any Greg. Huh. That's really—*oh*. *Greg*. Dude, it's been *forever*! Man, you used to sell me the best weed, and then you just disappeared. How you been? That's—oh. I'm so sorry to hear that. Uh-huh. That right? Three whole years in jail? That's rough. Yeah. What's that? Yes, I've heard about our lord and savior Jesus Christ. I don't know what that has to do with—Greg. Greg. Stop. *Greg*. Look, dude. I'm glad you found Jesus, man, but I still smoke out, so. I really don't think I'm going to hell because of—right. Uh-huh. Well, it's been great catching up with you, but—Greg. *Greg*. What the hell. Oh no, I'm about to go through a tunnel. It's… breaking… up." He hung up the phone and put it back in his pocket. He looked up to find Quincy gaping at him. "My bad, dude. What were we talking about?"

Chapter 8

A brief interlude before becoming a movie star.

"No."

"Gustavo."

"No."

"Gustavo."

"*No.*"

"*Gustavo.*"

"Did you find out where Michael Bay lives yet?" he demanded. "I tried to do it myself, but the Internet is useless and has failed me."

"Nah, man. It's not as easy as you think."

"You are an *actor*. Idiot people keep giving Michael Bay money to make tragic mistakes in *Hollywood*. How is this so difficult?"

"Gustavo," Josy said slowly. "Just because I'm an actor doesn't mean I know every other actor. That's not how it works."

Silence. Then, "It's not?"

"No. And I can't audition for one of his movies because you told me if I did, you would never speak to me again."

"Oh. Well, then. That's disappointing. What's the point of you, then?"

"You're a storm cloud. I'm sunshine. I heat you up and make you leak rain."

Josy could picture the scowl on Gustavo's face when he said, "That's not how weather works. The public school system has failed you."

"Casey told me you—"

"Casey is often stoned out of his mind and thinks everyone should love everyone else. Margo Montana tried to tell him hugs not drugs, and five minutes later they were hugging and smoking a doobie. He knows how I feel about alliterative librarians!"

"Everyone knows. Gustavo."

"No."

"Please?"

Gustavo sighed. "You're going to come anyway, aren't you."

"Yeah, man. Pretty much."

"Fine. Whatever. Do what you want. I don't care. You can't stay at my house. I have everything where I like it, and your feet smell terrible."

"This is so awesome!"

"I'm hanging up now. Don't call me again. Until next Tuesday. And congratulations. I don't know if you deserved it, but here we are."

Gustavo hung up on him.

Josy was the happiest he'd ever been.

"AND I *quit*!" Josy bellowed.

"I'll make sure you never work in this town again!" Frank screamed back at him. "At any Applebee's that isn't franchise-owned!"

"Whatever! I'm going to be famous! One day I'm going to come back here and you're going to *beg* for my autograph. And I'll give it to you, because I will never forget where I came from and I'm always going to be appreciative of my fans!"

"We'll see about that!"

"I guess we will! Oh, and I'm actually not quitting for another few weeks. I just wanted to give you notice in case you needed to hire someone in my place."

"Thank you. That's big of you. Can you check on table sixteen? Jasmine took her break, and I think they need refills."

"On it. Let me drop off these mozzarella sticks first and I'll get it."

Frank sneered at him. "Damn right you will." He turned and stalked away.

Josy really fucking hated that guy.

THE PHONE rang in his ear. He wasn't surprised when it went to voice mail. He was happy the phone number was the same, at least.

He waited for the beep. "Hey, uh. Mom and Dad. It's me. Josiah. Long time no talk! I hope everything is going well for you. I just... I just wanted to say that it's happening. Um. It's finally happening. I got a movie role! And it's not even in the background or anything. I'm one of the main characters. I get lines! Like, lots of lines. So. I just wanted you to hear it from me so you wouldn't be surprised if paparazzi appeared on your doorstep someday, asking questions about me. Ha ha, that was a joke. It—that probably won't happen. But this is a big deal for me. And I know you said that you didn't think it would ever happen and that I was wasting time and money on all this or whatever, but I did it. Okay? I did it. And no one can ever take that away from me. Just—my number hasn't changed, if you ever want to call. So. I guess... I'll talk to you later. But hey! Maybe one day you'll see me on the cover of a magazine and you can tell everyone that it's me. Your son. Anyway. That's it! So. Bye."

"WE'RE EXCITED," Casey said over Skype. "I can't believe you're going to come here and *stay* here. Man, it's going to be like old times." He grinned. "And maybe you won't ever want to leave. You could stay at Baked-Inn & Eggs, and we can smoke together like we used to and maybe eat pie. Lottie makes this really good rhubarb that tastes amazing when you're stoned. Not so much sober, but don't tell her that. Gus told her because he doesn't know how to not say what he's thinking, and she didn't bring him lunch for a week." He shook his head fondly. "You should have seen the look on his face when he went to apologize. It was far-out. Like, totally epic. Holy crap, I love him so much. I'm so happy. Goddamn, I need to hug someone. You need to get here fast so I can hug you!"

Josy liked that idea quite a bit.

"IT'S NOT a lot," Starla said, frowning down at the contract on her desk. "But it's still more than you've ever made before. And there's a clause in here about back-end stuff in case this movie goes big. And who the hell knows if that will happen. If you'd told me that *Madea Goes Boo at Kwanzaa Part Twelve* would have made as much money as it did, I would have thought you were nuts. But this... it's solid, kiddo. I'll have the attorney look it over, but I think it's solid. This is the real deal. Maybe Roger Fuller doesn't quite have the clout he once used to, but everyone loves a comeback story. I mean, look at Mel Gibson. He's anti-Semitic *and* misogynistic, but people keep putting him in crap. Roger isn't any of those things, but he is queer as balls and doesn't give a damn who knows. You know you live in America when people can hate who you love, but then can turn around and hug a damn racist. Fuck them. You go out and show them just how stupid they are."

A KNOCK at his door.
    A man stood on the other side. "Josiah Erickson?"
    Josy was ready. "No paparazzi!"
    "Um. What."
    "You can't take my photograph! I'm a human being, just like everyone else. This is my *home*. I just want to have a peaceful day without being harassed!" Josy grinned at him. "And that, my friend, was acting. Josiah Erickson, nice to meet you. I was just doing a scene. You're welcome. You can take my picture if you want."
    "I hate this town so fucking much," the man muttered. "I have a delivery for you." He reached into his courier bag and pulled out a thick folder. He placed a small tablet on top of it before he handed it over. "I just need you to sign right here on the line to confirm receipt."
    Josy winked at him. "Better ways to ask for my autograph, man. But anything for my fans."
    "I have no idea who you are."
    "Sure, sure." He signed the tablet with a flourish. "Hold on to that, okay? It's gonna be worth something someday. Just think! You'll get to say you knew Josiah Erickson at the very beginning. You know what? We should take a selfie together! That would be—and you're already leaving. Do I tip you, man? That sucks, because I don't have any cash. I have coupons for—is your moped not starting? Do you need help? I don't know anything about—you're just gonna walk? That's great, man. Walking is good for your body! Get those steps in!"
    He closed the door.
    Took a breath.
    And then opened the folder.
    Inside was a script.

FROM THE Beans and Weenie Morning Show:
    "—and *wow*, this must be a hard one today. Sorry, caller! That is *not* the right answer. Eighty thousand people are absolutely *not* bitten by vampires every year because vampires don't exist. Funny, that. Let's

move on to the next! Caller, you are on the air with Beans and Weenie in the Morning on 104.7 the Butt Rock Station. Are you ready to get your butt *rocked*?"

"I sure am!"

"Awesome!" Annoying sound effects. "What's your name, caller?"

"It's me, Josy!"

"Josy! We were getting worried, man. We haven't heard from you in three days. Are you dying?"

"Nope. Even *better*."

Pause. Then, "Wait. Hold up. That… doesn't make sense. What's better than dying?"

"I got a role in a movie!"

Many more annoying sound effects. "For real? Is it a porno?" Beans asked. "Are you gonna show your schlong?"

"Ha!" Weenie cried. "You're gonna show your weenie!"

"Boo-yah!" Beans shouted.

"It's not a porno," Josy said. "It's *better* than that, if you can imagine."

"No such thing," Beans said. "But since it's you, I'll take your word for it. What's it called?"

"I can't say, because it's being kept under wraps."

"Boo," Weenie moaned. "Are there going to be naked women and crap blowing up?"

"I… don't think so?"

"Sounds boring," Beans said. "I can't wait to see it. Josy, do you know the answer to the Beans and Weenie Super Hard Trivia Question brought to you today by Yarwood Honda? Let's remind everyone again."

"Eighty thousand people get bitten by this every year," Weenie said.

"Is it… other people?"

All the annoying sound effects in the world happened at once. "Ladies and gentlemen, Josy has done it again! It *is*. Eighty thousand people are bitten every year by *other* people, the freaking weirdos. Weenie, what has Josy won?"

"Josy has won a free tire rotation and oil change at Yarwood Honda!"

"Thank you," Josy said, getting choked up. "But I won't be needing it. There's no Yarwood Honda where I'm going. I'd like to donate it to charity. And also, I need to tell you that if it wasn't for Beans and Weenie in the Morning, I wouldn't have gotten this far. I'll never forget you. I'm sorry. I don't mean to cry. I have to go."

From Josiah Erickson's Instagram Story

"Hey, followers! I hope you're all doing well. I've got some big news! I signed on for a part in a big movie. Okay, it's not, like, *Hollywood* big, but it's big for me. It's an indie flick that I think is going to be amazing. I have to go meet with costume people and everything! I even get to keep my beard, which is pretty rad. I'll be posting a lot from the set, so I hope you're ready! Hashtag Instagay. Hashtag actor life. Hashtag my rising star. Hash—oh. Right. I'm not supposed to say hashtags out loud. I forgot. My bad."

HE WASN'T stalking.

He *wasn't*.

He was sort of friends with Quincy now.

So if Quincy (as Q-Bert) had a new blog post on his website, Josy should read it, right?

Right.

It wasn't stalking.

It was research.

Some changes are coming, something I've never done before. And I'm sorry this is going to be so vague, but it's still a work in progress, so until I get further into it, it almost doesn't seem real. I don't want to jinx it by speaking of it too soon.

I am stepping out of my comfort zone in a major way with a new project, something that I've always wanted to do but convinced myself would never happen. I tend to do that: tell myself the things I want are too big to be anything more than a dream. When I first started writing, I thought nothing would come of it. And when something did *come from it, I thought it was a fluke, a onetime thing that would never be repeated. But it has been, over and over again, and I still pinch myself, sometimes, sure that I'm asleep.*

Something happened last year. An idea that I couldn't get out of my head. I almost talked myself out of it, sure that I was dreaming too big again. But then I looked back on everything I've written on this blog, about my strengths and weaknesses, about taking charge of my own destiny. There are days when the anxiety is crippling, days when that old black dog is nipping at my heels, wanting to latch on and drag me back into bed to pull the covers over my head.

It's part of me, but it doesn't define me. Sometimes it wins. Sometimes the very idea of leaving my house makes it hard to breathe. There's a voice in my head that says my life is crap, that the work I do is crap, and that I should just stop now before I make things worse.

It's not easy.

But it doesn't define me.

Which is why I didn't let it take this moment away from me. This idea. This chance. So I pushed that voice to the back as much as I could and went for it.

I'm not going to lie. It was harder than I expected it to be. I made mistakes. But when I finished, I was proud of myself for what I'd created.

This is going to be something amazing, I think. Something unlike anything you've ever seen. And I've got a good group of people helping me make my dream a reality.

I know it's frustrating how much I'm not *telling you. And my updates might get a bit more sporadic. But I promise you it's for a good reason. Soon I'll be able to show you why.*

In the meantime, remember that you matter.

You are loved.

You are wonderful.

And if you have those bad days like I do, you will get through them, because you are stronger than you know.

I promise.

Talk soon,

Q-Bert

The comments were filled with all kinds of speculation.

Josy normally didn't like secrets.

But he thought this one was okay.

JOSY FELT like he was on top of the world and did his best to put it into words. "And, like, just... you know?"

"Yeah," Serge said, exhaling a heavy stream of smoke toward the ceiling.

"Exactly," Xander said, eyes glassy and bloodshot. He looked down at Josy, whose head was in his lap. "Right on."

"Yeah," Josy said, feeling fine. "And it's just gonna be... whoa."

"Whoa," Serge agreed. "Wait. Hold on. Do you ever think of—"

"Pizza?" Josy asked. "All the time."

"No," Serge said. "That's not what I was going to—I want pizza."

"Oh," Xander groaned. "Me too. Holy crap. And none of that stupid hipster crap with goat cheese and kale and bullshit. I want to get fucking *gross* with pepperoni."

Josy sat up quickly, eyes wide. "Xander! You can't say that. *We're* hipsters. We're supposed to like goat cheese and kale and bullshit pizza!"

Xander waved his hand in dismissal. He almost fell over. "Yeah, but like. Dude. It's... it's like. Okay. Think. Who... who *are* we?"

"Wow," Serge said. "I have no idea. And I spent eight months in India."

"We're us," Xander said. "But why are we us? People say we're hipsters, even though we don't call ourselves that, not really. What does that mean? Like, you know? What does that *mean*?"

"It means we're part of a demographic that tries to set itself apart from culture as a whole while paradoxically trying to remain in that culture at the same time," Josy said.

Xander and Serge stared at him.

Josy frowned. "I have no idea what I just said. I'm so stoned."

"I'm going to miss you," Serge said, reaching over and squishing Josy's face. "All parts of you. Your nose. Your face that's attached to your nose. Your hair. The way you laugh."

"You're going to make me cry," Josy said, sniffling. "And you know that I'm an ugly crier when I'm stoned. It's not forever. It's only for six weeks." His eyes widened. "You can come with me. Both of you can!"

"Yessss," Xander hissed. Then, "Wait. No. We can't. I have to draw on people with needles."

Serge groaned. "And I have to help white people with disposable income put their legs over their shoulders in poses that probably aren't good for their overall health."

"Dammit," Josy said. He lay back down on the pillows they'd spread out on the floor at Xander's house. "I didn't think of that. Well, when I get famous, I will hire you to be my assistants, and we'll travel all over the world and smoke in exotic places like Milwaukee and the Vatican."

Serge laid his head on Josy's shoulder. "Yeah, Josy. That sounds awesome."

Xander collapsed on Josy's legs. "We'll buy an RV and hotbox the shit out of it when we drive to Milwaukee and the Vatican. Do you think the Pope smokes?"

Josy shrugged. "Yeah, man. I'm sure he does. I mean, he has to, right? Otherwise he would get so bored doing… whatever the king of Jesus does. I don't know."

"It'll be awesome," Serge agreed. "And the next six weeks won't be so bad. You'll have Casey and Gustavo."

"And *Quincy*," Xander singsonged.

Josy felt his face grow hot. "Shut up."

"Who is your *friiiiend*."

"Shut up, Xander!"

They wrestled for a little while.

Then they ate potato chips and watched HGTV.

Five minutes later, they remembered to order pizza.

It had goat cheese and kale and bullshit on it.

Chapter 9

When Josiah Erickson landed in Eugene on a crisp morning in late October, three elderly women were waiting for him at the airport wearing sparkly pink jackets and holding signs with glitter on them.

The first woman was bony thin and taller than the others. She had a commanding presence and was obviously the leader of the trio. She was nearly eighty years old, and her poofy white hair sat like a cloud on her head. Her sign read: WELCOME TO.

The second woman was shorter and squatter. She suffered from female pattern baldness and today wore a platinum blonde wig that made her look like a high-powered executive. Her sign said: OREGON, YOU.

The last woman stood with her shoulders squared. Her head was shaved to a tight buzz cut, and she wore black chaps over her jeans. She also had on leather fingerless gloves with rhinestones on them. Her sign said: MOVIE STAR.

Bertha, Bernice, and Betty.

The We Three Queens.

Josy waved wildly at them.

Bertha and Bernice waved back just as hard.

Betty sized him up.

"Is that for me?" Josy demanded as he approached, pointing at their signs.

Bertha nodded. "It was Bernice's idea. She said that she always wanted someone to be waiting for her with a sign in an airport and thought you would like the same."

"I used too much glitter on mine," Bernice said, looking down at her sign. "I got glitter in places no one should. My rear looked like a disco ball by the time I finished."

"Cadet!" Betty growled. "Report!"

Josy snapped to attention. "The flight was good! I had water with no ice because ice hurts my teeth, and peanuts, and the woman next to me got drunk and asked me to go to her hotel room!"

"Oh dear," Bernice said. "I do hope you said no. I don't think we rode all this way just to wait outside for you to make love to a stranger. And a woman, no less. I always thought you were queer."

"I said no," Josy assured her. "That would be rude to make you wait. Also, I don't have sex with women."

"More for the rest of us," Bertha said. "Shall we?" She frowned. "Is that all you brought? Just a backpack?"

Josy shook his head. "Nope. I have two more bags." He squinted at them. "Did you bring a car, or…?"

The We Three Queens burst out laughing.

"A car," Bertha said.

"As if we would *ever*," Bernice said, wiping her eyes.

"Do we look like car people?" Betty asked.

That seemed like a dangerous question. "Uh… no?"

"We brought the Vespas, of course," Bernice said, tugging him toward the baggage claim. "Bertha has a trailer that attaches to the back of hers, and Betty has a sidecar attached to hers that you'll sit in. I get to just be pretty on mine without anything extraneous."

"That's right," Betty said. "You're gonna be my sidecar honey. You have a problem with that?"

"Nope," Josy said. "I didn't even know they made sidecars for Vespas, but I think I've always wanted to sit in one."

"They don't make them for people," Bernice said, patting his hand. "It's actually meant for a dog, but Casey said you're flexible. Just because you're a movie star now doesn't mean you're better than a dog."

Josy blushed. "I'm not a movie star."

"Not yet," Bertha said as they stepped onto an escalator. "But I've got a good feeling about this. I remember when I first met you. I said, 'That boy is going to be in a movie one day, and we'll be the ones picking him up from the airport.' Didn't I say that?"

"She did," Bernice said. "It's spooky when you think about it. Though I don't know why this didn't happen sooner. I asked Casey why you weren't cast in the Hungering Blood Moon saga. I've always thought you'd make a perfect Martindale." They stepped off the escalator and followed the signs for the baggage claim.

Josy shrugged. "He didn't have any say in the auditions. The producers didn't think I was vampire/werewolf postapocalyptic enough, I guess. But that's okay! Someone told me once that when one door closes, a window is left open so you can still break in and take what you want."

"Wow," Bernice said. "That sounds like it belongs on a calendar. Doesn't that sound like it belongs on a calendar?"

Betty snorted. "It's deep. And incorrect. But I had a good ride today into Eugene, so I'll let it slide. Got me out of Abby for a little while. Too noisy there the past few weeks."

Josy cocked his head. "Noisy?"

"Oh," Bertha said, "it's a trip. Abby is all abuzz since the movie people arrived with their cameras and their clapboards and their strange desire to have iced coffees in their hands at all times. There's never been anything like it before. Californians are so strange."

"Especially since they held auditions for minor roles in the movie," Bertha said as they stopped in front of the conveyor belt. "Everyone who is *anyone* in Abby auditioned for a role."

"Whoa," Josy said. "That's awesome. Did you guys audition too?"

Bernice sniffed. "Did we audition. Of *course* we auditioned. In fact, we were the first in line."

"She made us camp out the night before," Betty muttered. "Even though there was absolutely no need to."

"Oh please," Bertha said. "Like you complained about a chance to get out your old Army tent. In fact, you complained that Bernice and I were taking too long and that we'd be late."

Betty crossed her arms as she rolled her eyes. "I don't know what you're talking about."

"It was sweet," Bernice whispered to Josy. "All of us in a tiny little tent, just like when we were younger. I tried to make s'mores, but apparently it's illegal to light fires on sidewalks in Abby for some reason."

"Oh man," Josy said. "I know all about that. It's not just Abby. You can't light fires on sidewalks in LA either."

"Laws." Bernice shrugged. "But yes, we did audition, and I nailed it, of course. I can't speak for the other two, only myself. So when I say I was better, you know it's true. At least that was the impression I got from the director."

"Quincy?" Josy squeaked.

They turned slowly to stare at him. "Yes," Bertha said. "Quincy."

Josy swallowed thickly. "That's... super cool. He's so neat. Like, I'm his friend now. And stuff. You know."

"And stuff," Bertha said, watching him strangely.

"Hmm," Bernice said, rubbing at a hair on her chin.

"Indeed," Betty said, eyes glinting.

Josy needed a distraction. "Did you get the parts?"

"We did," Bertha said, puffing out her chest. "I am some kind of monster thing that gives your character advice. I get to wear a costume. It will be my greatest role. And also my only one."

"I'm a talking tree!" Bernice exclaimed. "I don't know why!"

They looked at Betty.

Betty ignored them.

Bertha nudged her shoulder.

Betty scowled. "I'm a cat."

"She has to lick herself," Bertha said, trying to smother her laughter. "I mean, it's not the first time she's had to lick—oh look, the bags are coming!"

And so they were.

THE PINK Vespas were waiting in the parking lot.

Sure enough, one had a sidecar attached. Josy didn't know how he was going to fit, but he was going to give it the ol' college try, even though he'd never been to college.

Betty put his luggage in the small trailer attached to Bertha's Vespa before turning back around. "Since you are my sidecar honey, you have to act the part. You're already an actor, so it shouldn't be too hard." She reached into a saddlebag on her own Vespa and pulled out a pink jacket, slightly bigger than theirs. She flipped it around. On the back, in bright bedazzled letters, were six words.

PROPERTY OF THE WE THREE QUEENS

"I get to wear that?" Josy asked. "That's.... No one has ever given me a pink jacket and told me I was their property before." He took it from Betty, running a finger over the letters. "This is gnarly. Thank you."

He put the jacket on.

"And a helmet," Bertha said. She handed him a pink helmet that had rainbows painted on it.

"And the goggles," Bernice said. She passed him a pair of pink goggles that looked like they would cover his entire face.

Since he was surrounded by a biker gang, he did the only thing he could: he put everything on.

"Wow," Bernice breathed when he finished. "You look ridiculous."

"We need a selfie," Josy demanded.

They agreed and smooshed in so he could take a picture.

His followers loved it, of course. Hashtag sidecar honey.

ON FRIDAY, October 23, 2015, Josiah Erickson arrived in Abby, Oregon. It was 2:36 in the afternoon. The air was crisp, the president of the United States was black and classy, and everything was wonderful.

Abby was in the deep throes of a bright and beautiful autumn. It was colder than it'd been in Eugene, and Josy was thankful for his kickass new jacket. He'd waved at everyone they'd passed, pleased that most people already seemed to be staring at him. They probably didn't know who he was (not yet, anyway), but a few of them waved back, and that was cool. When he waved at people in LA, they either ignored him or walked faster. One time a guy had pulled a knife, but Josy had knocked it out of his hand with a powerful karate chop.

Now that he thought about it, that last one might have been a dream.

But no matter.

Abby just felt different than back home did. He might not have liked the fact that Casey had moved so far away, but he understood it. Not only was it home to Gustavo Tiberius, it was also a beautiful place in its own right. The leaves were red and gold on the big maple trees, and the smell of Douglas firs was thick in the air. The streets were filled with fall and Halloween decorations, paper pumpkins and witches put in the doors and windows of businesses that lined the main stretch. Casey had told him that Mrs. Leslie Von Patterson of the Abby Fun Committee had been in charge of the decorations and tended not to take no for an answer, much to Gustavo's consternation. After the success of last year's Strawberry Festival, Mrs. Von Patterson had decided that Abby should be decorated at all times, even if there wasn't a specific festival and/or event going on. Mostly it went well. Other times, like this past April, they celebrated Plan Your Epitaph Day, where the businesses in Abby had to put in their windows what they wanted on their gravestones after they died.

Casey had sent him a picture of what Gustavo had put in the window of Pastor Tommy's Video Rental Emporium.

I DIED AND NOW I FINALLY GET TO BE LEFT ALONE. BYE.

Gustavo was wonderful.

Abby, Oregon, was wonderful.

(Also, Oregon had legalized recreational marijuana last October, so.)

Casey had told him that Lottie was in the process of getting her license to create an extension onto Lottie's Lattes that would act as a dispensary, both medical and recreational. It would be Abby's first. It would work in harmony with Baked-Inn & Eggs, and they hoped to make Abby a destination stop on kush tours. The ideas were still in the planning stages, but the bed-and-breakfast Casey had opened was the first part of it. He'd bought an old ramshackle house last spring, had it renovated, and when the ballot initiative passed, opened it for business. He worked the B and B himself for the first couple of months before hiring a small staff to take over for him so he could focus on his books.

That had mostly been Bernice's doing. She'd told him in no uncertain terms that if he didn't resolve DesRinaDale, she would go onto Yelp and leave him a negative review for Baked-Inn & Eggs. She apologized almost immediately, but when Casey still hadn't started a week later, a curiously vague review for the B and B appeared on Yelp from a user named IAmNotBernice that said it was haunted by the ghost of a loquacious Mormon. Casey immediately began working on the next book, and the review was removed before ghost hunters got wind of it. Everyone agreed that was for the best because ghost hunters were the absolute worst people in the world.

Josy loved LA. He loved the lights and the vibrancy and the people.

But here, in Abby, he felt like he could breathe again for the first time since he could remember.

The whine of the Vespas echoed off the buildings as they drove down the street. They passed Gustavo and Casey's house and then the video store, which had a Closed sign on the door, along with a note that Josy didn't catch. Betty honked the tiny horn as they passed by the coffee shop, where Lottie waved at them from the window, her frizzy dragqueen hair bouncing on her shoulders.

They left Main Street and turned up a small road that wound its way up a hill behind Abby. They came to a sign on the right that read:

BAKED-INN & EGGS
BED & BREAKFAST
WEED LOVE TO HAVE YOU!

According to Casey, Gustavo had threatened to knock down the sign in the middle of the night if the pot pun wasn't removed. He didn't seem to have gotten around to it.

The house itself was three stories but was still somehow cozy. It was an old Tudor with green leafy vines growing on the front. It had a garden in the back that was still a work in progress but would eventually have a gazebo and hammocks hanging from trees where people could smoke and relax. And since it was 420-friendly, there were no children allowed, which Josy was happy about. He was okay with kids as long as they belonged to someone else and stayed far, far away from him.

And there, standing on the porch, arms crossed and a scowl on his face, was one of the greatest people in the world.

"You're late," Gustavo Tiberius snapped. "You said you'd be here by two. It's now a quarter till three. Do you know how much business I might have lost at the video store? Why, I can't even begin to imagine."

Josy didn't hesitate. Even before the Vespa had come to a complete stop, he jumped out of the sidecar and ran. Gustavo gave a little shriek of fear and managed to say, "Who are you, pink stranger, stay away from me!" before Josy was on him, wrapping him in a tight hug.

"It's Josiah," Bertha called. "Who else would it be?"

Gustavo barely relaxed. "Why is he dressed like he just came from a rave in the late nineties?"

"It's how my sidecar honeys look," Betty said, grunting as she pulled Josy's bags from the trailer. Bernice tried to help but got distracted by a butterfly on one of the bushes Casey had planted along the driveway.

"How much longer must this last?" Gustavo asked.

"Hi," Josy said happily.

Gustavo sighed. "Hi, Josy." And then, wonder of all wonders, he brought his arms up and *loosely hugged Josy back for almost three seconds*.

It was almost as good as the moment when he'd been hired to star in a movie.

Which wasn't that long ago, so everything was coming up Josy.

Gustavo grumbled under his breath until Josy stepped back. "Take off that helmet. And the goggles." He frowned. "The jacket's okay, I guess."

Josy did just that. His beard was probably a mess, and his hair felt in disarray, but none of it mattered. He dropped the helmet and goggles on the porch, pulled his phone out of his pocket, and pressed his face against Gustavo's.

"What are you doing? No, Josy, I swear to god, if you don't unhand me, I will—"

"Please?"

Gustavo rolled his eyes. "You get one."

"Per hour?"

"Per *week*."

"But—"

"Take it or leave it."

"You suck, Gustavo. Is that any way to treat a guest?"

"You're not a guest. You're a leech that has somehow attached himself to my person, and I will not stand for it. Either take the picture for your Instatime or we're done."

"You have to smile. At least a little."

Gustavo bared his teeth. He looked like a rabid chipmunk. It was perfect.

Josy snapped the photo before letting Gustavo go. "You know what? I'm not even going to use a filter for that. It looks so good already."

"Wow," Gustavo said. "The joy I feel knows no bounds." He looked down the porch at the We Three Queens. "I know I'm supposed to ask if you need help because it's polite, but the last time I did that, Betty reminded me she knew six ways to break my neck. And since the bones of the neck are surprisingly weak, I believe her."

"Seven ways," Betty corrected as she hefted Josy's bags up the stairs. "And I got it. I may be old, but I'm still stronger than you. Being in love has made you soft, cadet."

"I still do push-ups," Gustavo said. "Sometimes Casey even sits on my back when I do them. I tell him to get off, but he says it's his duty as my boyfriend to sit on me."

Josy thought that was adorable but wisely kept it to himself. Gustavo Tiberius did not like being told he was adorable.

"I like your little muscles," Bernice said, pinching his arm before she followed Bertha and Betty inside.

Josy bent down and picked up the helmet and goggles. When he stood upright again, Gustavo was watching him.

Josy grinned. "It's good to see you, man."

Gustavo's lips twitched like they were fighting a losing battle not to smile. "I guess. There are a lot of strange people in town because of you."

Josy shrugged. "Good for business, right?"

"One of your movie people came into the store and asked if we had *Transformers: Age of Extinction*. Do you know what that is?"

Josy winced. "Uh, maybe?"

"It's a film," Gustavo said, "in which apparently a gigantic robot rides another gigantic robot that's actually a dinosaur. Do you want to know how I know that?"

"You… watched it?"

That was probably the wrong thing to say.

Gustavo narrowed his eyes. "I *know* that because this man proceeded to tell me how it was *super cool*, and that I needed to see it to believe it."

"Is he still alive?" Josy whispered, not understanding why either answer would be fine with him.

"Barely. But he is banned from the video store for life, and I cannot promise there won't be a ruckus in the streets if we come face-to-face. Casey ordered me a video from the Internet that tells me how to be more assertive. I haven't yet gotten to the part that teaches me how to incapacitate someone with the least amount of bloodshed, but I assume it's coming. Otherwise it is a waste of three monthly installments of $19.99."

"I missed you," Josy said honestly.

Gustavo looked vaguely uncomfortable. "We talk once a week."

"It's not the same as getting to see your face. It's a nice face."

"I don't know why you think so, but it could be worse. I could look like Michael Bay and have an expression of perpetual smugness that I don't deserve when I make robot dinosaurs for reasons that boggle the mind. I'm still disappointed you haven't found out where he lives. I took the THC mint off your pillow because of it."

Josy deflated. "Aw, man. Come on. Casey said—"

"And Quincy is here too."

That caught Josy off guard. His heart tripped a little. "He is? Like, right now?"

Gustavo nodded. "He's inside with Casey. He seems… nervous. About everything. He twitches. I respect that."

"Yeah, man. That's Quincy for you."

Gustavo squinted at him. "Why do you sound like that?"

"Like what?"

"You sounded weird just now when you talked about him."

"I don't know what you're talking about."

"Whatever. Like I've told all the other guests who stay here, there are to be no wild Hollywood parties at Baked-Inn & Eggs. I expect you to keep things under control. No hookers or heroin or whatever it is you do in California. Do you understand me?"

"Sex workers," Josy said automatically.

"Excuse me?"

"You're not supposed to say *hooker*. Or *prostitute*. It's rude. You call them *sex workers*. There is a negative connotation behind—"

Gustavo wasn't having it. "I don't *care* what you call them. I just don't want them here. If you must hire one for a—a *shindig*, then you take them to the motel down the road where everyone else is staying."

"We're not going to hire sex workers, Gustavo. I don't even know any sex workers. Wait, that was a lie. I know six. But I don't know any *here*." He squinted at Gustavo. "Are there sex workers in Abby?"

"I don't doubt it," Gustavo said. "Pastor Tommy probably knew, but he never told me about them. He knew everything about everyone."

"Pretty cool dude, huh?"

Gustavo sighed. "Yeah. He was. But regardless, I know you're famous now or whatever, but this is still a small town. Don't make things weird."

"I'm not famous yet," Josy assured him. "I mean, maybe I will be, but right at this moment? You don't have anything to worry about. Pretty much no one in this movie is well known."

"Tell that to Mason Grazer."

"Um. Okay? Why?"

Gustavo threw up his hands. "Oh my god. The first thing he did when he got here was demand bottled water be sent to his room, because apparently he doesn't do *tap*. And then he tried to flirt with Casey. I mean, what the hell."

"I hate that guy! I mean, sure, yeah, tap water is disgusting, but still! Did you maim him?"

Gustavo shook his head. "I thought about it, but Casey said the FBI can track it when you order arsenic online. And I don't know anyone that sells it around here."

"Oh. That sucks. I mean, it's probably for the best that you don't poison someone."

"That's what Casey said," Gustavo muttered. "But Casey told Mason, and I quote, 'totally in love with the best dude, like, you don't even know,' and then Mason left him alone."

"Aw. Gustavo, that's so special."

"It's terrible is what it is."

"You're smiling."

"I am not. I'm working out my facial muscles. Come inside. You're late, and I have to get back to the store soon."

He turned and headed inside.

Josy followed him. He was pretty sure he'd follow Gustavo anywhere.

THE INTERIOR of Baked-Inn & Eggs was warm and cozy, filled with couches and pillows and blankets and those moon chairs that Josy imagined every single person in the world had in their first apartment because they were so *adult*. He'd never had one because he had never been able to afford it, but he'd sat in one at an Ikea once. It had been an uncomfortably transcendent experience.

The We Three Queens were nowhere in sight. Josy hoped they weren't throwing his luggage into the woods behind the house.

There was a tiny desk set up near the main entrance, and standing beside it with a lopsided grin and a messy bun on top of his head was Casey Richards.

And next to him, looking flustered and anxious, was Quincy Moore.

"Best day ever," Josy whispered fervently.

No one heard him, but that was okay. Gustavo went over to Casey and leaned forward, kissing him on the cheek. Casey's smile widened. "You need to head back to the store?"

"Yes. It's Friday. Sometimes people rent movies on Fridays. I need to be there to meet the demand. I'll come back after I close since you insisted on having dinner with everyone."

"Yeah, dude. That's great. Don't forget the ferret with merit. Lottie texted and said that he ate part of her phonebook. I didn't even know they still made phonebooks."

Gustavo frowned. "Of course they do. How else are you supposed to know phone numbers of places you need to call?"

"Oh man, I love you."

"Yes, well, I expect you would," Gustavo said, sounding flustered. "I'm leaving now. I will be back at five thirty. Maybe later, depending on how long it takes for me to vacuum the floors. You know I have to vacuum on Fridays. Just because people are here doesn't mean I can't vacuum my store."

Casey shrugged. "I know. You do you. I'll be here when you're done."

Gus nodded, hesitated, and then leaned in and kissed Casey's cheek again. He muttered something under his breath that sounded suspiciously like *I love you too*, but Josy couldn't be sure.

Gustavo nodded at Quincy and then turned back toward the door.

"I'm not going to hug you again," he said to Josy. "I just hugged you five minutes ago, and we don't need to do it again."

"Are you sure?"

"I've never been surer about anything in my life."

"Fist bump?"

Gustavo scowled. "Of course not. Oh my god, I'm not your *bro*. I don't want to play hacky sack or drink a brewski with you. Why on earth would you think I'm the type that fist-bumps anything?"

He had a point. "High five, then."

Gustavo glared at him.

Josy dropped his hand.

"It's nice to see you," Gustavo muttered as he walked by him toward the door. "I'm happy you're here. I missed you. If you need to practice your lines, you know where to find me." He slammed the door behind him.

But Josy had no time to react to this astonishing revelation. As soon as the door shut, he had an armful of Casey. And that was pretty okay.

"Dude," Casey said happily near his ear.

"Dude!" Josy said back, equally as pleased as he squeezed Casey tight.

"Like, right?"

"Totally."

"So cool."

"I know!"

Casey pulled away so he could look at Josy. "I can't believe you're here! And for six whole weeks." His eyes widened. "That's a long time."

"So long," Josy agreed. "How's tricks?"

"Same old, same old. I think I'm living the dream, dude. Got a good guy, my own B and B, and Quincy here just helped me get over my writer's block."

Josy looked over Casey's shoulder to see Quincy looking as if he was about to run. "He did? Oh man, that's so rad."

Quincy cleared his throat and reached up to fiddle with his glasses. "I don't—I didn't do anything."

Casey stepped away. "Nah, dude, totally give yourself credit. You've earned it."

"Yes, but all I did was come down here and ask for another pillow."

"Right? And then we started talking about how cavemen probably used rocks as pillows—"

"Actually, *you* started talking about that—"

"—and then that led to a discussion on the Boston Tea Party—"

"And I don't even know *why*."

"—and now my writer's block is gone," Casey finished. "I've got so many ideas. I need to go email my agent before I forget. Quincy, I know you don't work here, but can you show Josy to his room? That would be awesome. I'll be back in a little bit. Thanks, man." He disappeared down the hall.

"Wow," Josy said, coming to stand next to Quincy. "That was nice of you. His writer's block was bumming him out."

Quincy shook his head. "I have no idea what happened."

"You did a good thing," Josy said. And then he was stumped. How did one greet a sort-of friend that was also technically his boss? Did they hug? Did they bump shoulders? Did they come up with a complicated handshake that goes on for a good solid minute? Josy wasn't sure.

So he did none of those things. He just stood there awkwardly.

Which made things *more* awkward, as Quincy did the same thing.

The silence stretched on for ten seconds. Josy knew this because he counted. And this was far longer than he was comfortable with. He needed to fix it. He said, "So."

Quincy cleared his throat. "So."

Okay, this was a good start. He could do this. "How is… everything?"

"Um. Fine? Everything is fine. I think."

Josy nodded. "Good. That's good."

"Yes. It is. Good."

"Good." Josy thought maybe he was drowning, but since he wasn't in water, he didn't know why he felt that way. So he said, "Did you try your THC mint that was left on your pillow?"

Quincy grimaced. "No. I don't do… that."

"Oh. Oh! That's… cool. I mean, I do, but you don't have to." He panicked slightly. "Not that I'll be high whenever I'm on set or needing to be on set. I would *never* do that. You don't have to worry about that."

"O… kay. That's good to know."

"And I'll never pressure you to do anything you don't want to do. Just because I enjoy something doesn't mean others will." He hesitated. Then, all in a rush, "Because that's not what friends do to each other."

Quincy blushed. "Oh. Um. Thanks?"

Josy nodded, pleased that Quincy didn't object to being friends. As Gustavo would say, today was an okay day. "And I enjoy it. I mean, I enjoy it a *lot*. Like, you don't even know."

"It's good to have hobbies?"

Josy sagged in relief. "Sweet. I'm glad we talked about this. I feel better. Do you like it here? I really like it here. It's quiet, you know? LA is all bam and blam, and Abby is all hey, man, take a breather. Take a break. Cool your jets, you know?"

"It's… different. I like it, though. The people are nice, mostly." He frowned. "There was a group of women who told me I'd wandered into a den of cougars. They growled at me. It was odd."

"Yeah," Josy said. "That happens here. Xander gave me anticougar spray as a joke before I left, but then he took it back because he thought I would actually spray them. Which, I mean, why give it to me in the first place?"

Quincy stared at him.

Josy smiled in return.

Quincy squeaked.

"You okay?"

"Fine!" he said. "Just… fine."

That was good. "Where is everyone else?"

"Roger and Dee went with some of the crew who got here this morning. Wanted to show them some of the locations they'd scouted. Mason was refusing to come out of his room until someone brings him a macchiato, but Dee told him to get it himself, and now he's pouting, I think? Especially after Gus told him that there was no espresso machine here because espresso machines are pointless and probably give off radiation."

"Gustavo is the bomb dot com."

"He seems interesting. Is that the right word?"

Josy shrugged. "There are no words that're good enough to describe Gustavo."

Quincy opened his mouth, and then it snapped shut. He looked down at his hands before apparently deciding to try again. "Yeah, he's.... When we got here, I was worried. For Grandad. He's independent. He likes to do things on his own. Always been that way. He doesn't let being in a wheelchair stop him from anything." He popped his knuckles. "I didn't see how he was going to get in the house without help. All those stairs." He smiled weakly. "But then Casey came out and told me they'd had a wheelchair ramp built on the back of the house." He looked up at Josy, a strange expression on his face. "Said it was your idea. That you called him and asked for it to be built."

Josy nodded. "Oh yeah! I forgot about that. Cool, right? Casey was always going to do it. He wanted the B and B to be for everyone who wanted to stay here. I just asked if he could build one sooner rather than later."

"Thank you," Quincy said quietly. "You… that was nice of you."

Josy rubbed the back of his neck, oddly embarrassed. "Yeah."

Quincy shuffled his feet. "Yeah."

"Oh my god," someone whispered. "It's happening again! Is it us? I think it has to be us. We have gifts."

They both looked up to see the faces of the We Three Queens peering down at them from over the banister on the floor above. Bernice was grinning. Bertha had her head cocked. Betty's eyes were narrowed.

Josy was confused. "What's happening?"

"Nothing at all," Bernice said sweetly. "You're doing amazing, sweetie." She looked at Bertha and Betty. "Did I say that right? I don't quite understand memes."

"Your room is ready," Bertha said.

"Double time!" Betty barked.

They double-timed up the stairs.

"Dude," Josy said in awe. "We get to share a room!"

"So it seems," Quincy mumbled.

"How about that," Bernice said.

"Weird how that worked out," Bertha said.

"I put your bags inside," Betty told Josy. "I was going to unpack for you, but then I remembered you're a man, even if you dress like a sixteen-year-old at a rock festival. So you need to do it yourself. And you will make your bed every morning. There are no maids here. I expect the corners to be tight. I won't say there will be random inspections, but I won't not say it either."

"She was in the Army," Bernice whispered to Quincy. "She likes to take charge. Sometimes I like it. Like when we can't figure out what we want for dinner."

Quincy stared at her. "Do you... do you all work here too? I could have sworn you said at the audition you were retired."

Bernice patted his arm. "That's nice."

Josy gave Betty a snappy salute. "Yes, ma'am."

Betty nodded. "Good. Since we're going to be working together, I will expect things to be done in a certain way. Now if you'll excuse us, we have lines to run. Ladies, let's leave them to it."

Bertha squeezed his arm as she followed Betty down the stairs. Bernice stopped at the landing, looking back over her shoulder. "You should know that I can be very intense about the things I love. And I think I will love you, Quincy. You're my first director. I will always remember you." She hummed as she descended the stairs.

"Who *are* they?" Quincy asked.

"Right? They're amazing."

"Are they...."

Josy waited.

"All together? Or...?"

"I mean, yeah. They're always together. I don't think they like being apart."

Quincy sighed. "That's not—you know what? It's none of my business. I need to go lie down. The past few days have been a little crazy. I'm getting a headache."

And since they were now confirmed to be friends, Josy said, "We're roommates, so I'll help you however you need. Like, a cold washcloth for your head. Or tea, because I know Casey has normal tea and not weed tea somewhere. Or if you just want someone to sit by you so you have company. Because I can sit by you and not talk. My friend Xander says I have a really good shoulder to lay your head on. And he doesn't lie about anything, even if it hurts your feelings."

Quincy smiled faintly. "That's good to know. But I'm okay. I just need quiet for a little while."

"I get that," Josy said seriously. "Sometimes I like to lay on my bed in the dark and stare at the ceiling and think about things, like how I'm happy I got my big break and why do taquitos taste so good, even the frozen kind."

"You're... serious."

"Yeah, man. Like, I know frozen food isn't healthy or anything, but you put some of those taquitos in the oven and holy crap, I could eat an entire box if it didn't give me the shits—"

"No. That's not what I was asking. I meant about this being your big break. That's what you think this is."

"Yeah, man," Josy said easily. "I'm in a movie. A *real* movie, you know? It's all I ever wanted, and now it's happened. How cool is that? My life is pretty great."

"It's that simple for you."

"Why wouldn't it be?"

Quincy slowly shook his head. "I—I wish I could see things like you do."

"But then you wouldn't see things like you do," Josy said. "And then there would be two of me and none of you, and that wouldn't be so good."

"It wouldn't?"

"Nope. Because I like you just the way you are."

Quincy coughed roughly. "I have to lie down."

"Okay. I'll head back downstairs to give you some peace and quiet. I'm going to go practice my lines and be ready for Monday. I'll see you at dinner."

Quincy looked like he wanted to say something else, but he went into the room instead, closing the door behind him.

Josy wondered what he was going to say.

He'd ask later.

Downstairs, Casey gave him another hug and slipped him a THC mint.

It was good to be back in Abby.

Chapter 10

The Stories of My Father (Working Title)
Day 1
Location: John Eagleton's home
Scene 3

IT WAS Josiah Erickson's first day on set.

He was nervous, but it was a good kind of nervous. He'd accidentally posted six selfies to Instagram this morning, but he needed some way to soothe his nerves. Yes, he quite possibly used more hashtags than he ever had in his life, but they made him feel better. Hashtags often did. Both Xander and Serge had commented on a couple of the photos, wishing him good luck.

"Wow," a voice said behind him. "I don't think I've ever seen a man get that much makeup on his face before. I mean, maybe drag queens, but not a hipster."

He was about to turn his head, but Dee growled at him and he kept still. She stood above him, eyeing him closely. He hadn't known that she was also in charge of the actors' makeup. She was a lesbian of many talents. Josy was impressed. She'd forced him into a chair in the living room while they prepared Roger for his role as Liam Eagleton's father upstairs. Josy had told her he had a distant cousin who was a drag queen in Tucson, and so he knew how to put makeup on, but she'd told him to shut up and let her work.

He needn't have worried about turning his head, however. Soon enough, bright red hair attached to a familiar face peered over Dee's shoulder.

"Lottie," Josy said, trying not to smile because Dee would snarl at him again. "What are you doing here?"

"Craft services," Lottie murmured. "Are you going to give him mascara? Because I've always had a thing for men with smoky eyes. I once made out with Robert Smith. Well, not *actually* Robert Smith. He was too busy being the only constant member of the Cure. It was a poster of him I had on my wall."

"Would you please step back?" Dee asked.

Lottie did.

"And no, he's not going to get mascara."

"Really?" Josy asked. "That sucks. I wore it once and someone said that it made me look like a demon angel."

"That was me," Lottie said. "The last time you were here. And you were high and let me put mascara on you."

"Oh right! Dude, my bad. I forgot. Did you bring sandwiches? I love sandwiches."

"Egg salad. With pickles. Gus won't eat it, so everyone else needs to. I always order too many pickles."

"Or you can just not make it," Dee told her, turning Josy's head side to side, checking her work.

Lottie scoffed. "Then what would I do with the pickles? I had a pickle barrel once, but no one would eat them. I even had special tongs and everything. It was quaint."

"This is such a weird town," Dee muttered.

Lottie leaned over her shoulder again. "What happened to your mustache? Why isn't it curled at the ends?"

"They made me trim it. Apparently Liam doesn't curl his mustache. He's very deep."

"Wow," Lottie said. "I don't know if I've ever heard anybody say those words before and sound so sad at the same time."

Dee glanced back over her shoulder. "You've heard someone say those words before and sound happy?"

Lottie shrugged. "I knew interesting people in the eighties."

Dee shook her head as she turned back around. "Josy, you're done. If you mess this up in the next five minutes before you're in front of the camera, I will make you sorry."

"I wouldn't do that to you. I know how hard you work." He looked into the mirror she held up. "Whoa. Dude! This looks great! I look like a Liam. You should feel proud of yourself. You were born for this."

Dee snorted. "Gee. Thanks."

Josy grinned at her.

"Literal sunshine," Lottie breathed. She coughed, shaking her head. "Where should I set up the food?"

"In here!" Casey called from down the hall. "I'm making room in the kitchen. Give me a second and I'll help you unload the truck."

"Are you also security?" Lottie asked Dee.

She frowned. "Security? For what?"

"All the people standing outside the B and B trying to take pictures."

"Oh my god," Josy whispered. "It's starting. Paparazzi."

"What? No. It's just nosy townsfolk."

That… wasn't as epic as some intrusive bastard who wanted to try to take photos of Josy when all he wanted to do was go out like regular people. Paps just didn't understand the perils of celebrity.

(But to be fair, neither did Josy.)

Dee went to the window. "What the hell?"

Josy stood from the chair and followed her, looking over her shoulder. Sure enough, standing around a truck for Lottie's Lattes was a group of townsfolk. There was the alliterative librarian, Margo Montana. Next to her was LaRonda Havisham, pushing up her cleavage for reasons Josy didn't understand. He thought it looked fine where it was. And next to *her* was Leslie Von Patterson, she of the Fun Committee and decorator of everything Gustavo despised. She had a small yellow-and-black rectangle in her hands, which she pointed in all directions before using her thumb to spin a dial.

"What is that?" Josy asked.

"A disposable camera."

"Really? That's so retro! I didn't know they made those anymore."

"She bought seventy boxes of them in 1999," Lottie told them. "Back when we all thought Y2K was actually going to be a thing, though for the life of me, I can't even remember what Y2K was. But she figured if the world ended, disposable cameras could be used as a bargaining chip in order to make her in charge of her own commune of survivors."

Dee turned to stare at her. "Please tell me you're joking."

"Not at all! Strangely enough, the thought apparently never crossed her mind that no one would be able to develop the film after the world ended, but then the turn of the century was a very strange time for everyone. We were so innocent then."

Others had amassed behind cougar town, curious onlookers craning their necks, trying to see into the house. It wasn't a *large* crowd, but Josy figured this was how it started. A few people here and then sold-out theaters across the country.

"Where are you going?" Dee called after him.

"Out to greet my people! They need to know how appreciative I am for supporting the arts."

"What? Josy, no! You get back—"

But it was too late. Dee was strong and wide. Josy was skinny. Ergo, he met less resistance when moving, making him faster. Also, he was determined, because potential fans could become outright fans, and they needed to know he cared about them as much as they cared about him.

He opened the door.

Mrs. Von Patterson immediately took his picture before furiously winding the camera. Ten seconds later, she was able to take another.

"Hello!" Josy said, smiling widely. "It's nice to see you. Hi! Hello! I'm sorry I don't have time for autographs right now. I'm getting ready to shoot my scene. But I will later, if you all want to stick aro—*urk*!"

Dee had grabbed him by the collar of his shirt and jerked him back inside. She took his place on the porch, crossing her arms over her chest. "This is a closed set!"

"We've been hired as extras," Margo Montana said, arching an eyebrow. "If you could let the director know that I'm here and ready for my close-up."

"We don't have extras on set today," Dee said. "You aren't scheduled until Wednesday."

"Oh dear," Mrs. Von Patterson said, taking another picture and winding it again. "We thought it was today." Another picture. More winding. "How upsetting."

Mrs. Havisham pushed out her bosom even farther. "Actually, *I'm* supposed to be here today. I have been assigned the pivotal role of Home Health Nurse."

Dee pulled out her phone and scrolled through something on the screen. "LaRonda Havisham?"

"'Tis I!"

"You're twenty minutes late. Get in here now before you're fired."

She hurried up the stairs.

Margo Montana and Mrs. Von Patterson scowled after her. The rest of the people whispered among themselves.

"I know how to fix this," Josy whispered as Mrs. Havisham pushed her way inside. "Let me take a selfie with them and they'll leave."

"If you ruin your makeup, I'll—"

"I know, I know. You'll make me sorry. Leave it to me."

He squared his shoulders, put a beatific smile on his face, and said, "I am costarring in this film! Who would like to take a selfie with me for Instagram in exchange for getting off the property?"

Everyone in the crowd raised their hands.

It was hard being in such demand, but he might as well start getting used to it.

ONE OF the bedrooms at the B and B had been slightly converted to act as John Eagleton's room. Machines that looked as if they belonged in a hospital had been set up next to the bed. Roger Fuller lay propped up by pillows, his wheelchair pushed out of sight. Dee stood above him, putting the finishing touches on his makeup, but it was still less than Josy had ever seen him wear. He'd been made to look older, frailer. It would be disconcerting if it wasn't movie magic.

Mrs. Havisham stood off to the side, palms pressed together as if she were praying before she started doing squats. She had changed into nurse scrubs from Wardrobe. Josy was thankful her cleavage had been hidden.

Quincy was talking with the boom mic operator, whispering back and forth. He looked harried, and there were circles under his eyes, as if he hadn't slept well. Josy could understand. He too had been nervous, but he'd smoked a blunt with Casey before he'd gone home to Gustavo and Harry S. Truman for the night. Josy had been out like a light by nine. He felt bad knowing that hadn't been the case for Quincy. When he'd gone up to the room, Quincy had been lying on his bed, facing the wall. Josy had assumed he was asleep, but maybe that hadn't been the case. He should have done more. They were friends now, and friends helped each other.

He didn't know if he should announce himself. Everyone looked busy, and he wasn't sure of his place. His stomach was twisting unpleasantly. He was nervous, more so than he'd ever been, and it worried him. He'd been in front of a camera before. Granted, this was bigger than anything else, but he was ready. He knew his lines. The shooting schedule had been given to him well in advance. He was ready.

But what if he wasn't? What if he messed up? What if the entire project collapsed because of him? What if he forgot how to act? He was already wearing clothes foreign to him: loose-fitting jeans, a plaid shirt, and scuffed boots. Nothing about it was ironic. It was bland and boring and perfectly within character for Liam Eagleton, a man who was estranged from his dying father and who worked in a cubicle selling vitamin supplements. He also had a second job working in a bookstore, just to make ends meet. He was on the road to nowhere, and what if Josy couldn't relate? He was on the road to *everywhere*. Well, he would be if he didn't fuck this up. Sure, do or do not, there is no try, but what if there *was* a try?

"Mason," he whispered loudly.

Mason, who was standing against the wall looking bored, ignored him. They were supposed to be achingly in love but unable to be together due to Liam's numerous commitment issues, in part because of his strained relationship with his father, and he was acting like he hadn't heard Josy!

"Mason!"

"What."

"I need your help."

Mason didn't even look at him. "With?"

"We need to be in love."

Mason snorted. "Yeah, I don't think that's going to happen."

"It has to be realistic," Josy insisted. He walked over to stand in front of Mason. "If we don't have chemistry, no one will believe I'm the love of your life."

"You're not."

Josy thought about pointing out how many times Mason had tried to flirt with him but decided against it. "Yes, well, that's why it's called acting. I mean, no offense, dude. You're not really my type. But we can fake it, you know? We kind of have to."

Mason rolled his eyes. "What do you want?"

"We need to stare lovingly into each other's eyes."

"Yeah, I'm not gonna do that."

Josy stared at him.

Mason didn't look at him.

Josy continued staring. He barely blinked.

Mason finally looked at him.

"I love you," Josy whispered.

Mason grimaced. "Seriously. Stop it."

"No. Dante, I love you."

"Josy, I swear to god—"

"I love you, and I'm sorry I broke your heart because of my numerous issues about commitment due to my strained relationship with my father."

"Why are you like this?" Mason demanded.

Josy—no, *Liam*—looked away. "My father is dying, and I don't know how to deal with it. My life is at a crossroads. One way leads to the dull path I've been on for years. The other... the other is a future with you just within my grasp—"

"Stop it."

Liam looked back at Dante. "Forgive me, my former lover who I still love." He blinked, Liam disappearing back into that place inside all actors of his caliber had. "Did you like what I did with my voice? I sound beaten, don't I?"

"I will make you sound that way for real if you don't leave me alone."

Josy put a hand on his shoulder. "It's okay to be nervous. I am, but we can help each other. After all, I've seen your penis."

Before Mason could agree with that bon mot, Josy's name was called.

He turned.

Quincy looked a little green.

"You okay?"

Quincy shrugged. "Oh sure. Just, you know. Everything."

Josy nodded. He understood greatly. "Yeah. But! Think of it this way: you won't know what you're capable of unless you try, man. Serge taught me that. Or I saw it on an inspirational poster that had a cat on it."

"Jesus Christ," Mason muttered behind him.

"Sure," Quincy said. "Um. Can you... are you ready? Both of you? I think it's almost time to begin."

"I won't let you down," Josy promised. "And if I do, tell me, because you're the director. I am open to critique. All I ask is that you make it constructive and not mean, because I don't like it when people are mean."

Quincy looked aghast. "I would *never* be mean. I don't even know *how*."

"Oh man, that's so good. One time a director yelled at me. Wait. No, three different directors yelled at me." Granted, Josy had been going completely off script with backstories he'd built in his head, but still. It hadn't been very nice.

"I don't yell," Quincy said, sounding stricken.

"It's true," Roger said. He grunted as Dee fluffed the pillows behind him. "Always such a quiet boy. Even when he skinned his knee, he barely made a sound. Oh, he cried, of course. These great big tears that just broke your heart—"

"Grandad!"

"Oops," Roger said. "My apologies. Today you are not my grandson. You're my director. I'll remember that from this point on. Did you take your medicine this morning?"

The crew snickered quietly.

"I did," Josy said, showing solidarity. "It was echinacea and honey in my tea to make sure my voice is strong."

"Wonderful," Roger said lightly. "Now, Quincy, I know this is your show. I will leave it up to you. We're in your capable hands."

Quincy nodded, head jerking. "That's… good."

"But I believe it's customary for the captain of our ship to address his crew before the maiden voyage."

Quincy squeaked.

Josy involuntarily took a step forward, barely able to stop himself from dragging Quincy to another room to build a blanket fort filled with pillows to block out the rest of the world. It was close.

Everyone waited, watching Quincy.

Quincy wrung his hands.

Roger coughed.

Quincy cleared his throat. "Um. Right. Okay. So. This is… my movie. That I wrote. And am directing. And will be helping to edit, even though I have no idea how to do that. And promoting. And distributing if we don't get picked up. But it's not just about me. It's about… all of us? Yes, it's about *all of us*. Because I'm the captain of this ship. But without a crew, the captain is alone and the ship will most likely run aground and be destroyed, killing hundreds of people on accident. But I don't want anyone to die, so let's not focus on that. Let's just make the best movie we can."

He had such a way with words. Josy wasn't surprised Quincy was an author. Though he did seem to have a problem with breathing, and his skin was turning red.

Josy did the only thing he could.

He clapped.

For a good seven seconds, he was the only one.

But then Roger joined in, and Dee, and the rest of the crew. Mason didn't, but Josy knew that while Mason was a good actor, he also didn't have a soul. He was just an attractive human husk put on this earth to send unsolicited dick pics and to test Josy's love of everything.

Quincy looked slightly shocked at the applause. Shocked, but almost pleased.

Josy liked that very much.

THE FIRST scene to be filmed in *The Stories of My Father (Working Title)* was an intimate one. Liam and Dante, separated but still desperately in love, returned to Josy's hometown to his father's bedside. The elder Eagleton was not long for this world and had summoned his son back to the house where he'd grown up. Some exterior shots had already been done over the weekend, but this was the first time there would be *actors* involved. The movie itself would start with Liam working his dead-end jobs and receiving the phone call that would bring him back. There would also be a strained car ride with Liam and Dante driving back across the country, with a voice-over from Liam describing their relationship woes, but that would come later. Films were rarely—if ever—shot in chronological order.

Josy was shown the mark on the floor he'd have to hit. Mason would remain in the background near the door, looking pensive and unsure.

"And I will be doing nurse things," Mrs. Havisham announced. "Like taking temperatures and administering injections."

"No," Dee said. "You're going to pull the blanket up a little higher on John Eagleton and then exit. Nothing else. You don't have any lines."

"I shall pull the blanket up," Mrs. Havisham announced. "No one will ever pull a blanket up as well as I."

Dee sighed as she looked at Quincy. "Later we're going to talk about a raise."

Quincy was sweating. "Okay. So. We are going to begin. Just… get right into it. Places, everyone. This is going to be a long take—"

Roger snorted. "Listen to him. Long take. How adorable."

"—*a long take*, and we need to make sure everyone hits their marks." He turned to Josy and Mason near the door. "Josy, you're seeing your dad for the first time in years. He's... he's never been so frail. Even though you had your differences, you always saw him as a larger-than-life figure. And now for the first time, you actually see him as human. Weak and fragile. You're angry, but you're also heartbroken."

"Sadly mad," Josy said. "Got it."

"Mason, you stay near the door. You're unsure. You're going to reach out and squeeze Josy's hand before he walks to his father's bedside. Just for a second."

"I should be able to handle that," Mason said dryly.

Josy wondered if it was too late to have certain roles recast.

Quincy turned toward his grandad. "And you—"

"I know what I'm doing," Roger said. "We talked this morning. Have trust in us, and we'll put our trust in you."

Quincy nodded tightly. He went to stand behind the camera, an Arri Alexa, something that was apparently extraordinarily expensive. Quincy had said Roger cashed in a few favors to get it. Josy didn't want to know what that meant but figured it was Hollywood lingo. One of the crew members had been fixed with a Steadicam as well. He looked like one of Gustavo's maligned Transformers.

Josy took a deep breath.

This was it.

This was his moment.

This was how he was going to be a movie star. For the rest of his life, he would look back at this very second. Hopefully it would be the start of a long and storied career, but even if he was seventy-six and working in a Burger King of the future (where they sold space fries made from asteroids or something), he would fondly remember this day where he had achieved his dream. Not many people got to do that.

(And space fries sounded *amazing*.)

"Ready?" Quincy asked.

Everyone nodded.

"Quiet!" one of the crew shouted.

A clapboard came out. A real live clapboard.

And the sound it made was just like in the movies.

"Action!"

Liam Eagleton stood in the doorway, looking at his dying father. A wave of the sad mads ran through him. This... this man hadn't been there for his son. He'd disappeared for days on end, leaving his only child with a nanny. He said he'd always come back, and he *did*, but he was a stranger, months passing by without any contact. By then, a young Liam had made his own family out of his imaginary friends.

Mr. Zucko, the half man, half zebra with a penchant for talking tough and fighting crime as a private investigator.

Dill, the gigantic cucumber who was scared of brine, as he didn't want to become a pickle. He was Mr. Zucko's secretary.

Boris Biggles, the sunflower with a mustache who was gruff and filled with a quiet pain at the loss of his sunflower family in the Great War against the Weeds. The weeds had won.

Grady, the man with the mane of a lion and the heart of a king who had tea with Liam on the days he felt loneliest.

These imaginary friends who Liam had forgotten until he saw his father on his deathbed.

Dante reached out and squeezed his hand.

Liam took a deep breath and took a step forward.

His father's eyes were closed. The machines around him beeped. His nurse pulled up the blanket to just under his chin. She looked up at Liam and smiled softly. "Your daddy is dyin'," she said in a deep Southern accent. "He's lost his livah due to the plague. Such a turrible thang."

"Cut!"

Josy blinked as Liam retreated within.

"You don't have any lines," Dee growled at Mrs. Havisham as Quincy looked toward the ceiling.

"I'm aware," Mrs. Havisham said, puffing out her chest. "But I thought if I'm to be in this little picture I should make the most of it. Also, I've always wanted to be a Southern belle, which is why I affected an accent. Y'all undastand?"

Josy had to admire that. He'd done the same thing many times before. Of course, he wouldn't say that out loud because he didn't want Dee yelling at him. She was really awesome with the way she cared for Quincy, but she was also terrifying.

Dee's eyes narrowed. "Don't. *Speak*."

"Eep," Mrs. Havisham said.

"Places!"

Imaginary friends. Dying father. The sad mads.

"Action!"

Unnamed Nurse pulled up the blanket a little roughly, and maybe she was glaring, but she kept her mouth shut. She stalked out of the way as Liam approached, leaving Dante behind him at the door.

He made his way to his father's bedside, hand shaking as he reached out to touch his father's arm. But the moment before he made contact, he curled his hand into a fist and pulled his arm away.

"Dad," he said quietly. "I'm here. It's me. Liam."

John Eagleton's eyes fluttered open. "Liam?" he croaked. He coughed roughly. "Liam, is that you?"

"Yeah, Dad. It's me."

"Oh, bless my stars. So it is. Let me look at you, my son. Come closer."

Liam hesitated, but then he leaned over.

Old, gnarled fingers came up to touch his face. They stroked his beard.

"Oh, my boy," John said, voice quivering. "Oh, my son. I'm so happy you're here. There isn't much time left. And I have so much to tell you."

"Cut! Okay, I want to try something different. Let's start again."

Now, it should be said that when one goes to the movies, one is witnessing the final product after months—maybe even *years*—of work. The takes are the best they can be.

But what most don't realize is that it's born of repetition. The same take happens again and again and again. A single uninterrupted shot that lasts ten seconds could take *hours* to film.

That, coupled with a novice director and a cast who, aside from Roger Fuller, had never really been part of a project of this magnitude... suffice it to say, it was exhausting.

They finally wrapped for the day just as the light was beginning to fade. They'd had a single break for lunch where Quincy had disappeared into their shared room with his laptop, muttering under his breath about how he needed to rework a couple of scenes, given the way Josy and Roger had played their reunion. Josy thought about bringing him up an egg salad sandwich with pickles, but Dee had stopped him, shaking her head. "It's better if he gets this out now," she told him quietly. "Let him be for a little bit."

Quincy had come back down near the end of the lunch break. He hesitated in the doorway to the kitchen until Josy waved him over to the seat he'd saved. He set a sandwich and some chips on a plate. "Eat," he said. "You'll feel better."

Quincy did.

And then they went back and did the same scene again.

And again.

And *again*.

When they'd finished for the day, Dee helped Roger back into his chair. Roger told Quincy to take a break, that he'd review the dailies and make some phone calls. He had business to tend to, after all.

"He's always networking," Quincy said, staring after his grandad as the rest of the crew started putting away the equipment.

"That's because he likes you," Josy told him. "That's pretty great, having someone like that."

Quincy turned to Josy. "It is?"

Josy shrugged. "Sure. I mean, I would think it is."

"Oh." He hesitated. Then, "Do you have that?"

"What do you mean?"

"Do you... have someone?"

"Like Roger?"

"Yeah."

Josy thought for a moment. "No, but that's because there's no one like Roger, I think. And that's okay, because it makes him special. That'd be cool, though, man."

"What about your parents?"

He reached up and scratched his face. The makeup was starting to itch. He was looking forward to washing it off. "They don't—they're not like Roger. They don't get me. Like, this whole acting thing, right? They told me a long time ago I was wasting my time. Which, okay, they can think whatever they want. They didn't believe I could do it. But that's fine, because I believe in myself enough for all of us."

Quincy stared at him. "I don't get you."

This was good. Two new friends talking, getting to know each other. Josy liked this a lot. "Why?"

"You're like... this guy."

"Yep. Sure am. I don't know what you're talking about."

Quincy looked frustrated. "I know how things go for me. How it works. I know what I'm capable of and what I'm not. I know what I have to do to push myself, and I know where the line is that I can't make myself cross. I have these boundaries set. Sometimes I can expand them, and sometimes they shrink. But you… you just… *do* whatever's in your head. You say it like it is without a second thought. Why do you do that?"

Josy squinted at him. "Who else am I supposed to be but who I already am?" He blinked. "Wow, that sounded like I went to India for eight months and learned about chakras. Holy crap."

Quincy gaped at him.

"My friend Serge went—never mind. I don't understand what you have to go through, you know? Because I'm not you. But how cool is it you can do all these things even when your boundaries shrink? That's pretty rad, man. Mad props and stuff."

"You're so weird," Quincy blurted. His eyes widened in horror. "I didn't mean—"

Josy waved a hand at him. "That's okay. I'm fine with that. I don't think that's a bad thing. And maybe I am. But I found a bunch of weirdos like me. I don't have a Roger. But I have a Serge and a Xander. I have a Gustavo and a Casey. There's the We Three Queens and Lottie, and you know what? They're good enough for me because I'm good enough for them." He grinned. "Hey, we should take a selfie together! How cool would that be? Commemorate this shit, you know? First day and everything. Is it okay if I touch you again? You don't have to say yes."

Quincy paled. "T-touch?"

Josy shrugged. "Selfies mean we get close together. I have to put my face near your face because that's how friends do it."

"Right. Friends." He nodded like he was steeling himself. "Yes. I can do that. I can do a selfie with you."

"Awesome." He pulled out his phone and moved until he stood next to Quincy. He put his arm slowly around Quincy's shoulders, giving him plenty of time in case he changed his mind. He didn't. Josy held out the phone in front of them. He liked the way they looked next to each other on the screen. Quincy was looking down, as if he couldn't bear to see himself. "You don't have to look if you don't want to," Josy told him quietly.

"Okay," Quincy mumbled. "Maybe not yet." And he turned his head toward Josy, his nose scraping along Josy's beard. It tickled. Josy laughed. He heard Quincy inhale sharply before he chuckled too.

That was it.

That was the picture.

He pressed his thumb against the screen, capturing the moment.

"Wow," Josy said, looking down at the screen. "I don't think we even need a filter for that one. Good job."

Quincy stiffened slightly as Josy removed his arm. He looked down at the screen. Josy had a wide smile on his face, mouth barely open with a hint of teeth. And Quincy's lips were quirked upward, nose against Josy's cheek.

"You don't think people will get the wrong idea?"

Josy was confused. "About what?"

Quincy shook his head. "Nothing. Never mind."

"First day on set," Josy muttered, typing on the phone. "Going great. Can't wait to show you more. Hashtag actor life. Hashtag no filter. Hashtag this guy is pretty great. Hashtag Liam Eagleton FTW. Annnnnd posted." He put his phone back in his pocket and looked up at Quincy, only to find him staring again. "What?"

"Uh. Nothing. I'm just… going to go." He practically ran toward the door.

"Do you want to come to dinner with me? I'm going to Casey and Gustavo's house. Gustavo said he learned how to make enchiladas, but Casey said they're gross. I can't wait."

"No," Quincy said over his shoulder. "I'm just—going to go to my room."

"*Our* room," Josy reminded him with a wink.

Quincy nearly tripped before he disappeared through the door.

LATER THAT night, when he opened the door to their room, a little stoned and very full of gross enchiladas, he was careful not to disturb Quincy, who seemed to already be asleep. He had kicked off his comforter at some point and was huddled on the bed. Since Josy didn't want his friend getting cold, he tiptoed over to Quincy's bed and pulled the comforter up and over him.

"Good night, dude," he whispered. "Have good dreams about directing and stuff."

Chapter 11

The Stories of My Father (Working Title)
Day 5
Location: Outside Eagleton Home
Scene 7

THERE WERE days when acting was hard. An actor had dialogue to memorize, makeup to be caked onto his face. He had to be fitted in Wardrobe, wearing clothes that he would never actually wear in real life because loose jeans were the worst. An actor had to follow direction, repeat specific lines over and over and over, and stand *here*, and stand *there*, and *don't cross your arms, Josy, that's not what you're supposed to be doing*.

But then there were days when Mason Grazer was a gigantic sunflower and all was right with the world.

Josy told himself it was rude to laugh.

But he also told himself he needed to get it out now so he could embody the wonderment Liam would feel at seeing his old imaginary friend come to life.

So he laughed.

He laughed his ass off.

The Stories of My Father didn't exactly have the biggest budget, but that was okay. Quincy, and in turn Roger, had insisted on as many practical effects as possible. Roger had spoken happily on what creature makeup was capable of, especially in the hands of a master. He told the crew how they managed to turn a tiny woman into a seven-foot-tall voracious vampire with shag carpeting, ketchup, and duct tape.

But since creature makeup masters were also expensive, they had to rely on Roger's expertise. That wasn't so bad, given Roger had played many roles in his lifetime: producer, director, script doctor, effects artist, queen of the B movies with feminist agendas and queer undertones through almost gratuitous nudity.

To be fair, had the transformation been done on any other person, Josy would have been astonished by the obvious skill that stood in front of him. Boris Biggles had been brought to life.

However, it was also Mason Grazer as Boris Biggles, which made it hysterical. He wore a tight green skinsuit that had been wrapped in plastic leaves and vines. On his head had been placed a crown of yellow petals that fell artfully around his face, which had also been painted yellow, with black flecks across his cheeks. He had a thick, bushy mustache.

He looked amazing.

And absolutely ridiculous.

Josy laughed until he could barely breathe.

Boris Biggles scowled at him and told him to fuck off, which was great, as he already seemed to be getting into character.

"If you try and take my picture, I will *end* you," Mason warned him. "I don't need to be on your tiny little Instagram account."

Josy wiped his eyes. "Man, you have, like, ten more followers than I do. And also, you're a sunflower with a mustache."

THE SCENE was a crazy one. Liam was in the shower. He heard a creak outside and thought it was Dante, who'd had to leave earlier than expected. He walked out of the bathroom and into the hallway of the old house. He saw a flash of green and yellow and followed it until he stumbled across his old imaginary friend, thus setting off the true adventure of *The Stories of My Father (Working Title)*.

And Liam had to do it wearing nothing but a towel.

Which meant *Josy* had to do it wearing nothing but a towel.

As an actor, Josiah Erickson was comfortable with nudity. He'd done it before for Japanese energy drinks.

But as a *person*, it was a little different.

Josy wasn't shy, per se; no, he'd had to get over *that* rather quickly. Otherwise Los Angeles would have eaten him alive in the first year. He wasn't an extrovert by nature, but he'd forced himself to become one in order to survive. After all, if he didn't speak up, his voice would never be heard. He would get trampled on, and *no* one walked all over Josiah Erickson.

Regardless, he was still a human being, and with that came doubts.

He'd spent the morning doing crunches in the bedroom he shared with Quincy while Mason was in makeup. He'd gotten on the floor and started grunting as he worked his core. Quincy had stared at him wide-eyed for a minute or two before sputtering about having to go make sure his grandad was getting Mason just right.

And while Mason Grazer looked absolutely ridiculous, Josy was wearing a robe. Underneath that robe was a tiny pair of flesh-colored underpants that left absolutely nothing to the imagination. Josy had stared at his reflection in the mirror for a long time, wondering if there was any way to hide the outline of his bulge. Turns out there wasn't, unless he decided to tuck. Which looked decidedly awkward when he tried to walk and ended up more painful than he imagined.

Dee knocked on the door, walked in without a greeting, stared at his junk, and said it would work just fine before throwing his robe at his head.

Except.

The scene called for Liam to be *in* the shower.

Which meant he couldn't wear the underpants, because it would be too obvious.

Josy would have to remove them.

Yes, he had just showered naked that very morning, but this was different. He hadn't had an audience then, nor a camera or two trained on him.

He'd only put them on *now* because the robe was scratchy on his beans and weenie.

(He missed Beans and Weenie in the Morning. Abby, Oregon, didn't have a radio station that held contests. There was a semilocal NPR station, but when he'd called in after one of the morning hosts asked *What is ISIS?* he'd found out it was a rhetorical question. Which, to be fair, was good, because he thought ISIS was a flower.)

Do or do not. There is no try.

He could do this. He *would* do this.

(Also, he was contractually obligated to do it. And Roger had told him about it before he'd gotten the part, after all. But that had been a lifetime ago. Many things had happened since then, and he'd forgotten.)

In the end, it wouldn't be that big of a deal. He would be given a modesty pouch for his junk, but nothing for his butt. Plenty of actors had done more. And it wasn't like it was a *love* scene or anything. Regardless, after the crunches, he'd done some squats, so he was good to go. He'd asked Dee if she needed to test the bounce of his bum, but she'd politely declined.

It would be fine.

At least he wasn't a sunflower.

"You good, man?" Casey asked him after Mason had stalked (ha!) away.

Josy sighed. "Yeah. Naked is naked, right? I'm naked all the time under my clothes. I was *born* naked."

"I've seen more of you than I care to think about, if it makes you feel any better."

"That's not my fault. You know how I get when I'm really, really high."

"You don't like clothes."

"I don't like clothes," he agreed. "Except for socks. Usually the ones with cows on them. I don't know why."

"Which is an image burned forever into my brain."

He bumped Casey's shoulder. "Thanks, dude."

"For what?"

"Letting me be filmed naked in your bed-and-breakfast."

"You know what? I honestly thought I'd hear that sentence from you sooner or later. No big deal, man."

"For real?"

Casey shrugged. "Call it a feeling, I guess. Intuition."

"Like mystical shit?"

"Maybe. Or maybe I just figured you'd be naked at one point in my bed-and-breakfast."

"Dude," Josy breathed. "It's like you're psychic."

"Lottie sees auras," Casey said thoughtfully. "Maybe knowing you'd be naked is my gift."

"Respect."

They fist-bumped. It was awesome having a best friend with superpowers.

The bathroom they were going to use was on the bottom floor. It was the biggest one in the house, given that they'd need room for the gaffer, the Steadicam operator, and, of course, the director.

Which... okay. He didn't know *why*, exactly, he was so fixated on the notion of Quincy seeing him in the buff. They were friends now. It was well known that if you were friends with Josy, at some point you would see him naked. Casey could attest to that. And maybe Quincy didn't know that about Josy yet, but it was bound to happen at some point, right?

He wasn't panicking.

He *wasn't*.

He grabbed Casey by the hand and tugged him out of the hallway and into an empty bedroom, then shut the door behind him. Once he was sure they were alone, he immediately untied the robe and dropped it to the floor. "Okay," he said seriously, "do I have blemishes? Dee spent a lot of time with me in makeup making sure I didn't have blemishes. *Butt* blemishes."

Casey choked. "Dude!"

Okay, maybe he was panicking a little. He looked down. The flesh underpants were… not covering very much. He had trimmed the night before, because the only bushes he wanted in the film were the ones that lined the sides of the house. But his stomach was flat, and he had sparse hair on his torso, and while he wasn't ripped, he was… skinny. Like, really skinny. "Oh my god," he mumbled. "Why didn't I work out more?"

"That underwear covers nothing!"

"I know, right? Well, it covers my dick, but that's about it. Why? Is it bad? Are there blemishes?"

Casey squeezed his eyes shut. "Just because I've seen you naked before doesn't mean I wanted to again!"

"But I need your help! You have to look up online how I can gain ten pounds of muscle in the next five minutes. Why did you never tell me I have chicken legs? Am I a twink? I can't be a twink. It's not even ironic!"

"You're not a twink," Casey said, opening one eye. "Twinks don't have beards or body hair."

Josy moaned. "It's so hard being queer. If you're not one thing, then you have to try and be another. Why do we have to fit in with stupid labels? It's ridiculous."

"You don't have blemishes."

"You're not even looking! Here. Wait. Hold on. You need to look at my butt." He dropped the underpants around his ankles and shuffled around awkwardly. He looked back at Casey over his shoulder. "Does it look all right?"

"It looks *fine*."

"Your eyes are closed again!"

Casey opened his eyes. He looked at Josy's butt for a split second before looking away. "It's fine. Your butt is blemish-free. And why the hell do you need butt makeup in the *shower*?"

"I don't know, man. Acting is weird. Dee wouldn't tell me if my butt was perky enough." He jumped up and down. "Did it bounce?" He jumped again.

"I can't believe this is my power," Casey moaned. "I predicted this. Lottie can see auras, and some people can light fires with their minds. I get to know when you'll be naked."

"Josy, we're ready for y—meep!"

It was about this time that Josy realized that the hinges on the doors of Baked-Inn & Eggs absolutely did not need to be lubricated, because they opened with nary a squeak. In fact, the *only* squeak came from Quincy Moore as he walked in to see Josy standing with his underpants around his ankles, jumping up and down so the owner of the B and B could make sure there was proper lift and fall with his buttocks.

"Um," Josy said. "It's not what it looks like? We're checking for blemishes and perkiness."

Quincy's face was bright red, and his mouth was hanging open.

Belatedly, Josy realized his junk was swinging free while he faced Quincy. He covered himself with his hands, which, unfortunately, were cold.

He was having a very strange morning.

Quincy averted his gaze toward the ceiling, swallowing thickly. "That's… um. You're… wow. Just… I don't."

And then, just because it needed to be worse, Dee came up behind Quincy, asking what the holdup was, only to see a room filled with three men, one of whom was covering his penis with cold hands. "Huh," she said, brow furrowing. "You have big hands. I've never realized that until now."

"Thank you," Josy said, because when a dyke complimented you, it was polite to acknowledge it. He had learned that his second day in Los Angeles.

"What are we looking at?" another voice said before the whir of an electronic wheelchair grew louder.

"Josy's naked," Dee said.

"What? Already? Let me in. I am the producer and must make sure he is—oh *my*." Roger grinned as he tilted his head around his grandson. "Making this film was one of my better ideas."

"Hi, Roger," Josy said, waving at him until he realized that made things worse.

Roger winked at him before turning his wheelchair around. "Carry on!" he called out as he rode away. "I respect your autonomy!"

"Just—get your asses out there," Dee said. "And Josy, put yours away until we actually need it." She followed Roger, muttering under her breath about actors and their processes.

"Oh, look at the time," Casey said, though he wasn't wearing a watch and there wasn't a single clock in the room. "I have someone new starting the front desk when this is over, and I need to train them on the reservation program. Josy, you look fine, man. No blemishes whatsoever." He patted Quincy on the shoulder as he left the room.

"Thanks!" Josy shouted after him, relieved.

Only Quincy and Josy remained.

Quincy was still staring at the ceiling. Josy looked up, but it appeared to be just a normal ceiling, so he wasn't quite sure what Quincy was staring at. "I was nervous," he said. "But I feel better now."

"That's... good?"

"Yep!"

Josy dropped his hands and bent over to pick up his underpants. Once they were snug in their proper place, he realized he had nothing to be worried about. He was an *actor*. This was *acting*.

"I'm good," he announced grandly. "Let's do this thing!"

Quincy all but ran from the room.

He must have been excited too.

WHEN PEOPLE shower in real life, it's to wash away the grime of sleep or of a long day. Sometimes they just stand in the warm water, letting it work out the knots in their muscles.

When people shower in the movies, it lasts only seconds, water sluicing down their bodies, steam curling up as the camera focuses on their backs and shoulders.

But when people shower while *making* a movie, it sucks.

Because it goes on *forever*.

"Shit," the gaffer muttered in the second hour. "We need to fix the lighting again."

"Cut!"

Josy was wet. *Still*. And while the water was still warm, he was positive he never wanted to take a shower again for the rest of his life.

Someone reached in and turned off the water.

The makeup artist came back in and started touching him up.

The modesty pouch was uncomfortable. It made him look like a wannabe exotic dancer.

His nipples were hard.

His beard felt droopy.

"Acting," he muttered to himself. "I am acting."

"Let's do it again," Roger said gleefully.

Quincy was watching the playback on a camera. "Uh, Josy?"

"Yeah?"

"Maybe... um. Maybe this time, you could. Uh. Like. Put your arm up on the shower wall. Facing away from us. And just... stand there."

Josy nodded because he could take direction. "I can do that. Should I flex any part of myself?"

"No! No. Absolutely not necessary. It's... nope. Don't need any flexing."

"All right," the gaffer said. "That should hold for now. You want to go again?"

Quincy nodded.

The makeup artist disappeared.

The water was turned back on.

"Remember," Quincy said as Josy turned around, putting his arm up against the tile. "Dante went back home. Your father, who you don't know anymore, is dying. You think he's lying about all the things he's told you. It's heavy. It's weighing on you. You're angry and sad."

"The sad mads in the shower," Josy said. "Got it."

It only took another hour.

LIAM EAGLETON was hurting. Everything was in shambles. John—because he couldn't bring himself to call him Dad—was frail. Dante was gone, and they'd left things so uncertain. Liam loved him, but he didn't know how to give him what he needed. He didn't even know what he was doing with his own life. What he was doing *here*.

He sighed, shaking the water from his hair and beard.

He was about to reach for the shampoo when he heard a noise.

He paused.

Silence.

It was probably nothing.

Then the noise came again.

It sounded like a giggle.

And in the far reaches of Liam's mind, there was a pulse of familiarity, like he *knew* that sound.

He turned off the water and reached for the towel. He rubbed it over his face and chest before wrapping it around his waist. He stepped out of the shower, dripping onto the bath mat under his feet. "Hello?" he said, voice rough with the pain and regret of a life in shambles. "Who's there?" He didn't know who it could be. His father was asleep upstairs, drugged to the gills. His nurse was reading quietly at his bedside last he checked. There was no one else in the house.

He took a step toward the door when the laughter came again.

He hesitated, nipples pebbled, the muscles in his chest flexing attractively.

The bathroom door was cracked slightly, enough to let out the steam from the shower. He peered through the crack and—

A yellow face stared back at him.

He yelled as he stumbled back, almost slipping on the floor.

Laughter trailed through the hallway as footsteps ran away from the bathroom.

Liam tightened the towel around his waist before throwing open the door. "Who's there?" he growled.

There was a flash of green and yellow near the sunlit window.

Someone was in the house.

He ran after them.

His feet smacked against the wooden floors as he followed the figure moving in his father's home, the same home he'd grown up in and left behind when he thought he was destined for bigger and better things. He was chasing after something, an unknown entity, but he was *also* chasing after a past he could never take back and a life he never wanted.

He heard quick footsteps in the kitchen, and the back door was flung open, rattling in its frame. He ran to the kitchen, where he and his father had made johnnycakes and good dreams, to see the door swinging on its hinges. Whoever had been in the house had gone to the backyard.

To where the property led to the forest. The forest that held a secret world his father believed was real.

But it *wasn't.*

It *couldn't* be.

He burst out into the cold sunlight, towel slipping suggestively around his hips. He was about to jump down from the porch into the grass when he saw something that shouldn't have been possible.

There, standing at the edge of the forest, was a gigantic sunflower.

And he recognized it.

It couldn't be, right?

It just couldn't.

"Boris Biggles," he breathed.

The sunflower waved forlornly at him, and—

"Drop the towel!" Margo Montana shouted. "Show me what you're working with!"

"Cut! What in the actual *fuck*—"

Josy blinked as he looked over to the side of the house.

A crowd had once again gathered at Baked-Inn & Eggs.

He waved at them.

Margo Montana, Mrs. Von Patterson, and Mrs. Havisham waved back.

They fled with the rest of the crowd as Dee started to walk toward them.

"Take it back," Quincy said with a sigh. "Let's try this again from the kitchen."

JOSY SPENT the rest of the day naked. He was tagged in twelve different photographs on Instagram, most of them blurry and taken from far away. But he was happy to see he appeared blemish-free, and that in one of them, he looked like he was posing for a luxury towel campaign.

He re-grammed a few of them. His followers seemed to like them well enough.

Chapter 12

"—and that's how I got over my fear of being naked in front of large crowd," Josy said. He took a hit off the spliff Casey had handed him as soon as he walked in the door. He held in the smoke for as long as he could before blowing out semirespectable rings.

"I didn't ask you about any of that," Gustavo muttered. "I only asked why you were wearing sandals with socks and thinking that was okay when you stepped into my home."

"Oh," Josy said, looking down. "I like it when I can see my toes wiggle. See?" He wiggled his toes. "That's the good stuff."

Casey snorted as he stood in front of the stove, stirring a pot of noodles. "That was a neat story, Josy."

"Thank you. But don't worry. I'll leave the book stuff to you and Quincy."

"That's nice of you."

His phone beeped. He frowned as he pulled it out of his pocket and swiped away the notifications.

"Someone's popular. That's been going off since you got here."

"Yeah," Josy said, muting his phone and putting it back in his pocket. "I posted a selfie of me and Quincy from the set. One of his followers found it and shared it, and now they're going nuts. I don't know why."

"Fans, dude. They love fiercely."

Gustavo was setting the table in the tiny kitchen. Josy had been over to their house a few times for dinner since he'd arrived in Abby. They told him he was welcome whenever he liked (well, Casey told him that; Gustavo was mostly silent in his invitation), but he didn't want to overdo it. They hadn't been living together long. When Casey had moved to Abby, he'd taken over Lottie's Lattes while Lottie did some traveling, but she quickly decided the world was too big. Then Casey purchased the B and B with the idea of renovating it. He was going to live there, but Gustavo told him he would die of asbestos and he might as well just move in with Gustavo.

Josy remembered the phone call he'd gotten that night, and it'd made his heart ache sweetly at the joy in his friend's voice. Gustavo had sounded less joyed, but not by much.

Josy had only been in Gustavo's home once before Casey had moved in. It had been neat and tidy with everything in its place, just the way Gustavo liked it. And while those things were still there, the house had become warmer. Bits and pieces of Gustavo and Casey were scattered all throughout the house. Their lives were melding together, and Josy couldn't be happier for them. His favorite thing was the framed picture of Gustavo and Casey standing in front of the B and B holding a SOLD! sign that hung on the wall in the living room. Casey was grinning wildly at the camera. Gustavo wasn't exactly smiling, but the look of awe on his face as he stared at Casey was just as good.

They completed each other.

And so, even though he could be over every night if he wanted, he thought they needed their space. They were still growing with each other, and while he liked witnessing it, he didn't want to overstay his welcome.

(Casey told him that Gustavo often complained about having more people in their house, but also said that he got grumpy when he heard Josy wasn't coming over.)

He watched as Gustavo set out one place setting, and then another, and then another…

…and then another.

Josy frowned.

He counted the people in the room. Three of them. Unless Harry S. Truman counted, but Gustavo didn't let him eat at the table.

Which meant—

"Who else is coming?" he asked.

The doorbell rang.

"Why don't you get that," Casey said as he poured the noodles into a strainer in the sink. "It's probably for you, anyway."

That sounded awfully close to being a surprise. It could be anyone. It could be an IRS agent saying Josy was going to be audited. It could be a doctor saying that Josy had whooping cough, though he couldn't remember the last time he'd actually *been* to the doctor. And he wasn't coughing. Or it could be Steven Spielberg, ready to make that war movie with Josy in the lead along with his trusty dog sidekick who would get injured in battle, causing Josy to sob over his body. In the end the dog would live, and they would move to the country to heal.

It wasn't Steven Spielberg.

It was someone better.

"Quincy!"

Quincy stood awkwardly on the porch, looking nervous. His ears were pink from the cold, and he was carrying a bottle of wine. "Uh, hi?"

"You're here," Josy breathed reverently. "At the house. Whoa."

"I was invited." He rubbed the back of his neck. "Unless you don't want me—"

"Are you kidding? This is the best day *ever*. Dude! Why didn't you tell me you were coming? We could have walked together! I could have shown you things. Like… buildings. Ignore me, I'm a little high. I wouldn't have if I knew you were coming. Which you did. Because you're here."

Quincy shrugged as he looked down at his feet. "I wasn't sure I was going to. Casey invited me, but he said it was up to me. It—ah, it took me a bit to work up the courage. I'm not very good at being in places I don't know."

"Don't worry about that," Josy reassured him. "This isn't just a place. It's one of the *best* places. And now that you're here, it's even better."

"Oh. That's… nice. Thank you. I brought wine." He thrust the bottle into Josy's hand. "I don't know how good it is. The We Three Queens saw me on the street when I was walking over here and insisted I bring it. I don't even know where they got it from. The label has a lizard on it. That can't be good."

"It's best not to ask. One time Bernice sent me socks she'd knitted in the mail. Somehow she knew one of my socks had lost its mate at the laundromat, and I was feeling bummed. I think they can read minds, but I don't know how to test it." Josy blanched. "Oh man, I'm so sorry. It's the weed talking. I'm being rude to a guest. May I take your coat?"

"I'm… not wearing a coat?"

He wasn't. He was wearing a gray sweater over jeans. He looked awesome. "Right," Josy said hastily. "I don't do the hosting thing very often. I must be out of practice."

Quincy shuffled his feet.

Josy grinned at him.

Quincy asked, "Can I come in, or…?"

"Yes! Yes. Come in. My casa is su casa. It's not my casa, but that's what people say, right?" Josy stepped back, giving Quincy room to enter. He wished Quincy *was* wearing a coat so he could take it and hang it up. That felt weirdly like an adult thing to do. He didn't know why he was so nervous. He bit his bottom lip to keep from blurting out something that would probably be embarrassing.

"Hey, Quincy," Casey said, coming out of the kitchen. "Glad you could make it."

"He brought wine," Josy blurted. "It has a *lizard* on it. Lizards can regrow their tails after losing them, so it's probably moderately expensive. Isn't that so cool?"

Casey stared at him for a moment before recovering. "The coolest." He took the wine from Josy, staring down at the label. "Oh, wow. Great, man. This will go really well with dinner. Good choice."

"The We Three Queens gave it to him," Josy said, fingers itching to take *someone's coat for fuck's sake*.

"Of course they did," Gustavo muttered. "They probably knew exactly what we were making."

A chittering noise came from their feet, and they all looked down to see an albino ferret twist its way around Gustavo's feet.

"What is *that*?" Quincy asked.

"That's Harry S. Truman," Gustavo said as the ferret started gnawing on his shoelaces. "He shouldn't be here. I grounded him this afternoon, as he chewed on a display at work like some sort of feral heathen."

Harry S. Truman squeaked at Gustavo.

"I don't care if they made another Sharknado movie, you can't just destroy something that doesn't belong to you. Go to your bed."

"He's the ferret with merit," Casey said. "Part of Gus's mystique."

Gustavo scowled at him. "I told you not to describe me as having mystique. It makes me sound like a fortune-teller or a Smurflike comic book villain, neither of which I am." He looked at Quincy. "Since you're an author, you must like encyclopedias. I have a collection to show you. Follow me."

Quincy did. He glanced back at Josy, who was still in a state of shock that Quincy was *here*, of all places. He was a famous writer who was directing what was sure to be a blockbuster film, and he chose to have dinner at the Tiberius house.

"You're not a vegetarian or a vegan, are you?" Casey asked before they went into the living room. "I didn't think to ask. If you are, that's cool. You just won't like any of the food I made. I tried being a vegetarian once because I'm woke, but man, I love hamburgers like you wouldn't believe. I feel bad about the cows, but not enough to avoid eating them."

"No," Quincy said. "I'm not a vegetarian or a vegan."

"Good," Gustavo said. "They can't be trusted. Please don't touch my encyclopedias. They're in alphabetical order, and even though it didn't take me long to put them that way, I didn't allot time this evening for corrections."

Casey grinned after them before he turned back toward Josy. He jerked his head toward the kitchen. Josy followed closely behind him.

"Why didn't you tell me he was coming?" Josy demanded the moment they were out of earshot. "I would have—okay, I don't know what I would have done exactly, but I would have done something. Maybe not smoke or whatever."

"I didn't know if he would," Casey said as he put the wine on the counter. "I floated the invite, told him no pressure." He started digging through a drawer near the sink. "That's okay, right?"

"Yeah. Absolutely. I just… it would have been nice to walk with him, you know?"

Casey pulled a wine opener from the drawer. "You get to walk back with him, if that helps."

Josy's eyes widened. "Holy crap. You're right. I do."

"You really like him, huh?"

"Oh, he's so cool," Josy said. "He likes books, and I now know two people who write them. He's a director, and I like being directed. He lets the We Three Queens give him street wine, and I have knitted socks. We have, like, so much in common."

"That's rad, man. He seems like an okay dude. If you like him, then I know I will too."

"I do," Josy said. "I thought I messed up with the whole I-don't-want-to-date-you-but-please-be-my-friend thing, but then Serge's kismet happened, and now I'm in Quincy's movie and we're friends." He hesitated. "Do you think he likes me? You know? Like *that*? Like a friend?"

"Oh yeah," Casey said easily. "It's obvious."

Josy was relieved to hear it. Casey didn't bullshit him. "Really?"

"Sure, man. Even if I couldn't see it with my own eyes, I'd still believe it because it's you."

"But I'm not good at it."

"Nah. You're actually the best. You just don't know it like I do. It's like—okay. So turtles, right?"

"Right."

"They exist."

Casey was so smart. "Yes."

"And they move really slow."

"So slow," Josy agreed.

"But they don't know that. To them, that's their normal speed, and everyone else moves superfast."

"That must be really weird."

"Totally. But the point is you're a turtle. You don't know any different because you don't need to. It's just who you are. You do things your own way. You take your time. And turtles have their homes already around them, so anyone who goes near them is already in their home. It's how I feel about you. I go near you, and I feel like I'm home."

"Dude," Josy breathed.

Casey shrugged. "It's true."

"Dude," Josy demanded. "That was like poetry!"

"I'm a writer, man. Stuff like that is in my head all the time."

"I can't even begin to imagine that. Like, it must be so cool being able to open your mouth and spit out greatness."

"Gimme some skin."

"Gladly." He slapped Casey's palm. Before he could pull away, Casey wrapped his fingers around his wrist. Josy liked holding hands, so this was a pretty good start to dinner.

"And if you ever decide to move in a certain direction, that's okay too. You know that, right?"

Josy cocked his head. "What do you mean?"

"If you found another turtle who you wanted to move slow with."

"My apartment back in LA doesn't let me have pets. I mean, the woman next door has, like, twelve cats, but no one calls the front office because we're pretty sure she's also a witch and will hex us."

Casey squeezed his hand before letting go. "Sure, man. Quincy seems like he's a good guy."

"He is," Josy said. "You could tell he was worried about me being naked in front of him all day by how much he kept leaving the room."

"Sounds like a righteous dude. Wanna pop the cork?"

Josy didn't think he'd ever been to such a mature dinner party. "Absolutely. I have no idea how to do it. Is it going to explode and shoot out like it's New Year's Eve? Should I do it outside? I don't want Gustavo to yell at me for breaking something again."

"I think that's just champagne."

"Oh. You sure?"

"Mostly."

It didn't explode. Casey knew so much.

THEY SAT down at the table, just four adults in the prime of their lives. Casey sat next to Gustavo, which meant Josy and Quincy would be sitting together on the other side of the table. It almost felt like a double date, or at least what Josy thought a double date would be like. He'd never actually been on one. And yeah, Gustavo and Casey were dating, but Josy and Quincy weren't. But this could be a *friend*-date. Josy had been on many of those in his lifetime.

Casey had made fettuccini Alfredo with chicken, and though Josy was sure it probably wasn't the best for his diet, he figured if the director of the film didn't have a problem with it, then he didn't either.

Quincy reached up to serve himself some salad but stopped when Gustavo shook his head. "Oh, I'm sorry. Are we saying grace or something?"

Gustavo sighed irritably. "No. We don't pray here. Organized religion is a detriment to humanity. Pastor Tommy said that being given false hope is like having a life vest made of cement, then getting tossed into the ocean."

"Pastor Tommy?"

"My dad. He's dead. And no, he wasn't a pastor. That was just what everyone called him."

"Oh. I'm sorry?"

"For what?"

"Him dying."

Gustavo frowned. "It was cancer, not you. So you don't have to apologize. We can't eat yet because they have to take pictures. You wouldn't understand because you're not a hipster." Gustavo squinted at him. "You're not a hipster, right?"

"I don't think so?"

Gustavo nodded. "Good answer. If you were, you would know. Anytime we make dinner, or go out, or are near food that isn't cereal or toast, they have to post it on Instabook."

Josy barely heard what they were talking about. He was busy taking a photo of the food Casey had made. He considered not using a filter, but then he realized it'd been a while since he'd used Mayfield, and it made the noodles look cool. He was generous with his hashtags and didn't give much thought on the last one, hashtag friend-date with the Q-Man.

Annnnd posted.

He put his phone away just as Casey did the same.

"Now we can eat," Gustavo told a baffled Quincy. "I made the salad. And by made it, I mean I opened the bag and poured it into the bowl. I hope you enjoy it."

IT WAS going well. Quincy was eating the food. He was a little quiet, but Josy knew that was often the case, so he wasn't too worried. The wine was gross, but then all wine was. However, because this was a mature and adult dinner party, Josy sipped it down, barely grimacing. He was quite proud of himself.

"How's the movie going?" Casey asked as Josy considered a second helping of noodles. He didn't have another nude scene until his love scene with Mason (gross), which was still a couple weeks away. He would probably need to do a thousand crunches to make up for all the carbs, but he was feeling fine. Maybe just a little bit more. "Seems like everything is going good. Aside from seeing Josy's junk today."

Gustavo's brow furrowed. "I'm sorry, what now?"

"I had to be naked today," Josy explained. He had thirteen noodles and a piece of chicken on his plate. That should be okay. "In the shower. Then I wore a towel and chased after Mason, who was in his sunflower makeup." That would never not bring him joy.

Gustavo's brow furrowed even more. "What kind of movie was this again?"

Quincy coughed as he wiped his mouth with a cloth napkin. Josy didn't know Gustavo was so fancy that he had cloth napkins. "It's a...

fantasy movie? About, um, imaginary friends coming to life? And there's… Josy in the shower?"

"And happy queers," Josy said. "Because Quincy wants queer people to be happy instead of sad or dead."

"In movies," Quincy said quickly. Then, "And also in real life too."

"Why did you have to see Josy naked?" Gustavo asked Casey.

Casey shrugged. "To make sure everything looked right, I guess."

"I was nervous," Josy said. "I needed him to tell me I looked okay."

Gustavo pointed his fork at Josy. "I don't ever want to see you naked."

"But what if I—"

"No."

"There could be a time when—"

"*No.*"

Josy scowled. "I would do it for you."

"I know. And that's a problem." Gustavo set down his fork and looked at Quincy. "Do you know Michael Bay?"

"Say no," Josy whispered. "Even if you do and you think he's a nice person, say no."

"No," Quincy said without hesitation.

Gustavo sat back in his chair. "Good. You can stay at the table."

"Thank you?"

"S'cool, man," Casey said. "Making happy queers. Representation, you know? It's important."

Quincy glanced nervously at Josy, who nodded in return. "Yeah, I… I just wanted to make something different. You know, that you don't normally get to see?"

"So you made gay sunflowers," Gustavo said.

Quincy shook his head. "It's not just—it's not *about* the sunflowers. It's a coming-of-age fantasy about a man who has lost his way and tries to reconnect with his father before he dies."

"It's gay *Big Fish*," Josy said.

"It's not gay *Big Fish!*"

"It sounds exactly like gay *Big Fish*," Gustavo said. "*Big Fish* was shut out of the seventy-sixth Academy Awards, aside from a nomination for Best Musical Score for Danny Elfman."

"Gustavo knows all the Oscars," Casey said fondly. "I tricked him into telling me he loved me by using that against him. It was awesome."

"*That*," Quincy said, sounding more fired up than Josy had ever heard him. "See? *That's* what I want to show. You guys are happy. I want other people to see that."

"Yeah," Gustavo said flatly. "I've never been happier. Sometimes I want to sing about it."

"Really?" Josy asked.

"No. Of course not. What the hell."

"I get it, man," Casey said, taking Gustavo's hand in his. "I tried to get more gay stuff in my movie, but the studio bigwigs didn't like it. Said since it was marketed toward teenagers, they wouldn't get it. Dumbest thing I've ever heard."

Quincy looked startled. "Your movie?"

"Hmm? Yeah. The one based on my first book. *The Hungering Blood Moon*."

"That was *you*? But that movie was so—adequate. It was very adequate." He paled. "I meant good. It was—"

Casey laughed. "It's all right, man. It was awful. I didn't have anything to do with it aside from it being off my book. The screenwriter butchered it. But I got a lot of money from it, and they're going to film the sequel next year. Fans seemed to like it, and that's the important thing. Gives me more incentive to finish the last book, especially since you helped me with my writer's block."

"I didn't even do anything," Quincy said faintly.

"Sure, man. If you say so. Gustavo's helping me too. He's watched the movie eight times—"

Gustavo looked offended. "I have *not*. Why on earth would I subject myself to that drivel? Oh my god."

Casey rolled his eyes. "He doesn't like it when I find out he's doing something super cool."

"Yes," Gustavo said. "Because *super cool* is something I aspire to be on a daily basis. And even if I've watched it repeatedly, it's only because it's a study on what not to do when adapting a literary work."

Josy's heart squeezed sweetly at the look Casey gave him. "Aw, man. Literary? You're so Vanilla Ice, you don't even know."

"Whatever," Gus mumbled. "I have notes on it I'll share with you later."

"I get what you're doing, man," Casey said to Quincy. "And I'm glad Josy's part of it. Happy queers are the best kind of queers."

Quincy seemed a little overwhelmed. "Yes, well, I'm… trying. And it's not always easy for me. I don't—being in charge of something like this makes me nervous. And I don't do well with being nervous. Or being in charge. Or being in public. Or having dinner at a stranger's house."

Casey eyed him up and down. "You seem to be doing okay to me."

"Even *better* than okay," Josy said. "You're, like, the best director I've ever worked with. And you're eating dinner like a champ. Rock on."

Quincy didn't look like he believed him, but that was okay. Josy was a turtle. Slow and steady gave first-time directors confidence, or however that saying went.

"Why are you nervous?" Gustavo asked.

Quincy looked down at the table. "I'm not used to—I don't…." He curled his hands into fists.

Gustavo frowned. "I didn't mean to make you uncomfortable. I sometimes do that without meaning to."

Casey glanced at Gustavo before turning back to Quincy. "Hey, man. It's okay. No biggie. You don't have to say anything you don't want to."

"They're good people," Josy whispered to him. "If you do. They're my friends. Just like you are."

Quincy looked at him, a strange expression on his face.

Josy smiled like he expected a turtle would.

It seemed to work. Quincy took a deep breath and let it out slowly. When he spoke, his voice was quiet. "I'm not very good at this kind of thing. I like writing, but writing is solitary. Some people think it's lonely, but it's not for me. And when I wrote the script, I didn't even think about wanting to direct it. But my grandad said it would be good for me and told me that he would help finance it and stuff if I did."

"Roger Fuller," Gustavo said.

"Yeah."

"He came to my store. I showed him all the movies of his I had for rent. He said it delighted him. I told him I wasn't there to delight him as I was running a business, but he just laughed at me."

Quincy sighed. "Sounds like him."

"You have anxiety."

Casey squeezed Gustavo's hand. "Hey, Gus. Maybe it's none of our business—"

"It's okay," Quincy said. Josy bumped their shoulders together. "Yes. I guess that's one way to put it. It was… worse when I was a kid.

Crippling, in fact. Coupled with depression, and I was probably more of a mess than I was worth. It took a long time for me to get to a place that was functional. Medication helped. Therapy did too. But it's not a cure-all. Still have good days and bad days."

"Your parents didn't help?" Gustavo asked.

"No."

Gustavo didn't push. "So you have anxiety and are sad. That sounds like my entire existence."

"He's not trivializing anything," Casey said quickly. "It's just how he—"

"I know," Quincy said. "He's blunt. That's okay." He glanced at Gustavo. "Are you…?"

Gustavo fiddled with a fork. "Am I what?"

Quincy looked uncomfortable. "Never mind. It's not—"

"Normal? No. I tried that, but it didn't work out."

"I dunno, man," Casey said. "Seems like it worked out okay in the end to me."

"Don't order the Internet," Gustavo told Quincy. "It makes life complicated, and then you end up wearing Hawaiian shirts for reasons you don't want to explain."

It was then everyone decided to ignore the Hawaiian shirt Gustavo was wearing. It was blue with white flowers. It looked nice.

"I'll keep that in mind," Quincy said diplomatically. Josy was proud of him.

"I don't have parents," Gustavo said. "Casey said I'm Orphan Gussy, but that's ridiculous, and I told him never to say that again."

"I said it twelve more times," Casey said, sounding gleeful.

"And his parents are jerks who don't deserve him. Same with Josy. He's an actor, and they didn't like it. But as long as he doesn't agree to be in a film about robots destroying yet another city without repercussions for the loss of life or property damage, he should do what he wants. No one should be able to tell him otherwise. Except for the robot thing. That's nonnegotiable."

"Gustavo loves me," Josy told Casey. "He's like the best friend and father I always wanted."

"Oh my god," Gustavo muttered. "I take it back. What the hell." He shook his head. "What I'm trying to say is that life sucks, and people say and do mean stuff because their own lives are awful. Maybe it's hard to make movies about happy queers or eat dinner, but do it for you and no one else." He stood abruptly. "I'm going to clear some dishes now."

And he did just that, stacking plates and silverware before heading toward the kitchen.

"Is he okay?" Quincy asked.

"Yeah, man," Casey said. "He's fine. Sometimes he needs some space. No big deal."

Quincy hesitated. Then, "Is he autistic? Or…?"

"Does it matter?" Casey asked, a challenge in his voice.

"No," Quincy said. "I'm sorry. That's none of my business. I shouldn't have asked. It isn't my place."

Casey's face softened. "It's fine. He's just… Gus, you know? Labels aren't a thing for him. And that's okay. He doesn't need to be defined. He knows who he is, and so do I. That's all that matters. It doesn't mean it's the same for everyone else, and I'm not trying to take away from anyone who is autistic. For Gus, everything else is just…." He shrugged as he waved dismissively. "Extraneous."

"He's pretty great."

Casey grinned. "He is, isn't he? Now, who wants to get high?"

QUINCY DIDN'T.

Josy did, but he didn't want to make his friend uncomfortable. Quincy told him it didn't matter, and Gustavo said he wasn't going to smoke. And smoking by yourself was never a good idea, and Josy couldn't do that to Casey.

Besides, Josy was keyed up from what had turned out to be a most excellent mature dinner event and knew he'd need some help to get to sleep. They were only working a half day tomorrow, but he still needed to get at least six hours in.

Josy and Casey passed the joint back and forth until the roach singed the tips of his fingers. It was sweet and mellow, and Josy felt good.

"I wish you had a jacket," Josy told Quincy as they stood near the door, getting ready to leave.

Quincy frowned. "Why? It's cold, but it's not too bad."

Josy shook his head. "No, so I could help you put it on. It's what friends do at the end of mature evenings."

"Oh. Um. Sorry?"

Gustavo was glancing back and forth between the two of them, his brow furrowed. "Do you guys like each—"

"Each of the courses we ate for dinner," Casey said cheerfully. "I mean, salad and noodles and cookies. That's three."

"It was great," Quincy said. "Thank you for inviting me."

"You can come back," Gustavo said. "At some point in the future. I'll let you know when. Or Casey will."

"Thank you."

Casey stepped forward and hugged Josy. "Good to have you, man. I'll see you tomorrow, okay?"

Josy patted Casey's back before letting go.

"No," Gustavo said.

"But—"

"No."

Josy sighed. "Fine. Our secret handshake?"

"We don't have a secret handshake," Gustavo said, arms across his chest. "What the hell, does that even *sound* like something I would do?"

"You made me practice it with you because you said you wanted to get it right," Casey said.

"Oh my god. I did *not*."

"My bad," Casey said, winking at Josy. "Must have been some other Grumpy Gus that I know."

"Whatever. I have to go make sure Harry S. Truman knows I forgive him." He turned and walked down the hall toward the bedroom.

Josy and Quincy barely made it off the porch before the door opened behind them. Gustavo came back out, and as Josy turned around, he held up his hand. "Yes!" Josy crowed. "Gustavo with the fake out."

They did their secret handshake. It was flawless.

Gustavo scowled at him as they finished. "I will never do that again. Please don't loiter on my porch." He slammed the door shut behind him, and a second later, the porch light switched off, leaving them in semidarkness.

And with that, the mature adult dinner party came to an end.

IT WAS a beautiful night to be walking outside while slightly stoned. Sure, it was cold, and maybe only one of them was slightly stoned, but still. The stars were out, and Abby's streetlights were lit. Josy thought it was perfect. Since he and Quincy were friends, Josy felt like they could talk about anything. He thought about what to say to get the conversation going.

"Do you think there are bears in the woods?" Josy asked.

Quincy's eyes widened. "What? I don't know. Do they have bears here?"

"Maybe. I mean, we're in the mountains. Bears live in mountains." Josy frowned. "Did you know they make bear Mace in case you're attacked by a bear? I don't have any, so if we are approached by a bear, you need to speak calmly and back away slowly. Don't run, because they'll chase you and then maul you."

"I don't want to get mauled!"

"You won't," Josy said seriously. "You're with me. I know what to do if we encounter one. I saw it on *National Geographic*. Did you know there's a country called Zimbabwe?"

"What does that have to do with bears?"

Josy shrugged. "I don't know. I don't think they have bears there. That's Lottie's Lattes. She's the one that brings craft services to the movie set. And that's Gustavo's video store. And that's pretty much all I know about Abby."

"Do you hear yourself talking?" Quincy asked him.

"No? Why? Can you not hear me either?" He wasn't *that* stoned that he was only thinking he was talking out loud, right? He hated when that happened.

Quincy sighed. "No, it's—never mind."

Josy nodded. For some reason, he couldn't think of anything else he could say to impress his friend. Maybe this was why he had so few to begin with. Finally he decided on, "Did you have a good time tonight?"

Quincy nodded. Their shoulders bumped together. "It was nice of them to include me."

"Yeah, man. I think so too. Casey knows how much I like you. You're so neat, you know?"

Quincy stared at him. "You really mean that, don't you."

"Yes? I wouldn't say it if I didn't believe it. What's the point of saying something you don't mean?"

"Right," Quincy said slowly. "What's the point." They passed Lottie's Lattes. The lights were off. Lottie had told him earlier that she had plans with the We Three Queens. They were going to play cards, which Josy thought might be code for something else, like a bank heist or charity work. He couldn't be sure. "Your friends are... they're good."

"Yeah. I think so too."

"They been together a long time?"

"A little while. Over a year. Casey knew right away that Gustavo was someone he wanted to know, and Gustavo was... well. He didn't know what to do about it. But they figured it out. Casey told me he was nervous at the beginning because of the whole ace thing—"

"The what?"

"Ace. Casey is asexual. It means he doesn't really experience sexual attraction."

Quincy was quiet. Then, "So how are they together?"

"What do you mean?"

"They don't...." He flushed as he looked away. "They don't... you know."

Josy blanked for a moment before he got what Quincy was saying. "Have sex? It's okay to say it, man. For someone who wrote about Sasquatch pile driving a frat boy, you're funny when it comes to sex."

"That's not *real*," Quincy snapped. "Gus and Casey are."

"And thank god for that. I don't know what I'd do if they weren't. Especially since I thought they were real this whole time. Talk about a twist."

"I shouldn't have asked."

"Nah, it's okay. Maybe they have sex sometimes. Or maybe they don't. And it's okay either way. You don't need sex to be in love with someone."

"But then how else do you show that you're in love?"

Josy looked up at the sky. The stars were bright. "Because you can look at the person and just know they're someone special. That you would do anything to see them smile. Sex is good for a lot of people, but not for others. And just because they feel that way doesn't mean they don't love like everyone else."

"I'm sorry. I didn't mean—"

"Remember how you weren't going to apologize for things anymore when you didn't need to?"

Quincy didn't respond.

Josy sighed. "You don't need to apologize for asking questions. You didn't know. Now you do. That's how people learn things. You're not being a jerk about it. You're curious. No one should make you feel bad for being curious. You don't know them very well, so maybe you wouldn't ask them. But you know me, and I don't mind. I think we're weird about sex when we don't need to be. It's not taboo to talk about it. Sex is sex is sex, you know?"

"What about you?" Quincy blurted. "Ah—that's not what I—"

"I like it," Josy said, cutting him off before he could get worked up again. "Every now and then. But only with someone I really care about. But even then, it's not a big deal for me. You know what's better?"

"What?"

"Lying on the floor under a Christmas tree with someone and looking up at the lights. Or going to the park and sitting on a blanket and reading comics to each other. Or watching a movie you've seen a billion times before and quoting the lines back and forth. It's that feeling, right? That feeling of knowing you're not alone because the person you're with doesn't want to be anywhere else but where they are."

There was a beat of silence. Then, "I like where I am right now."

Josy grinned. "Me too, dude. Abby's a pretty cool place, right? It's nice to get out of Los Angeles."

"No, I meant—yeah, Josy. Abby's a pretty cool place."

"Can I hold your hand? I mean, we're friends now, right? I like holding hands with my friends. It's okay to say no if you don't want to. I'm fine either way, man."

Quincy gaped at him. Josy thought he was far too precious for this world, and he needed to be protected at all costs. "Uh, yeah. Sure. That's—that's fine. Friends, right?"

"Friends," Josy said happily. He took Quincy's hand in his own, marveling at how well they seemed to fit together. His fingers were a little cold, so Josy squeezed tightly, trying to warm them up.

They held hands the rest of the way back to Baked-Inn & Eggs.

"So, this is me," Josy said, standing in front of the bedroom door. He felt oddly nervous for reasons he didn't quite understand. They were still holding hands, though Josy's palm was a little sweaty now.

Quincy squinted at him. "What?"

Josy nodded toward the door and waited. This almost felt like the end of a date, which was *weird*. Maybe friend dates were like regular dates. "This is my room. So. Good night."

"This is my room too," Quincy said slowly.

"Oh crap. Right. Dude, I totally forgot. It was probably the noodles. I don't eat carbs that much anymore. I think they made me forget." He frowned. "Or maybe it was the spliff. And then the joint. That could be it too." He looked down at their joined hands. Definitely sweaty, but if Quincy wasn't going to say anything, he wasn't either. "So. I guess… we should just… go inside."

"I guess so."

They stared at each other.

Josy coughed.

Quincy cleared his throat.

Then they both turned and tried to walk through the door at the same time. The *problem* with that was both of them side by side were wider than the doorway. And also the door was still closed. The end result was a collision of knees and shoulders against wood. It wasn't the dumbest thing Josy had ever done. (That would always be the time he was so stoned, he called to order Chinese food, only to discover two hours later when said Chinese food hadn't arrived that he'd dialed a box of Goldfish Crackers instead of his phone.)

"Mother*dicker*," he groaned, dropping Quincy's hand to rub his knee. "What the effin *frick*."

And then he heard the strangest sound.

Something he'd never heard before.

Quincy was laughing.

It wasn't the loud, gut-busting guffaw of someone who found something extraordinarily funny. It probably couldn't even be considered *laughter*. It was more of a dry, dusty chuckle of amusement, and Josy was *entranced* by the sound. Quincy was smiling and shaking his head, and he had these little crinkles around his eyes, and Josy wanted to see that expression on his face always.

It was a first for him, feeling that way.

He didn't know what it meant.

But that was okay too.

It was enough. For now.

He thought he woke up in the middle of the night to the glow of a laptop and furious typing on a keyboard, but in the morning, he figured it was just a dream.

Chapter 13

The Stories of My Father (Working Title)
Day 15
Location: The Woods
Scene 18

Liam Eagleton was lost. Metaphorically. Spiritually.
And literally.
He was literally lost in the woods.
He didn't know how long he'd been gone. Time moved weirdly ever since he'd found out that the imaginary friends he'd had in his childhood were real. It'd taken him time to come to terms with the fact that his father's stories were true and not part of some cerebral event that was indicative of a major stroke.
But maybe it was. Maybe he was in a hospital right this very second, attached to the same machines his father was at the house, and he was dreaming all of this.
It was crazy, right?
But what if it wasn't?
Boris Biggles had changed since Liam knew him as a child. Then he'd been rough and somber, the memories of the sunflower family he'd lost in the Great War against the Weeds still fresh in his mind. *That* Boris hadn't given two shits about anything but the pain that burned through him.
The Boris that had shown up to the house was... different. He'd led Liam through the woods, laughing and singing incoherently. It wasn't until Liam had caught up with him—sure he was finally losing it—that he'd realized that Boris wasn't how he'd been all those years before. *This* Boris was wild and overwrought, and had spun a tale of the land Liam's father had spoken of being in trouble.
(Granted, this came after extensive rewrites on the fly. Screenplays evolved. It happened.)

Boris had told Liam that he was needed to save their world. That since he'd forgotten them, forgotten the stories of his father, they were in danger.

And then he'd been reintroduced to Mr. Zucko, the half man, half zebra with a penchant for talking tough and fighting crime as a private investigator.

(Mason Grazer was not happy with this costume. At all.)

Which led to Dill, the gigantic cucumber and fearful fellow who acted as Mr. Zucko's secretary.

(Mason Grazer was, if possible, even less pleased with this costume.)

Which, in turn, led to Liam's current predicament: traveling through the woods with Grady, a lion of a man who had the heart of a king.

Grady, who reminded Liam of Dante.

It brought out very conflicting feelings.

Grady was more tired than Liam ever remembered seeing him as a child. Then he'd been majestic and kingly and would always chase away the loneliness Liam felt when his father was off following his dreams, having left his only son with yet another caregiver.

But Liam wasn't that child anymore.

And he could appreciate Grady in a whole new light.

Even if they were lost in the woods.

They had been tasked by Boris Biggles to find the Three Oracles of the Woods, beings of pure magic who could aid in their quest to claim the forest. It wasn't going very well.

"This is pointless," Grady snarled. "They're *playing* with us. Even now, these woods that have been my home since I could remember are being used against me!" He tilted his head back and roared.

(Granted, it came out like a strangled yell, but Quincy said they'd add sound effects in post.)

"We'll figure it out," Liam said, voice pleading. "You can't keep going on like this, Grady. It's tearing you apart."

Grady's eyes were blazing as he whirled on Liam. "You don't know anything about me, boy. You chose to forget us. You chose to forget *me*."

Liam reached up and ran his hand through Grady's mane, fingers disappearing into the auburn hair. His fangs were bared, brow furrowed as he rumbled angrily in his chest.

Liam's heart was racing. He shouldn't—*couldn't*—be feeling this way. Not about Grady, even if he was so much like Dante.

But the heart wanted what it wanted.

And Liam wanted to kiss the lion man.

He leaned forward and—

"Cut!"

Josy blinked.

Mason groaned as he stepped back, his face contorting underneath heavy makeup. "What was wrong with that one? We were doing *fine*."

The crew started moving around Quincy, who stood off near a tree, frowning down at one of the cameras. They weren't that far from the house, and as a bell rang, Josy could hear people starting to move about and talk.

"It was great," Quincy muttered. "It's just… time to break for lunch. I know how you get when you haven't had your protein powder."

"Whatever," Mason muttered. "I'm going back to the house to warm up. I'm freezing my ass off out here. Someone get me an umbrella!" He stalked off through the trees, a hapless crew member struggling to keep an umbrella over his head.

Mason wasn't wrong; it *was* cold today. And there was a slight drizzle coming down, which made things worse. November in the Oregon mountains wasn't exactly the best time to have an outdoor shoot. But Josy was an artist, and he knew that sometimes one must suffer for their art. Van Gogh had cut off his ear. Beethoven had been an alcoholic. Georgia O'Keefe had seen vaginas everywhere.

Josy could stand a little rain.

The true suffering, of course, came from the fact that today was supposed to be the first time he kissed Mason Grazer.

Mason who was in lion makeup.

Beethoven had nothing on Josiah Erickson.

They'd been at this one scene for two days now. Which, to be fair, wasn't anything new; Quincy was nothing if not a perfectionist. But if it continued on, they were going to get behind schedule. The We Three Queens were ready to play their parts and were supposed to be on set this morning, but after yesterday, that had been delayed. Oh, they were still ready and in their costumes (for the most part), but they'd done nothing but sit around the B and B. Bernice said it was fine because it gave them more time to practice their lines. Bertha agreed. Betty was less impressed.

Quincy was frowning down at his phone. Josy started to go over to him, but Dee intercepted him, leading him toward the house.

"Is he all right?" Josy asked, looking back over his shoulder.

"He's fine," Dee said breezily. "Just director stuff. You know how it is. Stressful. The rewrites aren't helping matters."

"Yeah, about that. I mean, I have no problem with it. Getting new stuff at the last minute is a small price to pay for being in a movie, but what's going on with it? Does he not like his own movie or something?"

Dee snorted as the house came into view. "Maybe someone shouldn't have told him some interesting ideas on what love means. Or what you have to do to actually show love."

Josy frowned. "Who told him that? Is that why he wrote out the sex scene between Liam and Dante? That's cool with me. I wasn't exactly looking forward to having Mason lying on top of me and grunting in my ear. I mean, Mason seemed pissed about it, but he seems pissed about everything."

"You really have no idea, do you?"

"About what?"

Dee shook her head. "Anything. Mason and the Q-Man go way back. They'll be fine."

That caught Josy's attention. "They do? I didn't know that. How far back?" Then a thought that terrified his very soul struck him. "Did they used to bone? Oh man, that is *not* something I wish my brain had made me think." He smacked the side of his head. "Stupid fucking brain."

"Oh Jesus. Of course that's where you went with it. No, Josy. They didn't used to bone." She paused, considering. "At least I don't think they did." She grimaced. "Now I'm thinking about it too. Ugh."

"Do they still have feelings for each other?" Josy demanded. "Did Quincy break Mason's heart and then cast him in the movie to try and win him back? Am I nothing but a pawn in their sick and twisted love game?" He blinked. "Wow. I didn't know I could use those words in that combination. That was like poetry."

"You're a special snowflake, aren't you?"

"My fourth-grade teacher wrote that exact phrase on my report card one semester. So I guess maybe I am."

"Quincy and Mason were never together," Dee said as she pulled him up the steps to the house. She stopped before reaching the door and turned to look at him, that evil smile back on her face. Josy didn't like it. "Would that bother you if they had been?"

Huh. Since he'd only gotten the idea a minute ago, he couldn't be quite sure. "No? Yes. Maybe." He scrunched up his face. "If it did bother me, it'd be because Mason isn't very nice and Quincy could do so much better. But as his friend, I would support him if that was his decision. But if Mason hurt him, it wouldn't matter if he was wearing makeup to look like a lion. I would still give him a piece of my mind. It's not cool to hurt people you care about."

Dee groaned. "I don't get you at all."

"I'm a Rubik's Cube," Josy said honestly. "I'm made up of rainbow colors, but they're all out of order, and you need to spin me around until I start making sense."

"I can't believe that I actually understood that," she muttered. "It's like I got a contact high."

"Hey, man, I haven't smoked in a couple of days. If you're high, it's not because of—"

She pulled him into the house toward a room that she'd commandeered as her space. He barely had a chance to wave at Casey, who sat in the kitchen in front of his laptop. Josy wished Dee wasn't being so vague. He felt like she was trying to tell him something, but he couldn't be sure what. He'd have to think about it.

"Sit," she ordered, shoving him into a chair. "I'll bring you a sandwich. If you move, I'll break your kneecaps."

"That was a very effective threat," he told her. "I actually believe you would do that."

"I would too," another voice said. "You can tell she's serious by the fire in her eyes."

Dee grunted and left the room, shutting the door behind her.

Josy turned around and was faced with a tree, a cat, and some strange monster thing.

And also Roger in bright red lipstick.

"Whoa," Josy breathed. "Sensory overload."

Bernice had leaves glued to her face and pinned to her dark-green wig.

Betty had whiskers. She was also glaring.

Bertha was... something. There were tentacles. And what looked like large elf ears over her regular ears.

"Dude," Josy said. "You guys look so rad."

"Thank you," Bernice said, smiling widely. "I still have no idea what's going on. I'm just along for the ride. Do you think I'll win many awards? They have a ceremony called the Razzies. It's given to stupid things. I want to win one."

"I don't know what I am," Bertha said, "but I'm just going with it. I find it's easier the older you get."

"I hate everything," Betty said. "And everyone. The only reason I'm still here is because Bernice called me an old fuddy-duddy, which I'm absolutely not."

"She's the best cat there ever was," Bernice said fondly.

"Lunch break?" Roger asked, fiddling with Bernice's leaves.

Josy shrugged. "Guess so. Past couple of days have been rough. But all the other days have been good, so it washes out. I just want to kiss Mason so we can get on with it."

They all stared at him.

Josy frowned as he thought back on what he said. "Wait, no. Not like that. Dude! Ack! No! Gross! I mean in the *movie*. I'm supposed to kiss him when he's a lion named Grady because he reminds me of Dante, who I love."

"Sounds complicated," Bernice said. "But I like it."

"You're making out with a lion?" Bertha asked.

"This is the stupidest thing we've ever done," Betty muttered, slumping in her chair.

"I don't want to make out with Mason," Josy said as he grimaced. "I'm only doing it because it's in the script."

"Which had the love scene written out," Roger said. "Interesting, don't you think?"

The We Three Queens turned slowly to look at him. It was quite eerie.

"Come again?" Bernice asked.

"Written out, you say?" Bertha asked.

"Recently?" Betty asked.

Roger's eyes were twinkling. "Quite. Apparently my grandson got it into his head that a sex scene would be gratuitous and wouldn't add anything that imagery and dialogue couldn't. The script supervisor wasn't pleased, but Quincy told him that sex wasn't needed to show love."

"Wow," Josy said. "That's deep. My name is Josiah Erickson, and I approve this message."

"Do you?" Roger asked. "Funny how that works out."

The We Three Queens seemed to be having a conversation with their eyebrows, something Josy was envious of. Anytime he tried to do the same, Xander and Serge asked if he had something in his eye.

Whatever they were saying to each other, the We Three Queens came to a consensus quickly. "How is Quincy?" Bertha asked.

"Good," Josy said. "I think. He seems a little frustrated today, but it happens."

Bernice smiled sweetly. "You two seem to be spending a lot of time together. Why, just the other night, we were out for a ride, and I saw the two of you walking down Main Street."

"Yeah. It's kind of our thing now. We go for a walk at night if it's not too cold."

"Cadet!" Betty barked. "Front and center!"

Josy stood in front of Betty before he realized he was even moving. Even though she had whiskers, she was still intimidating.

She sized him up. "Are they good walks?"

He snapped his head up and down. "They are!"

"Do you have stimulating conversation?"

"We do!"

"Do you enjoy it?"

"Yes, ma'am!"

"You may sit."

He did.

"Such fascinating creatures you are," Roger said. "I think I shall keep you."

"I'm a tree," Bernice told him. "I belong to no man."

Before they could continue, the door opened again and a lion walked in.

Not a *real* lion, of course. Why, the only lions in Oregon were in zoos or animal sanctuaries.

This was just Mason as Grady.

"I have problems with the script," he told Roger.

Roger arched an eyebrow. "You don't say. Please. Tell me why I should care."

Mason scowled at him. "It was fine the way it was. I don't know why Quincy is cutting my scenes down. *I'm* supposed to be the star here. Not Josy."

"Wow," Josy said. "Thank you for thinking I'm a star. That's nice of you."

"I didn't—that's not what I meant!"

"Oh. Sucks. My bad." Then a thought struck him. "We should probably practice kissing."

Josy was almost offended by the way Mason recoiled. "Excuse me?"

"I have to kiss you while you are wearing fangs and lion makeup," Josy explained patiently. "Don't you think we should try it out, just to make sure we get it right? I don't want our first attempt to be me slobbering all over you."

"You remember that television show from the eighties where Terminator made out with the Beast?" Bernice asked, staring at Mason. "That's what this reminds me of."

"She wasn't the Terminator," Betty scoffed. "She was Sarah Conner. She had biceps almost as big as mine."

"A lesbian icon," Bertha agreed. "Even if she had sex with men. Ahead of her time, she was."

"I would have let her throw me over her shoulder," Roger agreed. "Ron Perlman played the Beast. I did cocaine for most of that decade. But never when I babysat Quincy. Why, that would just be irresponsible of me."

"I don't want to make out with you," Mason growled.

"I don't want to make out with *you*," Josy snapped. "But we have to get it right so we don't have to keep doing it over and over."

"This is just like the TV show," Bernice said excitedly. "Even the undercurrent of bestiality is the same!"

Mason threw up his hands. "Fine!"

"Good!" Josy said, standing up.

"You know," Bertha said, "when I woke up this morning, I didn't think part of my day would entail watching Josy kiss a lion."

"We should move back to Ashland," Betty muttered.

"Pishposh," Roger said. "It would seem you have taken to your roles as a Greek chorus to heart. I do believe the world would collapse without your presence."

"More than you could ever know," Bertha told him. "We have a history with this sort of thing." She frowned as she looked at Mason and Josy. "Though I think this is with the wrong people, currently."

Josy barely heard them. In his head, he was working out the logistics of kissing Mason/Grady/Dante (he was unsure, exactly, of who this was supposed to be). He had fangs in his mouth and elaborate makeup on his face. It was of a good stock, meaning it wasn't supposed to smear easily, but Josy didn't want to take any chances lest he be faced with the wrath of Dee.

Mason was scowling at him, which added to the effect. He *looked* lionish.

And this was just a job.

Josy was an actor.

He could do this.

He was Liam Eagleton.

His father was dying.

His imaginary lion friend was real.

He missed Dante, but it was like he was almost here.

Grady's eyes widened as Liam took a step toward him. Liam couldn't exactly remember what he was supposed to say. He thought he should ad-lib. "I'd be lion if I said I didn't want to kiss you right now."

The tree in the room started choking wildly.

"Get away from me," Grady said, though Liam knew he was just trying to be brave.

Liam reached out and put his fingers in Grady's mane.

He leaned forward.

And kissed the lion king.

It was… chalky. And a fang poked his lip awkwardly.

He pulled away a little bit. "Huh."

Grady rolled his eyes. "You're not angling your head the right way." He reached up and tilted Liam's head to the right. They kissed again, mashing their lips together.

The mane tickled Liam's nose. He sneezed on Grady's face.

"What the fuck!" Mason cried.

"This is nothing like the fan fiction I spent the entire year of 1989 writing," Bernice said with a grimace. "I hate it when fantasy doesn't match the cold wet truth of reality."

"I'm sorry!" Josy said, rubbing his nose. "Your mane was all over my face!"

"So you *sneezed* in my mouth? What the hell is wrong with you!"

"It was a surprise! Like I *wanted* to sneeze on you! I just wanted to get this right, but it's not my fault you don't know how to kiss!"

Mason's eyes narrowed. "Say that again. I *dare* you."

Josy squared his shoulders. "You don't know how to kiss."

Mason grabbed him by the back of the neck, bringing him forward. The kiss was ferocious. Josy imagined this was what it would be like to make out with a real lion, though he'd never given that much thought before. The fangs still made things awkward, the mane got in the way, but still. It was better than it'd been before.

And then the door opened. "Hey, guys, I had some thoughts on—"

Josy pulled away from Mason to see Quincy standing in the doorway, mouth hanging open.

"Hey, dude," he said easily. "Just practicing to make sure we get it right for you." He smacked his lips. "It was awkward, but I think we got it."

Quincy closed his mouth and then opened it again. No sound came out.

"Oh boy," Bernice said.

Mason rolled his eyes. "Whatever. I didn't even want to do it in the first place. Josy made me. It's not my fault if he finds me attractive."

"Actually," Josy said, "it did nothing for me. I mean, I know we're supposed to be in love and stuff. Or at least like a version of you. But man, it was like making out with the stuffed bear I had when I was eight. Which I never did. Because that's weird."

Mason glared at him.

Josy grinned.

"Can I speak to Josy, please?" Quincy asked, sounding strained. "In private?"

"Sure," Bertha said. "But since we were here first and told not to leave, you can go somewhere else. It's a big house."

"Dude," Josy said. "I know just the place! We share a room, remember? The We Three Queens made sure of that."

Roger shook his head, smiling ruefully. "Listen to that chorus sing."

The We Three Queens chuckled quietly as Josy followed Quincy from the room.

THE FIRST thing Quincy said when they were safely behind closed doors was "My followers think we're dating because you said we were."

"Oh man," Josy said. "That's gnarly. How did that happen?"

Quincy waved his phone in Josy's direction. "You—you and your *hashtags*."

Josy blinked. "Say what."

Quincy looked down at his phone, scrolling furiously before shoving it in Josy's face again. The picture was the selfie he'd taken of the both of them, with Quincy turning toward Josy's face.

"That's a good one," Josy said, handing him the phone back. "Thanks for showing it to me."

Quincy groaned. "That's not why I—look. You remember when you took that picture of the food at Gus and Casey's house?"

Josy nodded. "I do. They were some good-looking noodles."

"We were sitting together next to each other."

"Right? Such a good time, man."

"You—argh! That's not what I'm saying!"

"Oh." Josy frowned. "I thought you had fun. Didn't you like hanging out with me?" The idea that Quincy *didn't* have a good time rubbed him the wrong way.

"What? What are you talking about? This is about the picture."

Josy squinted at him. "What about it? Should I not have taken it? Are you against noodles on the Internet?"

"I'm against hashtags where you say we're dating! And my followers know it's me because sometimes they can be a little obsessive and figured out I was sitting next to you in the picture by the fact you could see part of my hand and my knee."

"Whoa," Josy said. "They can tell who you are by your *hands*? Show me!"

"What?"

"Hold up your hands!"

Quincy looked confused. "Why are you—and now you're holding my hand."

Josy brought Quincy's hand up close to his face, studying it intensely. "I mean, it's a nice hand, sure. But I don't see how—oh, maybe it's that little freckle near your thumb. Dude, it kind of looks like a heart! That's awesome. I figured out how they knew it was you." He dropped Quincy's hand and smiled at him. "That's still a little creepy, but go them!"

"You told them we were *dating*."

Josy shook his head. "I don't think I did. I would remember if I wrote that. I wouldn't say something like that without talking to you first."

Quincy gaped at him.

Josy shrugged. "See? No worries." He gently took the phone from Quincy and looked down at it. "Look, not dating. It says it's a *friend*-date with the Q-Man. There's a difference."

"Not to people on the Internet who see what they want to!"

"Oh. Well, I can't really do anything about them. Casey told me once that you can't make everyone happy because it's impossible and people are dumb." He laughed. "S'funny, right?"

Quincy rubbed a hand over his face. "It's—that's not how that works, Josy. That coupled with the first picture—"

"The one where it looks like you're smelling my beard?"

Quincy flushed brightly. "I'm not smelling your beard."

"I mean, no worries if you were. That's what the beard oil is for. Makes it soft and smell good. Like mangos."

"Jesus fucking *Christ*."

"Wow," Josy said, scrolling through the post. "I mean, I saw some of the comments, but I muted it so I could focus on making the movie as best as I know how. This one says we're cute. This one says we should take more photos together because we have an interesting dynamic. This one got graphic really quickly, so I'm just going to skip over it. Look! This one says we're so adorable, she could just die." Josy frowned. "I hope she actually doesn't die. I would feel really bad. I'm just going to tell her not to die. Hold on a second… annnnd posted. Oh, this one is also graphic. Wow. I cannot bend that way."

"Don't you see the problem with this?"

Josy looked up at him. "No? I mean, it's the price of being in the spotlight, right? My agent, Starla, told me that if I ever got famous, paparazzi were going to jump out of the bushes and take my picture. She also said that if I ever went to Barbados, I couldn't sunbathe nude because they would climb trees to take a picture of my junk. Paps, man. I mean, I get they have a job to do, but not cool."

"What are you *talking* about?"

Josy shrugged. "People speculate about stuff, right? Like, tabloids and celebrity news blogs. They eat that stuff up. Doesn't mean it's true. Remember *Weekly World News*? They always had interviews with women who got pregnant by Bigfoot or aliens or—wait. That sounds like it's right up your alley. Oh man. Is that where you get your ideas? How do authors get ideas? That sounds like it's really tough. I can't write—"

"We aren't dating!" He started pacing.

Josy nodded. "I know that. And you know that. The people who like us know that. Who cares otherwise?"

"How can that not bother you? That people make assumptions about you that aren't true?"

"Because people have made assumptions about me my entire life."

Quincy stopped and stared at him.

Josy felt—well, not exactly *uncomfortable*, but a little off-centered. He didn't think this was something he was going to talk about today. If he'd known, he would have prepared himself better. But it was already out there, so he might as well get it over with. "Look, man. It's not a big deal. I know I'm not the smartest person in the world. I say dumb shit all the time. I'm a stoner, and I like socks with cows on them, and for reasons no one really knows, I'm pretty great at radio trivia. People look at me and see the beard and the clothes and say, 'Hey look, it's one of those hipster dudes.' And maybe that's true. I mean, sometimes I get it. I liked Arcade Fire *before* everyone else did. One time I bought something called a reclaimed apothecary matchstick container that cost two hundred dollars, even though it was just a glass jar with long sticks in it, because I *needed* it. But you know what? I don't care what those people think. I do the things I do because they make me happy. I am who I am because this is the person I want to be. It took me a long time to get this way, and I don't let little things like people assuming things on the Internet get to me."

Quincy looked taken aback. "I didn't mean—I like who you are."

This pleased Josy greatly. "Thank you. I like who you are too, even if I sometimes think you don't give yourself enough credit. Like, man, you're making a movie. From something you *wrote*. How many people in the world get to say that? Yeah, sure, sometimes your brain gets a little wacky and you think bad things about yourself, and that's okay. That happens to me too. I know it's probably not even close to being the same, but I think it helps me understand it a little. But no matter what happens, even when you start to think bad things, even if people start making shit up on the Internet, there's still someone who knows you're pretty rad. You took a jump outside of your comfort zone, and man, that's something to be proud of."

Quincy gave a shuddering sigh. "That's—that's nice of you to say."

Josy shrugged. "It's the truth. It's easier to say things that are the truth than to spend the time thinking up a lie. But you know what? We can fix this right now if it bothers you so much. You have a Facebook page, don't you? Because you're old-school." He looked down at the phone and flipped through the apps until he found the one he was looking for. "You have a much bigger follower count than I do. Good for you, man. Let's just use yours, then."

"Use mine? For what? Josy, what are you—"

"Do you trust me?"

Quincy didn't hesitate. "Yes. Of course I do."

That was better than any high.

"And we're on!" Josy said cheerfully, stretching out his arm and angling the phone toward them. "Hi, Q-Bert's followers! It's me, Josy! I've taken over the Q-Man's page, coming to you live from the set of our first film together! We're—wow. Twelve hundred people are watching already. And now there's thirteen hundred." He swallowed thickly. "That's a lot more than I expected this quickly. Or at all. Oh look, now it's up to sixteen hundred. It's the middle of a workday! How are you all watching this?"

"Oh my god," Quincy said faintly.

Josy shook his head. "That's okay. I can do this." He grinned into the camera, ignoring the little red box in the corner that showed the viewers increasing exponentially. Tiny little hearts and smiley faces and blue thumbs-ups began shooting across the screen. Josy didn't understand why Facebook needed that. It seemed unnecessarily complicated. "As I was saying, I am here with the man of the hour! We're making a movie. Q-Bert wrote it, and he's also directing it, and it's pretty cool. We're not going to tell you what it's about, because that would be spoilery, but I will say that it's about happy queer characters, because goshdarnit, we deserve it. Say hi, Q-Bert!"

He turned the phone toward Quincy, who stood wide-eyed. "Um. Hi?"

Josy moved until he was standing next to Quincy, their shoulders pressed together. Quincy was pale, and Josy knew he was nervous, so he reached out and took his hand. No one could see it as it was off-camera, but Quincy latched on tightly. Josy hoped it made him feel safe. "We're a couple of weeks in, and we've still got about a month to go. But I think it's going to be something like you've never seen before. Isn't that right, Q-Bert?"

Quincy opened his mouth once, twice, then shook his head and cleared his throat. "Yeah. That's... that's right. It's different. It's... well. It's something I've wanted to do for a long time, and I didn't say anything, because I didn't want to jinx it."

"Oh crap," Josy moaned. "Dude, I didn't even think about—"

Quincy squeezed his hand. "It's okay. This—I can do this. It's probably better I talk about it now, right? It was going to come out eventually." He took a deep breath, and while the smile on his face looked like the love child of a grin and a grimace, his voice evened out when he spoke again. "Hi. You know me as Q-Bert. I write monster porn. And I'm making a movie."

"Damn right you are!" Josy crowed.

"And while those two things aren't exactly related, the things I learned from my books helped me to tell the story I wanted to tell."

"And it's a good story," Josy added, eyeing the viewer count as it neared *four thousand.*

"A good story," Quincy echoed. "Josy—*Josiah*—plays one of the leads."

"I'm one of the happy queers!"

"Yes, you are. One of the happy queers. And I'm sorry I didn't tell you guys about this sooner, but I think it was because I couldn't really believe it was real. Some days I still don't think it is. I've... I've talked about stuff like this before. How hard it is for me. To speak to all of you. To come out of my shell without feeling like I'm being torn apart. Even now, there's a little voice in the back of my head that's telling me to run away, to hide in my bed and not move for a long time. I used to listen to that voice a lot. Sometimes I still do. Even when I got this idea to make a movie, I talked myself out of it time and time again. But then my grandad told me that if I gave in to that voice this time, I always would. That I shouldn't let it hold me back." His smile became softer, and Josy adored it. "He was right, of course. Mental health is no joke. And maybe Grandad was a little crude with how he went about it, but he still had a point. It's part of me. But it's not who I am."

"You're pretty great is who you are," Josy said.

"Thank you?"

"Yep yep. And look at all those comments! Wow. Like, hundreds of them. I can't keep up with them! That's—oh, that one! Yes, my beard is real, and no, it's not just for the movie. I always look like this. Q-Bert let me keep it because he's awesome like that. If I shave, I look like I'm twelve, and no one wants to see that. Next comment! Um, that one! No, we're not going to tell you the name of the movie yet. It's a secret. Next! What's that one say? 'I saw you on Josiah's Instagram, when are you getting married because you need to have babies.'" And didn't *that* just cause Josy's brain to short-circuit briefly. "Um, what?"

Quincy saved him. "What he's trying to say is that no, we're not getting married. We're not dating. We're just… friends."

"Right," Josy said, nodding furiously. "Just friends. *Good* friends, even. And now there's a bunch of angry emojis on the screen. Huh. I didn't expect that."

"Josiah Erickson is a wonderful actor," Quincy said quickly. "I want you all to remember that name, because he's going to be huge. There's no one else in the world who I could see playing the role he has. He's… he's perfect."

"Aww," Josy said. "I think you're pretty perfect too. And now there are heart emojis again. How fickle the minds of men. And women. And fans. I don't know what I'm talking about." He frowned. "Fickle is a weird word. It sounds dirty. I'm going to fickle you so hard—"

"And that's probably enough for now," Quincy said, taking the phone from Josy's hand. "Thank you to everyone who has allowed me to get to this moment. Since we're talking about the movie now, I'll be sure to post more about it."

"And we'll probably have at least three or four live videos a day," Josy added.

"Maybe one per week."

"Per day."

"We'll talk about it *later*."

"Oh. Right. Follow me on Instagram! I tried Twitter, but I don't have a lot of thoughts that can fit into a hundred and forty characters, so it's pretty dead over there. Bye!"

Quincy ended the live feed just as the number of viewers crossed over ten thousand.

It was about that time that Josy realized they were still holding hands.

And since Quincy didn't seem to notice, Josy certainly wasn't going to bring it up.

"That went well," he said seriously. "Thank you for trusting me."

Quincy sighed. "Like I could ever not. Come on. We've got a movie to make."

"Action!" Quincy said.

"We'll figure it out," Liam said as his voice cracked. "You can't keep going on like this, Grady. It's tearing you apart."

Grady spun around, his chest bumping into Liam's. "You don't know anything about me, boy. You chose to forget us. You chose to forget *me*."

Liam reached up and ran his hand through Grady's mane, fingers disappearing into the auburn hair. His heart was racing. He wanted Dante.

But he also wanted Grady.

He leaned forward and kissed the lion man.

"And *cut!*" Quincy yelled. "Good. That was good. I want to try it one more time. I have an idea. Mason, I want you to really grab on to Josy, okay? When he first kisses you, I want you to stay still and not respond. Count to three in your head, and then I want you to just *shove* him against the tree. Got it? Let's do it again!"

Chapter 14

From Josiah Erickson's Instagram Story

"Hey, everyone! Just checking in. Welcome to the 647 new followers I've gotten over the past week. It's great to have you here. I hope you like pictures of me and also of food because that's pretty much what you're going to get. And of course, stuff from the set! I'm here with three of my costars, who are in a Vespa gang. They're pretty great! Say hi!"

"Hello. Hi. *Hola.* My name is Bernice. I wasn't prepared for this, so I didn't have time to write a speech. But I think the first time I knew I was destined for stardom was when I was told I was going to be a talking tree a few weeks ago. I haven't looked back since. I have been banned from using our Instagram account, so you can send fan mail to my PO box, which is—"

"Don't give them our address! You don't know what kind of deranged stalkers are out there. To anyone watching, if you even *think* of harming one hair on Bernice's wig, just remember that I know sixteen ways to kill a man with my bare *hands* and—*mmph*."

"Sorry about that. Betty gets… protective. My name is Bertha, and I am the leader of the We Three Queens. You can't have our address, but you may worship us from afar. Also, we would accept donations in our name to Planned Parenthood, because the male Republicans who wish to dismantle it should have their testicles hooked up to a car battery. Maybe then they would understand what it feels like to be a woman in America."

"And that's it for today! I'll be on again soon. Once again, thanks for following me! Josy out."

"Action!"

"None of it is *real*," Liam snapped, head in his hands. "It's—it's just a dream, okay? I don't know how you're doing this to me. This—this shared *delusion*. But it's not real."

"My son," John Eagleton said weakly. The machines hissed and beeped around him. "You always thought with your head and never with your heart. The rational child, no matter how much evidence to the contrary was right in front of you."

"How would you know?" Liam asked, laughing bitterly. "You were never there to show me otherwise. Always gone in this fantasy of yours. Tell me, Dad. Where did you go? What were you doing that kept you away for weeks at a time?"

"I've told you—"

"You've told me *nothing*. You've made up this goddamn story about this fantasy world that can't be real. It *can't*."

"Just because you don't believe in it," his father whispered, "doesn't mean it can't believe in you."

JOSY LAY on his bed with his arms behind his head, staring up at the darkened ceiling. The only light in the room was from Quincy's laptop. He'd been typing on it for the past hour, though he was starting to slow down.

It was only a few minutes more before he sighed and closed it.

"All good?" Josy asked, proud of himself for staying quiet this whole time.

"Yeah," Quincy said, popping his neck. "I know I shouldn't be messing with the script any more, but Roger said fine-tuning happens all the time."

"Big changes?"

"Not really. Just… refining, I guess. Not too big a deal. You guys will have the pages in plenty of time."

"That's okay, man. I trust you."

A pause. Then, "Thanks."

"Sure. You're the director. You know what you're doing."

Quincy snorted. "I don't think that's how it works."

"Eh. It sounded right in my head."

Silence followed, long enough that Josy thought Quincy had fallen asleep. He was jerked out of his own dozing when Quincy spoke again. "I don't know how you do it."

Josy turned to his side, propping himself up on his elbow, hand against his head. He could see Quincy's outline on his own bed. "Do what?"

"You're just… happy. All the time. And positive. About everything."

"Gustavo said it's because I don't know any better."

Quincy laughed quietly. He seemed to be doing that more lately. "I don't think that's quite it."

"Oh. Then I guess I don't know why. I mean, I think I've always been like this, even when I didn't want to feel like it."

Quincy turned his head toward him. "What do you mean?"

"I don't know, man. Like, there's before Los Angeles and after Los Angeles."

"Which is better?"

"After," Josy said promptly. "No question. Sure, sometimes it sucks because I'm always broke and working crap jobs and getting passed over for roles. But they mostly went to people who deserved them, so I couldn't be too upset about it. I'm not the only one who works hard to become an actor."

"Not famous, though."

"What?"

"You said you're not the only one who works hard to become an actor. You could have said to become famous."

"Oh yeah, I guess I did. Well, it'd be awesome to be famous for doing something cool, but I'm starting to think that doesn't matter much to me anymore. Not like it once did. I like having followers on Instagram, and it'd be nice to be rich or whatever, but I don't think that's why I'm doing this anymore."

"Then what's the reason?"

Josy picked at a loose string on the comforter. "Because I like it. I like playing other people. Because it helps remind me I can be whoever I want to be. Like right now I'm playing this dude you wrote who doesn't know what to believe is real or not and makes out with lion men and junk, and then I get to go back to being the same old Josy when it's done. And I like that. I think I forgot that when I got lost in the idea of bigger and better things."

"Los Angeles can do that to you."

"I suppose. I moved out here without a clue what I was doing. I had, like, eight hundred bucks, three pairs of pants, and my portfolio of headshots that took me almost a year to save up for all packed in my car. Well, not the eight hundred bucks. That was in my bank account. I rented a really shitty apartment because it was cheap and found a job at a Mexican restaurant where no one spoke English." He paused, considering. "I still don't know how that happened. I was just looking for some tacos, and then I was washing dishes and getting paid."

Quincy snorted. "Sounds about right."

"Yeah, I guess it does. And it wasn't all sunshine, you know? Sometimes I felt sorry for myself when I could only eat crackers for dinner and I didn't know anyone. I even thought once about packing up and going home."

"Why didn't you?"

Josy shrugged. "Because I would have been letting myself down. Even though it sucks to fail, it can teach you things you might not have known before. But I wasn't ready to learn about those things yet. So I told myself that I would give it a few more weeks and rethink it then. You know what happened then?"

"What?"

"The very next night, I met Xander. He wanted to fuck around, but I said no, and we became best friends instead. And with him came Serge and Casey. And not long after that, I met my agent, Starla. I found people who believed in me. I figured I must be doing something right to have that. Not everyone does."

"Before Los Angeles?"

"It was harder," Josy admitted. "But I still did the best I could. I mean, my parents weren't—aren't—too happy with what I wanted to do. They wanted me to go to college, which, okay. That's cool, man, but it wasn't for me. I just didn't connect with school stuff, you know? Some of it was hard, and while I know I can push myself, I'd rather do it with something that I love."

"That sucks," Quincy said quietly. "The parent thing."

"Eh. I guess. They're old-school. Don't get me wrong, they're good people." Josy thought hard, trying to find the right words. "But… I think sometimes kids are born to the wrong parents. You know? Not because the parents do anything wrong but because they don't know how to just… parent. They always thought there was something wrong with me, that I was slow, even though I just thought about things in a different way. They didn't like when I smoked weed, even though it made me feel better than any medication they tried to give me. They didn't understand that I felt happiest on a stage or in front of a camera. I used to make all these movies with the big, clunky camcorder we had. Dumb things, but I liked them. They were never really interested in watching my movies, though. They had me, but they didn't *get* me. I love them. And I always will. Just because we disagree doesn't change that. But it doesn't mean I couldn't think for myself or make my own decisions. I told them that. And you know what they said to me? They said the door wouldn't always be open when I failed and needed to crawl back home."

"Jesus."

Josy shook his head. "Do or do not, there is no try. So I did. And here I am. It took a lot to get here, but I made it."

"That's a lot of pressure."

Josy laughed. "Nah, man. This? Here? This is *golden*. And you know what? Even if I never get another part again and have to go back to Frank at Applebee's and beg for my job back, I'll be okay. Because I got to be in a movie. And that's awesome. Pretty awards and flashing cameras are nice and all, but they're not everything to me. I'm glad I figured that out now and not before it was too late."

"You're happy."

Josy grinned. "Yeah, dude. I'm happy."

"Have you talked to them? Since you left?"

His smiled faded slightly. "A few times. But it's always awkward. The last time I talked to my dad, he asked if I was still 'hooked on the marijuana.' Which, you know. Stupid, right? But I haven't actually spoken to them in a long time. Almost a year, I think. I left them a message telling them I got the part in your movie and how cool it was, but they never called me back."

"They didn't?"

"Nah. But that's okay, man. I've been too busy to worry about it anyway."

"Doesn't it make you mad?"

Josy's answer surprised even himself. "Not really. More sad, but it goes back to me thinking I was born to the wrong people. And then I remember that I have the right people around me, and I did that all on my own. And then I feel better."

"Something has to piss you off. You can't be happy *all* the time."

"Oh sure, dude. A lot of things piss me off. The fact that weed is still criminalized in a lot of the country, and minorities feel the brunt of that. When Froot Loops decided to add marshmallows. Michael Bay, but only because it makes Gustavo feel better. People who put ketchup in the pantry instead of the fridge. People who don't like dogs. Racists who don't care that they're douchebags. How those little bags of potato chips you get at Subway are only, like, a quarter full. The gender wage gap. Taco Bell. Rodrigo Duterte."

"The Filipino president?"

Josy scowled. "He knows what he did."

"You're so…." Quincy didn't seem to know how to finish his sentence.

"Yeah, I get that a lot. I tell myself it's cool that a lot people can't find the right words to describe me. Makes me think I can't be put in any box. Some people try, though. They see me and the way I look and think I'm just this weird millennial hipster dude. Others hear me talk and think how stupid I am. I smoke weed, so I must be a burnout."

"I don't think you're stupid," Quincy mumbled.

Josy grinned in the dark. "Thanks, dude. I'm smart in some ways and not so smart in other ways. That's okay with me. No one should be smart about everything, because what would there be left to learn?"

"Why do you smoke weed?"

"It helps me relax. Keeps me focused."

"It does?"

Josy shrugged. "Sure, man. I mean, it's not for everyone. I would never pressure someone to do it if they didn't want to. But it's medically accepted for a lot of reasons, and I'm not hurting anyone when I smoke, so what's the big deal? People shouldn't be made to feel bad about the things they like to do if it doesn't hurt anyone else."

Quincy snorted. "That's easier said than done."

That frustrated Josy to hear, even if it was the truth. "Yeah, but it takes less energy to be nice than it does to be a dick. Like, a lot of those people who came to the library to hear you read. There was a girl there named… okay, I don't know what her name was, but she called herself Tigress, and she said being in that room with other people like her made her feel safe and happy. It made me think there were people in her real life that don't make her feel that way, and that makes me mad. Why do you have to shit on other people for doing what they love? Like, furries, man. I don't get it. Not my thing. But you know what? It's so fucking *cool* they have that. I'm not saying Tigress is a furry. At least I don't think. But who cares if she is or not? What's the point of making others feel bad about themselves?"

"She felt safe there?" Quincy asked, sounding awed. "She said that?"

"Yeah, man. And you could see it on her face too. All of their faces. I mean, when I was stalking you after that night—"

"Maybe don't call it that."

"Oh, right. When I was trying to learn everything I could about you without you knowing, I would read your blog and see all the comments there from people. They feel safe talking about whatever goes on in their heads because you gave them a space to do that. That's pretty cool, man. People shit all over the idea of safe spaces only because they're so filled with self-loathing they don't know how else to be. That's on them, and not anyone else."

Quincy turned his head toward the ceiling. When he spoke, his voice was rougher. "I didn't know that."

"Really?"

He shook his head. "Sort of, I guess. I knew they felt like they could say what was in their heads, but I thought it was just because I did too."

"It is, man. That's the reason. You put the words down that reminded them of themselves and helped them find their own voices to say what maybe they couldn't before. I think it takes a lot of courage to say the scary things that no one likes to talk about because they think it makes them look weak. That's the cool thing about it. When you stand up for yourself, you never know if you're standing up for someone who isn't ready to do the same. And you might be giving them the courage to do it somewhere down the road. And when they do, they help someone else. And it keeps on going down the line. Serge said it's good karma."

Quincy swallowed thickly. Then, "My parents died when I was a kid."

Josy winced. "Oh, man, I'm sorry. I didn't mean to—"

Quincy waved him away. "It's fine. I was young. I have a few memories, but… I don't know if they're real or just what I've been told."

"Did Roger raise you after that?"

"Yeah. Even though I'm sure he didn't think he'd spend his later years with a morose kid attached to his hip."

"I bet you twenty bucks that was just fine with him."

Quincy snorted. "Maybe. But he—I think he got more than he bargained for. I was a mess. I didn't make friends. I didn't do very well in school, even though I knew the material. I was all over the place. I didn't like to go outside. I didn't like strangers. Once, when I was—twelve, maybe?—I just couldn't get out of bed, no matter how hard I tried. There was this weight on my chest, and I couldn't find a way out from under it. He thought I was sick, and then it went to the second day, and the third day, and then on the fourth, we both knew something was really, really wrong. He asked me why I couldn't get up. I told him I wanted to die."

Josy exhaled sharply.

"And not in that emo teenage everything-sucks-and-kill-me-now kind of way, though maybe there's some truth to it. I honestly wanted to be dead. I even knew how I'd do it. And it was strange, too, because it was like part of me was thinking that I wanted it to fail. I could have easily gone into Grandad's bathroom and grabbed a handful of his pills and swallowed them down. It'd work because I've never been able to make myself throw up. There'd be no way out unless I got my stomach pumped. So I barely even considered doing it that way."

Josy didn't want to know, but he had to ask anyway. "How were you going to—"

"Someone gave me a guitar for the birthday before that I never learned how to play. I was going to take one of the strings and wrap one end around the rod in the closet and another around my neck. I told him that. Because even though I wanted it badly, there was a small part of me screaming to make it stop. To fight it. And that little part of me spoke to him on the fourth day. He dragged me out of bed. He was slight, even then, but he's scary strong when he wants to be. He didn't need the wheelchair yet. He carried me down the stairs and out into the car. I spent the next month in a hospital. It was… terrible. All of it. I told him I hated him and myself. That I never wanted to see him again. That I wished I was dead. That *he* was dead. And you know what he told me?"

Josy shook his head, not trusting himself to speak.

"He told me I was allowed to hate myself all I wanted. Because he loved me enough for the both of us. And he wouldn't let me go without a fight." Quincy wiped his eyes. "He was in the middle a production. Some cheesy stupid direct-to-video thing. But he let someone else take over so he could be there every day. For that entire month. And when I finally got to go back home, the guitar was gone and he'd taken the door to my room off its hinges. The closet had been gutted, and anything and everything that I could use to hurt myself was hidden away or destroyed."

"On lockdown, man."

"Exactly," Quincy said hoarsely. "Lockdown. I didn't understand then, though I do now. I thought he didn't trust me, which, even if that was it, he was in the right. Not trusting someone isn't the same as not loving them. It was *because* he loved me enough for the both of us. I figured that out. Eventually."

"I'm glad you did," Josy whispered. "I like that you exist in the world. I think a lot of people would say the same thing."

"I like that you exist too."

Warmth bloomed in Josy's chest. "Thanks, man. That's cool of you to say." An idea struck him. "Do you still trust me?"

"Yeah. Of course."

"Close your eyes. Like, you can't open them until I say. No matter what you hear."

Quincy closed his eyes.

Josy got up from the bed and went to the large closet. He pulled out spare blankets and pillows. He laid them on his bed before grabbing the two chairs from the desk in the room. He positioned them between the beds. It wouldn't be the best—he needed more chairs—but he didn't want to wake anyone else up by trying to get some.

He draped the blankets over the chairs, tucking the ends between the mattress and the box spring on his bed. He took the pillows and spread them out on the ground. To finish it off, he took the lamp from the desk and set it on the floor near one of the chairs. He switched it on and sat back on his knees. It was a rush job, but he thought it'd be okay. He crawled out of the blankets and reached over, tugging on Quincy's hand. "Keep your eyes closed. Put your feet on the floor and then hunker down."

Quincy moved. He was wearing loose shorts and an oversized shirt. His legs and arms were bony, all sharp angles. He slid to the floor, eyes still closed. It was awkward, trying to get him inside without hitting anything, but somehow Josy made it work.

He pulled Quincy inside, dropping his hand and pressing against his shoulders, pushing him down on his back on the pillows. Quincy scrunched up his face, but he didn't peek. Josy exited one last time, grabbing the comforter off his bed and pulling it down with him. He lay next to Quincy as he covered the both of them. It was a little cramped, and his head hit one of the legs of the chair, but that was all right.

"Okay," he said. "You can open your eyes now."

Quincy blinked slowly as he looked around. "What is…. Did you make a blanket fort? Seriously?"

Josy grinned, head tilted toward Quincy. "Yeah, man. I wanted to do that for you on the first day of the movie. You looked all shy and scared when you were talking to all of us, and I wanted to keep you safe. A couple of years ago I tried out for this commercial. I don't even remember what it was for, just that one of the casting people was really mean to me. They said I should just give up and go back to whatever Podunk town I came from. That I didn't have what it took to be an actor. Normally shit like that doesn't bother me much, but for some reason, it did this time. I was sad. And my friends don't like it when I'm sad. So Xander and Serge picked me up from my apartment and took me to Casey's house. In his living room, he'd made a huge blanket fort for me. It had lights on strings and joints and cookies, and we stayed in there all night. The next morning I still wasn't ready to leave, so Xander and Serge called in sick, and Casey ordered Chinese food at seven in the morning, because you can do that in Los Angeles. We ate noodles and those tiny corns that seem really pointless but I like for some reason. And I felt better. Sometimes you need to hide away from the rest of the world. And it's okay to do that, just as long as you don't forget the world is waiting for you when you're done."

Quincy turned his head. The low light reflected in his eyes. "Thanks, Josy."

"No problem, man. I like being in here with you."

And for the first time, it was Quincy who reached out and took Josy's hand.

They slept, eventually.

From Q-Bert's Blog

Yesterday was a harder day than I expected it to be. It hit without rhyme or reason, and even though I tried to power through it, it still got the best of me. I was angry with myself for allowing it to happen, for letting it trample all over me and suck me down like the swiftest of quicksand. But then I remembered that sometimes these things happen, no matter how strong I try to be. It's not about winning every battle. It's about how you face the war. It's okay to have bad days, just as long as you remember to not let the bad days last forever. Winston Churchill referred to his depression as a black dog, and I get that, because I can feel it nipping at my heels. And while this dog may never be put down, it can still be muzzled and placed on a short leash. I can take the fight out of it because I am *stronger than it is, and you are too.*

Couple that with anxiety and well… it sucks, frankly. Living with it is like having a person constantly following you, heckling you with every step you take. They know all your faults. All your insecurities. And they don't just whisper them in your ear. No, they shout them until they're the only voice you can hear, even if you're standing in the middle of a crowded room.

I get a lot of comments on here asking for ways to beat it back. Some of you tell me that you feel like you're drowning. If you ever *feel this way and can't seem to get it back under control, seek help immediately. There's no shame in it. A doctor. A friend. A clergy person. Pick up the phone and dial one of the phone numbers I have listed under the* GET HELP *tab on this website. Do* something, *because a world where you don't exist is a world that will always be dimmer. I was reminded recently that you've helped me build a wonderful community here. I see the comments of those having bad days getting responses from others offering solace and ways to help.*

Remember this one thing: you are never *alone.*

"OKAY, IN this scene, Josy, I need you to look just *crazy* with awe, okay? Liam has never seen anything like the Three Oracles before. Even with all that he's been told, even with everything he's been through, this is still a big moment for him. It's hitting him like nothing has been able to. Even with what he's heard from his father, even with Boris and Grady and Dill and Mr. Zucko, *this* is the moment when it becomes real for him. We're going to add SFX in post, but it's not going to be much. Some fairy lights and such, which is what the tennis ball is for. Follow it with your eyes as it moves around you. Got it?"

Josy nodded. "Got it."

"I'm a tree," Bernice said happily. "I get it now. I am the oldest living thing in the forest, and you two are my weird monster and my cat. Oh, the joy I feel."

"I'm not going to lick myself," Betty growled. "So you can get that out of your head right this second."

"I think one of my tentacles is coming loose," Bertha said with a frown. "Unless it's supposed to break off and I grow a new one. I'm still not quite sure what I'm supposed to be."

Quincy took a deep breath. "Okay. Let's do this."

THE BELL chimed overhead as Josy opened the door to Lottie's Lattes. He bowed and said, "After you, my good sir."

Quincy rolled his eyes as he went inside. He hung his jacket on the coatrack but kept the scarf wound around his neck. Josy thought it looked good on him. He was a big fan of scarves. He didn't own one himself. Los Angeles wasn't really a scarf kind of place.

There were a few people at the tables inside. Two teenage girls sitting near the door saw them as they came in. Their eyes widened and they immediately put their heads together, whispering furiously.

Lottie stood behind the counter, her red drag-queen hair as frizzy as it'd ever been. She grinned at the sight of them. "Welcome to Lottie's Lattes, where we like you a lottie."

Quincy blinked. "What?"

"It's her catchphrase," Josy said, pulling him toward the counter. They held hands a lot these days, sometimes without even thinking.

"It's part of my brand," Lottie agreed. "If I ever decide to open another store somewhere, the employees will be required to say it for every customer. Gus says it's stupid and the foundation for a terrible business plan, but he runs a video store in 2015, so I'm not too worried about what he thinks on the matter."

"Doesn't he own most of the town?" Quincy asked.

Lottie shrugged. "Just like his daddy before him. He's a good landlord. Jimmy, who owns the hardware store, ran into some financial trouble last year, and Gus helped bail him out. We take care of our own here. What can I get for you? Fair warning, everything is pumpkin spice flavored, because that's what one does in the fall. It's an epidemic of catastrophic proportions."

"The muffins?" Josy asked.

"Pumpkin spice."

"Coffee."

"Pumpkin spice."

"The egg and bacon sandwich?"

Lottie leaned forward and whispered, "Pumpkin spice."

"Whoa," Josy said. "That sounds awesome. And gross."

"That explains the lasagna you brought for lunch last week," Quincy said with a grimace.

She shrugged. "People buy it. I mean, *I* don't eat them, but for some reason, from October to just after Thanksgiving, people turn into junkies looking for their next fix. And I'm the dealer waiting to take their money. And then it's peppermint everything, because Christmas and Jesus and stuff. Should the licensing go through, I already have plans next year for pumpkin spice and peppermint cannabis."

"How's that going?" Josy asked as Quincy looked at the baked goods behind the glass. It really was all pumpkin spice. Josy was suitably impressed.

Lottie scowled. "Oh, the government is taking their sweet time, of course. Just because Oregonians overwhelmingly approved the legalization of recreational marijuana doesn't mean the powers that be won't drag their feet. I'm being told February 1 now, at the earliest. It's going to be strictly regulated, but I'm not worried about that."

Quincy looked up. "How is Casey able to do what he does at the B and B?"

"He doesn't sell it, at least not yet. He found a workaround. People pay to stay at the B and B at a slightly higher rate, and he's able to give his consumables as gifts. While it's not sustainable for the long run, it works for now. See something you like? I wouldn't recommend the egg and bacon sandwich. It's disgusting and—"

A loud crash came from the kitchen.

Lottie sighed as she tilted her face toward the ceiling.

"That was nothing!" a voice called out. It sounded like Bernice. "Everything is fine and nothing is broken, such as the mixer!"

"The We Three Queens are practicing their recipes for No-Thanks Giving," Lottie told them. "They said that they can't do it at their house because the last time they experimented, Bernice misread the recipe and used seventeen onions instead of one."

"I get that," Josy said. "It's why I don't cook anything except for when I have to use the microwave."

"What's No-Thanks Giving?" Quincy asked, pushing his glasses back up.

Lottie stared at him.

He shifted nervously.

"Josy," she said slowly. "Does your friend not know about No-Thanks Giving?"

Josy scrunched up his face, thinking back if he'd told Quincy or not. "I don't think so? We've been really busy making a movie. I don't know if you know this since you're not an actor, but it's a lot of work."

"Oh, *I* know it is. I was in a movie once."

"What? You were?"

"Oh yes," Lottie said with a nod. "The seventies were a very sexually liberating time. I think I still have a bootleg copy of it somewhere, if you'd like to see. But you should probably keep in mind that back then, we had very different ideas on how much body hair was socially acceptable."

"That's okay," Quincy said hastily. "Don't even worry about trying to find it."

"Are you sure? It's no trouble at all. There was this one scene with me and three guys who—"

"Seriously. Not a problem. Don't look for it. At all."

"No-Thanks Giving is what's celebrated in Abby," Josy explained. "They're really big on festivals here."

"Sometimes it's about strawberries," Lottie said. "And sometimes about the eradication of the native people by white men."

Quincy looked between the two of them. "I'm learning not to question the things that happen here."

"That's probably for the best," Josy said. "This will be my first No-Thanks Giving. I couldn't afford to come up here last year, but Casey told me about it. I tried to ask Gustavo, but he said I'm not allowed to ask him about festivals because they're the worst."

"He's very opinionated about festivals," Lottie agreed. "While the rest of America gets together and celebrates the fact that our ancestors took land that didn't belong to them by shoving bread up a turkey's asshole, Abby puts on a festival in protest. There are booths for food and crafts and a bunch of other things. We have a stage set up where people can get in front of everyone and talk about what they're not thankful for, or thankful for, or tell a joke or whatever they want, as long as they keep it mostly appropriate. Everyone chips in, and the people who have booths donate half of all proceeds to a specific charity. This year it's the Native American Rights Fund. They're sending a couple of representatives to give a presentation, and they'll have their own booth as well."

"I don't know what to say to any of that," Quincy admitted.

"It's okay," Lottie said, reaching across the counter and patting the back of his hand. "It's just the years of systemic racism you've been taught by the American school system. You'll learn."

Another crash.

"Don't worry about that!" Bernice yelled. "That was just… well, definitely wasn't the mixer this time!"

Lottie huffed out a breath through her nose. "Would you excuse me for a moment? I'll be right back to take your orders." She whirled around and stalked into the kitchen, making colorful threats involving pumpkin spice being shoved into places that Josy didn't think needed the festive fall flavor.

"This town is so weird," Quincy said, staring after her.

"Right? It's awesome. I love it here." He nodded toward an empty table. They sat down, and the two girls near them giggled and flushed brightly when Josy winked at them.

Quincy drummed his fingers on the table. "You do, don't you."

"What?"

"Love it here."

"Yeah, man. I mean, it's nice. Quiet, you know? Don't get me wrong, LA is okay too. But even when you're surrounded by millions of people, it can sometimes be lonely. I don't feel like that here."

"Why do you stay in LA, then?"

Josy hadn't ever really thought of it that way. "I kind of have to. Not many calls for auditions up here. It's my job."

"Say you could, though. Say that you were a famous actor and you could live wherever you wanted."

Josy thought hard. "Would I get to have my own private plane?"

"Sure."

"And a popcorn machine?"

"Uh, yes?"

"Maybe. Casey and Gustavo are here. And Lottie and the We Three Queens. But Xander and Serge aren't. And you're not either."

Quincy twitched. "How's that now?"

"You live in Los Angeles, right? If I moved here, I wouldn't get to see you as much when we went back home. It's like Casey and Gustavo living here. It sucks, because I love them and don't get to see them as much as I want."

"You want to see me after we go back?" he asked, voice hushed.

Josy cocked his head. "Well, yeah, man. Of course I do. Why wouldn't I?" A terrible thought struck him. "I mean, unless you don't want to hang out with me when we go back. I know you'll be busy with the movie and editing and life and—"

"No," Quincy said quickly. "I want to see you. All the time."

"Really? *All* the time?"

"Well, maybe not *all* the time, but most of the time."

"Dude," Josy breathed. "That's just what I was thinking! Like, not *all* the time, because I have to sleep and sometimes I have to practice my facial expressions in the mirror, but most of the time is good for me. And you get to meet Xander and Serge! I think you'll like them. They can be scary. Well, that's mostly Xander, but only because he likes to pretend he's all badass even though he's like Mallomars."

"What's a Mallomar?"

"It's a cookie that's hard chocolate on the outside and marshmallow on the inside. They're really good when you're high, but disgusting when you're not."

"And that's like Xander?"

Josy shrugged. "A little bit."

"I don't—"

The two girls suddenly appeared at their table, breathing heavily. "Hello," the one on the left said in a quiet voice.

"Hi," the one on the right whispered breathlessly.

"We're really big fans of yours."

"Like, the biggest fans."

"Can we please have your autograph?"

Josy grinned. "Oh, that's so cool. Do you want me to take a picture of the three of you too?"

"They're not asking me, Josy," Quincy said, sounding amused.

Josy looked at him, then back at the girls. "They're not? Who are they talking about, then?"

"You," the girl on the left said.

"So you," the girl on the right said. "We follow you on Instagram, and we watched all your commercials on YouTube."

"I have your picture on my wall," the girl on the left said. "You're my *favorite*."

Now, it should be said that Josiah Erickson had thought about this moment before. Granted, it'd always been late at night just before he dropped off to sleep, a little flight of fancy that left a smile on his face. He knew that even if he worked as hard as he could, sometimes dreams stayed just that: dreams. At most, he hoped he could become one of those actors that everyone vaguely recognized but didn't know from where. He'd always told himself that it'd be better that way, so he could go to the grocery store in the middle of the night after some good bong rips to get Cheetos without being hounded by gaggles of fans.

But dreams were dreams for a reason. They were a happy place, a wish for something more.

And here, now, were two giggling teenage girls making his dream come true in a small town in Oregon where everything was apparently made of pumpkin spice.

"Are you *crying*?" Quincy asked incredulously.

"No," Josy mumbled, wiping his eyes. "The We Three Queens must have used more onions than they should have again." He blinked rapidly up at the girls. "You really want my autograph?"

They nodded furiously.

"So bad," the girl on the left said.

"You don't even know," the girl on the right said.

So he learned their names (Kristina and Becca). He signed their napkins (THANK YOU FOR BEING SO AWESOME XOXOXO JOSIAH ERICKSON). He posed with them as Quincy took pictures with each of their phones ("Josy, maybe wipe your nose a little more first"). They told him they couldn't wait to see the movie ("I like it when boys kiss other boys," the girl on the right sighed dreamily). They were sweet and kind, and as they thanked him and walked away, squealing excitedly, Josy stared after them, a dopey expression on his face.

"Did that really just happen?" he asked.

"It did."

"To me."

"To you."

He collapsed in his chair. "Wow. That was... wow."

"First time?"

Josy nodded dumbly. "First time."

"It's overwhelming."

"My face feels fuzzy."

"That's because you have a beard, genius."

Josy didn't know what to do with that. "Did you just—did you just dad joke me?"

Quincy groaned, putting his face in his hands.

"You *did*. What the hell!"

Quincy dropped his hands. His mouth was twitching.

Josy grinned at him.

Quincy smiled back.

"Oh," a voice whispered loudly. "Now I'm convinced it's us. Look at them. So precious."

They looked over to see the We Three Queens and Lottie peering out at them from the kitchen.

Josy waved.

They ducked immediately. "Do you think they saw us?"

"I don't know," Betty said. "But it won't matter if you keep talking so loudly!"

"I'm not talking loudly! *You're* talking loudly!"

"Both of you are loud," Bertha said.

"How did you get gravy on the ceiling?" Lottie asked. "You know what? I don't want to know."

"They know we can hear them, right?" Quincy asked.

"Yeah," Josy said. "But I don't even know what they're talking about, so. I think I'm going to try the pumpkin spice egg and bacon sandwich. Want to split it with me?"

"Absolutely not."

Yeah, Josy was having an okay day.

AND IT lasted for three more days before it came to a screeching halt.

All because of Xander and Serge.

"—and now we're getting closer to the end, and the movie is going to be so cool, you don't even know. I mean, yeah, there's been a ton of rewrites, and I'm not sure what's happening anymore. But I trust Quincy, you know? And *yeah*, I've had to kiss Mason Grazer, like, six times, but still! It's going to be awesome. Quincy said that we might finish right on time. And Quincy also said that it's getting some interest from some distributors. And Quincy told me that we could go on the film festival circuit. And Quincy—"

"Jesus Christ." Xander sounded pained.

Josy finally took a breath. He looked down at the Skype screen where Xander and Serge sat side by side all the way in Los Angeles, staring at him with what looked like a mixture of amusement and disgust. "What? What'd I say?"

"Oh, I don't know," Xander said. "Something about Quincy? In fact, everything you've said has been about Quincy."

"Well, yeah. He's my friend." Josy frowned. "And I'm not talking about him *that* much."

"You've said his name twenty times in six minutes," Serge said.

"Really? That's weird. He's just a cool guy, I guess."

Xander snorted. "Cool guy, huh? That's what you're going with."

"He is!"

"Josy, have you looked at your Instagram lately?" Serge asked.

Josy rolled his eyes. "Have I looked at my Instagram lately. *Duh*. It's *my* Instagram. I look at it every day. Do you see how many followers I have now? I might hit ten thousand by the time I come back to Los Angeles. Soon that meaningless blue check mark will be mine and I will lord it over the both of you while feeling empty inside."

The skin under Xander's right eye twitched. "He's asking about the *content*, Josy. The pictures you've been posting."

Josy picked up his phone. "What about them?" He launched the Instagram app and pulled up his profile. He'd gotten thirty more followers in the past hour, which was rad. A bunch of new comments and likes. He was getting behind in reading them all. He wondered if he needed to hire a personal assistant to handle his social media soon, but then thought that made him sound like a dick. His followers needed him and not some underpaid staffer named Stephanie.

"What's the last picture you posted?" Serge asked.

"Umm… me and Quincy on set this morning."

"And the one before that?"

"Me and Quincy having dinner last night with Gustavo and Casey."

"And the one before that."

"Quincy hanging from a tree branch, trying to fix the lighting the way he wanted. He looked so funny. I don't know why people don't believe in evolution. We obviously descended from primates."

"And the one before that."

"Me and Quincy laying in a pile of leaves. Oh man, that was great. We jumped in it and everything."

Xander sighed. "Now look at Casey's profile. What's the common denominator for most of his pictures?"

He searched for Casey's Instagram and opened it. "Let's see. There's him and Gustavo. Gustavo. Gustavo. Him and Gustavo. Harry S. Truman. The We Three Queens. Gustavo. Gustavo. Gustavo and Casey. Gustavo and Casey. A loaded pipe. The B and B. Gustavo. Gustavo. Gustavo. Wow. You know, for someone who hates social media as much as Gustavo does, he's sure in here a lot."

"And what does your page have in common with Casey's?" Serge asked.

Josy squinted down at his phone. "We use a lot of the same filters?"

He heard a banging noise from the laptop and looked up to see Xander repeatedly hitting his forehead on the table.

Josy knew what that meant. He'd seen it often enough. "I'm missing something, aren't I."

Serge shook his head. "A little."

"What is it? Tell me."

"I'm going to ask you some questions, and I want you to answer them with the first thing that comes to mind. Okay?"

"Got it."

"Who is the first person you talk to when you wake up in the morning and the last before you go to sleep?"

"Quincy," Josy said promptly. "Because we share a room."

"Who do you eat with on most days?"

"Quincy. He likes most of the same things I do."

"Who do you spend most of your time with?"

"Quincy. Because we like hanging out with each other."

"Something exciting happens. Aside from posting it online, who is the first person you tell?"

"Quincy," Josy said. He paused. His brow furrowed. "Huh. That's weird. Normally it's you guys, but I guess it's because you're not here. How about that."

"Couple more questions, okay?" Serge asked. "First thing that comes to mind."

"Yeah, sure," Josy said, though there was a strange buzzing noise in his head.

"Who makes you happy?"

"Quincy."

"Who do you miss when you they're not around?"

"You guys," Josy said. "A lot."

"But...."

"But also Quincy."

"Who do you try and make laugh all the time just because you like the sound?"

"Quincy."

"Who do you have feelings for?"

Josiah Erickson said, "Quincy," like it was the easiest thing in the world.

And then he promptly choked on his tongue.

Serge and Xander looked slightly alarmed as he gasped for air. He gripped the sides of the desk in the room he shared with Quincy, the blanket fort he shared with Quincy partially collapsed, as he'd temporarily taken the chair out. And when he had, didn't he think to remind himself to put it back when he was done? Because *that's* where they slept now, wasn't it? Oh, the beds were still there, but they hadn't been used since the night he'd built the fort.

For *Quincy*.

"What in the fucking fuck?" he managed to say. "What sort of mystic bullshit is this? I told you I don't like yoga, Serge!"

"That's not yoga, Josy. Those are *feelings*."

He shook his head furiously. "What? No, they're not! Sure, we spend a lot of time together, and *yes*, it's mostly just the two of us, and *yes*, I like it when he smiles and laughs and it makes me feel good whenever I see him and ohhhh. Myyyyy. *God*."

"I can't believe this is my life," Xander muttered.

"Guys!" Josy said, voice high and breaking. "What is happening!"

Serge rolled his eyes. "You're realizing that you've been dating someone for a while now. Probably longer than even we know."

"We're not *dating*," Josy wheezed. "Dating is when you hold hands—"

"You do that."

"When you talk about them all the time—"

"You do that."

"When you *know* you're dating," Josy finished triumphantly. "You can't date someone without *knowing*."

"That's it," Xander said, starting to get up. "I'm done."

Serge pulled him back down. "Knock it off. You said we'd hash this out now before it got worse."

Josy was slightly horrified. "Before *what* got worse?"

"*You*," Xander cried. "You and this—this *Quincy*. That's all it is. Quincy this and Quincy that. Josy and Quincy. Both of your names end in *y*. That should *not* be as cute as it is. I feel like I'm dying."

"But my name ends in *h*! It's Josiah. It doesn't end in—ohhhh. Josy. Ah. I get it now. Ha. That is kind of cute. Thank you for saying—*no*. You won't get me that easy, Xander!"

"It's okay if you like him," Serge said, not unkindly. "You know that, right? You're allowed."

"But—but that's not what this—I'm demisexual. I don't experience attraction like normal people. I'm—"

"Hey!" Xander barked. "There's nothing wrong with who you are. If that's your normal, then it's as normal as can be." He paused, considering. "Okay, you're absolutely not normal, but you get what I'm trying to say."

"Demi means you need to have a connection with someone before you can have romantic and/or sexual attraction," Serge said. "And dude, you have a connection with him. Like a hard-core connection. You're connecting all over the place."

"That's not what this is," Josy said faintly, though he was starting to doubt his own words.

"You care about him, right?"

"Yeah."

"Do you want to hold his hand?"

"Oh yeah."

"Hug him?"

"Such good hugs," Josy whispered fervently.

"Kiss him?"

Yes. Yes he did.

"Holy freaking crap," Josy breathed. "I find Quincy Moore attractive."

Xander threw up his hands. "Good god, *finally*."

"I think he's sexy."

"Good for you, man," Serge said.

"I want to put my mouth on his mouth."

"Okay," Serge said. "That's... good."

"He's hot," Josy said. "Like, frigging hot. I mean, the whole sex thing can wait or whatever, but goddamn. Have you *seen* him? I wish I was a blanket so I could lay on top of him all the time and keep him warm."

"That might be enough," Xander said, wincing slightly. "We got it."

"You need to be sure about this, Josy," Serge said. "It's a pretty big deal."

"It is?"

Serge shrugged. "I think so. I mean, it's sex stuff, right? I know you're not wired like Casey is, but you guys have pretty similar views on sex. Casey found someone who… well. He found someone who understood. What if Quincy doesn't?"

Josy was confused. "Why wouldn't he? I mean, maybe we'll have sex eventually, but why do we have to do it right away? Why can't it wait until we're both ready?"

Serge and Xander exchanged a glance Josy couldn't read. "It can," Xander said slowly. "And if Quincy likes you as much as you like him, he'll understand that. Sex isn't the same for everyone. But you need to be ready in case it doesn't work for him. You remember what it was like for me and Casey. I wish… I wish I could have done things differently. But I needed things he couldn't give me. And that's not his fault, nor is it mine. If Quincy thinks the same way, you can't blame him for that."

Josy blinked. "Of course I wouldn't. Why would I blame someone for being who they are? Sex can be complicated, but it doesn't have to be if you're up-front about it. I want to make out with him. Like, you don't even know how much. I want to kiss him and eat his breath and—"

"Abort," Xander muttered, tapping the screen on his end. "Why isn't this aborting?"

"It's not a touch screen," Serge hissed. "Stop getting your fingerprints all over it!"

"What do I do?" Josy asked, starting to feel hysterical. "I mean, how do you tell someone you're accidentally dating that you want to make it real dating, preferably for a long time to come?"

"You just *tell* him—"

"I need an expert," Josy said. "I need someone who knows what they're talking about. Someone who has been through something *exactly* like this before." He looked up at his friends who were hundreds of miles away. "And I know who to go to."

"What?" Xander asked, sounding alarmed. "Oh god, no. Josy, don't you *dare*—"

"I love you!" Josy yelled as he stood up, the chair falling back behind him. "I wish you could be here for No-Thanks Giving! I miss you! Thanks for helping me realize I want a boyfriend named Quincy! Bye!"

He slammed the laptop closed.

There was only one person in the world who could help him now.

Chapter 15

"I NEED your help with a love-life emergency!" Josy bellowed as soon as he burst through the doors of Pastor Tommy's Video Rental Emporium. "I need you to tell me—oh. Sorry. You actually have a customer. Wow. I don't think I've ever seen that before. Hullo, Mrs. Von Patterson. What's that you got there? Is that a… paper turkey?"

Gustavo glared at him.

"Yes it is," Mrs. Von Patterson said with a sniff. "I know you're all… Hollyweird and think things should be done exactly when you say, but it'll have to wait until Mr. Tiberius accepts the fact that I will hang this turkey in his window as acting president of the Fun Committee for No-Thanks Giving, or we *will* be talking about this at the next town council meeting."

"Do you not see the irony in what you just said?" Gustavo asked.

"Even I could see it," Josy said. "And I miss mostly everything."

Mrs. Von Patterson ignored them. "This paper turkey is a symbol of No-Thanks Giving, and if not placed in your window, it'll seem as if you don't stand for everything No-Thanks Giving is about. You don't want people to think you're against No-Thanks Giving, do you, Mr. Tiberius?"

"I'm not against the holiday. It's the decorations I have a problem with—"

"Can you please let her put the turkey in the window?" Josy asked. "I have a life-or-death emergency, and I'm worried that it's about to be more death than life."

Gustavo looked startled. "What? What's going on? Is everything okay?"

Josy sighed. "I don't know. Maybe. But maybe not."

"That doesn't—ugh. Fine. Put it in the window if you must. But then leave the premises. You are loitering, and that is against city ordinance fourteen dash one nine seven—"

"Already done," Mrs. Von Patterson said.

Sure enough, the turkey was plastered against the window. Josy was impressed. "Wow. I didn't even see you move."

"A good president knows when to take matters into her own hands," Mrs. Von Patterson said. "And I'll not take no for an answer. Mr. Tiberius, if that turkey is removed at any point before No-Thanks Giving, I will use the might of my presidency to rain down hellfire upon you until all that remains is the smoking ruins of this thing you call a life. Happy holidays."

She disappeared out the front door.

GUSTAVO SCOWLED at the turkey. "It had actually better be life and death. If it's not, I will have my revenge."

"It *is*," Josy moaned, flopping down on the counter, laying his head on his arms.

"Is something wrong with the movie?"

"No. Worse."

"Is someone sick?"

"My allergies gave me trouble yesterday, but I took a Zyrtec. But that's not it. It's *worse*."

"Did someone die?"

"They might as well have! You're getting warmer!"

"Is someone *about* to die?"

"Yes!" Josy cried, lifting his head. "And it's *me*!"

Gustavo stared at him before nodding slowly. He leaned to the left, looking over Josy's shoulder toward the front of the store. Josy followed his gaze. The sidewalk was empty.

"I always knew this would happen," Gustavo said. "I'm glad you've come to me."

"You knew?" Josy asked. "Goddammit. Did everyone know?"

"I don't know about anyone else. But I figured it out right away. I mean, it makes sense, if you really think about it."

Josy frowned. "It does?"

Gustavo nodded. "I mean, it was bound to happen sooner or later. You're in too deep."

"How do you know that?" Josy demanded. "I didn't even figure it out before today!"

"Because I know many things," Gustavo said. "It's what happens when you read encyclopedias."

"Whoa," Josy breathed. "I didn't know that. Encyclopedias sound amazing. I've never used one before because I live in the twenty-first century, but still."

Gustavo leaned forward on the counter. Josy felt better already. "First thing you need to do is to make sure you're not being followed."

This was good advice. "I wasn't. No one even stopped me for a picture, which was really disappointing. I think I let those two girls who wanted my autograph go to my head. I'm a fame whore now."

"I don't know what you're talking about. But it doesn't matter. The second thing you need to do is destroy all your credit cards. They can trace you that way."

Josy's eyes widened. "They *can*?"

"Yes. Everything is traceable. Which brings me to the big one. You're going to have to ditch the phone. That means no more social media."

Josy gasped. "I can't do that. What happens if someone posts a picture of their colorful sushi and I don't see it?"

"It's a price you'll have to pay," Gustavo said gravely. "If you're going to go off the grid, you need to cut all ties with who you used to be."

"Gustavo, *no*."

"Josy, *yes*. They will find you unless you do exactly what I say."

Josy was getting paranoid. "But—but what if I only looked at Instagram, like, three times a day?" He shook his head. "No, that's crazy. Maybe twelve times a day."

Gustavo scoffed. "You obviously don't care if you die, then."

"I do! I do care if I die!"

Gustavo slammed his hands down on the counter. "Then you need to start *acting* like it! Maybe a few years down the road when you've established a new life under a different name, you can think about making a new account, but only if you remember one thing, and one thing only. Are you ready to remember that one thing?"

Josy nodded furiously. "So ready."

Gustavo leaned forward. "Here it is: selfies will get you killed."

Josy took a step back. "No. That's not… that can't be true."

"It *is*. If you're going to go into hiding, then you need to remember that Josiah Erickson is *dead*. Whatever new name you pick for yourself, *that* is who you're supposed to be. You'll need to shave off your beard—"

"Anything but that! Why are you doing this? Why are you tearing me apart?"

"I'm trying to save your life!" Gustavo shouted. "The Hollywood Mafia is after you, and now that you've finally come to me to get free, I am doing everything I can. But you're not *listening*."

"I am listening! I swear. But you're—wait. What."

Gustavo squinted at him. "What what?"

"Who is after me?"

"The Hollywood Mafia."

"They are? Why?"

Gustavo threw up his hands. "I don't know! Probably because you're in too deep! You've sold your soul for fame and money, and now you're about to pay the price!"

Josy didn't know he'd done any of that. It was a good thing he'd come here. "But... it's just a movie!"

"That's how it starts. First it's a commercial. Then it's a part in a TV show where you play a corpse."

"Oh no," Josy whispered. "I did those things."

"And *then* you get the starring role in a movie about having sexual relations with animals—"

"Hold up. Time out. That's not what the movie is about."

"You made out with a man dressed like a lion."

"Yeah, but it's *whimsical*. Grady is an imaginary friend that became real who reminds my character of his one true love. It's kind of like *Calvin and Hobbes*."

Gustavo snorted. "Calvin never wanted to fuck the tiger."

Josy gaped at him. "That's—I don't know that I've ever heard you say fuck before, man. It's really tripping me out. Also, that sentence really messed with my childhood memories."

"And now you're coming to me for help because you know the Hollywood Mafia is after you because you've stumbled upon their terrible secrets."

Josy blinked. "That's not why I'm here."

"It's not?"

"Uh, no? The mafia isn't after me. At least I don't think."

"But you said it was life-or-death!"

"It is! Xander and Serge made me realize that I'm accidentally dating Quincy, and now I need your help figuring out how to make it real dating."

Gustavo stared at him.

Josy smiled back.

Gustavo was quicker than Josy expected. He practically shoved Josy out the door before he even realized what was happening. "Hey, man! What are you doing?"

"Get out," Gustavo snapped. "You are banned from Pastor Tommy's Video Rental Emporium for life. And don't even think about trying to sneak back in. I have your face memorized."

"Aw, that's so nice. I have your face memorized too. Stop pushing me!"

"No!"

Josy dug his heels in. Gustavo was freakishly strong, but Josy had done squats this morning, so his thighs were ready for the challenge. A man and a woman walked by the front of the store and stopped to stare at them.

Josy waved.

Gustavo growled.

They left quickly.

"Gustavo," Josy moaned, tilting his head back to rest on Gustavo's shoulder. "You're the only one I trust to help me with my love life."

"That was the worst thing a human being has ever said to me. Don't do it again."

"But you're in love! You got Casey, and now I need your help with Quincy!"

"Then talk to Casey!"

"I'm trying to talk to you!"

It was about that time that Gustavo must have figured out that Josy wasn't going to leave. They were both panting and sweating slightly. Gustavo had him in a headlock, and Josy was hanging on to the front pockets of Gustavo's pants. Either Josy's neck would break or Gustavo's pants would rip.

They were at a stalemate.

"Truce?" Josy managed to say.

"Truce. Let go on one… two… *three*."

They let go of each other.

Gustavo glared.

Josy grinned. "That was awesome. You could be a bouncer at a swanky club."

Gustavo sniffed. "Yes. Well. I will keep that in mind if my current career path doesn't pan out. And if a swanky club ever opens in Abby. Which I doubt, given the lack of space for such a thing."

"I don't think the Hollywood Mafia is a real thing."

"It is. Just because you haven't been invited to be in it doesn't mean it doesn't exist. Frank Sinatra and Sammy Davis Jr. started it. That's what Pastor Tommy said. And he knew everything, so."

"He did," Josy agreed. "And he sounds like he was awesome. Since you're his son, that means he taught you everything he knows. Which means you're awesome too. And that's why I came to you for help."

Gustavo tucked his shirt back in. "That makes sense. But I must decline. I'm very busy, as you must know."

"Please?"

Gustavo sighed. "You're not going to leave, are you."

Josy scuffed his shoe against the carpet. "Probably not."

"And this is important to you?"

"Like, so important."

"And you think I can help you?"

"The only person," Josy said earnestly. "Because you're in love with an awesome dude, and he loves you back. I mean, I *could* ask Casey, but it's not the same. I'm more like you than I am like him."

Gustavo scowled at him. "That's not even remotely true."

"We're practically twins."

"I don't have ridiculous facial hair, nor do I dress like a traveling carney."

"*Feelings* twins," Josy amended. "We think alike."

Gustavo looked horrified. "Why would you *say* that?"

Josy shrugged. "Because I always tell the truth about stuff. You know that."

Gustavo stumbled toward the counter. "Oh my god. I do know that. What the hell."

Josy followed him. "And now you know why it's life-or-death."

"I think I'm going to be sick. Yes, that sounds right. I believe I need to close the store down early today and go home. I'll leave a note on the door. I'll put on my Yasser Arapants and get back in bed. I probably have a fever."

Josy frowned. "You do look a little pale."

Gustavo bent over, putting his head between his knees. "Is the room getting smaller? It feels like it's getting smaller."

Josy looked around. "I don't think so? It looks the same size to me."

"I smell lemons. Is that a sign of a stroke? Everything smells like lemons!"

Josy sniffed. "No, I smell lemons too. Unless we're both having a stroke. Oh no! Are we both having strokes?"

Gustavo stood upright. "No. Well, maybe. But I just remembered that I was cleaning the counters before you got here. And the disinfectant wipes smelled like lemons. I hate them, but Casey had a coupon for them, and he said that using coupons made him feel like an adult, so I didn't say anything."

"See! That's what I want, but with Quincy!"

"You want… lemon-scented disinfectant wipes that you bought using a coupon?"

"With Quincy!" Josy exclaimed.

"And you really think I can help you with that."

"Yeah, dude."

"Don't call me dude. *If* I do this, you have to promise me to never ask for my help with anything ever again."

"What if I have to move and need your help?"

"Ask someone else."

"What if I need a ride after my car breaks down?"

"Call a tow truck."

"What if I get married one day and need you to be my best man?"

Gustavo flushed brightly. "That's… that's just dumb. I would never agree to such a thing. Why would you even say that? You have Xander and Serge and Casey for such frivolous things."

"But what if I want you?"

"I don't like speaking in front of crowds. I wouldn't give a speech."

"That's okay," Josy said. "Speeches are boring. We could do a choreographed dance instead."

"Absolutely not. And the idea of planning a bachelor party gives me hives."

"We can just watch TV and smoke out and eat Cheetos and waffles."

"And I don't like posing for pictures."

"I won't make you pose for anything."

Gustavo looked relieved at that. "Okay." He took a deep breath. "I'll be your best man. Thank you. That was very nice of you to ask."

Josy beamed at him. "Thanks, man! God, I'm so happy you agreed. I can't believe I'm getting married and—" He felt the blood rush from his face. "Oh no."

"What is it?"

"Gustavo!"

"What!"

"I'm not getting married! I haven't even figured out how to ask him if we can date for real!"

"Then why would you even ask me?" Gustavo demanded.

"I don't know!"

"Oh my *god*. What the *hell*. Now I *have* to make sure you and Quincy date and fall in love so that I can be the best man. This is quite possibly the worst day of my life."

"Yes!" Josy bellowed, pumping his fist. Then, "How are you going to do that?"

Gustavo stared off into the distance, a look of pain crossing his face. "I'm going to have to do something I swore I'd never do again."

Josy felt goose bumps prickle along his arms and the back of his neck. "What's that?"

Gustavo Tiberius squared his shoulders. "I have to ask the Internet for help. To the laptop!"

RECORDING OF a customer call taken by Pacific Northwest Cable technical support representative Mitzi Reniger on 11/20/15 at 12:41 P.M. THIS RECORDING IS USED FOR INTERNAL REVIEW ONLY. DO NOT RELEASE RECORDINGS TO THE PUBLIC.

"Thank you for calling Pacific Northwest Cable technical support. This is Mitzi, and this call may be recorded for quality assurance. How may I provide you with exceptional technical support today?"

"Hello, Mitzi."

"No. No, it can't be. It's not possible—"

"Mitzi, Mitzi, Mitzi. It's *always* possible."

"I helped you. I gave you the Internet when you asked. I canceled it for you at your request. And then when you called back to have it set up again, I did it without complaint. I was done. I was *safe*. I switched to technical support so I would never—"

"You know who this is."

"I should have known. I should have known I couldn't hide. That no matter where I went, you would find me."

"Say it. Say my name."

"Gustavo Tiberius."

"*Yes*, this is Gustavo Tiberius, a customer of Pacific Northwest Cable's Super Xtreme Broadband Internet Service with Megacheck Security. And I am *not* having a cabletastic day, in case you were wondering."

"Hi! I'm Josy! I'm also here too. You're on speakerphone! It's nice to meet you, Mitzi! I've heard a lot about you."

"Are you the asexual hipster?"

"Um, no? I'm the demisexual hipster."

"There are *more* of you?"

"Mitzi! Ignore him! Focus on the sound of my voice! I am having connection issues, and I need your assistance. My account number is—"

"Oh, I know your account number. It's been forever burned into my memory. Don't you ever doubt that."

"Oh, well. That's good, if a little intrusive. Then if you please, pull up my account so we can move forward with this farce. The sooner you do, the sooner I can once again forget that you exist."

"There is nothing I would want more."

"Excuse me?"

"I said, just one moment and I'll be happy to assist you, Mr. Tiberius."

"That's what I thought."

"Mitzi. Mitzi!"

"Yes… Josy, was it?"

"Yeah, that's me. How's your day going?"

"I don't quite know now. Surreal is probably the best I can come up with."

"Oh. That's… deep."

"Josy, would you stop talking to her and let her focus? I can't be sure that multitasking is in her wheelhouse. Or even *near* her wheelhouse."

"What's a wheelhouse?"

"It's a—it's when you—it's just an *expression*. Would you stop talking?"

"Your ears are really red."

"Josy!"

"Mr. Tiberius, I have your account pulled up. What seems to be the problem?"

"It's about time. My *problem*, Mitzi, is that I'm attempting to connect to the Internet with the service *you* have provided me, but it's not letting me. It says I have connectivity problems."

"That's an understatement."

"What was that?"

"I said, that sounds terrible. I would be happy to help you as best I can. At what location are you trying to connect? I see we have three separate routers set up for you. Your residence, your place of business, and something called… Baked-Inn & Eggs. Is that a restaurant?"

"Are you stalking me, Mitzi?"

"Absolutely not, Mr. Tiberius."

"Then why have you gathered so much information about me? What kind of racket is this? You'll never get what you want! I'll burn everything to the ground before I let you find—*mmph*!"

"Hi, Mitzi! It's Josy again. Sorry about that. We're at the video store. And Baked-Inn & Eggs is Gustavo's boyfriend's 420-friendly bed-and-breakfast."

"The asexual hipster."

"Yeah, dude. That's him. Wow. You sure seem to know a lot about them. What great customer service. We will gladly take the survey at the end of the call to rate your performance. You're a ten in my book."

"Unhand me, Josy! Take your hand from my person, you—"

"Thank you. That's very kind. I am happy to know you think I've provided you with ten-level service."

"Do *not* get an undeserved sense of accomplishment, Mitzi. Oh my god, you have yet to solve my problems. Josy, you sit there and do not speak. Mitzi, connect me or I shall cancel my Internet again. I really will!"

"Please. No. Anything but that."

"Are you mocking me, Mitzi?"

"Of course not, Mr. Tiberius. I wouldn't dare. Now, what seems to be the problem?"

"I can't connect! And if I can't connect, I won't be able to look up online how to find out how a demisexual hipster can turn accidental dating into real dating with the twitchy director. And if I can't do *that*, then I can't make Josy leave me alone!"

"…."

"Mitzi?"

"…."

"*Mitzi*!"

"How are you a real person?"

"Excuse me?"

"I just don't—I don't *get* it. Years. I have done this for *years*. And I have never come across someone like you. I told my therapist there are days I think I've made you up, that you can't possibly be real. But here you are. A voice on the other end of the line and I don't know *how you can exist*."

"Maybe if you spent less time with your pseudophilosophical quandaries and more time on fixing my Internet, you wouldn't have to worry about it! You're not some grad student sitting on a quad with a hacky sack and a beret!"

"I can't believe you're making sense. That's absolutely right, Mr. Tiberius. Let us begin. Connectivity issues. Is your desktop or laptop turned on?"

"Oh gee. Would you look at that. It wasn't. That solved everything!"

"Really?"

"*No.* I'm not stupid, Mitzi. Of course my laptop is turned on!"

"…."

"Mitzi!"

"Sorry about that moment of silence, Mr. Tiberius. I had to mute you to… clear my throat."

"Well. Thank you for not making me hear that. I don't need to listen as you evacuate your phlegm."

"Of course, Mr. Tiberius. And your Wi-Fi router is turned on?"

"I… think so? It's blinking."

"So you see the little symbol that looks like a globe with lines through it?"

"I do."

"Is the light on?"

"It is. It's orange."

"It should be green. Let me run a test to see if I can get the router to respond."

"You can do that from where you are?"

"Yes, Mr. Tiberius."

"So you admit to stalking me!"

"That's not stalking, Mr. Tiberius. It's a simple test to—"

"Oh, that's what you'd like me to believe, isn't it, Mitzi? That's what a *spy* would say. Well, the joke's on you! I've got nothing for you to spy on! I'm an open book!"

"I highly doubt that, Mr. Tiberius. The test is running."

"I'm taping a piece of paper over the webcam hole on the laptop. That way you won't be able to see me."

"That's not something I can do."

"Like I believe that. A few months ago I looked up a product on the Internet, and for the next three weeks, all I saw were ads for that *same product* whenever I got online. I know what it is you people are up to. I've read the blogs. It's called spyware for a reason."

"It's actually called adware, Mr. Tiberius."

"I knew it! You *are* spying on me! That was a trap, and you walked right into it—oh. The little light turned green. That's good, right?"

"It is, Mr. Tiberius. I am showing you should be able to connect now. If this problem happens again in the future, you can switch off the router and then turn it back on."

"Why didn't you tell me that in the first place? I only have so many minutes per month on my cell phone, and now I've wasted at least *six* on you. What happens if there's a real emergency and I run the risk of going over my minutes and getting charged an exorbitant amount? Is that something you revel in? Is that what you—I'm online now, Mitzi. I no longer have connectivity issues. You have performed your job as deftly as I'm sure you know how. Rest easy tonight in the knowledge that you're adequate in this profession you have chosen."

"I shall sleep deeply at the thought. Is there anything else I can help you with, Mr. Tiberius?"

"No. That will be—wait. Hypothetically, what if there was a demisexual hipster who—"

Call dropped

Supervisor note: I followed up with Mitzi to ask why the call was disconnected on our end, given that it's a Pacific Northwest Cable practice to never hang up on a customer. She said it was accidental, that her finger slipped. I asked why she didn't call the customer back if that was the case. She laughed and said, "Oh, he'll call back if he needs something else. He'll find me. He always does."

I attempted to call back the customer to apologize and to make sure nothing further was needed, but when I identified myself, the man who answered the phone told me quite vehemently to, and I quote, "Stop stalking me, oh my god, what the hell," before disconnecting.

Mitzi asked for time off.

I approved it.

Chapter 16

At 12:57 p.m. on Friday, November 20, 2015, Gustavo Tiberius and Josiah Erickson connected to the Internet after having brief technical issues.

Several tabs were open on Gustavo's ancient laptop. He attempted to go through and delete each one. He made a strangled noise when a specific tab opened, showing a screen filled with jewelry. Specifically rings, silver and gold and platinum.

"What's that for?" Josy asked.

"Nothing!" Gustavo said, sounding strangely frantic. He smashed the keys on the keyboard until the tab disappeared. "Research!"

"For what?"

"A—a *play* I'm writing. Yes, a play that involves a ring of thieves and a heist. Nothing more!"

"Wow. I didn't know you wrote plays. Can I read it? Can I audition for it? Dude, you have to let me be in your play. That would just be wicked awesome."

"It's not—it's still in its infancy. Hence the research. I might not even write it. In fact, I probably won't and we should forget about it altogether. It's for the best."

"You can't! You have to write it. I've never heard of a play about thieves who steal wedding rings before. Especially wedding rings for men!"

"That's not what those were! They were just regular rings that anyone can wear for any reason. And you can't tell anyone you saw it."

Josy frowned. "Why not?"

Gustavo's face looked pinched. "Because. Because I don't want anyone to know that I am potentially considering writing a play about thieves who steal wedding rings—"

"So they *are* wedding rings—"

"A slip of the tongue! Regular rings! But you can't tell anyone, because then I won't write it, and you won't get to audition for it, and then where would we be?"

"In a bad place."

"*Exactly*. So forget you ever saw it and don't speak a word of it to anyone."

"Sure, man. If that's what you want. I got your back, Gustavo."

"I know. It vexes me. Moving on. This is… delicate. I know it's going to be difficult to hear, but you can't believe everything you read on the Internet."

"You can't?"

Gustavo shook his head. "No. Imagine my surprise when I figured that out. Apparently people can lie about anything they want and post it online. It's not regulated."

"Why would you do something like that?"

"I have no idea. It's confounding. But thankfully, I found a place that doesn't lie to you. All it does is give advice. Sometimes the advice isn't good, but at least it's honest."

"Whoa," Josy said. "That's crazy."

"Yes. I know." He typed into the search bar. A moment later, a website that Josy had never seen before came up. It was bright and colorful and filled with different illustrated links that could be clicked on. One said HOW TO START A BARBER SHOP. Another read HOW TO REMOVE SAP FROM CLOTHES. Still another proclaimed it could teach you HOW TO RELAX BY PLAYING AIR GUITAR.

"What is this place?" Josy whispered.

"It can be overwhelming at first," Gustavo said almost reverently. "And most of it is pure and utter crap that no one should ever be asking about. Like this one. HOW TO TAME A FULLY GROWN QUAIL. Why on earth would you need to know that?"

Josy shrugged. "Maybe you hit a quail with your car and hurt it and then have to nurse it back to health on your own. And then you name it Dan Quail and you can't help but care for it, even though you try and fight it. Then you get news from the vet that Dan Quail can never be released back in the wild because it now has a developmental disability due to its injuries. The vet says it would be best to put it down. But then Dan Quail looks at you and you just *know* you can't do that. So you keep it, but it's still wild, so you have to learn how to tame it."

Silence. Then, "My question was rhetorical."

"Oh. My bad, man."

"Yes. I'm positive it was your bad. As I was saying, a lot of this is unnecessary, but some of it can be helpful if you know what you're looking for. You just have to ask the right question."

"Really? That's badass. It's like one of those Magic 8 Balls. What should we ask it?"

"What do you want to know?"

Josy thought hard. It only took a moment for him to think of the question he needed to ask. He leaned forward until his face was inches from the screen. "How do I know if I'm already dating someone?"

He waited.

Nothing happened.

Gustavo shoved his head away. "You have to type it."

"Oh. Sorry."

Gustavo muttered something about useless people under his breath as he typed on the keyboard. He hit Enter with a flourish.

The top of the screen said HOW TO KNOW IF I'M ALREADY DATING SOMEONE.

And underneath: 0 RESULTS.

Josy's shoulders slumped. "Aw, man. That sucks."

Gustavo looked surprised. "That's never happened before."

"It's okay. I guess there's not an answer for everything, you know? Thanks for trying, though."

Gustavo glared at the laptop. "You can't give up! Not yet. We just didn't phrase the question right. You like him, right?"

"Yeah, dude. Like, so much. I didn't even know how much until the website told me it couldn't help me. Now it's all I think about."

"That was ten seconds ago."

"I know, right?" Josy groaned. "I don't even know if he likes me back. I mean, I could ask him, but what if he says no? I'm fragile, Gustavo."

"You're not fragile. You would survive. Even if he said no, you would still be his friend because you're a good person."

"Thanks, dude."

"I told you not to call me that. Didn't he ask you on a date?"

Josy shrugged. "That was before we even knew each other. Maybe he doesn't like me that way now that he knows me."

"That's certainly possible." Gustavo perked up. "That's it!" He typed on the keyboard and hit Enter.

"Oh man," Josy breathed once he saw what was on the screen. "Jackpot."

How to Tell if a Guy Likes You Back

Isn't this a pickle to be in, right, ladies and gentlemen? There's this guy, and he makes your stomach feel all swooshy and you get sweaty in the backs of your knees at the very sight of him. Congratulations! You have a crush. Or maybe it's past that and you're into the land of Full-Blown Feelings. It's a great place to be, but does he like you back?

Here are some surefire ways to find out if he shares the same feelings for you. Remember, if he doesn't, that's okay! There is someone out there who will like you for everything you are. But if you find out that he does, make sure you read the companion guide HOW TO TELL SOMEONE YOU HAVE FEELINGS FOR THEM for examples on how to nab yourself the person of your dreams!

Body Language

Men can be mysterious and fickle creatures. Fortunately, they can also be rather obvious in their desires. Sometimes it's as simple as noticing an erection. Other times it might be subtler, in that they won't stop staring at you and licking their lips.

Body language is important to finding out if he likes you back. Interestingly enough, body language experts believe that women have over fifty body language tells to indicate interest, while men have only ten. While this might not be backed by a factual scientific study, it's still something to consider. If this is something you believe, it'll make things easier.

However, if someone does appear interested based upon the suggestion below, it doesn't mean they are actually *interested. This is but one part of a whole. If someone tells you no, then you must accept that. If you think you might have a problem with that, there is a guide for you called HOW TO NOT BE CREEPY that should be able to help.*

Now, for some examples of body language that could indicate interest, consider the following:

—Where does he look when you're together? Do you find him watching you? When you glance at him and catch him, does he raise his eyebrows slightly? If so, this is known as "the eyebrow flash." He might not even be aware that he's doing it. It's a body's natural reaction to show interest. It lasts only a fifth of a second, so you have to know what to look for.

—Does he make a lot of eye contact? And if he does, does he also lean toward you when doing so? Maintaining eye contact and leaning into your personal space could be a sign of feelings involved. Be careful, though, because it could also be a sign of failing vision and hearing, and he's leaning toward you in order to see and hear you better.

—Check to see how he's sitting. Does he sit with his legs spread? Does he stand with his hands on his hips? These are considered to be "manly gestures" and indicate he is trying to impress you. If he points his pelvis toward you, he's definitely probably potentially interested.

"WHY ARE you staring at my grandson?" Roger whispered. They were filming a scene that happened toward the end of the movie, with Dante returning to the Eagleton house unbeknownst to Liam. John Eagleton was about to pass, and Liam had found peace with it. His father's stories were true, and Liam had helped to save Boris and Dill and Mr. Zucko and put Grady back in his rightful place as the ruler of the forest. It was slightly bittersweet because Liam knew where he belonged, and it wasn't with Grady. It was with Dante.

Josy wasn't quite sure he understood what was happening in the movie, but he trusted his director.

Whom he had been staring at for the past hour as Quincy worked with Mason Grazer outside the B and B, filming his arrival back at the house.

"I'm trying to see if he angles his pelvis toward me," Josy told Roger. "And flashes me with his eyebrows."

Roger coughed. "Come again?"

"I'm working on it," Josy muttered. It wasn't going so well today. He'd been given the tools, but he wasn't sure quite how to use them. Quincy had been focused on the scene at hand and hadn't really even so much as glanced at Josy for at least four minutes. Josy didn't know what that meant.

"You know he's special," Roger said quietly.

Josy finally tore his gaze away from Quincy to look at the man beside him. Roger had a fond expression on his face as he watched his grandson. His lipstick today was bright green. It was rather lovely, in an assault-on-the-senses kind of way. "I know."

Roger nodded. "I've always thought so. He was.... It was difficult raising him. I wasn't prepared. His mother was always so independent. And then I had this child who was like painted glass. Beautiful but fragile, even more than I expected. I didn't know if I could do right by him."

"But you did," Josy pointed out.

"That's because you fight with everything you have for those you love. I saw I was losing him and—has he told you? I don't want to speak of things that aren't mine to tell."

Josy swallowed thickly. "About the guitar."

Roger sighed. "Yes. That damnable guitar. It hurt when he told me. It hurt me down to my very soul. Here was this... this *child*, this little boy having thoughts no little boy should ever have. I couldn't believe I hadn't seen it sooner. I shudder to think if I hadn't seen it at all."

"But you did. And he knew enough about himself to tell you."

Roger patted Josy's hand. "That's true. And I knew then I'd been given a precious gift. I promised myself that I would treasure it forever. Oh, would you look at that. We seem to have captured some attention."

Josy looked back out at the front of the house.

Quincy was heading toward them.

"He's pointing his pelvis at me," Josy whispered excitedly.

"Well, yes. That's what happens when people walk toward you. Funny how that works."

Before Josy could reply, Quincy climbed the steps to where they sat on the porch. He grabbed an empty chair and pulled it until it was in front of them. He sat down, his knees bumping against Josy's. He didn't try to move away. He ran a hand through his hair and looked at Josy, making eye contact.

His eyebrows rose slightly.

Josy could barely breathe.

The eyebrow flash.

"What are you guys talking about?" he asked. "You look serious."

Josy couldn't speak. Quincy sat back in his chair, legs spreading slightly so that Josy's own legs were trapped between his. And then, just as soon as his back hit the wood of the chair, he sat forward again, leaning toward Josy, hands dangling between his legs.

"Whoa," Josy breathed.

Quincy squinted at him. "What?"

Josy shook his head. "Um. Hi?"

"Oh boy," Roger said.

"Okay?" Quincy asked.

"Sure," Josy managed to say. If he was being honest, he had somehow managed to convince a small part of himself that the Internet was a liar. But here, right in front of him, was potential evidence that it could quite possibly be right.

Eye contact? Check.

Invasion of personal space? Check.

Eyebrow flash? Check that shit.

Directional pelvic interest? Check to the motherfucking check.

"Why are you staring at my pants?" Quincy asked. "Do I have something on them?"

Oops. Josy looked up sharply. "I wasn't staring at your pelvis!"

Roger coughed roughly.

Quincy's eyebrows rose again. For almost *three full seconds*. "You weren't staring at my pelvis."

"Nope! That would just be weird! Ha ha, why would anyone do something like that?"

"Right," Quincy said slowly. "Are you okay?"

"Mostly," Josy said. "My armpits are suddenly sweaty and my mouth is dry, but other than that? Super good."

"Uh-huh. Well, if it's okay with you, I'd like to borrow my grandad for a moment. I need help setting up this shot. I can't get it like I want it."

"And as acting director of photography, I should love to do nothing more," Roger said. "I'll meet you out front shortly. Why don't you keep Josy here company while I fetch my scarf?" He hummed under his breath as he turned his wheelchair around and went inside. "Oh, and Josy!" he called back over his shoulder. "Remember what I said. You fight. You never stop, because it's always worth it."

"What's he talking about?" Quincy asked as the sounds of the wheelchair faded into the house.

"I have no idea," Josy said.

"Okay. You all right?" Quincy's fingers tapped against Josy's knee, seemingly an unconscious action.

Josy was transfixed by it. "Yes," he finally said. "I think I am."

WHAT'S HE SAYING?

Look, it's well known that men like to talk about themselves. They can't help it; give a man an inch, and he'll take a mile. But men are often insecure and need to talk themselves up to prove themselves. Oh yes, there are those types of men out the there. You know the ones I'm talking about. They're the men who take it too far, and instead of trying to prove themselves to a potential romantic partner, they cross the line into bragging. It's unfortunate, but it happens. Things would be much easier if human beings had evolved as some birds did, with bright plumage that we could puff out and wave around in order to indicate interest. But since we don't have bright plumages, we tend to overcompensate with our words or actions.

But you know you might have a good match when the man has interest in what you have to say. Even if he's nervous and telling you about the time he bowled a perfect game or saved ten hostages being held by a gunman in a bank with minimal loss of life, it's how he reacts to what you talk about that's most important. If he brushes off what you say and continues talking about himself, it's a sign that he's probably a douchebag. Relationships, romantic or platonic, are two-way streets. Yes, sometimes a person might cross over the double yellow line and strike you head-on, but at least they're going in the opposite direction.

It makes sense if you really think about it.

An exercise to try:

Get close to him and whisper something interesting about yourself. Make sure your shoulders brush together and speak quietly. If you are feeling particularly brave and the person is okay with being touched, put your hand on the small of his back. If he leans closer, he's potentially interested. If he steps away with a look of disgust on his face, either he's not interested or you don't practice good dental hygiene. Consider reading about how to correct this in HOW TO FLOSS AND BRUSH YOUR TEETH.

JOSY FLOSSED twice.

He brushed his teeth for five minutes.

He gargled with mouthwash until his eyes watered.

He stared at himself in the bathroom mirror. He could do this.

He could *do* this.

He opened the door.

"Hey, man," Casey said easily. "I was just coming to check on you. You've been in here for a long time, and dinner's ready."

"I had to brush my teeth using your toothbrush," Josy admitted.

A complicated look crossed Casey's face. "O… kay? I mean, that's not cool. Like, at all. In fact, it's really gross."

"Yeah. I'm not proud of it."

"Can I ask why?"

"It's this… whole *thing*."

"Does it have anything to do with what you went to the store to see Gus about that he won't tell me?"

"Probably. Gustavo is my secret-keeper."

"Uh-huh. Well, maybe not tell him you used my toothbrush. He'll probably have a meltdown. You know how he gets."

Josy did.

But his mouth was minty fresh, and he was ready.

He followed Casey out to the kitchen. Quincy was sitting at the table, fidgeting nervously. Gustavo was sitting across from him, his brow furrowed. "What took you so long?"

"Josy was looking for ChapStick," Casey said quickly, and Josy couldn't love him more if he tried. "Helped him find some."

"Why?" Gustavo asked. "Are your lips chapped? They don't look chapped." Then, "Oh. *Oh*. I see. That's… disgusting. Don't do that here. It's not something I want to see. Ever."

Josy didn't know what he was talking about, but that was okay. He sat down next to Quincy. "Sorry it took me so long."

"Yes, well, you should be," Gustavo said. "I forgive you. Quincy was telling me about his books. I asked him if he was as successful as Casey, but I didn't get an answer."

"That's because it's rude," Casey said lightly.

Gustavo frowned at him. "How is that rude? I just wanted to know if he sells a lot of books. You do, and it's something to be proud of. I wanted to know if we should be proud of Quincy too or not."

Quincy rubbed the back of his neck. "I do all right." He seemed embarrassed. And nervous. Granted, he pretty much always seemed nervous, but still. "Maybe not as good as Casey, but—"

"We write for different audiences," Casey said, sitting down next to Gus. "There might be some crossover, but it's apples to oranges."

Gustavo scowled. "You know how I feel about fruit metaphors." He picked up his water glass to take a drink.

Quincy glanced quickly at Josy, then looked back at Gustavo and Casey, a strangely determined expression on his face. "I don't usually do physical copies of books, which is what gets you on the big bestseller lists. Most of my stuff is in e-books. But I sell my fair share, enough that I can do it full-time and be able to put some aside for the future."

"That's better than saving hostages at a bank," Josy breathed.

Gustavo choked on his water, spilling it on the table.

Casey rubbed his back. "Okay?"

Gustavo nodded as he wiped his mouth. "Yes. Just went down the wrong tube."

Josy leaned over to Quincy, their shoulders brushing together. Quincy looked over at him. His face softened. His eyes were bright and warm. Josy reached over and pressed his hand to the small of Quincy's back. It was going perfectly. His mouth felt fresh and clean. Now all he had to do was whisper something interesting about himself. "I don't like salamanders because wet lizards creep me out."

Quincy gaped at him.

Josy nodded and rubbed his back once before pulling away.

Success.

INTERESTS!

It's wonderful to learn something new. A piece of trivia or finding a new hobby can bring joy to one's life.

When it comes to matters of the heart, it's no different. Your potential romantic partner probably won't like all of the same things you do. But if the guy you have your eye on suddenly starts expressing interest in the things you like, it could be a sign of intent.

Say that you're a professional skydiver and the man is afraid of heights. It's not okay to pressure him to do something he's not comfortable with. But what happens when he comes to you and says he wants to jump out of a plane? It could mean that he's willing to set aside his own fears and reservations so that you could do something together.

That doesn't mean he has to do it. If it's outside of his comfort zone, he might just be saying it to impress you. If you can see it makes him nervous or uncomfortable, you shouldn't actually push him to do it. In the example above, if you can tell the idea of him jumping out of plane doesn't sit well with him, reassure him that he doesn't have to do something just because you do it. Thank him for volunteering, and then suggest a more suitable activity that both of you can do together.

You could say, "Hey, thanks, friend. But you don't need to skydive just because I do. Why don't we do something that we would both enjoy, like going to a nondenominational church picnic or searching for treasure with this treasure map I just found in a dusty book at the library."

Trust me when I say you'll be happier doing something you'll both enjoy.

CASEY PASSED Josy the spliff, exhaling a thick stream of smoke.

And that's when Quincy asked, "Is it hard? To hold in the smoke? I've always wondered about pot."

Josy almost dropped the spliff on the carpet. He managed to burn the tip of one of his fingers. He hissed and stuck it in his mouth.

"You okay, man?" Casey asked.

Josy nodded. "Just slipped."

They were sitting in the living room of casa de Gustavo and Casey. Casey had lit up but had first asked Quincy if he minded, as that was the polite thing to do when smoking in front of guests. Quincy had shaken his head, saying it was fine.

Gustavo wasn't smoking. He sat in his recliner with an open encyclopedia (Josy thought it was the beginning of the *R* section), Harry S. Truman chittering at his feet as he played with a ball that had a bell inside. Casey sat on the arm of the recliner. Quincy and Josy were on the couch.

"It takes some getting used to," Casey said. "I remember when I first started smoking, I managed to cough everything up. It didn't help that it was ragweed, you know? All dry and seeds and shit." He chuckled as he shook his head. "I didn't know what I was doing. But you get used to it, especially when you have the good kush. Right, Josy?"

"Um. Yes?"

Casey stared at him funny. "You all right, man?"

Maybe. He couldn't be quite sure. "Yep. Everything is fine. Everything is perfectly fine."

"I've just never been inclined," Quincy said, sitting back against the couch. Their knees were touching again. It was nerve-racking. "Smoking doesn't appeal to me."

Casey shrugged. "And that's cool, dude. It's not for everyone, though you don't have to smoke it if you don't want to. There are edibles and tinctures. Tablets too. But again, it's about choice. You don't have to do anything you're not comfortable with."

Quincy hesitated. Then, "I have a friend. Back in LA. He... he's a little like me. Only it's worse for him. Or it used to be, at least. His anxiety was devastating. And the SSRIs he was on didn't help much. He got his medical marijuana card as a sort of last resort. And it changed so much for him."

Casey nodded. "Yeah, it helps. Not everyone, of course. But it can. I was reading this story a few months back. There was this little girl who had terrible seizures. They couldn't find the right combination of meds to stop it. We're talking, like, twenty or thirty seizures a day. I can't even imagine the kind of life she led. And medical marijuana wasn't legal where they lived, but when the parents heard of cannibid oil, they had to try it. And since you have to have a residence in the state where you get your medical marijuana card, they had to move. Except the dad had a good job where their health insurance came from, so he couldn't go with them. He stayed while the mom and little girl moved." He shook his head. "The girl got cannibid oil, and the number of seizures she had were halved almost immediately. Once they figured out the right dosage, she had even less. And it sucks, because she had to leave a parent behind in order to get help."

Quincy glanced at Josy, who sat with the spliff burning in his hand. "Maybe... one day. I don't know. I'll have to think about it. See if it's something I want to try. I mean, it can't hurt, right?"

"We should go to the church treasure hunt," Josy blurted. "It's nondenominational. Yay Jesus!"

Quincy stared at him.

Casey turned slowly to look at Gustavo, eyes narrowing.

Gustavo nodded sagely. "Sounds about right."

Social Media Interaction

It's all about the Internet these days, isn't it? Gone is the time when you would send a letter and have to wait a couple of weeks for a response. Now we're connected to people from all over the world and can hear from them in a matter of seconds. It's intimidating, but it also gives us an opportunity to speak to people and learn things that we might have not had the opportunity before.

Social media is at the forefront of these interactions, and even that is ever changing. Now, instead of emailing, we can Snap and Insta and Whisper and WhatsApp and Facebook and Twitter whoever we want! It's a double-edged sword, because one doesn't want to be too *involved on social media. There are laws against stalking in place for this very reason. If you don't believe someone returns your affection, it's not socially acceptable to comment on their posts how attractive you find them, and that you wish you could smell their hair. Once again, that falls under HOW TO NOT BE CREEPY, in case you think you need it.*

But it doesn't hurt to look *at his social media. If he's active, it will be yet another clue into his interests. It also might show you if he's talking about you at all. If he tags you in posts, it means he's found something he wants you to see, or he's talking about you.*

For example: You get a notification on your phone. It's from Facebook, telling you that he's talking about and/or to you. You click on the notification and you see he's tagged you in a post about tiger sharks, saying that you should watch this video of a feeding frenzy. When you watch it, you can either give the post a "like" or you can leave a comment. If you choose to comment, keep it simple but directed at what you were tagged in! It will show that you actually watched the video, and also are responding to some part of it. It could help too if you leave some kind of emoji at the end. If you feel like being a little flirtatious, you could leave a winking emoji. It will look like this:

"Wow, this sure is interesting! That's a lot of blood and ripped flesh in the water. ;-)"

See how that works? It's to the point, but also ends with something fun!

JOSY'S PHONE beeped three days before No-Thanks Giving.

He was brushing his teeth in the bathroom, getting ready for bed. It'd been a long day, and he was ready for sleep.

Until he saw the little Instagram icon in the corner of his screen.

Q-Bert tagged you in a post.

Josy stared down at his phone.

Quincy was downstairs on a conference call with Roger and a man in Los Angeles who would be editing the film. Roger had used him for multiple films, and he was going through the dailies, figuring out what takes worked the best. But here Quincy was, tagging Josy in an Instagram post.

Josy's hand shook as he clicked the notification.

Instagram opened.

He didn't know when the photo had been taken or who had taken it. Quincy had used a black-and-white filter, which Josy appreciated as an artist.

The photo was of Josy and Quincy standing in the woods. Quincy had headphones around his neck and a small smile on his face. He was looking at Josy, whose head was tilted back as he laughed. He remembered this. Quincy had told him that it was a big moment for Liam, that he was realizing he could have what his heart truly wanted. "And I really need you to sell it. Liam is realizing he's in love with Dante, and it makes him happy. Mason's not *that* bad, right?"

He'd laughed, because yeah, Mason was terrible.

And that's when the photo had been taken.

There was a caption underneath.

Getting close to the end of filming my first movie with this guy. We've spent every day for the last month together. It's going to be an adjustment not seeing him as much when it's all over. @TheRealJosiahErickson, thank you for making this whole journey worth it. I can't wait for everyone to see just how great you really are. You're an actor of the highest caliber.

Josy's eyes stung.

Only three people had told him that in his lifetime.

One was on parole.

The second smoked Virginia Slim 120s.

The third wore awesome suits and pretty makeup.

And here, now, was a fourth.

He double-tapped the photo. A little heart bloomed at the center, right between the two of them.

It hit him, then. It really hit him.

What this could mean.

What they could be.

The comment section was filling up. People excited about the movie. People happy to see Q-Bert looking so happy and healthy. There were a lot of heart emojis. He saw one that said I MET JOSIAH AT THE LIBRARY! I WAS TIGRESS, AND HE WAS SO NICE TO ME!

Josy wiped his eyes.

He gnawed on his bottom lip as he closed Instagram.

He pulled up the web app and went to Q-Bert's website.

There was a new blog post from just this morning.

As Josy stood in the bathroom, toothbrush hanging between his teeth and toothpaste dribbling on his chin, he read.

From Q-Bert's Blog

It's been... daunting. This whole thing. I didn't even really know it was a dream of mine until I was told it was something I might be able to do. I was a writer first, and that had already been a dream come true. Sure, my stories are absurd, and sometimes the allegories are as subtle as a sledgehammer to the face, but I was able to tell them the way I wanted to, the way I thought they should be told.

(Except for when my editors told me I was wrong. I listened to them. Mostly.)

There are times I wish I'd told you all about this whole movie thing sooner, rather than hiding behind my grandad. I wasn't sure how it'd be received. I worried that people would laugh at me. Or tell me I couldn't do it and was out of my depth.

Or that I should just stick with what I know. With what was working. I can write books. I can. I can sit down and tell a story. That's easy, even if some days are frustrating as all hell. But even though no one actually told me these things, I thought what if? What if they did? How would I respond?

Even a few years ago, it would have destroyed me. Sent me spiraling into doubt and self-flagellation. I used to take reviews of my books to heart, and every bad one was like a spear in my chest. There was one I remember reading which said they couldn't understand why I was popular, that I was obviously a hack and blah, blah, blah.

That one hurt. For days.

But I'm not that person anymore. These past few months have given me confidence I didn't know I had. I still make mistakes. I still have moments where I doubt myself. But I have a group of people behind me that believe in me and this project. And that's a funny thing, because I never thought it would be this way.

Mason Grazer is going to knock your socks off. He plays a bunch of different roles, and he's a chameleon with every single one of them.

Roger Fuller, my grandad, returns to the screen after a long absence. And he has found depths within himself that I didn't even know were possible. He will bring you to tears.

There are three women who play... oracles, of sorts. They have never acted in front of a camera in their lives and yet make it seem effortless.

There are a bunch of smaller roles, some of which are only a single line. But each of the actors has given it their all.

And then there's Josiah Erickson. He plays a character named Liam. And I'm not being hyperbolic when I say this actor is a revelation. I think some people are old souls, and you can tell just by looking at them. It's something in their eyes, a brightness that you can't find anywhere else. That's Josy. Remember that name, because I know it's going to be everywhere soon enough. And I can't wait to see just how far he goes.

It's not all better. Anxiety and depression don't work that way. There are days even now when I struggle to breathe. However, if I could have you remember one thing, it would be this: There are bad days, yes, and they may be many. But they become but shadows in the sunshine of the good days. The days when you remember that you're worth something. When you have people who think you matter. When you push yourself out of bed even though it's hard because you know it's the right thing to do.

You are important.
You are worth everything.
You matter.
Never, ever forget that.
Q-Bert
PS: Thanks for your patience on a new book. In three weeks I'll be releasing a brand-new story called My Billionaire Boss is a Coffee Mug and Asked for Two of My Creams. *Here is the cover. Yes, that is a half-naked man holding a gigantic coffee cup with a face superimposed on it. Pre-orders are now available at the links below!*

HE POUNDED furiously on the door.

It took a moment before the porch light came on. The door opened, and Casey and Gustavo stood blinking blearily out at him. Casey was wearing shorts. Gustavo had on his Yasser Arapants.

"The prophecy has been fulfilled!" Josy exclaimed wildly.

"Do you have any idea what time it is?" Gustavo snapped.

"Uh, no?" Josy pushed his way into the house. "I had to wait until Quincy fell asleep so he didn't suspect that I know what I think I know about knowing what he thinks."

"That… huh." Casey rubbed a hand over his face as Gustavo closed the door. "I actually understood that. I might still be dreaming."

"He likes me!" Josy cried. "And he also wrote a book about a rich coffee cup wanting to have sex with one of its employees in what I expect is a searing look at power dynamics in the workplace."

They stared at him.

"The liking-me thing is the more important part of what I just said," Josy said hastily.

Gustavo's eyebrows did that thing they always did. "You asked him?"

"Well, no. But still! All the signs are there, just like the Internet said."

Casey sighed. "Please tell me you didn't go to Gustavo and both of you went online to look up how to figure out if Quincy liked you."

Gustavo said, "No," while Josy said, "Sure did!" at the same time.

Casey did something Josy didn't expect.

He took Gustavo's face in his hands, stared at him for a moment, then leaned forward and kissed him. It wasn't that Josy didn't see them show each other affection. Anyone who knew them as well as he did could see just how much they loved each other. But Josy also knew that Casey didn't like kissing all that much. Even Gustavo seemed a little surprised.

"Man," Casey said as he pulled away, "you are just... I don't even know. I love you. You're such a dweeb, and I love you more than anything. You dork."

Gustavo blushed as he scowled. "Oh my god. I'm not a dweeb. Or a dork. What the hell." He glanced at Josy, then looked back at Casey. He leaned forward and kissed Casey on the cheek. "I love you too. Shut up."

"This is so special," Josy said. "But can we talk about me some more? Because I don't know what to do now."

"He likes you," Casey said. "You like him. You tell him."

"Or we could look on the Internet again just to make sure," Josy said.

Gustavo glared at him. "Which you could have done back at the B and B without coming here and waking us up."

Josy grinned. "I don't know why I like it so much when you say B and B. It's, like, so anti-you."

"That's it. Leave."

"But I need you!"

"You *don't*," Gustavo retorted. "You can look up stuff on your own. I have already had my fill of the Internet for the month."

"But—"

"No."

Casey sighed. "Better help him, man. That's his I'm-not-leaving face. I've seen it a few times before."

Josy had no idea what Casey was talking about but figured he might as well run with it. "Exactly. This is that face." He frowned. Then his nose itched. Then he sneezed. Then he stroked his beard. He wasn't leaving.

"Oh my god," Gustavo muttered. "This is—I can't wait until every one of you Hollywood people goes back to California where you belong. People don't need to worry about millennials killing everything off because I'm going to kill all millennials." He stalked toward the bedroom.

"Wow," Josy said, impressed. "That was a pretty woke thing to say."

"Yeah," Casey said. "He's learning. He likes to pretend he's not, but he is. I caught him looking up pop culture news the other day after I told him about an actor I liked for a role in the next Hungering Moon movie."

"Whoa. Really?"

"Yeah. It was sweet. Until he accidentally clicked on a link for the actor's alleged sex tape. That's why he's had his fill of the Internet. The actor was very… enthusiastic in getting an arm shoved up inside him."

"I don't understand fisting."

Casey shrugged. "I don't understand sex, but to each his own." He picked up Harry S. Truman, who was winding his way between Casey's legs.

Before Josy could ask who the actor was (he had an idea or two—you could tell sometimes by the way they walked), Gustavo returned, his scowl ever-present, his ancient laptop in his hands.

"If I help you do this, you don't get to ask me for anything ever again," he told Josy.

Josy rolled his eyes. "We both know that's not gonna happen, man."

"Whatever." He sat down in his recliner and booted up the laptop. Casey sprawled on the couch and almost immediately started dozing, Harry S. Truman curled against his chest while Josy sat on the recliner's armrest.

"I don't know what to ask the website," Josy admitted. "I've never really been here before. Not when it mattered."

"I know what to ask," Gustavo muttered. "And if you tell anyone I said that, I'll deny it and ban you from Abby."

"What? You can't do that!"

"Watch me."

"Ugh. Fine. You have my word, dude."

"Don't call me dude." Gustavo didn't type in the web address like Josy expected. Instead, he pulled up the Favorites tab and clicked on a link already bookmarked.

When Josy saw what came up in the browser, he started laughing.

"Shut up," Gustavo snapped.

"Oh man," Josy said, wiping his eyes. "You're the best."

How to Tell Your Crush You Like Them

Congratulations! You have found yourself in a position of love, and it seems like it could possibly be reciprocated. What a wonderful feeling, isn't it? You find yourself walking down the street, and there's an extra little spring in your step. The sun is shining, and the birds are singing and—

Uh-oh.

Hold on a second.

There's a problem!

You haven't yet told *your crush about it!*

Oh, there's fleeting glances and secret smiles. They touch your shoulder and your hand, and maybe they even share their fried pork wontons, even though everyone knows fried pork wontons are the greatest food in the world.

So what are you going to do about it? What are you going to say to make sure your crush understands the depths of your feelings?

This guide will provide easy steps to make sure that you and your crush are on your way to living a happily ever after like you deserve. But, as always, keep in mind that if you're mistaken and/or a stalker, it's not right to pursue the object of your desires if the feelings are not returned. If you're mistaken, apologize and back off. We'll discuss that more in part one. If you're a stalker, please click on HOW TO TURN YOURSELF IN TO THE LOCAL POLICE or HOW TO SURVIVE IN FEDERAL PRISON.

"Whoa," Josy breathed. "Click on that last one."

"No," Gustavo said. "We can't. It's a trap. Trust me. I've been there before. I learned things about cats I never wanted to know. We have to resist."

It was probably for the best.

Rejection

Sometimes things don't turn out the way we expect them to. Maybe we misread signals or mistake friend gestures for flirting. It's okay. It happens to the best of us. But it's what happens next *that separates the good from the bad. Remember: if a person doesn't return your affection, it's not the end of the world, even if it feels like an atomic bomb was just dropped on your heart. If you were rebuffed, you should still be proud of yourself for being confident enough to express your desires. If your crush says no, respect that and put some distance between the two of you. It'll help in the long run. Some of examples of responses are as follows:*

—Cool, my guy. I respect that. I'm just going to go help build a house with Habitat for Humanity in a foreign country for six to eight weeks.

—Hey, friend, you are a good person. Thanks for listening. If you'll excuse me, I have to catch a plane to Disney World for a planned family reunion.

"Oh my god," Josy moaned, face in his hand. "What if I'm wrong and he rejects me? I have to go all the way to *Florida*? But that's, like, one of the worst places in the world!"

"I know," Gustavo said, squinting at the screen. "We'll send you to Alabama instead or something."

Josy sighed in relief. "Good. Anywhere but Florida."

Look Your Best

Appearances aren't everything, but if you are planning on telling your crush how you feel, it's best that you present yourself in a manner that shows you value cleanliness and hygiene. At the same time, don't be too obvious about it. If you normally dress casually, do not go out and buy a suit. If your wardrobe consists of business attire, do not buy cargo shorts and Crocs to show how "laid-back" you can be. There is nothing "laid-back" about Crocs.

You don't want your crush to think you're trying too hard to impress them. They might immediately notice something has changed and call you out on it before you're ready to talk about it.

Consider your wardrobe: What do you own that shows you're cool and confident, while also saying you're just a regular person who might be interested in dating? Perhaps it's a scarf. Or maybe it's a pair of knitted trousers.

"Oh thank Christ. I finally have an excuse to wear my tweed suit coat over an ironic printed T-shirt I got a thrift store, skinny jeans, and the fedora I bought at the swap meet two years ago. Everything's coming up Josy!"

"Oh my god," Gustavo muttered. "What the hell is wrong with you?"

Time and Place

As the saying goes, there's a time and place for everything. You could get up from wherever you're reading this and go find your crush and tell them right this second, but where's the fun in that? It helps, especially if you're nervous, to have it planned out. Pick a time and place to speak to your crush about your feelings. That way you'll know when it's going to happen, giving yourself time to think about what you're going to say.

Don't do it through a phone call or text message. It's impersonal, misses the nuances that a face-to-face conversation will have.

Also, when thinking about where *and* when *to do it, consider the following: If you go to the residence of your crush, you might feel uncomfortable if you're rejected. Blinded by tears, you might get lost in their house if you're not familiar with the layout, which will end up making things worse.*

It's best to pick a neutral setting, like a coffee shop or a zoo. Perhaps there is a farmers' market you could both attend, or a festival celebrating the opposite of what a holiday actually entails put on by people coming from a place of privilege. That way, if it doesn't go the way you anticipate, you can thank the person for their time and go find a stall that sells pie to make yourself feel better.

"The No-Thanks Giving Festival," Josy whispered.

Gustavo frowned. "That did get oddly specific for only a potential situation. But it's...." He leaned toward the computer screen. Then, "Hello? Can you hear me?"

"Yes," the computer said in a robotic voice. "I can hear everything you say, Gustavo Tiberius."

Gustavo and Josy screamed.

Casey laughed. "Got you. Man, you guys are so easy." He rolled over to face the back of the couch, Harry S. Truman chittering softly.

THE ACT OF TELLING

Okay, so you look good. You've picked a time and place. You're ready to do this.

What next?

Two things.

First, you need to figure out what you're going to say.

Second, you need to figure out how to say it.

Ah, love. Love is splendid thing. But it has razed cities and brought even the greatest of men to their knees. It can be difficult to even get the words out, even if it's not quite *love yet. But even a very strong affection is hard to articulate.*

There are several ways to go about this. If you are of the humorous sort, open with a good joke. Nothing puts people at ease like shared laughter. It's best to avoid puns, because some people think puns are the lowest form of humor. Try to avoid sensitive topics such as politics, race, sex, or male-female dynamics.

For example, what do you call a belt made of watches? A waist of time!

Or, if you're feeling a little more confident: A horse walks into a bar, and the bartender says, "Why the long face?" The horse replies, "My alcoholism is destroying my family."

However, it should be noted that if you are not of the humorous sort, it's best to avoid trying to tell a joke, as it could fall flat.

Think of what your strengths are and build upon that.

Once you're both at ease, it's time for the main event.

It's scary. Putting yourself out there usually is. Maybe you need a big declaration. Maybe you want to put together a flash mob where people randomly start dancing around you until you join in, even if you're not the best dancer.

Maybe you know magic tricks and can conjure up a flower out of thin air and present it to your crush.

Big declarations are cool and all, but you know what?

Sometimes the biggest declaration can come from the smallest of actions.

Sometimes it can be very simple.

Sometimes all you need to say is, "I think you're wonderful. There is no one in the world like you, and I can't imagine not being by your side. I'm not going to tell you a joke about an alcoholic horse, because you're already smiling, and that's all I could ever ask for."

And that's where the how *comes in. Because all the jokes and fancy tricks and pretty words mean nothing if there's no heart behind it. You have to believe in yourself and what you're saying. Love is scary. It's intimidating and can rip our hearts from our chests.*

But it is also kind and warm and makes this crazy thing we call life that much brighter.

You can do this.
I know you can.
Because love is important, and you deserve to be loved.
Good luck!

CASEY WAS snoring softly on the couch when Gustavo closed the laptop. He handed it to Josy as he stood. He walked over to the couch and stood above Casey, staring down at him and Harry S. Truman with a strange look on his face.

Finally he said, "I didn't think I could have something like this."

"Like what? Casey?"

He nodded. "After… after Pastor Tommy died, I was a little lost. I remember the day it happened. I came home and the house was so quiet. Normally when Pastor Tommy was home, you could always tell where he was. Either he'd be singing or messing around in the kitchen or yelling at *House Hunters* on the television. He always thought the stupidest people were on that show. It's probably for the best he didn't live to see *Tiny House Hunters*, because those people are even worse, oh my god. They actually go into something called a *tiny house* and complain how small it is."

Josy smiled but didn't speak.

Gustavo sighed. "And it stayed quiet for a long time. Even with the We Three Queens and Lottie, it was… I don't know. A half life, I think."

"And then you found Casey."

"And then I found Casey," Gustavo agreed. "I didn't get him at first. And when I tried to, it only made things worse. Because I thought I needed to be someone different. But you know what?"

"You didn't."

"No. I didn't. Because he liked me for the me I was and not the me I was trying to be."

"That makes so much sense, dude. Like, you don't even know."

"Does it?"

"Yeah. You're very likable for the you you are, not the you you're not."

"Right. That's exactly right. I didn't know that. But I learned. I can be abnormal and weird and strange, and that's okay with him."

Casey snored loudly.

Then Gustavo Tiberius changed everything. "I lied to you about something. About the rings I was looking up. I'm going to ask him to marry me."

Josy's eyes bulged as he slapped a hand over his mouth to keep from screaming.

Gustavo looked up sharply.

Josy was having trouble breathing. "Dude!" he squeaked between his fingers.

Gustavo nodded solemnly. "Dude. You can't say anything. You're the only one who knows."

Josy drew an X over his heart. "I so swear." He stood and walked over to Gustavo, grabbed him by the arm, and dragged him toward the front door. He pulled Gustavo outside and shut the door behind him. Once he was sure Casey couldn't hear, he threw his arms around Gustavo and started jumping up and down.

Gustavo did not, in fact, jump up and down, but he did return the hug.

"This is the *best*!" Josy crowed. "You don't even know!"

"I think I do," Gustavo said stiffly. "It was my idea, after all." He hesitated. Then, "Do you think he'll say yes?"

Josy stopped jumping and took a step back, hands still clasped on Gustavo's arms. "Hell yeah, man. Of course he will. He'll say yes so fast your head will spin."

Gustavo looked relieved. "Good. I'm not worried or anything, but it's still good you think so."

"I'm so happy for you."

"Me too. About you."

Josy beamed at him. "Really?"

Gustavo shrugged awkwardly. "Yes. Quincy is… he's nice. And twitchy. He writes monster porn, but I guess nobody's perfect. But he likes you, and you smile really big whenever he's around, and that's what's most important."

"I'm so happy Casey found you," Josy said seriously. "Sometimes I get sad that he's so far away, but then I remember he's with you, and that makes it better. Then I remember you're *both* far away, and I get sad again."

"Yes, well. That sucks."

"It does, dude."

Gustavo scowled at him. Then he mumbled something Josy didn't catch.

"What was that? Couldn't hear you, man."

Gustavo sighed and looked skyward. "I said, I miss you when you're not here too. You're one of Casey's best friends, and I tolerate you most of the time. It's going to be hard when the movie is over and you go back to Califor—oh my god, are you *crying*?"

"No," Josy sniffled, wiping his face. "And even if I was, it was because I thought of a video I saw about a dog that was adopted after being rejected many times. I love you, dude. And I can't wait for you and Casey to get married. I get to be in the wedding. And there better be a weed bar."

Gustavo groaned. "You know there will be. Look. Just—do you really want to know what to do about Quincy?"

"Yeah, man. I mean, I sort of have an idea, but you're, like, this love guru—"

"First, what the hell, never call me that again. That's terrible, and you should be ashamed of yourself."

"And second?"

"Second, go for broke. Don't worry about what to say because you'll know it when it happens."

"You told Casey you wanted to be a lesbian with him and that you wanted to shave his pinewood beaver—"

"Oh my god, that was an *accident*—"

"Hey, man, I'm not judging, I'm just saying that maybe worrying about what to say is kind of important—"

"It made sense at the time. There was *context*—"

"I still want to audition for that movie if it ever becomes a real thing—"

"Would you shut up and *listen to me*?"

Josy grinned. "Always, man."

Gustavo took a deep breath. "Just… do it."

Josy blinked at him. "Tell him the slogan for Nike? What will that—"

Gustavo threw up his hands. "You know what? You're on your own. Get off my property before I call the police."

Josy laughed as he walked down the stairs. The air was cold and the stars were twinkling overhead. He felt good. He felt… better. It would work out. And even if it didn't, he'd be okay.

(After bouts of crying and making Casey and Gustavo bring him joints and ice cream.)

He stopped when he reached the sidewalk and turned around. Gustavo stood on the porch, arms across his thin chest. "Thanks, man. You're one of the good ones."

Gustavo rolled his eyes. "I own that part of the sidewalk too. Keep walking."

And so Josy did.

QUINCY WOKE up briefly when Josy returned to their room at the B and B.

"Hey," he said, voice rough. "All right?"

Josy had to stop from blurting out everything right then. "Yeah. Just couldn't sleep. Went for a walk."

"Blanket fort?"

That sounded good. "Blanket fort."

Quincy was asleep the moment his head hit the pillow again inside their blanket fort.

Josy watched him sleep for a minute or two, not wanting to make it weird. He really didn't want to have to look up HOW TO NOT BE CREEPY.

Soon, he too slept.

Chapter 17

From Josiah Erickson's Instagram Story

"Hey there, followers! Happy Turkey Day, or as we say here in Abby, No-Thanks Giving. Did you know that the natives of this country were eradicated and marginalized as the colonists took over? It still happens to this day. That sucks. Not trying to make you feel bad, but remember when you're eating your turkey that a lot of our ancestors were terrible people. And what's even worse is that there are *still* terrible people in this country. What's up with that? I have no idea. I was going to borrow a friend's encyclopedia to read up on it, but then I remembered it's 2015 and so I just used my phone. White people suck. And yes, I know I'm white, but I can still say it because it's true. We deserve to be called out for our stupid shit. We have to be better. So… do that.

"In other news, today's a big day! For… um. Reasons. Reasons that I can't quite say anything about. But hopefully it'll be good, and then I'll be able to tell you all about it later! Or maybe I'll be crying and eating ice cream, so just be prepared for that. I don't know that anyone looks good crying and eating ice cream at the same time, but I'll try my best."

"Hey, Mom and Dad! It's me, Josy. Just… leaving you another message. I don't know if you got my last one about the movie since I didn't hear from you, but it's going well! In fact, we've only got a couple of weeks left on it. I can't wait for you to see it. I don't know if they'll play it in Wooster, so you might have to go to Cleveland if you want to… see it… and—

"You know what? Don't even worry about it, man. I know you won't go see it. And that's really shitty of you. Maybe I didn't turn out how you wanted me to be. Maybe I'm not the best son in the world. But that shouldn't matter. I took a chance and it turned out okay. I've got a good life. I've got the best friends. I've got a roof over my head. Well, it's not *my* roof because I'm in Oregon for the movie, but I still have one in Los Angeles! That I paid for *myself*. I didn't ask for help from you or anyone else. I did it on my own.

And guess what. I made something of myself. *For* myself. You might not approve, but I don't need it. Not anymore. I've got these people, okay? And they're *good*. They think I matter. They think I'm *important*. And there's this guy. He's awesome and has depression and anxiety, but he's so kickass about it. He's such a fighter. And I really like him. I might even love him a little. I'm going to tell him today. All of it. Because when you care about someone, they deserve to hear it. I'm nervous and scared, but I'm also excited, because good things happen to good people. And I'm a good person. So yeah. I guess that's all I want to say.

"Oh, and happy Thanksgiving! And merry Christmas! Bye."

"WHAT ARE you going to do?" Starla demanded as soon as he answered the phone. "I just saw your Instagram. You can't do anything to jeopardize your part in this movie, Josiah. I swear to god if you light something on fire, I will *end* you—"

"I might be in love," Josy said, staring in the mirror as he fixed the fedora on his head. "And I'm going to tell the object of my affection my intentions to ask him to be my boyfriend."

Silence. Then, "Oh sweet Jesus."

"Totally, right?"

"It's that director, isn't it?"

"Yes, ma'am." The tweed coat fit just as well as it had when he'd bought it for ten dollars from a store that played music by a band he liked before they got popular, then stopped listening to, then started again once they didn't sell as well on their second album. His was a complex life. "How'd you know?"

"Because of the heart eyes on every single picture I see of the two of you."

"That obvious, huh?"

"Plain as day." He heard her inhale on her cigarette. He felt a little ache in his chest. He missed her quite a lot. "Good for you, Josy. But if this gets in the way of the film and blows up in your face, I'm letting you go as a client."

"No, you won't."

"No, I probably won't," she admitted. "I've got a feeling your star is on the rise. Roger Fuller's been talking you up in certain circles. I've got some inquiries coming in about having you audition after the New Year."

Josy blinked. "Really?"

"Really. I'm not going to say much more because I want you to focus on finishing up there. But we'll talk when you get back. Most of it is crap, but there's a couple of scripts that might work."

"Whoa. That's—"

"Neither here nor there right now. You've got a job to finish and apparently a man to nab. Now, if you'll excuse me, I have family to deal with. They told me they're taking my phone away from me. I'm cutting them from my will, so I suppose we're even. Don't fuck this up."

And then she hung up on him.

Josy adored her.

"Wow," Casey said as he entered the kitchen. It smelled of baked goods, and the counters were lined with trays of cookies and pies. "You look good, man. Cleaned up real nice."

Josy fidgeted with the coat. "Yeah? It's not too much?"

"Nope. I think it's just right."

"My socks have cartoon cats on them. I don't know where I got them."

Casey looked amused. "Gave those to you a couple of Christmases ago."

"Oh. Well. Thank you for that."

"Speaking of, you outta here after the movie, or you gonna stick around for Christmas?"

Josy shrugged. "I don't know. I'm still paying for the apartment. Got four months left on the lease. Seems a waste not to. And my agent says she's got some other stuff for me after this."

"That's great, dude. You're going to be famous and shit."

"Maybe. I don't care about that a lot, though. At least not anymore. I just like acting. Being in front of the camera this last month has made me realize how much more I want it. Even if it's just commercials again."

Casey snorted. "You're so weird. It's awesome."

"Thanks." He reached for a cookie, only to have his hand slapped away. "Dude! Not cool!"

"Those have weed in them," Casey said. "See the stickers on the plates? It's to keep them separate from the regular batches. If today's your big day, I think you should be sober."

"You got stoned on your first date with Gustavo," Josy reminded him. "Like, a lot."

"Yeah, but that was because I was nervous."

"I'm nervous too!"

Casey shrugged. "If that's what you want. They're not too strong, but it's sativa, so it'll amp you up a little bit. Lottie wants them as a sort of demonstration as to what she'll serve once her license is approved."

Josy thought hard. While he *was* nervous, he wasn't the biggest fan of sativa. It was a euphoric head high. He preferred indica, which was a body-centered stoned effect. He got too rambly and touchy when he had sativa. He didn't think that'd go over well. He did have a few joints left upstairs, but Casey had a point.

"Maybe you're right," he said begrudgingly.

Casey patted his hand. "There will be plenty left when it's done."

"Maybe I'll be sad then. You know I don't like being stoned when I'm sad. Makes it worse."

Casey rolled his eyes. "I don't think you have anything to worry about."

"Really? That's—"

"What are you worried about?"

Josy whirled around.

There, standing in the doorway, was Quincy.

And he was wearing a *tie*. With *rabbits* on it.

And that *did* things for Josy.

"Holy guacamole," Josy breathed.

Quincy frowned. "What?"

Josy shook his head. "Nothing! Absolutely nothing at all. You look… nice. Like, so nice."

Quincy blushed and looked down at the floor. "Thanks. I like your hat."

"It's a fedora," Josy blurted. "I bought it at a swap meet for six dollars. The guy who sold it to me said it was worn by a gangster in the 1920s, but he was lying because there's a tag inside that says it was made in China in 2007."

"Oh. That's… something."

"Yeah," Josy said, nodding furiously. "So cool. Like you. You might even be the coolest person I know. And I know lots of cool people."

"I'm not *that* cool," Quincy said, pulling at his tie like he was uncomfortable.

"Dear god," Casey muttered. Then, "I need to go get changed before Gustavo gets here. Can you start packing these cookies up for me? The

Tupperware has matching stickers on it so you know what goes where. Don't mix them up, okay?"

"Sure," Josy said, not looking away from Quincy. "You got it. Pack the stickers with cookie Tupperware."

Casey sighed. "Maybe just hold off until I get back." He squeezed Quincy's arm as he left the kitchen.

They were alone.

Was this it? Was this the perfect moment?

He opened his mouth to say *something* about how they should probably spend the rest of their lives together if that was all right with Quincy, but his mouth had other ideas. "Where's Roger and Dee?"

"With the We Three Queens. Bernice wanted to do his makeup, and Dee went with him because she was worried he would come to the festival looking like a clown."

"That's probably accurate," Josy said. He didn't know it was possible for thighs to sweat this much, but he was sure finding out now. "They like him. Dee too."

"Yeah. They're good people. Strange, but still good."

Then came the awkward silence.

They shuffled their feet.

They glanced at each other and looked away.

Josy cleared his throat.

Quincy fiddled with his glasses and coughed.

Josy racked his brain for something to say. *Anything*. And it would be so goddamn *easy*, wouldn't it? Just right now. No big declarations. Keep it simple.

But fuck, was he nervous.

Before he could do anything, Quincy's phone beeped. He pulled it out of his pocket and glanced down at it. "It's Dee. Says Roger looks like a working girl. That's... I don't know what that means."

"It's probably okay. Maybe. Hopefully. Can you just... wait right here? I left my phone upstairs. I need to go grab it. Then maybe we can walk to No-Thanks Giving together?"

Quincy smiled. "I'd like that."

Josy was relieved. "Me too." He was about to hurry by Quincy when he stopped, kissed him on the cheek, and then fled the kitchen and practically ran upstairs.

He hadn't planned that.

Holy crap.

Holy crap.

He smacked himself on the forehead as he reached the top of the stairs. "Come on, Josy. Man up. You can do this. Maybe next time don't kiss him and run away. Jesus Christ." He found his phone sitting on his bed where he'd left it. He pocketed it, gave himself a last once-over in the mirror, took a deep breath, and headed back downstairs.

Each step he took increased his resolve.

Keep it simple.

It didn't have to be big.

It just had to be *right*.

And this was right.

He felt it down to his very bones.

He wanted to build Quincy blanket forts for a very long time to come.

That sounded good to him. Maybe he could say it just like that.

He entered the kitchen and said, "Quincy, there's something I need you to know. I want to build blanket—oh no."

Quincy stood next to the counter. In his hand was the last little bit of a cookie.

He chewed.

He swallowed.

"Sorry," he said. He started to raise the last bite to his mouth. "I was hungry, and I didn't think Casey would mind—what the fuck!"

Josy gave a hoarse battle cry as he charged toward Quincy. He managed to knock the remainder of the cookie out of his hand just in time. He gripped Quincy's jaw as lightly as he could to open his mouth. There were bits of cookie on his teeth, but he was already too late.

"Did you eat the sticker cookies?" Josy demanded.

Quincy squinted at him. "I took one from the plate. Why? What's wrong?"

"I know this is going to sound weird, but I need to stick my fingers in your mouth to make you throw up."

"*What?*"

He pulled Quincy toward the sink. "I am going to stick my fingers in your mouth. I respect your autonomy so much. Like, you don't even know, man. But you gotta throw up."

Quincy pulled away. "I *can't*."

Josy blinked. "What?"

"I told you that before. I can't throw up like that. I've never been able to! I don't have a gag reflex."

All of Josy's synapses misfired with an audible pop. "Um. Whoa."

Quincy flushed. "That's not—I'm not trying to—why do I need to throw up?"

Josy's brain was still in the process of rebooting. He didn't know that a cute dude in a rabbit tie telling him he couldn't throw up because he had no gag reflex was totally his jam until that very moment. "What."

"Why do I need to throw up!"

Josy shook his head. "I don't know what you're—oh! Because of the *cookie*, dude. You ate a sticker cookie!"

Quincy frowned. "What's the big deal? Were those being saved for—"

"They have *marijuana* in them."

"Oh no," Quincy whispered. He spun around and bent over the sink, sticking his entire fist into his mouth. It did not help Josy's newfound appreciation for all things Quincy. Especially when Quincy barely even choked on his hand.

"Ipecac!" Josy cried. "You need to drink ipecac to throw up!"

Quincy coughed as he pulled his hand from his mouth. "They haven't made ipecac in *years*."

"Really? That's weird. Remember when we were kids and our parents sometimes gave it to us when we swallowed magnets because we wanted to see if it would give us superpowers?"

"No one did that, Josy."

Josy's gaze shifted side to side. "Riiiight. No one. That would just be… stupid. Okay, there has to be a way to make you throw up. Think, Josy. Think. What if—I know! Whenever *I* see someone throw up, it always makes *me* throw up."

"And?"

"I'll vomit for you," Josy said seriously. "I swear, I will vomit so much for you."

Quincy grimaced. "That doesn't sound as helpful as you think it does."

"What's with all the shouting, man?" Casey said, coming back into the kitchen. "Is something on fire? Gus is going to kill me if that happened again."

Josy whirled around. "Quincy ate one of your pot cookies!"

Casey squinted at them. "Okay. Is that, like, against his religion or something?"

"I'm not religious," Quincy said, sounding slightly offended.

Casey shrugged. "Cool. I mean, whatever floats your boat. It shouldn't be too bad, I don't think. And it shouldn't have any harmful interaction with your SSRIs."

Josy put his face in his hands and groaned. "I totally forgot about those! We need to get him to the hospital so he can have his stomach pumped!"

"Hey," Casey said, coming to stand in front of them. He pulled Josy's hands away from his face. "He's going to be fine. Quincy, have you ever consumed an edible before?"

Quincy shook his head. He looked a little pale.

"That's okay. They weren't strong by any stretch of the imagination, but edibles do affect people differently. It'll take about an hour or so to kick in. It's sativa, so it's a head high. Happy, man. It'll make you feel happy. I promise it's not going to be bad. How much of the cookie did you eat?"

"Almost all of it," Josy said frantically. "I was going to stick my fingers in his mouth to make him throw up, but he doesn't have a gag reflex."

Casey stared at him. "That's... huh. All right. Well, first and foremost, Josy, calm down. You've consumed a hell of a lot more than is in a single cookie. You freaking out isn't going to help, man."

Josy nodded tightly. "Right. I have. And look at me! I'm just fine."

"You're wearing a tweed jacket over a shirt that says you survived the 1997 Whittemore family reunion," Quincy pointed out.

Josy grinned. "Do you like it? I found it at a thrift store. It cost a quarter."

Quincy mumbled how he thought it fit Josy well.

Casey sighed. "If you're going to be stoned for the first time, then you couldn't ask for better people to be around. We know what we're doing. I promise. You've got nothing to worry about." Then his eyes widened. "Oh crap. Josy, I'm so sorry. You were going to tell him about—*mmph*!"

Josy kept his hand firmly on his mouth. "Casey? Can I talk to you? In the living room. Now? Like, *right* now?" He started dragging Casey from the kitchen. He looked back at Quincy over his shoulder. "Be right back! Don't eat any more cookies!"

"Shit," Casey said once they were out of earshot. "Dude, I didn't even think. Oh man, I'm so sorry."

Josy shook his head. "Don't worry about it. It's not... it's not a big deal."

Casey squeezed his hand. "It is, Josy. It's a big deal for you, so it's a big deal for all of us. You might have to wait a few more hours, but it can still happen today."

"You don't think it's a sign or something?"

"Nah, man. I don't. You guys are so meant to be. Lottie told me this morning that your auras complement each other. They, like, glow together."

"She said that?"

Casey nodded. "Yep. And she said the same thing about me and Gus. Look how that turned out."

Josy thought of Gus standing above a sleeping Casey, speaking of rings and love. "Yeah. I guess that turned out okay."

"See?" Casey smiled. "It's going to be just fine. Hell, we'll all be able to look back at this and laugh our asses off at your fiftieth-anniversary party."

"Oh man, we'll be so old then."

"Right? Still be best friends, though. I just know it. And Xander and Serge think so too. About you and Quincy, that is."

Josy's heart ached sweetly. "They do?"

"Yeah. I was just talking to them while getting dressed. They were asking about you. Xander told me to tell you not to fuck this up. And coming from him, that's the biggest compliment."

"He said we were cute because our names ended in y."

Casey's smile widened. "Super cute. They're rooting for you. So are me and Gus and Lottie and the We Three Queens. And I bet Roger and Dee are too. You've got all of us, man. Right here behind you."

Josy hugged him.

"Oh yeah," Casey whispered. "Hugs are the best." He held on tight.

"All right," Josy said when he finally let go. "So I'll have to wait a little bit. That's okay. I'll like him just as much later today as I do right now."

Casey waggled his eyebrows. "Maybe even a little more. What's this about not having a gag reflex?"

"You're the worst asexual," Josy grumbled.

"I'M NOT feeling anything," Quincy announced as they came back into the kitchen. "I feel perfectly fine."

"It won't hit you yet," Casey said. "Give it some time. You might even be one of those people that isn't affected at all."

"Really?" Quincy asked hopefully.

Casey shrugged. "Maybe. It happens. I mean, *I* think that sucks, but to each their own."

"I won't… hallucinate? Or something?"

"No, man. You won't hallucinate. There isn't a whole lot of THC in it. You'll just feel really… good. Floaty. Like you're a little drunk, but without having to worry about a hangover."

Quincy gnawed on his bottom lip. His glasses were crooked, and Josy wanted to fix them. He somehow managed to keep his hands to himself. "I can deal with that."

"I know you can," Casey said, patting Quincy on the shoulder. "And you'll have Josy next to you the whole time. Isn't that right, Josy?"

"Yep!" Josy said. "Every minute. Unless you have to go to the bathroom. I'll let you do that by yourself if you want."

Quincy snorted. "Thanks. I think." He looked at Josy. "Maybe it won't be so bad. It might even be fun."

Josy grinned. "That's the spirit. Maybe I should eat a couple too and—"

"Nope," Casey said, starting to pack the baked goods in Tupperware. "Today you get to be sober. Just like we talked about before. Remember?"

Right. Because of the whole I-want-to-be-your-boyfriend-forever thing. Goddammit. "I can do that," Josy said morosely.

"I know you can. Now help me pack these up so we can load them into the car. Lottie will kill me if we're late."

ABBY, OREGON, was a quaint little town. Nestled high in the Cascades, it was picturesque, with big trees and rollicking streams. It had an old-fashioned charm, the buildings along Main Street made of brick with large awnings that hung over the sidewalks. The people were friendly, if a little eccentric. People that came to visit Abby always left with a sense of happiness, promising themselves they would return as soon as they were able.

Now, it should be said that Abby, Oregon, prided itself on many things. It had two working payphones in booths that only had a little graffiti on them (and it wasn't even offensive graffiti; one message, spray-painted in bright orange, told people that the end of days was approaching, which was nice to be warned about). Abby also had a coffee shop that made the best fruit smoothies and a video store where people could rent seminal films such as *Weekend at Bernie's II* (where two men desecrated a corpse for a second time for monetary gain) and *Robo Vampire* (a rip-off of a still somewhat awful film about a man-turned–super robot who has to rescue a beautiful woman from the Vampire Beast). It also had a well-run library, an antique store that sold what were most likely haunted porcelain dolls, and gift shops that sold art and knickknacks created by the townspeople.

One could say that Abby, Oregon, was a near-perfect place.

But there was one thing one absolutely could *not* say.

And that was how Abby, Oregon, didn't know how to throw a festival.

Because it *did*.

"Holy freaking crap," Josy said, sounding awed. They'd parked Gustavo's 1995 Ford Taurus ("He lets you drive this? Man, you're so lucky!") behind the coffee shop. They'd filled their arms with Tupperware and walked through the back door to Lottie's Lattes, passing through the kitchen before reaching the front dining room. And through the entryway, they could see Main Street was filled with people milling about, a couple dozen booths lining each sidewalk, the most crowded of which was for the Native American Rights Fund and another that seemed to be selling something mysterious known as Cup O'Quiche.

Streamers hung from the streetlights, and Mrs. Von Patterson had filled the windows of every business with paper turkeys and autumn leaves and cutouts of what appeared to have once been strawberries, but now had been fashioned to potentially be yams. There was a stage set up near Pastor Tommy's Video Rental Emporium where live music would be played at some point and, for the brave soul with stones of steel, the chance to get up in front of everyone and tell them why they were thankful for No-Thanks Giving.

It was all very festive.

Except—

"Is that person dressed like a unicorn?" Josy asked. "Where have I seen that before?"

Sure enough, a man was walking down the street in rainbow tights, a white tail hanging from the back, and a horn sticking out of his head.

Quincy frowned. "That looks like the character from one of my books. Weird."

Lottie was out in front of her store at a booth the We Three Queens had helped her build with a sign that proclaimed LOTTIE'S LATTES, WHERE WE LIKE YOU A LOTTIE. Next to her stood Gustavo, hands on his hips and a scowl on his face.

Lottie glanced behind her into the store, throwing up her hands at the sight of them. She pushed open the door to the shop. "Finally! You're late! People are craving my pastries, and I *shan't* disappoint them."

"Sorry," Casey said. "We had a bit of an emergency."

Lottie looked worried. "Is everything okay?"

"Uh, yeah," Casey said. "Should be. Just… Quincy ate a pot cookie."

Lottie blinked. "O… kay? Is that not good?"

"I've never tried marijuana," Quincy said. He wasn't as pale as he'd been before.

"Huh. Odd. I thought everyone in California smoked weed. It's why they're not evil and don't vote Republican for the most part. You'll be fine, Quincy. You've got some pros by your side. I wouldn't worry too much about it." She frowned. "Although…."

That didn't sound good. "Although what?" Josy asked.

She glanced over her shoulder. "So, here's the thing. Do you know what geotagging is?"

Josy was so good at trivia. "It's where things like photos posted on social media let people know where you're at by listing your location."

"Right," Lottie said. "You should have a cookie."

"No," Casey said.

"Aw, man, but—"

"So apparently pretty much everyone in town has been posting photos from the movie," Lottie said. "Of the cameras and the crew and the actors. And of our Quincy here."

"Oh no," Quincy whispered.

"Yeah," Lottie said sympathetically. "You have very… loyal fans. So loyal, in fact, that many of them looked at the geotags, discovered where you were, went online to learn about Abby, and found out about No-Thanks Giving on the town's website. It must have appealed to their… sense of adventure, because many decided to make the trek up the mountain to our little town. What fun! Well, *I* think so, anyway. Gus was told this by a man dressed as what appeared to be a sexy anthropomorphic sugar container. The man said it was from your novel *Pour Some Sugar on Me: Sexy Diner Adventures*. Apparently it's a series? Good for you. I like interconnected stories."

"Oh no," Quincy said a little louder.

"It's fine!" Josy said, trying to stave off Quincy's panic attack. "They like you so much they came uninvited to a public event that's open to everyone!"

"I can't see them," Quincy hissed. "I'm about to be high!"

"I like talking to people when I'm high," Josy said. "It makes for interesting conversations. The first time I talked to you, I was high."

Quincy looked slightly horrified. "You were high? At a *library*?"

Josy shrugged. "Yeah, I told you that, remember? And it's not the weirdest place I've been stoned. That would probably be the time I was—"

Casey coughed pointedly.

"Right," Josy said hastily. "Doesn't even matter. It's going to be fine, okay? I promise. You don't even have to talk to them if you don't want to. And hey! If you want to leave, you and me can go back to the B and B and play Stoner Scrabble or something."

"It's the best game in the world," Casey agreed. "Might even learn a thing or two about stuff."

Quincy shook his head. "No, it's—it's fine. I can do this. It's just… it's just people, right?"

"Right," Josy said.

Quincy looked at him shyly. "And you'll be there?"

Oh man, Josy wanted to kiss him so hard. "I promise, man. I'm not going anywhere."

"Aw," Lottie said. "You two are so—Gustavo! Stop shaking your fists at that mermaid! You'll scare away potential customers!" She rushed out of the front of the store.

"Here," Casey said, shuffling the Tupperware in his arms so he could take the ones from Quincy. "Stay in here for a minute. Take some deep breaths and then come out when you're ready. It's gonna be fine, dude. You'll see. Josy won't let anything bad happen to you." He followed his aunt to the booth.

Quincy stared after him. Then, "I'm not fragile."

"I know," Josy said easily. "No one thinks that."

"It's just... a lot."

"Yeah, man. I get it. The world is a big place, and sometimes you just want to feel small. Doesn't mean you break easy."

Quincy glanced at him. "How do you do that?"

"Do what?"

"Say the right thing all the time."

Josy laughed. "Oh man, just you wait. That doesn't happen as often as you think."

"Seems like it does to me."

"Oh. Well, I guess that's okay, then. As long as it makes you feel better, I can dig it."

Quincy squared his shoulders. "This is going to be fun."

"I think so."

"And we're going to have a good day."

"The best, even," Josy said, sending up a little prayer to god, hoping she was listening.

"And I'm going to be stoned."

"Hell yeah!"

Quincy nodded. "Okay. Let's do this."

"Rock and roll!" Josy crowed.

ON THIS most holy of holidays, No-Thanks Giving, in the year of our Lord 2015, it took approximately sixty-seven minutes from the moment Quincy Moore first consumed one of Casey's sativa cookies before he began to feel the effects.

At first it was barely noticeable to those who didn't know what they were looking for. But since Josiah Erickson was an expert in such matters—having been under the influence of sativa many times before, though he would always prefer indica strains—he was able to pinpoint the exact moment it started.

Quincy was standing at his side—his smile slightly forced but still engaged—as fans flocked around him, waiting for their turn to take a picture with their literary hero. They came to this small mountain town for their idol, not necessarily knowing Abby was in the throes of a celebration first thought up by a man named Pastor Tommy Tiberius. Pastor Tommy, who, in all his infinite wisdom, wanted a way to bring his town together in rejecting a traditional Thanksgiving, but to also give his young and cripplingly shy son a reason to go out and see the world wasn't always a scary place.

One moment Quincy was posing for a picture with a man dressed as a deer and a woman with a very large septum piercing, his smile more a grimace, and the next his shoulders began to loosen and Josy thought he saw the hint of teeth through the smile.

Now, it could be said that Quincy was just getting comfortable with his surroundings, but Josy knew better. He watched as the rigidness left Quincy's spine, and how his eyes drooped a little. And he *definitely* knew something was happening when Quincy let out a loud bray of laughter when a man dressed as Sassy the Sasquatch (which seemed to be a repurposed Chewbacca costume) told him that rhyming bipedal ape creatures were the greatest thing ever created.

He didn't think he'd ever heard Quincy laugh so freely.

It was lovely to hear.

Quincy must have thought otherwise, as he immediately slammed his hands over his mouth. But he was still unable to keep from squeaking, his eyes crinkled and leaking slightly. His forehead turned red and he was *shaking*, but he looked… happy.

Josy could barely breathe. He liked this Quincy, but then he liked all the Quincys he'd ever seen. The serious one. The director one. The author one, the normal one, the *abnormal* one. The sad one and the happy one, and the one who had told him that he sometimes felt a black dog still biting at his heels, but he no longer felt like letting it catch up with him.

Josy hadn't caught his breath by the time Quincy had calmed some, though still giggling as he posed with Sassy for a picture. Quincy looked over at him and motioned for him to come over.

Josy, not necessarily graceful on the best of days, managed to not trip over his feet as he did what Quincy asked. "You need to be in the picture too," Quincy said, eyes bright. "Remember? We met because of Sasquatch, and so I want you to be here with me."

And how could Josy say no to that?

He couldn't, of course.

Sassy said, "Oh my god, you're Josiah Erickson! From the movie! I follow you on Instagram!"

Josy managed to say thank you, distracted by Quincy's arm around his shoulder, pulling him close. He reminded himself that Quincy was stoned—or on his way to *being* stoned—so he had to be careful not to take advantage of the situation. It wouldn't be right. And it wasn't as if he'd have to wait long. He thought he would wait for Quincy however long it took.

"Say monster porn!" Sassy said.

"Monster porn!" Quincy bellowed right in Josy's ear.

"Monster porn," Josy echoed quietly.

And now that the floodgates had opened and Q-Bert's fans were aware that *the* Josiah Erickson was also present at the No-Thanks Giving Festival, they were swarmed for hours. People asked for photographs and autographs. Josy signed some boobs, which made him feel like a rock star, but also kind of uncomfortable.

Not to be outdone, of course, Mason Grazer made an appearance, saying that he too was in the movie, and for anyone who wanted a photograph with him, he would waive the fee for today only.

Josy rolled his eyes but let it go.

It was a day of no-thanks, after all.

But there was a moment that cemented it all for him, a moment when he realized just how lucky he was to have someone like Quincy, even if it didn't turn out the way he wanted. If Quincy was only going to be his friend, he would treasure him.

It came when a trembling young black woman approached Quincy, eyes darting side to side. She had been waiting in line until her turn came, and when it did, she looked panicked, as if the idea of fleeing was better than anything else.

Quincy saw her just as Josy did, and though his smile was getting dopier by the minute, he stepped away from the last group of people he'd taken pictures with and moved toward her.

Her eyes widened, and she wrung her hands. She wasn't dressed in a costume of any sort. She was wearing jeans and a heavy coat, a beanie pulled down over her dark curly hair.

Josy knew this was most likely going to be private, and apparently Dee did too. She had come to help control the line of people wanting to speak to Q-Bert, and immediately started pushing them back a little. She hadn't been too happy when she'd found out that Quincy was about to be stoned, but Quincy had told her he'd be all right. She'd seemed surprised but hadn't said another word about it.

Josy was about to leave and head back to the booth to give Quincy and the woman some space, but Quincy reached back and grabbed his arm. His hand slid down Josy's wrist until their fingers intertwined. He didn't let go, and Josy stood just behind him, squeezing back tightly.

"Hi," Quincy said quietly, the sound of the crowd around them fading to the background. "I'm Q-Bert. It's nice to meet you."

"I know," the woman said, barely able to hold Quincy's gaze. "I mean… sorry. I just… I know what you look like. Oh god, sorry. I'm being stupid about this."

Quincy smiled at her, and it was soft and sweet. "No. You're not. You're doing just fine."

She nodded once, her hands balled into little fists. "It's just… I live in Eugene. And I've always wanted to meet you. And then I saw you were here, and I thought I would try. I know you probably didn't want all these people—"

"What's your name?"

She looked up at him, surprised. "Mia."

"It's nice to meet you, Mia. Can I shake your hand?"

She hesitated. Then, "Yes."

He did. Her fingers were long and thin. The sleeve of her coat pulled back slightly, and Josy thought he saw twisted white scars on her wrist.

Mia took a deep breath and it out slow as she pulled her hand back.

"Did you come by yourself?" Quincy asked her.

She shook her head. "My mom came with me." She glanced back over her shoulder, and Josy saw a woman clutching her hands to her chest, a reassuring smile on her face. She gave a little nod to her daughter before Mia turned back around. "She knew it was important."

"That's great."

"I need you to know something," Mia said. "I don't talk about it a lot. Is that okay?"

"Yes," Quincy said immediately. "That's okay."

Mia blinked rapidly as she looked away. "So, this is probably going to sound weird. But I need you to know you helped me. I was—stupid. I hurt myself. On purpose. Because everything was too loud and I didn't know how else to make it stop. It felt like it was night all the time." She took a shuddering breath. "I don't know how I found you. But I did, and then I read more and more, and it was dumb and stupid, but it made me laugh. And then I looked at your website and saw you talking about all these things that I felt. Anxiety and depression, and so many people commenting about feeling the same, and I felt like—I just need you to know that it made the night go away a little bit. I didn't feel so dark anymore."

Quincy squeezed Josy's hand until Josy thought his bones creaked, but he didn't dare pull away.

Mia gave him a watery smile. "You didn't fix me. I don't know that I'll ever be fixed, not all the way. But you gave me the courage to try. You and all the others. I've made some really good friends with people in our community, and they told me what did and didn't work for them. And so I tried. I got the help I needed. I still have bad days, but I have good days now too, and that's because you helped to show me how. You and all the others. So, um. Just. Thank you for that."

"You're welcome," Quincy said, voice thick. "That means more to me than you could ever know."

She nodded, already taking a step back. "That's it. That's all I wanted to say. I don't want a picture or anything. I just—I'm going to go now." She glanced at Josy before spinning on her heels and hurrying toward her mother. The woman didn't look back, but her mother did as she wrapped an arm around her daughter's shoulders. She mouthed *thank you* to Quincy before they disappeared into the crowd.

"Holy shit," Quincy breathed, reaching up to wipe his eyes. "That was…."

"Yeah, man," Josy said, moving to stand at his side. He still held Quincy's hand. He didn't ever want to let go. "That's was pretty gnarly. I told you that you mattered, remember?"

"I just—I believed you? But—Christ."

"You're a good dude."

Quincy turned his head, eyes wide. "Oh my god."

"What?"

"Josy! That was heartfelt and amazing!"

"I know!" Josy didn't know why they were yelling, but he went with it.

"No, you don't! That was *life-changing*. And I am fucking *stoned*."

Josy gaped at him.

"I was listening to everything she said. And it was heartbreaking and hopeful and I *hurt* hearing her words, but I kept thinking, 'Quincy, you're really high right now, you have to be serious because this is *real*. You absolutely cannot tell her to buy one of Lottie's cookies, even though *everyone should eat one*.' I was touched by everything she said, but I also started thinking about Cup O'Quiche, and *why* is that a thing? Is this what munchies are? Do I have the munchies? Josy, that girl was brave, and I'm thinking about quiche in a cup!"

"Yeah," Josy said. "That's just swell." He turned to look at Dee, who was watching them both with a frown. He shook his head at her, and Dee turned around, telling the crowd that Q-Bert was going to take a break but he'd be back later. "Tell you what, why don't we go see if we can get you some of that quiche, man. Fill you up real good."

"I'm a stoner," Quincy announced to no one in particular. "I am a stoner because I'm stoned."

"Hell yeah, Q-Bert!" Sassy yelled at him. "Me too! Party on, Q-Man!"

"Bodacious!" Quincy yelled back as Josy tried to pull him away. "Or whatever!"

"Oh my god," Josy muttered. "What the hell."

"Wow," Bertha said.

"Oh my goodness," Bertha whispered.

"This is unsanitary," Betty muttered.

"I love everything about today," Roger said with a sigh.

"Oh my *crap*," Quincy moaned through a mouthful of quiche in a cup, eyes rolling back in his head. "Is god a mass murderer? Because this tastes like it was made from angels."

Josy didn't know quite what to do with that. He didn't know really what to do with any of this. Quincy was on his second Cup O'Quiche, having demolished the first one even before Josy had finished paying for it. Rather than risk losing his hand, Josy had handed over his own, which Quincy promptly started to devour. He had a bit of quiche on the tip of his nose. Josy should not have found that as adorable as he did.

"Oh, I'm sorry," Quincy said, cheeks bulging. "Do you want some?" He held out a bite on a plastic fork.

Josy somehow managed not to grimace. "No, thanks, man. That's all you. You kill that quiche."

"I *will*," Quincy said savagely. "I'll kill it so good." He shoved more in his mouth. "Do you think I should have more? I think I should have more. Also, do you think the Teenage Mutant Ninja Turtles are circumcised?"

Yeah, Josy was so fucked.

"Don't we have that thing we have to get to?" Betty asked Bertha and Bernice. "Remember? That thing we have to go to so we don't have to be here?"

"What thing?" Bernice frowned. "I don't remember there being a thing."

"That *thing*," Betty growled.

"*Oh*," Bertha said. "That thing. No, that got postponed until some other day. We have absolutely nowhere else to be, so we'll stay right here."

"What *is* quiche, exactly?" Quincy asked. "I mean, who decided that it should be created? Who is its *maker*? It's such a weird word too. The first three letters are the same as the first three letters of my name, and I don't think I'm this delicious." He looked sad about that. "Do I taste this good?"

"I think we should let Josy answer that question," Bernice said, and Josy was startled to learn that she was evil.

Quincy looked him with wide, glassy eyes. "Josy, do I taste good?"

Josy's heart stumbled in his chest. "Um. Yes?"

Quincy grinned. He had spinach in his teeth. He looked like he had spent the last hour fellating the Hulk. "Wow. That makes me feel good. But that also might be the pot. I am having all these *ideas*. Like, okay. Ready? Idea one: a man named John McClane fights against German terrorists holding hostages in a large tower in the middle of a city. While it's an action movie, it's also secretly a Christmas movie."

"That's *Die Hard*," Josy said.

"Oh. Shit. Okay. I got it! Idea two: we write a book about the creation of the universe and mankind by an omnipotent being that no one ever sees but still believe exists. And here's the kicker! The text of the book is actually full of contradictions that people will pick and choose what they believe in because they're mostly hypocrites."

"That's the Bible," Josy said. He was so good at trivia.

"*Dammit*. Okay, idea three: we somehow get superpowers and wear costumes where we fight politicians who are trying to take away rights from marginalized people."

"That's... huh. I don't know what that is."

"That's my brain on drugs!" Quincy bellowed before eating more quiche.

"Once, when he was seven, he fell down and scraped his knee," Roger told the We Three Queens. "He was convinced he was going to die and demanded that I amputate his leg. I always thought that was going to be my favorite memory of him. This is so much better."

"Marijuana certainly lets people have a good time," Bertha said.

"Especially for those who don't do it," Bertha said, squinting at Quincy as if he were some kind of bug she'd never seen before.

"I still think we need to go do that thing," Betty muttered.

"Oh no!" Quincy gasped. "The quiche is gone!" He turned the cup upside down, and sure enough, only crumbs fell out onto the ground. He looked heartbroken. "What will I do now? Maybe we should go get some more."

"Yeah," Josy said, taking the cup and fork from him. "How about we wait a little? I don't think that much quiche is good for anyone."

Quincy looked like he was going to argue, but then he shook his head. "Right. Of course. That's just crazy talk. I don't know what I was thinking. You are—"

"You do realize we can see you backing away toward the quiche stand, don't you?" Bernice asked, sounding delighted.

Quincy stared at her. "You can? I thought I was being subtle. Being high has really messed with what I think I'm capable of." He sighed. "Josy, you should probably hold my hand so I don't try and escape to get more quiche."

"Yes, Josy," Roger said. "You should probably hold his hand."

The We Three Queens chuckled quietly.

"Yeah, sure, man," Josy said. "I totally got you."

"You do, don't you?" Quincy asked as he took Josy's hand. "You got me."

Josy reminded himself that Quincy wasn't sober and therefore should not be kissed within an inch of his life in the middle of a crowd. "Yeah," he managed to say. "I do."

"I'll take that," Bertha said, plucking the empty quiche cup from Josy. "You two just stand and there and hold hands."

"I just had the *best* idea," Quincy whispered fervently.

"I do hope it's about another movie that already exists," Bernice said. "I'm going to beat Josy on this one."

"We should take a selfie!"

And since Quincy was singing the song of his people, Josy was helpless to resist. "Dude, yes. Yes to all of that."

"*Except* we're not going to do it ourselves!" Quincy said grandly. "We're going to let *other* people take it for us."

Josy blinked. "But… that's not a selfie. That's just a photograph."

"Then we should take *that*." Quincy pulled his phone out of his pocket and thrust it at a random passerby. "Excuse me, stranger. I must call upon you to take the best picture of your *life*. Do you accept the task I have bestowed upon you?"

"Uh, yes?" The man looked down at the phone. "No one has ever trusted me to take a photograph of them before. I will accept the task wholeheartedly."

Josy believed Abby, Oregon, was a weird and wonderful place.

"Thank you, kind sir! Grandad, you stay right there. We Three Queens, next to him. Josy, you stay by me."

They all did as he said. When one is being instructed by someone stoned for the first time, one listens. It's the rules.

The man pointed the phone at them. "Everyone say 'Thanksgiving is a lie to cover up the destruction of a peaceful populace!'"

When all was said and done, the photograph would show the tiniest slice of life on this cold winter's day in a small mountain town. There was a man in a wheelchair, his makeup expertly applied, if a bit heavy. He was smiling serenely and looked at peace. There were three women standing next to each other, pink jackets flashing brightly in the bright sun. One of the women stood with military precision between the other two, fighting a losing battle against a smile as the women on either side of her leaned in and kissed her cheeks.

There were two more people in the photograph, young men with their arms around each other's waists. The man in glasses was smiling goofily, spinach in his teeth. The other man, fedora cocked to the side, was staring at him with such a soft look on his face that it caused anyone who would see it frozen in time to think only the happiest of thoughts.

"He's in love," they would say. "You can tell that he's in love."

But none of them saw the photograph right away. Because as soon as the phone was handed back to them, the sound system screeched, causing everyone in the crowd to turn toward the stage.

Leslie Von Patterson stood on the stage, inexplicably dressed in turkey motif. Her dress was brown and orange and yellow, and she had a fan of feathers across her back. She wore a red scarf to act as a wattle, and she wore yellow lipstick that appeared to be acting as a beak. It was quite the sight.

Casey suddenly appeared at their side, Lottie trailing behind him. "Hey, man. You've seen Gus?"

Josy shook his head. "I thought he was with you."

Casey frowned. "He said he had to do something, but I haven't seen him since."

Mrs. Von Patterson tapped the microphone. "Testing. Testing. A little hot. I'm getting a lot of feedback. Can we—Pat, can you turn this thing *down*. Christ, is it so hard to—there. That's better. Maybe if you had done what I'd asked in the first place, I wouldn't have had to shout at you. I hope you remember that for next time." She turned from glaring at someone offstage to smiling primly at the crowd gathering before her. "My name is Leslie Von Patterson. I am the president of the Abby Fun Committee. Thank you for attending our twenty-first annual No-Thanks Giving." She paused as the audience applauded. "I see that we have a much larger crowd than we normally do, and some of them appear to be furries. Welcome. You'll find that we accept all eccentricities here in Abby. But please remember there is to be no fornicating in public, or whatever it is furries do."

"We're not furries!" a mermaid yelled. "We're characters from books! Not that there's anything wrong with being furries!"

Mrs. Von Patterson barely blinked. "Well, whatever you are, welcome! It's certainly… illuminating to have you here. Since today is a day of no-thanks, I will refrain from pointing out the person who I assume is responsible for your presence."

"Oh man," Quincy whispered to Josy. "I wonder who she's talking about."

"That's probably for the best," Josy whispered back.

"No-Thanks Giving is a time-honored tradition here in Abby," Mrs. Von Patterson continued. "It was started with the idea that Thanksgiving, while widely celebrated, is built upon the backs of our horrendous ancestors, who decided to take something that didn't belong to them. And while keeping in mind to check our own privilege, half the proceeds from every No-Thanks Giving are donated to a charity supporting Native American people. This year, the donations are going to the Native American Rights Fund, and it appears that we will be able to give our highest donation yet!"

"This is such a rad town," Sassy muttered to someone who appeared to be Mrs. Sassy. She nodded in agreement.

Then Mrs. Von Patterson's expression softened slightly. Josy didn't know she could look anything but mostly terrifying. It was quite astonishing. "I've only taken over as master of ceremonies in the last few years. No-Thanks Giving was originally hosted by its creator, Pastor Tommy Tiberius, may he rest in power. He was a wonderful man who cared deeply for this town. I would like to request a moment of silence in his memory, something which we will do for as long as there is a No-Thanks Giving."

Everyone bowed their heads.

Quincy reached out and took Josy's hand in his again. It was very warm.

"Thank you," Mrs. Von Patterson finally said, and everyone looked back up at her. "Every year since we lost Pastor Tommy, I ask his son if he'd like to get up and say a few words. Every year, he... declines. And quite forcefully too. This year, however, much to my surprise, he accepted."

"No freaking way," Casey whispered, eyes widening.

"Gus, would you please join me onstage?"

"Dude," Josy said.

"*Dude*," Casey agreed.

Gustavo Tiberius walked on the stage, looking extraordinarily uncomfortable in a bright pink Hawaiian shirt under his coat. He was grimacing, brow furrowed, eyebrows moving as if they'd become sentient beings and were in the process of taking over his forehead. He scowled at the crowd as they cheered, Casey loudest of all, head tilted back as he howled toward the sky. Mrs. Von Patterson covered the top of the microphone with her hand and leaned over to whisper something in Gustavo's ear. Josy thought Gustavo was going to karate chop her face off, but somehow he resisted. She stepped away from the mic, letting Gustavo have the stage.

"Hi," he said into the mic, and it screeched around his voice.

"Pat!" Leslie bellowed. "We talked about this!"

"Sorry!" came the reply. "Try it now."

Gustavo cleared his throat. "Is that better?"

Mrs. Von Patterson gave him a thumbs-up.

Gustavo scowled harder as he nodded. He took a deep breath, then said, "I don't like people."

The crowd stared at him.

"I love him so goddamn much," Casey whispered. "He's just… this *guy*."

"People have never been my thing," Gustavo continued. "And Pastor Tommy told me that was okay. But then he left me and I… I didn't know how to be. How to be happy. How to be right. How to be normal. Then these women whined into town on their Vespas and for some reason decided they were going to stay."

"He's talking about us," Bernice said to the people around her. "We will be available for autographs after. Cash only."

"And they became my… friends. I didn't even *like* them, but they didn't care. And Lottie was there too, and she brought me sandwiches. Even when I wasn't hungry. But she made me eat, because she said I was too skinny and that if I didn't eat, I was going to die."

Lottie wiped her eyes as she laid her head on Casey's shoulder. "He hates pickles so much."

"And it was… okay. I read stuff on a calendar that I didn't want, but I told myself I was going to have an okay day. And I did. I had Harry S. Truman—my ferret, not the president—and my encyclopedias, and I thought it was enough. And it was. But then an asexual stoner hipster decided he wanted to be my friend, and I—I realized that I wasn't okay. At least not as okay as I wanted to be. I wanted something more. And even though he was annoying and wouldn't leave me alone, I thought maybe he wasn't so bad, aside from the way he dressed and talked and other things that I didn't appreciate. I mean, what the hell, right? Oh my god. But he was… nice. And good. And I love him a lot." Gustavo blushed as the We Three Queens catcalled him from the crowd.

"Holy shit," Josy breathed. "Is he going to…?"

Casey glanced at him. "Is he going to what?"

But Josy could see it when it happened. The moment Gustavo changed his mind. He looked stricken, hands in fists at his sides. His mouth was in a thin line, and he shook his head. "He showed me I didn't have to be normal. That I could be me, and that was okay. And that's what Pastor Tommy wanted to show for No-Thanks Giving. That we could do things our own way and still be fine. Thank you for celebrating this for my dad."

Gustavo hurried off the stage. Mrs. Von Patterson clapped along with the audience as she went back to the mic. "Thank you, Gus. That certainly was… what it was. Now we will allow those that would like to come onstage and give their thanks, their no-thanks, or whatever comes into their head. You have one minute, and you must keep it clean, as there are children in the crowd. That means you, hairy ape creature."

"I can dig it!" Sassy shouted at her.

Gustavo was pushing his way through the crowd toward them, a frown on his face. Casey rushed toward him, and Gustavo barely had a moment to react before he was practically tackled. Casey leapt at him, wrapping his legs around his waist, hands on his shoulders. "Dude," Casey demanded. "That was epic!"

Gustavo rolled his eyes. "It was just words."

"The *best* words, man. Like, I had no idea you were going to do that!"

"I wanted it to be a surprise," Gustavo mumbled.

"Awesome surprise, Grumpy Gus. Best day ever."

"Really?"

Casey nodded as he put his feet back on the ground. He leaned forward and kissed Gustavo firmly. "Really. I'm proud of you, man. You have no idea how much."

"Thanks. I think."

Quincy was watching them. "They really love each other."

"Yeah," Josy said. "They do. They're good for each other, you know? Keep each other happy."

Quincy nodded slowly but didn't say anything more.

PEOPLE TOOK to the stage for their allotted minute. Thanks was given for a dog named Fred, a washing machine, a woman named Kimberly, condiments, a new mattress, a doctor, Disney World, firefighters, Christmas, narwhals, Darth Vader, shag carpeting, the polio vaccine, the fact that Barack Obama was president and not some narcissistic maniacal liar, and strangely, two people sang a song about fighting crime with Jesus.

Others gave no-thanks to mean people, bank robbers, the way sometimes a toaster toasted one side of the bread more than the other, a broken toe, a broken heart, a broken lamp, people who were antiweed, flat tires, mayonnaise, an inability to climb into a hammock the first time without falling out, lemon-flavored cough drops, and strangely, a guy named Billy Ray who would never be forgiven for that thing he did one time, you bastard, who the hell do you think you are?

Some people told jokes, most of which were terrible, but at least a third of the crowd was high, so that was all right.

Someone played a flute.

Still another person tap-danced.

And yet another spoke in what sound like Dutch, but Josy couldn't be sure how he knew what Dutch sounded like.

Casey squeezed Gustavo's hand and headed toward the stage. Gustavo watched him leave, an indiscernible expression on his face.

"You okay?" Josy asked him.

Gustavo shrugged. "I don't know."

"You did good."

"I chickened out."

"I thought maybe you were thinking some thoughts."

Gustavo snorted. "Is that right?"

"Sure, man. But it's okay, you know? When it's right, you'll know."

"I thought it was, but I got up there and… I just couldn't make the words come out."

"What's he talking about?" Quincy whispered.

"Nothing," Josy said easily. "Just love stuff."

"Oh. I like love stuff."

"Awesome, dude. Me too."

"Oh my god," Gustavo muttered. "Do that somewhere else. What the hell."

"Give us a minute, will you?" Josy asked Quincy.

He nodded. "Sure. I'll just go be stoned by Roger."

Josy grinned. "Sounds like a plan."

He waited until Quincy was walking toward his grandad before he turned back to Gustavo. "You got the ring?"

Gustavo nodded stiffly. "In my pocket."

"Keep it there, man. Keep it safe. It'll still be there when you're ready. I promise. You're a good dude, Gustavo. And you know he's going to say yes no matter when you decide to ask him."

"You think so?"

"I know so. He's, like, totally in love with you."

"Like, totally," Gustavo mocked.

Josy shoved him. "You know what I mean."

Gustavo sighed. "Unfortunately. Maybe I'm not as ready as I thought I was."

"And that's okay. Maybe you will be tomorrow. Or the next day. Or next month or next year. But you know he's going to be there when you are, so it's all good, dude."

"Don't call me dude."

"Yeah, no, man. Probably never going to stop that."

"Lucky me. Look. Casey's up next."

The audience cheered as Casey walked up to the mic. He smiled at them and gave a little wave, a lock of hair coming loose from the bun on his head and falling around his face. "Oh, hey, that's real nice. Thanks. Just wanted to take a minute to thank Mrs. Von Patterson and the Fun Committee for putting on the No-Thanks Giving, and to say how rad it is that Oregon decided to legalize recreational marijuana. My aunt and I have got big plans for Abby, and we appreciate the support we've received."

"I'm going to get so many people stoned through pastries," Lottie said behind them. "Muffins and cookies and scones and—"

"I've got one no-thanks and a bunch of thankful stuff," Casey said. "I try to be positive as much as I can, but sometimes even I can get a little pissed off. So, I give my no-thanks to people who try and tear others down. Like, what the fuck, man? Why do you have to be such a douchebag? Just because other people are different doesn't give you the right to be a jerk. So just stop it, or whatever. Live and let live."

"Succinct as usual," Gustavo mumbled.

"But I'm thankful for this community, and for the people in it who have helped make it one," Casey continued. "Everyone here has welcomed me, and I'm so happy to call Abby my home. The ferret with merit and Lottie and the Queens. They're my family now. It's awesome to know that sometimes it's not about the blood in your veins but the people who got your back no matter what."

"We love you!" Bernice shrieked. "Still waiting on DesRinaDale, but I forgive the delay! Mostly!"

"Oh, I hear that. Soon, I hope. And I've got my friends too. Josy and Xander and Serge. They helped me become the man I am today, and I think I turned out all right, so thanks to them."

"He's talking about me," Josy said excitedly, looking around to find out if Quincy heard. But Roger was next to the Queens with no Quincy in sight.

Josy hoped he hadn't wandered off to find a pond with ducks in it. He'd done that once back in Los Angeles, and it hadn't turned out well for anyone involved. The police hadn't been amused when they'd arrived.

"And then there's my dude. My man. My guy. Gustavo. I don't know if you know this, but he's pretty much the best."

"Aw," Josy said. "That's so nice."

Gustavo was blushing and muttering under his breath.

Casey looked at him, smiling quietly. "And I just want him to know that I might have accidentally seen some things on his laptop that maybe I shouldn't have, and that maybe he was going to ask something today but decided not to. I just want him to know that when he's ready, I'm all-in. For life. Because Abby may be my home, but you're my heart, dude. Just so you know."

Gustavo looked shocked.

Josy absolutely was not crying.

"And that's it," Casey said with a shrug. "Be good to each other and we'll all have okay days." He gave a little bow, and the crowd clapped him off the stage.

"See?" Josy said, wiping his eyes. "Told you. I can't believe we're going to be related!"

"That's not how any of that works," Gustavo muttered.

"What? Of course it does, we're—"

The crowd roared.

Josy blinked as he looked around. "What the hell is—"

Quincy was on the stage, looking determined and terrified all at once.

"Oh no," Josy whispered. "He's high. I've got to save him!"

Gustavo grabbed his arm before he could make his way toward the stage. "Let him talk. He wouldn't be up there if he didn't want to be."

"He's *stoned*. He doesn't know what he's doing!"

Gustavo rolled his eyes. "He's not *that* stoned. Trust him a little bit."

"Do you trust me when I'm high?"

"Yes," Gustavo said slowly. "Even though I would rather be anywhere else because you talk about stupid crap."

"Monkey Island," Josy reminded him.

Gustavo crossed his arms over his chest as he scowled. "That was a good idea. Shut up. Casey's still by the stage. If something happens, he'll help."

Josy groaned but stayed where he was. He hoped Quincy wouldn't regret this later.

"Hi," Quincy squeaked into the microphone. He coughed, then tried again. "Hello."

"We love you, Q-Bert!" the mermaid screamed.

"Thank you? Yes. Thank you. That's… very nice of you to say. Just so you know, I ate a marijuana cookie, and now I'm stoned."

The audience cheered.

"Not that I'm always stoned," Quincy said quickly. "I mean, it's okay, but it was on accident, and I can't throw up on purpose, so here I am."

"He's going to murder me," Josy moaned. "And then he won't want to be my boyfriend because I'm dead, and no one wants to date a dead guy except for necrophiliacs and teenage girls."

Gus was scandalized. "What the hell?"

"But I'm still going to do this," Quincy said. "Because no matter what, taking chances is always going to be scary. That won't ever change. Sometimes you put yourself out there and it doesn't work out. Maybe because it wasn't the right time or place or it wasn't meant to be. But you can always say you tried, and I think that's what's important."

The crowd was silent.

Josy swallowed thickly.

Quincy reached up and gripped the mic. For a wild moment, Josy thought he was going to start singing. But instead he said, "We get these people in our lives. People who change the way we see things. They are so bright, just like the sun. And all you want to do is stay in their light, because it makes everything warm. They make everything better. I still get lost in my head. And I get sad for reasons that aren't even clear to me, but as long as I know there's still going to be sun after those cloudy days, it makes it all worth it."

Josy's skin was thrumming.

He couldn't be talking about… it wasn't about… right? Because that would just be—

"Josiah Erickson," Quincy said, "I have something to say to you."

Everyone turned to look at him.

Quincy took a deep breath. "You must be a fake Twitter account peddling realistic disinformation, because I've fallen for you."

The crowd gasped.

Josy gaped up at him.

Quincy nodded. "Are you a magician? Because whenever I look at you, everything else disappears."

Josy was having trouble breathing.

"Do you work at Lottie's Lattes? Because I like you a lottie."

"Oh my god," Josy managed to say.

"What the hell," Gustavo agreed. "He came to me a couple of days ago and we looked up online how to tell a hipster you like them. We found a bunch. They're all pretty good."

"I want to live in your cow socks so I can be with you every step of the way."

Gustavo sighed. "Except for that one. That one sounded creepy. I told him not to use it, or the one about—"

"Are you an orphanage? Because I want to give you kids. Oh crap. Wait, I wasn't supposed to say that one. I take that back. That's just weird."

Casey's face was in his hands.

People in the crowd starting chuckling.

Quincy looked panicked. "I have better ones! Is your name ChapStick? Because you're da balm. Jesus Christ, that's so *stupid*. Who would name their kid ChapStick, aside from most of the celebrities that live in Hollywood? Oh! I got a better one. Do you smoke pot? Because weed be good together."

Josy's heart was in this throat. No one had ever cared so much about him to make a weed pun.

"Did you read Dr. Seuss as kid? Because green eggs and *damn* you're fine." Quincy winced. "Wow, this isn't going like I thought it would. Gus! I'm not doing it right!"

"Do the asexual one!"

"Are you a hardware store? Because I think you're ace."

"No, not *that* one. The other one!"

"What other—oh! I'm a pack of cards, and I want you to be the ace in my deck!"

"Okay, there's something wrong with your delivery. Maybe try the hipster ones."

"You're so hot, I better date you before you're cool!" Quincy shouted. "My feelings for you are one hundred percent organic and locally sourced! Are you gluten-free tonight, because I'd like to take you on a date! I'd still care about you even if you went mainstream! Roses are red, your shirt is ironic, your drink of choice is probably a mason jar filled with a vodka tonic!"

Josy was almost to the stage even before he knew he was moving. He could hear Quincy asking if he was a pair of Warby Parkers, because he'd like to see Josy up close, but he was already on the stairs.

Quincy was facing him, and he looked *terrified*. Josy couldn't have that.

He said, "Yes. Yes to all of it. Yes, of course yes, I want to be the ace in your deck and your Warby Parkers and I am so gluten-free tonight for you. And every night after."

And then he wrapped Quincy in a hug.

The audience cheered.

Quincy sagged against him, taking a shuddering breath, his nose pressed against Josy's beard. They'd hugged before, of course. And since Josy was Josy, he'd kept track of such things. Since the day he'd met Quincy Moore, they'd hugged eighteen times. And this, the nineteenth, was the best one of all. They *fit* together, and as he brought his hand up to the back of Quincy's head, fingers in his hair, he didn't think he'd ever want to fit this way with anyone else ever again.

Quincy sighed and tilted his head back, eyes darting down to Josy's lips. He leaned in and—

"No," Josy said, pulling his head back.

Quincy's eyes widened. "Oh my god. I'm so sorry. I didn't mean—I thought you would want—"

"I do, man," Josy said firmly. "More than anything. But you're high, and I don't want to do that. When you sober up, if you still want to kiss me, then I promise I'll make it worth it."

"I will," Quincy said. "Even if I'm pretty sure I'm going to regret everything that just happened, I will."

Josy grinned. "It was pretty gnarly. You're such a nerd."

Quincy groaned and laid his forehead on Josy's shoulder.

And as the people of Abby (along with an assortment of brightly costumed weirdos already planning on making this an annual trip because this was *so amazing*) cheered, Josy couldn't think of anywhere else he'd rather be.

Chapter 18

"Do you think sea lions have feelings?" Quincy asked him as they made their way up the stairs at Baked-Inn & Eggs. "I think about that a lot. I mean, they have to, right?"

"Probably," Josy grunted, pushing Quincy up another step. It was slow going, as Quincy had decided twice so far that lying down right where he was seemed to be the best idea. "They have whiskers. I think everything with whiskers has feelings."

"Oh. That makes sense. You're so smart. I know you don't always think you are, but you can trust me on that. I'm a writer. I know things."

"Thanks, man. That's awesome of you to say."

"Giraffes don't have whiskers. They must be soulless demons. Do you think giraffes are dinosaurs? Long necks, right?"

"I have no idea, but that makes sense."

Quincy laughed. "It does, doesn't it? Marijuana is *awesome*. I want to be high all the time. Like, I want to be high when I write. Can you imagine what my books would be like? Just… so good."

"They're already good."

Quincy looked over his shoulder with wide eyes. "You've read my books?"

"Yeah. Some of them."

"When you were stalking me?"

Josy sighed. "It wasn't stalking. It was intense interest."

"Oh. That sounds like the same thing."

"Maybe one is less creepy."

Quincy shrugged, almost sending them both tumbling down the stairs. "I don't think you're creepy. I think you're tubular. Or whatever hipsters say."

"I don't think anyone says tubular."

"Ninja Turtles do. And don't think I've forgotten that no one has ever answered me about the state of their genitalia."

"I don't think anyone can forget that."

They finally made it to the top of the stairs. Josy was breathing heavily. Quincy wasn't as light as he looked, especially when his entire body seemed to have turned to jelly. Josy took his hand and pulled him toward their bedroom.

The blanket fort was still set up in the middle of the room. Josy switched on the light, and the lamp underneath the comforter lit up with a low glow. Josy let Quincy go and went to the fort, then leaned in to make sure the pillows and blankets hadn't been removed. He heard Quincy toeing off his shoes behind him.

"Oh man," Quincy groaned. "I shouldn't have eaten all that quiche. Why did no one try and stop me? I don't want to be wearing clothes right now."

Josy turned around in time to see Quincy drop his slacks to the floor, attempt to kick them off, and almost fall flat on his face. His legs were pale and skinny, covered in light, curly hair. Josy's mouth went dry as Quincy fussed with his tie, managing to loosen the knot enough to slip it over his head and throw it to the floor. He fought with his dress shirt, getting a few buttons undone before trying to lift it off. His right arm got stuck above his head, and his left was somehow wrapped behind his back.

"Dammit," Quincy said, voice muffled. "This isn't going as well as I'd hoped."

"Seems like it's going all right to me," Josy said quietly. He stood up and went to Quincy to help him from the confines of his shirt. He chuckled under his breath as they eventually got the shirt off. Quincy blinked at him, glasses askew.

His skin was lovely. Freckles dotted his shoulders, and hair sparsely covered his chest and stomach. There was desire there, and maybe it was stronger than Josy had felt for anyone in his entire life, but it wasn't important. At least not right now. It could simmer for however long it needed to.

It seemed to dawn on Quincy slowly that he was wearing nothing but green boxers. He flushed brightly, the warmth spreading from his cheeks down his neck to the top of his chest. He fiddled with his glasses, swallowing thickly. "So."

"So," Josy said.

"Here we are."

"Yeah."

He glanced at Josy before looking away. "No kissing, right?"

"No kissing," Josy agreed. "Not yet, at least."

Quincy nodded. "That's okay."

"Yeah?"

"Yeah."

Josy grinned. "That's good. Do you want to put on pajamas?"

"No. I'm weirdly anticlothes right now. I don't know why. It must be the pot."

"Must be." Josy jerked his head toward the fort. "Why don't you climb inside, man. Get comfy."

"You're coming too?"

"Right behind you."

He absolutely did not stare at Quincy's butt as he bent over and went inside the blanket fort.

He picked up Quincy's clothes off the floor and laid them on the bed that hadn't been used in days. His skin felt like it was thrumming. He felt stoned, though he hadn't so much as touched a single joint the entire day. He was undressing when Quincy spoke from behind the comforter.

"That all just happened, right? It wasn't something I made up in my head?"

"It all happened," Josy said, hanging his tweed jacket on the bedpost.

"In front of everyone."

"Yep."

"Oh." Then, "That's cool."

"I think so too."

"You do?"

"Yeah, man."

"Cool."

Josy snorted. He thought about pulling on a pair of sweats but decided against it. If Quincy could be in his underwear, then Josy could too. He stood above the blanket fort. "I'm coming in now."

"Hurray."

Hurray, indeed. Josy pulled back the comforter and sank to his knees. Quincy was already wrapped up in blankets, head lying on his pillow. His eyes widened slightly as he saw Josy's state of undress, and he coughed roughly.

"All right?"

"Mostly!" Quincy squeaked. "Just… ah. I see your nipples, is all."

Josy frowned as he looked down at his chest. "Is that okay?"

Quincy nodded furiously. "They're very good as far as nipples go."

"Thank you. That might be the nicest thing anyone has ever said about them." Josy crawled inside until he collapsed next to Quincy. He sighed happily, all the strength draining from his body. He didn't move as Quincy pulled the blanket out from underneath him and pulled it over the both of them. He felt warm. And safe.

He turned over to face Quincy. Somehow they were sharing the same pillow, and their faces were inches apart. Quincy was blinking owlishly, eyes glazed.

"Wow," he said softly. "You're so pretty."

Josy huffed out a laugh. "Ditto, dude." He reached up and took Quincy's glasses off, then folded them up and set them aside.

"I have something to tell you," Quincy said seriously.

"Go for it."

"I like marijuana."

"You do?"

"Yes. But I never want to do it again today."

"But tomorrow?"

Quincy scrunched up his face. "Maybe not tomorrow either. Or next week. Maybe next month. For Christmas or something. To celebrate Jesus, or whatever." He blanched. "But *you* can do it anytime you want. I'm not going to try and change you."

"That's good."

"Because I like you just the way you are."

"I like you too," Josy said, and it felt so damn good to finally be able to say it out loud. "Like, a lot."

"Ohhhh," Quincy whispered. "Maybe even more than like?"

Josy thought he would shake apart. "Maybe even more. But we'll wait until tomorrow, huh? When you're thinking clearly."

Quincy looked disappointed. "But—"

"Are you going anywhere?"

"Uh, no?"

"Neither am I, man. I'll be right here in the morning. And if you still want to talk about it, we can."

"I will," Quincy said. "I'll probably want to talk about it all the time."

"I can deal with that."

Quincy nodded. Then he reached out and pressed a finger to the tip of Josy's nose and said, "Boop." He erupted into giggles, turning his face into the pillow.

Josy was certain of a few things in his life. He wanted to be an actor. He had an agent who cared about his future. He had friends he'd somehow managed to carve into a family. He liked weed and funky socks with animals on them. He was good at radio trivia (which for some reason didn't translate so well to bar trivia). He had a bong named Vlad the Inhaler, and maybe his parents would never come around to seeing that while his life would never be what they wanted, it was still a life worth living.

And Josiah Erickson was certain that what he felt for Quincy Moore went beyond simple affection. Regardless of what happened tomorrow or any day after, he would remember this moment when he felt so full of light he thought he'd burst.

Quincy wiped his eyes, still chuckling quietly. "I am going to be so embarrassed tomorrow about all of this."

"You don't have to be."

"Remember when I asked you out and you said no?"

Josy winced. "Yeah. Man, I'm sorry about—"

Quincy put a finger against Josy's lips. "Shh. Shh, shh. Listen. *Listen.*"

Josy listened.

Quincy didn't move his hand. "It was scary for me. I'd never really done anything like that before. Ever. I'm not—I'm not that type of person. You know why I did?"

Josy shook his head.

"You were cute. Like, *really* cute. A little ridiculous, because seriously, a Hypercolor T-shirt? *Seriously?*"

Josy wasn't offended in the slightest.

Quincy pulled his hand away. "I liked your beard and your eyebrows, but it was the way you smiled at me after I smashed a cupcake on your forehead that really knocked me for a loop. You just seemed so happy that you were covered in frosting. It was weird."

"Can I tell you something?"

"Sure."

"I was really disappointed I didn't get to eat the cupcake."

Quincy laughed again. "Sorry. It's just this whole *thing*. I don't even remember how it started."

"It's such a waste of cupcake. You should be ashamed of yourself."

"I'm really not."

"Heathen."

"You had frosting on your face and you were smiling at me," Quincy said, voice barely above a whisper. "And I didn't think I'd ever seen anyone smile at me that way before. You didn't know me, but I thought maybe you could see me. Even beyond all the crap in my head."

"It's not—"

Quincy shook his head. "I know it's dumb to think that way, but it's how I felt. And even though you were smiling and I thought my heart was going to beat right out of my chest, I wasn't going to do a thing about it. It was too big. It was too much. I didn't think I was ready. I was standing in front of a crowd that terrified me, and you were there like… like sunshine."

"Then why did you?" Josy asked.

Quincy rolled his eyes. "Because Dee knows me and she saw how affected I was by you. And she reminded me that all the chances we don't take are the chances for something great we'll miss."

"And then I shot you down. Dude, that *sucks*."

"A little. But it's okay."

Josy needed this to be clear. "I wanted to be your friend. Like, you don't even know how much. I'm not good with making friends, and I saw you for the first time on the stage and I just… I wanted to know you. You seemed like someone I needed."

"Strange, right? I thought the same thing about you."

"So strange," Josy agreed.

"I yelled at Dee when I went back to her. Did I ever tell you that?"

Josy shook his head.

"Well, I did. Or I *started* to yell at her, but then she told me to stop being such a dick and to be proud of myself for going out on a limb."

"She's kind of scary."

"It's the neck tattoos. She's really sort of squishy." He looked slightly panicked. "Don't ever tell her I said that."

"Promise. I don't want you to die."

Quincy relaxed. "And then you started stalking me and liking old photos on Instagram—"

"It wasn't *stalking*. That was my manager's fault at Applebee's. If he hadn't come into the bathroom yelling at me, I wouldn't have accidentally liked the picture."

Quincy squinted at him. "That was such a weird sentence."

"It's true!"

"So we have to thank your manager who scared you in the bathroom at Applebee's for all of this?"

"What? No! That's just—oh my god."

"Right?"

"Oh my god!"

"And then Dee showed me your commercial where you had genital herpes—"

"I don't *actually* have genital herpes."

"—and you were wearing these really tiny basketball shorts, and I thought she was making fun of me."

"She probably was. She's evil."

"You came to the audition. I didn't know you were going to be there."

"I was going to ask you to be my friend again when I saw it was you."

"That's all?"

Josy sighed. "I also wanted to be in the movie."

"There it is."

"But I really did want to be your friend. Like, so much."

"And we became friends."

"Yeah. It's pretty great, man."

"It only made me like you more." Quincy closed his eyes. "And I told myself it would be enough. If that's all you wanted, then I was going to be okay with it. It was hard. A lot harder than I thought. You're very… handsy."

"I do touch things a lot."

"But then Roger and Dee said you would watch me when I wasn't looking, and I thought… okay. I could deal with that."

"I was being very creepy," Josy said. "My bad."

"And then I started thinking about what would happen when the movie was over. I wouldn't get to see you every day. I wouldn't get to see the way you stumble in the mornings when you're not quite awake, or when you eat, like, six pancakes in one sitting."

"I do like pancakes. Just not with a lot of syrup, you know? Makes them soggy."

"I didn't like it."

"Soggy pancakes? Oh, dude, I totally feel you on that—"

"The thought of not seeing you when I felt like you were one of the few people in the world who could actually see me."

Anything Josy could say in response suddenly died on his tongue.

Quincy tapped the side of his head. "It's loud in here sometimes. I get in my own way. I'm stronger than I used to be, but that doesn't mean I always win. Sometimes I lose, and it's horrible. But it's what I do after I lose that makes me different than how I used to be. I can pick myself up now. It might take me a while, and it hurts, but I can stand again. I don't need to be propped up by anyone because I can do it myself."

"That's real good, man," Josy managed to say. "I'm so proud of you."

The smile he got was dazzling. "I'm proud of me too. It took me a long time to get where I am, but I think I'm okay with how I turned out."

"I like who you are. Every part. Even the not-so-good things. It shows you're a fighter."

"You hugged me. And we started holding hands."

"I like being near you. I just didn't know how much until it was pointed out to me. And then I saw you and how you directed your pelvis at me—"

"Until I did *what*?"

"—and I knew that I didn't need to be worried, because everything was going to be okay. I was going to tell you today, but then you got stoned."

"What the hell does my pelvis have to do with *anything*?"

Josy shrugged. "It showed you had feelings for me. That's what the Internet said. And the eyebrow flash. You do that a lot at me."

"I don't have any idea what you're talking about." His eyebrows rose slightly.

"There it is," Josy said happily. "Eyebrow flash. So rad."

"That doesn't make any sense!"

"Or does it make all the sense?"

Quincy groaned. "I'm too stoned for this."

"That's all right, man. I can wait."

"That's what Gus said when I went to ask him for advice about you. He said that you were patient and kind and would never do anything to hurt anyone."

Josy didn't like surprises, but he figured this one was okay. "He said that?"

"Yeah. He also said you were annoying and talked too much, but it was obvious he likes that about you."

"Why did you go to Gustavo?"

Quincy looked confused. "He's your best friend."

Josy refused to get choked up. "You know that?"

"Ye-es. I mean, you've got the Queens and Lottie. And you've got Casey too, but Gus is like… he's like your opposite. You guys are two sides of the same coin, you know? Everyone can see that. Of course I went to him." Quincy frowned. "Though he made me go on the Internet and look up things that absolutely did not help."

"You're so hot, I better date you before you're cool," Josy teased.

Quincy sighed. "Don't remind me."

"I thought it was pretty cool, man. Like, no one has ever done something like that for me before."

Quincy swallowed thickly. "I really want to kiss you right now."

Josy reached out and touched the side of his face. "Me too. But I promise you I'll still want to kiss you in the morning. Maybe even more. It'll be worth it."

"Promise?"

"Yeah, man. I promise."

Quincy yawned so wide, his jaw cracked. "Holy shit, I'm tired. And stoned. Christ, I'm still stoned. I can't believe the first time I got high, I ended up getting a boyfriend." He didn't even seem to realize what he said, because the next moment, his eyes were closed, and he started snoring softly.

"What the fuck," Josy whispered. "You can't say something like that and fall asleep!"

But that's exactly what he'd done.

It was all right, though. Josy made a promise. And he intended to keep it.

Eventually, his eyes slid shut and he slept too.

AS THEY slept, Josy's phone buzzed from the pocket in his discarded pants. He'd see the message the next afternoon. It was a video from Serge and Xander. Serge was laughing at him and Xander was scowling slightly, but they both told him how happy they were for him. Xander did add that he'd have to meet Quincy again, this time to make sure he was up to snuff. But his expression softened, and he said that Josy had done good.

But that would come later.

For now, Josy and Quincy slept in a blanket fort, hands curled together between them.

LIFE ISN'T like the movies, no matter how hard we wish it so. There is no tidy resolution in ninety minutes. Michael Bay doesn't direct us to run in slow motion as gigantic robots explode behind us for reasons that make no coherent sense, given he's nothing but a hack who *maybe* made one nearly watchable movie in his lifetime.

Life stings. It can bite and claw and kick you when you're down. It can lift you up in celebration and clutch your heart until you think it'll rip from your chest. It's glorious and wonderful and oh so devastating. We sing and we laugh and we dance until we can move no more, and it's all worth it. Every single piece. Every single part. Because life isn't made up of the breaths we take, but the moments that take our breath away.

Like this:

Josy opened his eyes slowly, face smooshed into his pillow. The morning light was weak through the comforter overhead. He stretched, the muscles in his back popping. He scratched his chin through his beard. He smacked his lips.

"Hey."

He blinked up.

Quincy sat next to him cross-legged, the blanket pooled around his waist. His hair was sticking up in different directions, and his glasses were perched on the tip of his nose. He had scruff on his jaw, and he looked nervous.

Josy had never seen someone more wonderful than Quincy at that moment.

Quincy said, "I know we said we'd wait until this morning. And I get it if you changed your mind—"

"You sober?"

Quincy stared at him. "Yeah."

Josy pushed himself up.

He took Quincy's face in his hands.

And he kissed him.

It wasn't like the movies.

There was no orchestral swell.

There was no burst of fireworks.

People didn't sing and dance around them.

Quincy's breath tasted like stale quiche.

Josy was sure he didn't have the best breath himself.

So no, it wasn't like the movies at all.

But it was *real*.

And that made it better.

They barely moved. It was the firm press of lips and nothing more.

And it felt like everything.

It went on for six rapid heartbeats before Josy pulled away, tilting his forehead until it pressed against Quincy's.

"Wow," Quincy whispered.

Josy laughed.

"No. Seriously. *Wow*. That was—"

Josy did the only thing he could.

He tackled Quincy to the floor just to see how many times he could make him say *wow* again.

(It turned out to be eight more times. Making out was *awesome*.)

Chapter 19

The Stories of My Father (Working Title)
Day 41
Location: Eagleton House
Scene 52

LIAM SAT on the porch of his father's house.
    He'd found peace.
    He'd returned to his father after his adventures in the woods.
    "It was real," he'd said to his father. "It was all real."
    John Eagleton had laughed, a single tear trickling down his cheek. "I know. I know. I know, and I love you more than anything."
    He'd passed an hour later, one breath in and a long, slow breath out.
    And now Liam was waiting. He had choices to make, but they didn't seem as insurmountable as they did before. He felt… different. Calmer. More settled. The things he'd seen… well, they felt like a dream. Already the little details were fading. But he would hold on to them as long as he could. And when finally he had to let them go, he'd be ready.
    A familiar car pulled up in the driveway, gravel crunching underneath the tires.
    He stood slowly.
    He could see Dante inside. He looked… worried.
    Liam loved him. Completely. He knew that now.
    "Hey," he said as Dante stepped out of the car. Liam stepped off the porch.
    "Hey," Dante said, shutting the door behind him.
    "Thanks for coming."
    Dante shrugged. "You know I always will. Whatever you need."
    Liam nodded. Yeah, he knew that all right.
    Dante hesitated. Then, "I'm sorry. About your dad."
    "Thanks. It's okay, I think. I heard him. In the end. Everything he ever wanted to say."

"He loved you."

Liam smiled. "I know."

"I don't—I don't know what happened to you. I don't understand what you've seen."

"I know. But I don't need you to." Liam took a deep breath. "I just need to know one thing."

"Anything."

"Do you still love me?"

Dante was shocked. "What?"

Liam glanced away. "Because I love you. More than anything."

When he looked back up at Dante, he could see the tears in his eyes. "I never stopped," Dante said hoarsely. "Never. Not once. I don't care what's happened to us, what's happened to *you*. I'm still going to love you with everything I have."

Liam laughed wetly. "Yeah?"

Dante shrugged. "Yeah."

Liam stepped forward to get his happy ending and—

"Cut!"

Mason sighed as he took a step back. "What was wrong with that one? I thought it was good."

The crew around them began to move. Quincy was frowning down at the screen on the camera. "You guys were fine. Lighting was a bit off." He shook his head. "Sorry, guys. I know we've done this a few times, but I need this shot to be perfect."

"My little diva," Roger said fondly, patting his grandson on the arm.

"Whatever," Mason grumbled. "Just get it right next time. Someone bring me a coffee. And I swear to god, if it doesn't have the right amount of sugar in it, there will be *hell* to pay!" He stalked away.

"Don't go too far!" Quincy called after him. "Five minutes. That's it." He glanced at Josy. "Good?"

"Sure, dude. That's fine with me."

Quincy nodded and started muttering with Roger.

Josy made his way over to the tent that had been set up next to the B and B. He waved at Dee, who was in the driveway, in charge of crowd control. A few dozen people had shown up, more than they typically saw, but it was a big day, so he expected it. Margo Montana was scowling at Dee, but Josy figured that was just a librarian thing. She and Mrs. Von Patterson and Mrs. Havisham were dressed as Christmas elves. Josy had asked Dee what that was all about, and Dee had told him they were MILFs on a shelf. He didn't know what that meant. He thought he was better off that way.

In the tent, the We Three Queens and Lottie were sitting in ratty lawn chairs around a space heater, wrapped in heavy coats and scarves. It was supposed to snow later, and the clouds overhead were thick and white.

Casey held a cup of his THC-infused tea that Josy gazed at longingly, but he knew he needed to have a clear head for this final scene. Gustavo was next to him, which surprised Josy. Aside from when Josy had first arrived in Abby, and a couple of times when he and Casey were still figuring things out, Josy had never known Gustavo to close the video store. Casey had told him that Gustavo wanted to be here for the last day of filming. Josy was absurdly touched, even though Gustavo was scowling at him.

Bernice greeted him first. "I think I like watching movies better than making them. This is very boring, watching you do the same thing over and over again. Well, it wasn't boring when *I* was in it, but now it is."

Josy shrugged. "*Repetitio est mater studiorum.*"

They all stared at him.

"What?" he asked.

"Was that… was that *Latin*?" Gustavo asked incredulously.

"Yeah, man. It means 'repetition is the mother of all learning.'" Josy frowned. "How the hell do I know that? Am I fluent in Latin? Quick! Ask me to say something else in Latin!"

"Say something else in Latin," Lottie demanded.

Josy opened his mouth… and nothing came out. "Okay, guess not. Whew. That scared me for a second."

"Wicked," Casey said, offering him a high five, which he gladly accepted.

"This is the last scene, right?" Bertha asked him.

"Yeah. Quincy's a perfectionist, so he wants to get it right."

"*Quincy*," they all said with a dreamy sigh.

"I don't sound like that when I say his name!"

That was pretty much a lie, but he still had to save face. His people had teased him endlessly for the way he'd practically been floating the past couple of weeks. It probably didn't help that Josy thought it was a good idea to tell everyone (including perfect strangers on the street) how amazing and wonderful his boyfriend was. It wasn't his fault that Quincy was the best thing ever. He was right up there with Gustavo. And Casey. And Xander and Serge and Lottie and the We Three Queens.

He was important. So important.

"You kind of do, man," Casey said, a goofy grin on his face. "It's epic."

"Yeah, dude," Gustavo muttered. "So epic."

Casey rolled his eyes as he nudged his shoulder against Gustavo. "This guy gets it."

"Isn't it strange?" Lottie asked him as she fixed the bandana around her drag-queen hair. "Having to kiss someone who's not your partner? I've always wondered that about actors. Don't their significant others get jealous? And don't even get me started on sex scenes. If I had Channing Tatum pretending to writhe on top of me, I would not be responsible for my lady boner."

"Oh my god," Gus said, sounding scandalized. "What the *hell*."

Josy shrugged. "I don't think so? I mean, it's a job, right? I don't have feelings for Mason. I keep it professional. I mean, yeah, I would prefer not to kiss him, but it's not really me, you know? It's Liam and Dante, not Josy and Mason."

"How interesting," Betty said. "No jealousy whatsoever. That's good to know. I wonder why the scene keeps stopping right before you have to kiss Mason?"

Josy blinked. "What?"

The We Three Queens smiled at him in unison. It was eerie.

He glanced back at Quincy. He was leaning down toward Roger, who was jabbing a finger in his direction. "Oh man. Seriously?"

"It is a little suspect," Gustavo said.

Casey glanced at him. "Would you get mad if I had to kiss someone else for a job?"

Gustavo shrugged. "You only like kissing me, so."

Casey beamed at him. "Respect."

Josy sighed. "That's so stupid. There's no reason to get jealous. I don't—hey, Mason!"

Mason looked up from where a harried assistant was thrusting a cup of coffee into his hand. "What?"

"I don't like kissing you! I don't even *like* you!"

"Good! I don't like kissing you either! You're stupid!"

"Hey, Quincy!"

Quincy looked up at him.

"You are awesome, and I like putting my mouth on your mouth! No need to be jealous about anything because I think you're the bee's knees!"

Quincy flushed brightly and looked at the ground, shuffling his feet in the gravel.

"There," Josy said, turning back to his friends. "All better. See? If everyone just talked about what they were feeling instead of hiding it, things would be so much easier. Miscommunication is such a waste of time."

"I taught him that," Gustavo said.

"And where did you learn it from?" Casey asked.

"I don't know what you're talking about." Then, "The Internet. Whatever. Fine. Shut up."

"There it is."

"All right," Quincy called out. "Let's do it again. One more time!"

"Gotta go make a movie," Josy said cheerfully. "Later days!"

He walked back toward Quincy and Roger, who was sitting back in his wheelchair, a fond expression on his face. "I think we're good to go now," he told Josy.

"Rock on. Hey, Quincy?"

Quincy was still red. "Yeah?"

"No one but you, okay?"

Quincy nodded furiously. "Okay."

"Good. Let's do this thing! Places, everyone! Let's rock this bitch!"

LIAM GLANCED away. "Because I love you. More than anything."

When he looked back up at Dante, his eyes were glistening. "I never stopped," Dante said, voice cracking. "Never. Not once. I don't care what's happened to us. What's happened to *you*. I'm still going to love you with everything I have."

Liam laughed wetly. "Yeah?"

Dante shrugged. "Yeah."

Liam stepped forward and kissed Dante with all he had. Dante wrapped his arms around him and lifted him slightly off his feet, and it was here, now, that Liam got his happy ending.

(Later, in post, they would splice the scene to show Mr. Zucko, Dill, Boris Biggles, and the Great Lion known as Grady watching from the woods, small smiles on their faces. Eventually they would turn around and disappear into the trees, going back to the woods where they lived for the rest of their days, never to be seen again in this world.)

(Unless there was a sequel. Because everyone loves a sequel.)

JOSY AND Mason broke apart as soon as they heard *cut* shouted from behind them.

"Dude," Josy said with a grimace. "You taste like coffee."

"You taste like *regret*," Mason snapped.

"Yeah, regret that I'd ever had to kiss—"

"Uh, guys?"

They turned to look at Quincy. He was staring at them, a strange look on his face.

"Yeah?"

"That's it." He cleared his throat as he pushed his glasses back up on his nose. "That's a wrap."

Josy raised his arms over his head and shouted, "*Yes*! Did you hear that, everyone? That's a freaking *wrap*!"

Lottie and the We Three Queens tilted their heads back and howled. Casey fist-pumped. Gustavo crossed his arms. Roger and the crew applauded as the crowd Dee was trying to hold back began to cheer.

Josy tilted his head toward the sky, closed his eyes, and breathed.

QUINCY FOUND him standing in the driveway long after everything had been packed up. The sky was starting to darken, and the air was cold.

"Hey," he said, reaching out to take Josy's hand. "I was looking for you. Dinner's ready. Everyone's waiting for you."

Josy smiled at him. "Just wanted a moment, you know? Take it all in. I might never get to do this again."

Quincy shook his head. "You will."

"You think so?"

"I know so. You were—are—amazing, Josy. And I can't wait for everyone to see it. I have a feeling things are only going to go up from here."

Josy squeezed his hand. "Maybe. Or maybe not. But even if nothing comes from it, I still got to have this. Here. Now. I was in a movie, man. That's just gnarly."

"If only little block-of-cheese Josy in Wooster, Ohio, could see you now."

"He wouldn't even believe his eyes," Josy said. He looked back up at the sky. "Thank you."

"For what?"

"Letting me have this."

"You earned it," Quincy said, jostling his arm a little. "It had nothing to do with what I felt about you. You were better than everyone else who auditioned—"

Josy shook his head. "Not that, though it's pretty awesome."

"Then what did I let you have?"

Josy looked at him and shrugged. "You."

Quincy took a shuddering breath. "Josy."

"Movies are great, you know? Getting to pretend to be someone you're not. But it's nothing compared to what's real. I think having something real is the best thing of all."

Quincy kissed him.

And even though it wasn't a movie, right at that moment, it started to snow.

The orchestra swelled.

Fireworks burst overhead.

People sang and danced around them.

(Nobody tasted like quiche.)

The camera panned toward the sky, and as the bright and wonderful world filled with swirling white flakes, two words appeared across the screen.

The End.

Epilogue

Okay, just kidding.
    There's still more.

    From Indie Film Digest
    December 2016
    How to Be a Movie Star
    By Jake Chambers

Have you ever watched the *Wizard of Oz* and wished Dorothy was a queer dude who made out with the Cowardly Lion? Except, for the purposes of this article, the Cowardly Lion was actually the Hunky Lion and an allegory for growing up and letting go and accepting your place in the world?
    Yes?
    Well, then do I have an absolutely *bonkers* movie for you.
    Chances are you've never heard of it, or its director and stars, but if word on the gilded streets is correct, that's about to change in a very big way.
    When I first became aware of this movie over the summer, I told myself there was no possible way it could be real. There were rumblings from the festival circuit of a film that defied all logic. It was produced by a name I hadn't heard in a long time: Roger Fuller, or as his die-hard fans lovingly refer to him, the *Queen of the Bs*. Known through the seventies and eighties for having half-naked women destroying the patriarchy while growing seventy feet tall, and mostly naked men fighting aardvarks on the *Titanic* with deeply queer undertones, or even shot-on-a-shoestring-

budget creature features that pondered a world where scientists and their grand experimentations were stand-ins for the aftermath of the Cold War (sometimes all three at the same time), Roger Fuller is something of a legend. His infamy is well known through the tiny little burg of La La Land, and no two people have the same opinion of him.

"It's exactly the way I like it," he tells me from the offices of his newly formed production company, Queer Films Inc. We're sitting at a desk surrounded by the bric-a-brac of a strange and frankly bizarre life. There are photographs hung on the wall of a much younger Roger Fuller surrounded by scream queens and leading men alike.

Back in the spring of 2015, a young man named Quincy Moore came to him with an idea. "He was nervous," Fuller says. "All jittery and twitchy. He usually was, but this time it felt different. He had an idea, bizarre though it was. And trust me when I say that I know bizarre." He sounds proud, like a doting grandfather.

Which is exactly what he is. Because the jittery and twitchy young man named Quincy Moore is Roger Fuller's grandson. Known to a legion of fans as Q-Bert, an author in the inexplicable genre known as monster porn, Moore is no stranger to the bizarre. With books that describe in explicit detail sexual relationships between hunky men and billionaire anthropomorphic coffee cups, or the burgeoning sexuality of a frat boy with Sasquatch, he's carved out a place for himself in a niche market that has only grown. His fans adore him and have built up a community around him that numbers in the hundreds of thousands. On any given day, his website's message board gets tens of thousands of views and hundreds of comments. And they're not all about coffee cups screwing a guy over a desk in his office (a sentence that *actually makes sense* if you've read the book). It's like the Island of Misfit Toys, though some don't like that description.

A woman who goes by the handle Tigress is one of Moore's forum moderators. "We're not outcasts," she wrote to me in an email. "We're not abnormal or weird or strange. We've found a group of like-minded people from all walks of life. We support each other. We help each other. There are professionals and blue-collar workers, stay-at-home moms or dads and people with doctorates in quantum physics. Three of them, in fact."

"Sounds like a cult," I wrote back.

"Not at all," she replied. "A cult implies we can't think for ourselves. And I can tell you, for one of the first times in my life, I do just that. As we sometimes say, there's unlimited wealth in taking care of your mental health."

In perusing the message boards, I see what Tigress is talking about. There are topics covering everything from how to get through panic attacks to someone available twenty-four seven if a member of the community is feeling suicidal. One topic, with thousands of comments stretching back five years, is filled with people talking about something that made them happy during their day.

It's remarkable. And if it's a cult, then hand me the Kool-Aid.

Quincy Moore went to his grandad with an idea.

Fuller heard his pitch, even though Moore would say later he wasn't trying to pitch *anything*. Little did he know, things were about to change. I get the idea that most people don't say no to Roger Fuller.

"Suddenly," Moore tells me one day last month, "there was a Kickstarter page, and money was pouring in quicker than I could keep up. I hadn't even finished the script, but Grandad didn't care about that. In the blink of an eye, we had over two hundred grand to make a movie."

Moore is handsome in an unconventional way. He's skinny and constantly moving. He can't seem to sit still. He's obviously nervous and doesn't like being the center of attention. We're sitting in his apartment, and he keeps glancing toward the kitchen as if he's looking for someone to save him.

Someone *will* come save him, but that's still a few minutes away. I ask him why he wanted to make this film. Why he decided to step outside of what is clearly his comfort zone.

"Do you know what the 'bury your gays' trope is?" he asks me.

I do. A nasty little thing. Along with queerbaiting, bury your gays is one of the worst tropes in film and television. It stems from the idea that queer characters aren't allowed to have happy endings. Also known as dead lesbian syndrome, it results when queer characters are introduced only to meet with catastrophe. If there are queer relationships, they end because tragic queer characters win Oscars and ratings. Even now, at the end of 2016, it's still prevalent in film and television.

He's looking down at his hands when he says, "I hated it. I still do. I mean, what do we have? *Brokeback Mountain*? Great! Two straight actors playing queer and then one of them dies. *Philadelphia*? Oh look, a straight actor playing queer and dying of AIDS. And apparently it's not possible to get an actual trans actor to play a trans character."

I remind him that these movies are at least a decade old.

"Right. But tell me the last time a queer actor played a queer character and lived happily ever after."

I admit that I can't, at least not off the top of my head.

He's not smug about it. If anything, he looks upset. "That's exactly why," he says quietly. "I just wanted people to be happy, you know? Something I didn't think I'd get to have for a long time. My head didn't let me. That's the rub when it comes to anxiety and depression. I tell myself I'm worth something, and then that voice in my head tells me I'm not. And it doesn't help when I look to books or television or movies and see people like me not getting to have what everyone else does. It's why I started writing in the first place. And why I wanted to make the movie. Maybe I went about trying to change the status quo in an absurd way, but at least I'm trying."

Absurd might be an understatement.

There is a scene in *The Stories of My Father* (a title that Fuller tells me he warmed to, given that it sounds so innocuous) where the character of Liam is talking to a gigantic cucumber named Dill (natch) who is an imaginary character from his youth. And the kicker? He's played by the same actor—Mason Grazer—who plays Dante, Liam's love interest. Grazer also happens to play a talking sunflower, a centaur-type thing that's half zebra, and also the aforementioned Hunky Lion known as Grady.

Sounds crazy, right?

But it all works.

Grazer plays all the roles with gusto. And between himself and the other lead actor, it's obviously the flashier role. After all, not everyone can be a talking cucumber and be *sympathetic* about it.

But it's the other lead that has everyone talking. In the past couple of weeks, he's even started popping up on Best Of lists by film critics in New York and Los Angeles, seemingly out of nowhere.

His name is Josiah Erickson.

And I guarantee you he's going to be a star.

He's also extraordinarily ridiculous in the best way possible and happens to be Moore's boyfriend.

Moore relaxes almost immediately when Erickson comes back from the kitchen, rejoining our interview. He's loose and affable, wearing a shirt declaring him to be part of the 1989 Wichita Lions Club and socks with cartoon cows on them. I asked him when I first arrived if he'd ever been to Wichita. He told me no, he's never been to Canada. That about sums up Josiah Erickson in a nutshell.

"Hey, man," he says, sitting back down next to Moore. "Sorry that took so long. I forgot we were talking and started making ravioli. Weird, right?"

Erickson is funny. And a stoner. And sometimes I think he might be smarter than I could ever be, even if he thinks Wichita is in Canada. He's also one of the most charismatic and mesmerizing actors I've seen in years. Watching him in *The Stories of My Father* is a kinetic, enthralling experience, one that I'm not alone in singling out. It's almost startling to think of Erickson as Liam versus Erickson as… well, Erickson.

When I first got to their home (one Erickson proudly told me they've shared for exactly twenty-six days), he made it clear that he was following Moore's lead. It's obvious to anyone with eyes (and maybe even to those without) the love these two share. They are aware of each other in ways that I haven't quite seen before. If I'd met them separately, without knowledge of their relationship, I would have never placed them together. But now that I see them together in front of me, it makes sense in ways I can't do justice. They just *are*.

Erickson puts his arm around Moore's shoulders and pulls him close. He kisses the top of his head without even the slightest hint of artifice and then grins at me. "What's up, man?" he says like we haven't been chatting for the past two hours.

I'm helpless to say anything but *hey* back. He has that effect on people.

"What were we talking about?"

I ask him about the rumors of his potential Golden Globe nomination in the coming weeks.

He shrugs. "That'd be cool."

But…?

"But that kind of stuff really doesn't matter to me anymore. I mean, it's neat and all. And my agent *really* likes it. But I'm just happy acting, man. Being in front of the camera and playing all these different types of people, that's all I ever wanted. Like, a couple of years ago I'd have given my left nut for a blue check mark next to my name on Instagram. I got one a few weeks ago, and I was all like, 'Oh. Fun.' And then I forgot all about it until right this second."

He's completely serious. If it were anyone else, I might think it's some kind of PR-spun bullshit, but from Erickson? The thought doesn't even cross my mind.

I tell him word on the street is that he's about to blow up.

For the first time, he looks uncomfortable. "You think so?"

Maybe.

"That's rad, I guess. But who cares?"

It takes me a moment to recover. I tell him a lot of people would kill to be in his position.

"Whoa. Do you think I need to hire a bodyguard? I don't want to get murdered."

Reminding myself not to go off on a tangent (it's so damn *easy* to do just that with him), I ask him how one becomes a movie star.

He looks over at Moore, and his expression softens. He says, "I don't know, man. I don't think it matters. I'm pretty good with what I've got already. You know? Happiness isn't little statues given to you by pretty people, though I suppose that isn't the worst thing in the world. Getting it would be nice if it happens, but I don't need it. I've got what I want already right here. Anything else is just cake." His eyes widen. "Oh man, I could really go for some cake. Like, with frosting and crap."

It's treacly bullshit. But it's *believable* treacly bullshit. Not necessarily because *I* believe it but because Erickson does.

I tell him that it can't hurt, though. He's just finished filming a supporting role in a film for Sir Ridley Scott ("He's, like, super cool"), and rumor is that he's being pursued for the lead in Michael Bay's latest installment of metal robots fighting other metal robots.

"Nah," he says, looking back at me. "I've already turned that down. My best friend would murder me. Michael Bay is his greatest enemy. I wouldn't do that to him."

It's weird, really. This whole thing. People like Josiah Erickson shouldn't exist. This *movie* shouldn't exist. But they do, and I think we're all better for it. *The Stories of My Father* is brash and contemplative and in-your-face and so far beyond what we expect from our filmgoing experience that it defies proper description. When I went to my first screening, I didn't know what to expect. When the credits started rolling, I didn't know what the hell I'd just experienced. It was stupid. And wonderful. And I was filled with joy, this odd and cathartic *joy*, that a movie like this was real. It warmed this old queer's heart to think the younger generation could have something I didn't when I was their age.

It was *happy*. Oh yes, there are tears and angst, but goddammit, that's life. And it's not perfect by any means. There are some pacing issues, especially in the beginning, and parts of it are a little hokey, but I don't ever want to live in a world where the perfect film exists. *The Stories of My Father* was shot guerrilla-style in the fall of 2015 with a bare-bones crew and a bunch of locals in the small town where they filmed filling out most of the smaller roles, and yet it *works*.

I ask them both how this is possible, because it's a question I'm still grappling with.

Erickson and Moore share a look before Erickson says, "I guess it comes down to what my friend Serge taught me after he spent eight months in India. Do or do not. There is no try."

You read that right. He quoted Yoda and attributed it to his friend named Serge, who went to India.

And, god help me, it makes sense.

Do or do not. Because there is no try.

Here, in this movie, we don't bury our gays. We let them breathe and move with such artful grace. They make mistakes but become better people because of them. Quincy Moore made them real in a screenplay that should be getting more attention than it is. Roger Fuller plays the role of the sick and dying father with a gravitas I didn't think he was capable of. Mason Grazer moves from role to role with effortless ease.

And Josiah Erickson.

Josy.

Whether he wants to believe it or not (or even wants it), this is how you become a movie star.

And I, for one, can't wait to see just how far he goes.

THE ALARM went off at six in the morning.

Josy groaned, pulling the blanket up and over his head. "Whyyyy. Why is this happening to me?"

He waited for the beeping to stop, but it kept going.

He shoved the comforter off and blinked at the empty space in the bed beside him. He reached over and slapped the top of the digital clock until it died a deserved death. He slumped back against his pillow, stretching his arms up and over his head as he yawned. He didn't know why he had to be up so early. He didn't start filming for the adaptation of Casey's second postapocalyptic werewolf/vampire book-turned-movie until after the holidays, and—

Oh.

Oh crap.

He sat up.

He reminded himself that shit like this didn't matter. And even if it did, it was nothing to get worked up about. If he didn't get it, it would be fine. He never thought he'd get to this point, anyway. He wasn't lying when he'd told that reporter the rest was just cake.

"And now I want cake again," he muttered, scratching his stomach.

"Your trainer would murder you if you had cake," a sleepy voice said from the bedroom doorway.

Josy's heart stumbled in his chest at the sight of a disheveled Quincy moving slowly toward the bed carrying two steaming mugs. One would be coffee and the other tea. He was wearing low-slung sweats, and his bony feet shuffled against the carpet.

"Oh man," Josy said in a rough voice. "Are you a sight for sore eyes." He frowned. "What does that even mean? Why would that make sore eyes better? You're not Visine. I don't get it."

Quincy set the mugs down on the nightstand before he leaned down and kissed Josy. He tasted like toothpaste and Josy most likely tasted like ass, but that was okay. Quincy didn't seem to mind. "It's too early for you to be talking about anything."

Josy grunted as he pulled Quincy down on top of him. He liked being the blanket, but sometimes he needed Quincy to be. Quincy didn't seem to mind about that either. "I don't know why we have to be up."

Quincy reached up and thumped him on the forehead. "You know why."

"Yeah, but it doesn't matter."

"Of course it does. Maybe not to you, but think about some queer kid in Wooster, Ohio, who dreams of moments like this. That's why it's important."

Josy sighed as he wrapped his arms around Quincy's bare back. "I like it when you make sense."

"You must like me a lot, then."

"So much," Josy agreed. "I'm pretty sure it's love."

Quincy snorted. "That's good to know, seeing as how you've told me that many, many times."

"'S because it's true."

Quincy smacked a kiss against his forehead before rolling off him. "Damn right it is." He pulled the comforter back up and over their heads, and it was almost like they were in a blanket fort. Josy approved. He rolled over to face Quincy, their faces only inches apart.

"I'm a little scared," he admitted quietly. "I know I shouldn't be, but I am."

"I know. But even if it doesn't happen, it's okay. You'll see."

Josy reached up and traced a finger over Quincy's eyebrows. "Thanks."

"For?"

Josy shrugged. "Being alive and stuff."

"Oh. Is that all?"

Josy kissed him. He couldn't not after that. Quincy's pelvis was pointed at him, after all.

Sometime later, Quincy pulled away with a gasp, lips swollen, brow furrowed. "What time is it? Oh my god, we're going to miss it!"

"Noooo," Josy moaned. "Less talking, more kissing."

Quincy shoved him away, throwing the comforter off them. He reached for the remote on the nightstand on his side of the bed and straightened out his glasses as he sat up against the headboard. He pressed the Power button and the TV mounted on the wall in front of their bed came to life.

Josy stared at the ceiling as Quincy started flipping through the channels. He thought of the kid in the block-of-cheese costume.

He thought of standing in his underwear outside a laundromat with a woman named Starla.

He thought of the We Three Queens, their pink jackets sparkling in the sun as their Vespas raced down the road at thirty miles an hour.

He thought of Lottie and her drag-queen hair.

He thought of Xander and Serge and Casey taking him in and never letting him go.

He thought of Gustavo Tiberius, who believed in him more than anyone.

And he thought of Quincy, of course. He always did. He probably always would.

It was going to be a good day. No matter what happened, it was going to be a good day.

"Your phone buzzed last night," Quincy muttered. "After you went to sleep. Think it was a text."

Josy sat up next to him, their shoulders brushing. "Okay," he said. "I'm ready."

Quincy smiled brightly. "I know you are. Me too."

They grinned goofily at each other before Josy reached over for his phone.

Four text messages, the screen read.

From Gustavo.

Which was *weird*, because Gustavo never texted unless Josy did first.

"There it is," Quincy whispered. "I think they're about to announce your category."

Josy opened the text messages.

The first: *I did it.*

The second: *I asked him.*
The third: *He said yes.*
The last: *Will you be my best man?*

"Holy shit," Josy breathed.

"What the—are you *crying*?"

"Yeah," he said through his tears. "I absolutely am."

And on the screen, an actress looking far too perky for the early-morning hour said, "The Golden Globe nominations for Best Performance by an Actor in a Motion Picture Musical and Comedy are—"

When TJ KLUNE was eight, he picked up a pen and paper and began to write his first story (which turned out to be his own sweeping epic version of the video game *Super Metroid*—he didn't think the game ended very well and wanted to offer his own take on it. He never heard back from the video-game company, much to his chagrin). Now, over two decades later, the cast of characters in his head has only gotten louder. But that's okay, because he's recently become a full-time writer and can give them the time they deserve.

Since being published, TJ has won the Lambda Literary Award for Best Gay Romance, fought off three lions that threatened to attack him and his village, and was chosen by Amazon as having written one of the best GLBT books of 2011.

And one of those things isn't true.

(It's the lion thing. The lion thing isn't true.)

Facebook: TJ Klune
Blog: tjklunebooks.com
Email: tjklunebooks@yahoo.com

HOW TO BE A NORMAL PERSON

TJ Klune

A How to Be Novel

Gustavo Tiberius is not normal. He knows this. Everyone in his small town of Abby, Oregon, knows this. He reads encyclopedias every night before bed. He has a pet ferret called Harry S. Truman. He owns a video rental store that no one goes to. His closest friends are a lady named Lottie with drag queen hair and a trio of elderly Vespa riders known as the We Three Queens.

Gus is not normal. And he's fine with that. All he wants is to be left alone.

Until Casey, an asexual stoner hipster and the newest employee at Lottie's Lattes, enters his life. For some reason, Casey thinks Gus is the greatest thing ever. And maybe Gus is starting to think the same thing about Casey, even if Casey is obsessive about Instagramming his food.

But Gus isn't normal and Casey deserves someone who can be. Suddenly wanting to be that someone, Gus steps out of his comfort zone and plans to become the most normal person ever.

After all, what could possibly go wrong?

www.dreamspinnerpress.com

OLIVE

JUICE

TJ KLUNE

It begins with a message that David cannot ignore:
I want to see you.

He agrees, and on a cold winter's night, David and Phillip will come together to sift through the wreckage of the memory of a life no longer lived.

David is burdened, carrying with him the heavy guilt of the past six years upon his shoulders.

Phillip offers redemption.

www.dreamspinnerpress.com

TJ KLUNE

Tell Me It's Real

Do you believe in love at first sight?

Paul Auster doesn't. Paul doesn't believe in much at all. He's thirty, slightly overweight, and his best features are his acerbic wit and the color commentary he provides as life passes him by. His closest friends are a two-legged dog named Wheels and a quasibipolar drag queen named Helena Handbasket. He works a dead-end job in a soul-sucking cubicle, and if his grandmother's homophobic parrot insults him one more time, Paul is going to wring its stupid neck.

Enter Vince Taylor.

Vince is everything Paul isn't: sexy, confident, and dumber than the proverbial box of rocks. And for some reason, Vince pursues Paul relentlessly. Vince must be messing with him, because there is no way Vince could want someone like Paul.

But when Paul hits Vince with his car—in a completely unintentional if-he-died-it'd-only-be-manslaughter kind of way—he's forced to see Vince in a whole new light. The only thing stopping Paul from believing in Vince is himself—and that is one obstacle Paul can't quite seem to overcome. But when tragedy strikes Vince's family, Paul must put aside any notions he has about himself and stand next to the man who thinks he's perfect the way he is.

www.dreamspinnerpress.com

The Queen & the Homo Jock King

TJ KLUNE

Sequel to *Tell Me It's Real*

Do you believe in love at first sight?

Sanford Stewart sure doesn't. In fact, he pretty much believes in the exact opposite, thanks to the Homo Jock King. It seems Darren Mayne lives for nothing more than to create chaos in Sandy's perfectly ordered life, just for the hell of it. Sandy despises him, and nothing will ever change his mind.

Or so he tells himself.

It's not until the owner of Jack It—the club where Sandy performs as drag queen Helena Handbasket—comes to him with a desperate proposition that Sandy realizes he might have to put his feelings about Darren aside. Because Jack It will close unless someone can convince Andrew Taylor, the mayor of Tucson, to keep it open.

Someone like Darren, the mayor's illegitimate son.

The foolproof plan is this: seduce Darren and push him to convince his father to renew Jack It's contract with the city.

Simple, right?

Wrong.

www.dreamspinnerpress.com

TJ KLUNE

Until YOU

Sequel to *The Queen & the Homo Jock King*

Together with their families and friends
Paul Auster
and
Vincent Taylor
request the honor of your company at the celebration of their marriage.

www.dreamspinnerpress.com

FOR **MORE** OF THE **BEST GAY ROMANCE**

DREAMSPINNER PRESS
dreamspinnerpress.com